Tracy Borman

The King's Witch

HODDER

First published in Great Britain in 2018 by Hodder & Stoughton
An Hachette UK company

This paperback edition first published in 2019

1

A CIP catalogue record for this title is available from the British Library

Paperback ISBN 978 1 473 66233 9
eBook ISBN 978 1 473 66232 2

Typeset in Sabon MT by Hewer Text UK Ltd, Edinburgh
Printed and bound by CPI Group (UK) Ltd, Croydon, CR0 4YY

Hodder & Stoughton policy is to use papers that are natural, renewable
and recyclable products and made from wood grown in sustainable
forests. The logging and manufacturing processes are expected to
conform to the environmental regulations of the country of origin.

Hodder & Stoughton Ltd
Carmelite House
50 Victoria Embankment
London EC4Y 0DZ

www.hodder.co.uk

To Stephen Kuhrt,
with deepest thanks

1603

21 March

Her fingers worked feverishly. Rosemary, hartshorn, rue. The familiar, pungent aroma rose from the mortar as she ground the tiny sprigs together. A little oil for binding. The mixture glistened green and gold as she dripped it slowly from the pestle, testing the consistency.

The chamber was sombrely lit, with two candles flickering on sconces on either side of the queen's bed, and hardly more light coming through the heavily draped mullioned window from the leaden skies beyond. Neither Frances's herbs nor the lavender strewn on the rush matting around the bed could disguise the sickly smell of decay.

The queen's breath came rapid, rasping, her chest rising and falling in short, jerking movements. There could be little time. Frances hastened to her side, and, without observing the usual ceremony, peeled back her mistress's gown, exposing her ragged, wasted chest. 'Crooked carcass,' the Earl of Essex had scoffed. He had lived to regret it.

She smoothed the oil over the queen's waxy skin, uttering a prayer as she did, so that it might soon take effect. Gradually, Elizabeth's breathing slowed, became more melodic, quieter. Her eyes fluttered open.

'Helena.'

At once, Frances's mother rushed to her mistress's side. 'Ma'am,' she whispered. Slowly, the queen surveyed the gloomy confines of her chamber. Her bony fingers trailed distractedly over the sumptuous damask bedclothes, tracing the intricately embroidered spheres of moons and pearls. Her bright red wig had long since been discarded, along with the other youthful adornments of her wardrobe, and her thin grey hair lay in lank, wispy clusters, barely covering the scalp underneath.

'Are my councillors gone again? All?'

'Yes, ma'am. For now.'

The queen's mouth curled into a small, sardonic smile, showing her sparse, blackened teeth. 'Of course,' she lisped. 'Why worship the setting sun when the Scottish dawn is upon us?'

'Your Majesty—' Helena began, her voice cracked with sorrow.

'Ah Helena, you have always served me faithfully,' Elizabeth soothed. 'Would that the same were true of all my court.'

Her chest heaved in silent mirth, but was soon racked with a choking cough that left her gasping for breath. Frances started forwards, but her mother was there before her. Gently, she raised her mistress's head and placed a silver goblet to her lips. With difficulty, the queen swallowed. After several moments, the fit passed and she sank back down into her pillows. Frances watched as a glistening droplet of the tincture slid from one corner of Elizabeth's mouth, tracing its way slowly along the deep wrinkles of her neck.

'Frances.'

She started from her careful appraisal of the queen and turned to her mother.

'You must not gaze so directly at Her Majesty,' Helena whispered. Chastened, Frances lowered her eyes and returned to her work, making fresh unguents for the queen's comfort.

The chill March wind, which bent the skeletal trees to and fro in the park beyond, could not penetrate the thick glazed windows of Richmond – the queen's 'warm box', as she called it. Braziers had been lit in every room, and thick tapestries lined the walls of the royal bedchamber, rendering it hot and oppressive. Impatiently, Frances brushed a stray lock of chestnut brown hair from her clammy forehead as she continued her labours. *Please let her live. Just a little longer.*

The silent gloom was suddenly broken by the sound of footsteps pounding up the stairs to the chamber. The door was flung open, though the force of the gesture was at odds with the man who made it. Robert Cecil, the queen's diminutive chief adviser, walked haltingly into the room, his gait made awkward by his twisted back. He was flanked by members of Elizabeth's council. Frances recognised the tall frame of the Earl of Nottingham, the queen's great admiral. His thin face appeared even more pinched than usual, and there were dark circles under his eyes. His wife had been one of Elizabeth's closest favourites, and her death a few weeks before had hastened the queen's own decline. To his right was the Lord Chancellor, Thomas Egerton, who surveyed the room with his small black eyes. Frances noticed his nose wrinkle at the smell, and he took a place furthest from the bed. The rest of the men fanned around the bedside, reminding her of crows on a winter's day. She looked at their faces, searching for concern, or grief, or obeisance. But she saw only impatience.

The dying queen had already closed her eyes against them, feigning sleep. Frances smiled. *Ever mistress of her fate – and of those around her.*

'Lady Frances,' drawled Cecil. 'How fares Her Majesty today?'

That he should address the daughter was a deliberate slight. Frances glanced towards her mother, who gave a barely perceptible nod.

'The same, my lord,' Frances replied. She ignored Cecil's expression of disapproval, and added: 'We pray for improvement.'

'Indeed? Indeed.'

Frances saw her mother's lips tighten. 'My lord, Her Majesty must rest in order to speed her recovery,' Helena said curtly, looking pointedly at the councillors clustered around the queen's bed.

'Naturally,' he replied soothingly. He showed no inclination to leave.

Frances focused intently upon her work, her fingers moving deftly between tiny glass phials, scales, and pots.

'And you, my lady. What occupies you there?'

Silence followed. Frances knew the question was directed at her, but she kept her back turned and became conscious that she was holding her breath. She had hoped to escape Cecil's notice. He had always made her feel uncomfortable, and she knew he resented her family for their favour with the queen. Little wonder he was so impatient for the old woman's death.

Her mother made a gentle cough, prompting. Slowly, Frances turned to face the assembled company.

'Well?' Cecil urged, clearly enjoying her discomfort. He watched her intently, his eyes narrowing as they met hers.

'I am making salves for Her Majesty's comfort, my lord.'

A pause. 'Do you think the ministrations of Her Majesty's physicians inadequate, then?'

'No, my lord, of course not,' Frances said, feeling her colour rise and silently chiding herself for it. She cast about for an explanation that would satisfy her interrogator, for such he seemed. 'Her Majesty willed it,' she added weakly.

'You should have a care, my lady,' Cecil murmured, his voice low. 'Our new king might mark you as a witch.' Then he let out a peal of laughter, so loud and prolonged that his fellow ministers felt obliged to join in, somewhat uncertainly.

'He is not our king yet, my lord.' Her mother's voice cut through the mirth.

'Indeed not. But we must always have an eye to the future, eh, my lady marchioness?'

Helena sniffed and busied herself with turning down the queen's covers, swiping at the folds with unnecessary force. Grateful for the diversion, Frances turned quickly back to her work. But her hands betrayed her, sending the mortar slipping from her grasp, the sound exploding as it crashed to the ground.

In the silence that followed, all turned back towards her. Even the queen, who had slipped into unconsciousness, twitched slightly, as if startled by a dream.

Cecil looked back at Frances, a small smile playing about his lips. Then, with a stiff bow to the sleeping queen, he walked slowly from the room.

CHAPTER I

28 March

'Mother says she passed easily,' Frances remarked quietly, her fingers tracing the intricate leadwork of the casement window. The glass misted as she spoke, momentarily obscuring the view of the knot garden below. She drew her cloak more tightly around her, then turned to look at her father.

'As mildly as a lamb,' he agreed softly, his grey eyes appraising her kindly. Casting a glance over his shoulder, he lifted his hand and made a small sign of the cross, then closed his eyes and mouthed a silent prayer.

'Leave that now,' he said to the boy who was sweeping out the ashes from the fireplace. 'There is much else to attend to.'

The boy bowed quickly, then scurried from the room, leaving a trail of soot from the brush in his hand. Sir Thomas sighed, and, wincing slightly, bent down to clean it up with a linen kerchief. Frowning, Frances stepped nimbly forward and helped him to his feet.

'Have you not used the salve that I prepared?' she chided. 'It will ease the discomfort.'

Sir Thomas grinned at his daughter. 'Even your skills cannot stave off the effects of age, Fran. Besides, my bones are merely protesting at the sudden cold. Every fire in the privy apartments was extinguished as soon as the queen breathed her last.'

With a sigh, he turned back to the tapestry that he had been carefully rolling in a fine linen cloth.

'Is the palace to be stripped of all its treasures?' Frances asked.

Her father nodded, but kept his eyes focused on the tapestry, the exquisite gold thread catching the light as it moved.

'The court is moving to Whitehall. Our new king will not wish to begin his reign in a place of death.'

'But Her Majesty lies here still,' Frances protested. 'Her rooms ought to be preserved at their finest until she has been taken to Westminster.'

'And so your mother wanted it, my dear,' Sir Thomas soothed, 'but my Lord Privy Seal would not be gainsaid. I suppose, as keeper of Her Majesty's purse, I ought to appreciate his desire for economy.'

'Indeed you should, Sir Thomas.'

Frances and her father swung around to see Cecil standing in the doorway of the presence chamber. His mouth lifted into a slow smile, but his piercing black eyes glittered dangerously. Frances felt her father's hand press the small of her back. Remembering herself, she bobbed a curtsey and lowered her gaze, while Sir Thomas swept a bow. She kept her eyes fixed on the silver buckles of the minister's shoes as he stepped silently forward.

'My Lord Privy Seal.' Her father's tone was light but respectful. 'I thought you were already at Whitehall, making preparations for His Majesty's arrival.'

'And so I was, Sir Thomas, but the barges and wagons come so slowly from Richmond that I thought I would find out what could be done to hasten them.'

'As you can see, my lord, there is much to be set in order,' her father replied evenly, gesturing to the tapestries that still hung on the walls, and the luxurious red and gold Turkish carpet that stretched from the foot of the dais to the door of the privy gallery. 'But we lack only a few days before the last of the wagons will be loaded.'

Cecil slowly arched an eyebrow and crossed his arms over his black velvet doublet. Frances knew that the sombreness of his attire was no compliment to the late queen. He had always favoured dark colours, as if – for all his ambition – he wished to fade into the shadows rather than strut like the peacocks of the court, her own uncle among them. His small stature added to his apparent inferiority. Even most women at court, Frances included, were taller than him. But her family, and many others besides, had learned how dangerous it was to underestimate him.

He turned his gaze to her now, and she squirmed inwardly. The lines on his high, wide forehead deepened slightly as he watched her, and she noticed a muscle twitch in his jaw. His small, thin lips were pressed tightly together, framed by his moustache and beard, the latter neatly trimmed to a point so that it accentuated his already long chin. He raised a delicate white hand to it now, and stroked it distractedly, his eyes never leaving Frances.

'Regretfully, Sir Thomas, we do not have a few days to spare,' he said at length, turning to her father. 'Already, His Majesty has progressed as far as York. He will be in London before the week is out.'

'Our new king must have very fast horses,' Sir Thomas observed. 'Anyone would think that he set out before Her Majesty had breathed her last.'

Frances smiled, but her father shot her a warning look.

'He is most eager to greet his new subjects, of course,' Cecil replied smoothly. 'And he is a very able rider – more so even than her late Majesty. It is one of many ways in which he exceeds her.'

'His sex being first among them, I presume?' Frances cut in, her colour rising.

Cecil took a step closer. She could feel his breath on her neck as he stood watching her.

'Your daughter has very decided opinions for one of her tender years, Sir Thomas,' he said quietly.

'You must forgive her, my lord,' her father soothed. 'She has spent but little time at court, preferring the tranquillity of our estate in Wiltshire.'

A slow smile crossed Cecil's face.

'I am sure there are many other advantages to be gained from living so far distant from the prying eyes of court, eh, Sir Thomas? Why, only yesterday my commissioners told me of a squire in Yorkshire who had been living with his family as if we were still a nation of Catholics. For years, they had been hearing Mass every day, thanks to a priest hidden beneath their staircase, and they had an entire closet filled with relics, rosaries, and other papist trinkets.' He laughed and shook his head. 'Their ingenuity is to be admired, even if it will cost them their liberty – perhaps even their lives. We must await our new king's judgement on the matter.'

Frances glanced at her father, who held Cecil's gaze steadily.

'The late queen had no wish to pry into men's thoughts,' he replied quietly, 'and His Majesty has already given cause to hope that he will be of the same mind.'

Cecil fell silent for a few moments. Frances became aware of the ticking of the small silver lantern clock that still hung above the fireplace. She tried to steady her breathing to its rhythm.

'You refer, I suppose, to the king's late declaration that any subject who will give an outward appearance of conformity shall not be persecuted,' the Lord Privy Seal said at last. When her father did not answer, he continued: 'I know of other Catholics who have drawn comfort from this, Sir Thomas. But they are fools. King James has made his revulsion for papist practices clear to all of us who will serve him in council. Already, he has instructed me to draft new laws against them so that none will escape condemnation if they are discovered.'

'*Other* Catholics?' her father repeated softly. 'You do not suppose me to be among their number, my lord?'

'Of course not, Sir Thomas,' he replied after a pause. 'For all her moderation, our late queen would hardly have shown such favour to you and your wife if she had known you to be papists. After all, she set you above all others – even those who might have been more deserving of her esteem.' His jaw twitched again. 'You would have had to go to great lengths to avoid her suspicion, and I can hardly imagine you had the time for such diversions, given all your duties at court.'

'My family and I have ever been loyal subjects, my lord.' Frances caught the edge to her father's voice, though his face remained impassive.

'Well now,' Cecil said brightly, clapping his hands together. The sound reverberated around the almost empty chamber, making Frances start. 'I must not disturb your labours any longer, since you still have much to do. Be sure to have the wagons loaded by morning, Sir Thomas. We cannot brook any further delay. King James will not take kindly to arriving in a sparsely furnished palace, and the old queen can no longer have need of such trimmings.'

He swept his hand across the neatly stacked rolls of tapestries, causing them to tumble to the floor, unravelling as they went. Without troubling to look back at the chaos that he had caused, he walked purposefully towards the door that led to the private rooms beyond. Frances looked anxiously up at her father, but he was staring resolutely ahead.

'Oh, I almost forgot,' Cecil called as he reached the doorway. He drew something out of his pocket. Frances strained to see what it was, but Cecil had it clasped too tightly in the palm of his hand. 'Lady Howard found this among the late queen's possessions.'

Without warning, he threw it towards Frances. Scrambling clumsily forward, she caught the small glass phial before it could shatter onto the stone floor. With trembling fingers, she pulled out the linen stopper and held it to her nose. She recognised the scent of lavender and marjoram almost before it reached her nostrils.

'Apparently it was hidden beneath Her Majesty's pillow,' Cecil remarked lightly. 'You should take greater care of your possessions, Lady Frances. Who knows what suspicions they might arouse, in the wrong hands?'

Not pausing for a reply, he turned on his heels and walked briskly from the room.

2 April

Frances felt her heart soar as the coach rounded the corner and she caught her first glimpse of the castle, its pale golden stones bathed in the mellow light of the spring afternoon. She let out a long, slow breath, feeling every part of her body relax. It was always like this, returning to Longford. All of her senses seemed to awaken as she made her way along the elegant, curving drive, and she took joy in every familiar sight, smell, and touch. Inhaling deeply, she closed her eyes and caught the sharp tang of the box hedges that encircled the formal gardens in front of the house. She knew that if she leaned out of the carriage window to her right, she would see the dark outline of the woods against the soft yellow sky. Straining to listen over the wheels crunching along the gravel, she smiled at the shrill chirping of a tree sparrow, and the low thrumming of the river in the distance.

Already, she was anticipating the moment when she would walk into her beloved home. She knew each knot in the panelling that lined the rooms; the creak of her old tester bed, with the curtains that she had helped her mother embroider as a child – her imperfect stems weaving crookedly among the superior petals of her mother's needle. If she closed her eyes, she could tell by scent alone whether she was in the smoky parlour downstairs, her mother's fragrant dressing chamber, with its rosemary and lavender pomanders, or her favourite room of all – the library, with the mellow, comforting smell of the hundreds of books that lined the circular walls.

She opened her eyes. An image of the library at Richmond had suddenly come into her mind, jolting her back to the moment when, two days before, she had taken her leave of her parents. Her heart contracted with sorrow as she remembered her mother's fierce embrace, the haunted look in her tired eyes as she urged her to make haste, even as she clung to her wrists as if she would never let go. Her father had said little, but his face had been uncharacteristically grave as he had bidden her farewell. They had promised to follow her to Longford as soon as they were able, but Frances knew that she could not hope to see them for several weeks – perhaps longer. They would need to be there to greet the new king, and join the unseemly scramble for places in his court.

With a jolt, the carriage came to a stop inside the courtyard of the castle. The coachman jumped down to open the door, and Frances stepped out, blinking against the bright light that was reflected from the circular walls of the courtyard. She felt the familiar sense of belonging. The very stones seemed to breathe their calming welcome.

'Lady Frances.'

She smiled broadly as she recognised the small, plump form of her childhood nurse bustling towards her.

'Ellen.'

She stepped forward and kissed her cheek, which was flushed. Ellen could only have received word of her arrival a few hours before, so she had no doubt been busy making preparations. Frances's smile broadened as she imagined her barking instructions at the cooks and chambermaids, then following in their wake and chiding them if they overlooked any detail.

'What a journey you must have had. There has been no rain this past fortnight. Your bones must ache from being jostled and jolted along the roads,' the older woman rattled on as she drew off Frances's cloak and handed it to an attendant. 'Come, take your ease in the parlour. I have had cook prepare your favourite sweetmeats.'

Frances paused in the hallway, feeling the warmth from the sunlight that streamed through the high windows. She turned slowly so that she could look all around her, taking in the familiar portraits that lined the walls, the faded hangings above the windows, and the silver-gilt sconces with their beeswax candles. She caught their scent as she breathed in deeply. Then, with a contented sigh, she followed in Ellen's wake.

Frances stared down at the delicate blooms that lay in neat piles on the wooden tray resting on her lap. The tiny, exquisite blue petals of the forget-me-nots nestled alongside the pale yellow and white anemones and – her favourites – the irises, their purple petals as soft as goose down. Distractedly, she twined a length of coarse thread through her fingers. She knew that she must work quickly to tie up the flowers before their colours began to fade, and then hang them to dry in the old leather coffer that she had fashioned for the purpose. But this gentle, methodical task seemed to have lost all of its soothing power today.

Sighing, she set the tray aside and walked over to the casement window. She gazed out towards the ancient woodland that bordered the estate, remembering the countless hours she had spent as a child, fascinated – even then – by the flowers and herbs that grew lustrous all around. She had loved to close her eyes and let her other senses guide her to the delicate scent of bluebells, the sweet fragrance of honeysuckle, or the sharp tang of dandelions. Every day, she had gathered these and many more for Ellen, who had tended her and her siblings' fevers and grazes with her potions, salves, and tinctures.

'My little woodland sprite,' her father had called her, with a mixture of amusement and affection. To her sister Elizabeth, who preferred the more conventional pursuits of a gentleman's daughter, she had been a source of bewilderment and scorn. Her adored elder brother, Francis, whom she so closely resembled, would always defend her in the quarrels that so often ensued, while their four younger siblings looked on, fascinated. She felt the familiar pang at his loss.

Frances slowly traced her finger down the misted pane and sighed.

'Don't take on so, my lady,' Ellen soothed. Her childhood nurse could read her moods as surely as old Doctor Dee could read the stars.

'But if I had had more skill, I might have spared her – for a time at least. She could have felt the May sunshine on her skin, rather than dying in the despair of winter.'

'Your herbs can achieve many wonders, my lady,' Ellen said, 'but they cannot defy the Lord. He has more power than all earthly remedies. He alone can decide who shall live and who shall die. You can merely do your best to ease their suffering.'

Frances looked fondly at her old nurse. Ellen had grown stouter this past year, and Frances noticed that her breath came shorter each time she mounted the stairs. Her light brown hair was now flecked with grey, and the skin around her mouth had started to sag.

'Our new king would approve of your counsel, Ellen,' she replied gently.

A fleeting look of distaste passed over the older woman's features, but she pressed her lips together and remained silent.

'I wish my lady mother were here,' Frances said with a sigh, her thoughts drawn back once more to the gloomy chamber at Richmond. In the hasty note that she had sent to her daughter at Longford, the marchioness had told her that she was with her old mistress still, overseeing the small coterie of the old queen's most trusted ladies who had been appointed to watch over the corpse where it now lay at Whitehall.

'I dare say my lady wishes that too. It is high time the old queen was laid to rest,' Ellen remarked with obvious disapproval.

'I am sure King James will soon see that it is arranged,' Frances replied calmly, then plucked a forget-me-not from the tray and studied it intently.

'Well, at least the matter of St Peter's is settled,' Ellen continued.

'Oh?' Frances asked, feeling an unexpected surge of unease.

Since the Reverend Samuels's death last December, the vacancy at Britford had been left open by Cecil and his men, along with numerous others across the country, on the excuse of needing to settle some administrative matters. 'They wait to see which way the wind will blow,' Frances's father had told her. Though he had feigned nonchalance, she had sensed his discomfiture.

'Yes, Dymock had it from the blacksmith's boy. Name's Reverend Pritchard, apparently. First sermon is on Sunday. He'll stay with the Bishop of Salisbury for a few days, until his house is made ready.'

'My parents ought to have been informed, no matter the need for haste. St Peter's lies in their estates, after all.' Frances frowned. 'Do we know anything of the new priest?'

'Not a great deal.' Ellen sniffed. 'But the new king will want to make his mark in such matters. They say he has bent every kirk in Scotland to his will.'

'I am sure we are far enough from court not to be greatly troubled, Ellen,' Frances replied distractedly.

'We were blessed with the Reverend Samuels,' her old nurse persisted.

'God rest his soul,' Frances said quietly.

Ellen turned her attention back to her needlework. Frances noticed the lines at the corner of the older woman's eyes deepen as she tried to make out the fine threads in the gathering gloom of the afternoon.

'I think I will take a walk to the village,' Frances declared at length.

'But the clouds are thickening and the talk is of rain. You'd best stay here by the warmth of the fire.'

'I promised Mrs Godwin that I would look in on Peter,' she replied firmly. Her old nurse knew better than to argue. She fetched Frances's cape and gloves.

*   *   *

As Frances strolled along the River Avon, which bordered the Longford estate, she inhaled the smell of the wet grass underfoot. In the woodland beyond, she could just glimpse the first green shoots of bluebells. Soon they would cover the forest floor in a luxurious, shimmering carpet, and she would be revelling in the beauty of late spring.

Taking long strides now, she quickened her pace so that she almost ran towards Britford. The village had changed a great deal since her childhood, and was now a thriving community, thanks to the benevolent interest of her father towards his tenants. There were more than thirty well-appointed dwellings, their neatly trimmed thatched roofs and whitewashed walls presenting a pleasing uniformity. Most of the inhabitants worked the land surrounding Longford. Neither they nor their families had need to venture far from the village, for there was a school, an inn, and a smithy, as well as the ancient church of St Peter's.

Its squat tower was just visible now above the trees that lined her path, its pale yellow stones interspersed with flint bricks at regular intervals, echoing the design of Longford. The church had stood on the same spot since Saxon times, and had marked the arrival, unions, celebrations, and passing of numerous villagers ever since.

Her father had remarked many times that St Peter's had witnessed more upheaval in this last century than in the previous ten, thanks to King Henry's reforms, and the turmoil that had followed in their wake. 'God frowns upon these times, Frances,' he had told her. 'The queen does not like to make windows into men's hearts and secret thoughts, but even she cannot resolve the differences between the reformers and those of the old faith. If her successor is less moderate, there will be great strife.' Frances felt a rush of affection for her father. For all his calm good sense, he was sometimes given over to such flights of fancy. He should know that the world had always gone differently here, as she supposed it had in most other villages that lay distant from court. Even the most turbulent changes were tempered by the time that they reached this tranquil place.

She paused as she reached the lychgate, its timbers so black-ened with age that they reminded her of the charred embers in the great fireplace of Longford. Glancing across the churchyard, the uneven grass punctuated with headstones set at precarious angles, she thought of the old priest. The Reverend Samuels had baptised her, along with her many siblings, and had been fond of recalling that while they had mewed and cried as the water had been poured over their downy scalps, Frances had only gazed at him steadily with her large dark eyes. She had visited him frequently as a child, eager to hear stories from the Bible, which to her seemed more fantastical and mesmerising than the fairy tales so beloved of her brothers and sisters.

It was the Reverend Samuels who had encouraged Frances's interest in the natural world. His skill at healing was renowned, if somewhat unorthodox. Eschewing the traditional practices of physicians across the kingdom, with their purges and potions, his cures were drawn from the forests, fields, and hedgerows surrounding Britford. It was he who had taught Frances that rosehip might ease the ague, or that peppermint could soothe a griping stomach. She had listened, rapt, to every word of his lessons, always asking questions, always hungry for more knowledge. He had responded with unwavering patience and care.

'Be ever watchful, Frances,' he had told her. 'There is no mystery in illness. Every sickness betrays an outward sign – often more than one. The clues are there for you to observe. The closer you watch, the more likely you are to find a cure.'

Eventually, the Reverend Samuels had agreed that she could accompany him on his visits. As the villagers had watched this serious, dutiful little girl help minister to the sick, not flinching – for all her noble upbringing – at the abhorrent sights and stenches that she encountered, their trust in her had grown. By the age of eleven, Frances had even conducted visits on her own, the old priest recognising her natural ability and trusting her to examine the afflicted so that she could report back their symptoms. Indeed, he had somewhat ruefully acknowledged that her observation and skill now surpassed his own.

'It is God-given, Frances,' he had told her. 'He wishes you to use your skill to help others. You must never deny Him.'

Frances was nearing the old vicarage now. Observing the hedges that bordered the garden and the once neatly kept rows of flowers and herbs, grown a little unruly these past months, that lined each side of the pathway, she felt a surge of sadness and longing. She had tended to her old tutor when the ague had first taken him at Michaelmas, mixing salves of elder bark and wild mint to lay across his chest so that his breath might come more easily, and tinctures of honey and nettle to draw out the fever. He had watched with gentle indulgence as she had moved about his chamber, working swiftly but quietly. She recalled the look of calm acceptance in his eyes now. He had known that he would not see out the winter.

'Lady Frances! You are back.'

Frances turned to see Mrs Godwin hurrying towards her. The older woman made a deep curtsey.

'Oh, my lady. How glad I am to see you!' she cried.

'How is your boy?' Frances asked softly.

'Worse. Much worse, I'm afraid.'

Gently, Frances reached out and took one of the woman's hands in both of her own. The palm was worn smooth, like leather, but was warm to the touch.

'Take me to him, Kate.'

The woman bustled off at once, Frances following close behind as she made her way through the village towards the cluster of dwellings next to the woods of Longford. The Godwins' cottage was at the end of the row. Although the walls were newly whitewashed and the tiny garden in front was well tended, Frances noticed that there were holes in the thatch. She ducked into the dark little room that served as kitchen, dining room, sleeping quarters, and – occasionally – bathroom for this family of six. Only the privy was separate, in a little wooden shack at the back of the house.

In the gloom, Frances could just make out the young boy sitting on the truckle bed, his knees drawn up to his chest and his hands clasped together, as if in silent prayer. His skin had the pallor of wax, and, although it was an unseasonably mild day, he was shivering violently. Frances noticed that his lips were tinged with purple, and his breathing came rapidly. She pressed her cool hand gently against his forehead, which was hot and clammy.

'Has he eaten?'

'No, my lady. But he has such a thirst – always he asks for water. John says I must not give it, that it might choke him.'

'Well he is wrong. The boy needs water. Please, draw some fresh from the cistern.' When the woman hesitated, Frances turned to face her. 'At once, Kate.'

Mrs Godwin hastened away, and Frances busied herself with wrapping Peter in what coverings she could find, then set to work mixing a tincture of woundwort, thyme, and hyssop. After his mother had returned with a pail full of water and given the boy several small sips of it, Frances cradled his head in her hand, and, with the other, slowly administered the potion. Peter flinched, his brow creasing and his lips pressing tightly together. But after a few moments, his features relaxed, and he drank the rest of the bitter concoction without complaint. Frances drew him closer to her breast and gently rocked him to and fro until he began to doze.

'Sleep will enable my herbs to do their work,' she told the anxious mother, who was standing helplessly next to the bed, wringing her hands. 'He's a strong boy, Kate. All will be well.' She smiled, with a conviction that she did not quite feel.

'God bless you, my lady,' replied the woman in a quiet voice.

'God bless Peter too. He will keep him safe,' Frances assured her. 'I will return on Sunday, before church.'

3 April

Frances blinked sleepily as the grey light of early morning stole through the narrow slit between her curtains. Breathing in the familiar scent of woodsmoke and rose oil, she gathered the coverlet around her and experienced a sense of profound contentment at being home. She would happily live out her days at Longford, far away from the noise and bustle of the court.

Slowly, Frances pulled herself up, the bed creaking softly as she did so. On the table at the side of her bed lay a copy of John Gerard's *Great Herbal*. It had been a gift for her seventeenth birthday. Frances could still recall the excitement she had felt as she had untied the silk thread and peeled back the velvet cloth, the book tumbling onto her lap. She had read the frontispiece over and over, as if trying to comprehend how she could own such a jewel.

The crimson silk binding, which was embossed with 'FG' in gold, was a little frayed at the corners now, and the pages were so well thumbed that their edges were crinkled. In between many of them were tiny sprigs of carefully preserved plants and herbs, each one pressed against their description in the book. At the top of the frontispiece, Frances had written in her neat, curling script: 'And the prayer of faith shall save the sick, and the Lord shall raise him up.' She ran her fingers over the words now, and, thinking of the Godwin boy, closed her eyes for a moment in silent prayer.

She began to turn the pages.

'Among the manifold creatures of God,' she read aloud, the words soft and melodic like a chant, 'none have provoked men's studies more, or satisfied their desires so much, as plants have done.'

She smiled. Few people shared the same respectful fascination with plants as Gerard, despite his confident assertion, but she was one of them. Frances remembered that after giving her mother and father a hurried, joyous embrace, she had immediately rushed to her room with her present to begin reading. For hours she had remained there, her eyes alight with revelation at each new discovery, the tip of her quill scratching notes across the pages. Her parents had been hard-pressed to persuade her to join the dinner held in honour of her birthday that evening. Even then, she had brought the book with her, placing it discreetly on her lap so that she might snatch brief glimpses of Gerard's words, and his exquisite sketches of all manner of different species, common and exotic.

Frances flicked through the pages quickly now, her mind drawn from happier recollections to the poor Godwin boy.

'For a fever, combine the leaves of catmint with a little oil, then grind in the stems of meadowsweet,' she read. 'They will be quick to take effect.'

Pulling back the heavy coverlet, she slipped out of bed, wincing slightly at the cold air on her legs. Even in summer, her room, which faced north towards the woods, was cool. Crossing to the dresser, she opened the top drawer and pulled out the small wooden box that contained her pestle and mortar, along with some phials of oil. Placing it carefully in a canvas bag, she set it by the door, then went to wash her face and hands in the ewer that Ellen had set out the night before. The cold water quickened her movements as she patted herself dry and drew on her cool linen shift. If she had risen at the customary hour, Ellen would have come in to warm it by the fire, but there was no time for such indulgence this morning. From the oak chest beneath her window, she drew out a black kirtle and skirt. She supposed those at court had been obliged to set aside their mourning clothes already in order to honour the new king's arrival. Not for the first time, she experienced a rush of relief that she was no longer amongst them.

Most of the household was still asleep, so Frances padded silently into the kitchen and wrapped some bread and cheese in a piece of cloth, which she put into a basket. She added a selection of herbs that she had gathered the night before on her customary stroll through the woods in the fading light of dusk, then hastened to the hall. Sliding back the bolt of the great oak door, she heaved it open just wide enough to slip through, then closed it silently behind her. The stables were next to the old manor house that lay in the castle grounds. Hartshorn gave a low whinny as she approached. He gently nudged her as she hauled the side-saddle and wooden plancher into place. Then, tightening the reins, she stroked his nose and offered him a handful of oats, before pulling herself up onto the saddle.

The ride to the village took only a few minutes, but Frances was grateful for the warmth of Hartshorn's back in the chill morning air. Reaching the Godwins' house, she tied the horse to a tree on the edge of the forest, next to the garden of the little cottage. She knocked gently on the door, which was immediately opened.

'He is a little better, I think, my lady,' Mrs Godwin said, pulling Frances into the room. Three hopeful little faces looked up at her from their bed on the opposite side of the room, and when their father saw her, he sprang up from the table where he had been taking his breakfast.

'You have worked a miracle, my lady. Truly, you have,' he burst out, then gave a stiff, hasty bow.

Frances smiled, but said nothing. She turned to the corner where Peter's bed was wedged between an old dresser and a rickety table with a cracked ewer balanced precariously on top. The boy stirred as she walked towards him, and, opening his eyes, smiled weakly up at her. He was still pale, but a hint of rosy hue was beginning to return to his wasted cheeks.

Frances leaned forward and gently placed her hand on his forehead.

'Keep him warm, Kate. He is still very weak.'

She rummaged in her basket and pulled out a small glass vial. 'You must administer three drops of this as soon as he wakes each morning and before he goes to sleep at night. Be sure to give him plenty of water, and as much food as he can stomach – little by little, mind.'

Mrs Godwin nodded briskly, and immediately busied herself with preparing some broth.

'Will you stay for some breakfast?'

Frances hesitated, knowing that even with the food she had brought they had little enough between them. The sudden peal of church bells gave her the excuse she needed.

'Thank you, but I must go,' she said, setting the loaf and cheese down on the table. 'I cannot be late for our new priest.'

'Please, my lady, tell the reverend we will come just as soon as Peter is better?'

'Don't worry, Kate, I will assure him that you are as God-fearing a family as all the rest in Britford,' she replied with a smile.

Drawing on her cape, Frances turned to bid the family farewell. Peter, she noticed, had slipped back into sleep. She would pray for him at church.

Leaving Hartshorn grazing contentedly by the forest's edge, Frances walked the short distance to St Peter's. The villagers made their solemn progress to the church door in a steady stream, their steps in time with the tolling of the bells. Frances drew comfort from the simple rhythm of life, well away from the sycophants and schemers of court. Here she was at liberty to study her plants and remedies, to walk or ride unaccompanied through the woods and parkland. She need not tighten her bodice or pin back her hair before entering company, or suffer the niceties of rehearsed conversation over dinner.

As Frances passed under the lychgate, she caught her first glimpse of the new priest, who was standing by the entrance to the church with a proprietorial air. He was a tall, wiry man with jet black hair, and as she drew closer she noticed his long thin face and small black eyes.

Ellen had been waiting for her by the path, and now stepped forward so that she could accompany her.

'You must be Lady Frances Gorges.'

He mispronounced the name, as most others did. Only those who were well acquainted with Longford or the court knew that it was Gor*gees*, like the great river in India, as her father was fond of explaining. It was an understandable mistake, but Frances was grateful for the momentary advantage it gave her.

'Reverend Pritchard. My parents, the lady marchioness and Sir Thomas Gorges' – she paused for effect and was gratified to see him flinch – 'asked me to convey their welcome. They are detained at court at present, awaiting His Majesty's arrival.'

'Naturally,' the cleric replied with a smile. 'As are all faithful courtiers. You must be sorely grieved not to be with them, Lady Frances.'

'My parents wished me to remain at Longford. The family must be represented here at all times, as I am sure you understand, reverend,' Frances replied pleasantly, holding his gaze.

'Indeed, Lady Frances. Although you must be desirous for the guidance of your father or one of your brothers.'

Frances forced a smile. 'I crave their presence very much, reverend. For the pleasure of their company.'

The cleric opened his mouth to speak, but Frances interrupted. 'I trust you have been made welcome at Britford?'

'Oh, indeed. My parishioners have been most solicitous – Mrs Tomlinson in particular. I believe she knows your man Dymock, my lady? Thanks to her, I feel that I am already well acquainted with every inhabitant of the village, and of Longford.'

Frances pushed away her growing sense of irritation. Smoothing down her skirts, she asked lightly: 'And the vicarage is to your liking?'

She noticed a fleeting look of distaste pass over the Reverend Pritchard's pinched features. 'Mrs Tomlinson did her best, of course, in the little time allowed.' He paused. 'But no matter, I will soon have it appointed to my liking. Once my furniture has arrived from Salisbury and I have had it arranged, I will turn my attention to the garden. It is most curious.'

'Oh?' Frances raised an eyebrow.

'Yes, it is so filled with herbs that there is barely an inch spare for flowers or hedgerows. The scent is quite overwhelming – it makes my head throb. I will have them taken up as soon as possible,' he added, watching Frances closely. 'Of course, if your ladyship would desire any of the contents for your own herb garden, you would be most welcome.'

Frances could feel the heat rise up her neck, but she held his gaze.

'You are most kind, reverend, but the gardens at Longford are plentiful,' she replied quietly, then turned to go. Remembering, she paused. 'John Godwin and his wife will not be attending your service today. Their son Peter has been gravely ill, and is not yet recovered. I assured them that you would be forgiving.'

Pritchard sniffed, his pointed chin rising a fraction higher, and his thin lips pursed in disapproval.

'I thank you, Lady Frances. I trust the boy has been attended by a physician, rather than falling prey to the spells and tinctures of some local wise woman.'

Before Frances could answer, he made a swift bow and stepped aside so that she could pass. She stared at him a moment, then went to take her place in the family pew at the front of the nave.

Frances had attended Sunday worship at St Peter's for as long as she could remember. Even as a child, while her younger siblings fidgeted and jostled through the prayers and incantations, she had found the words melodic and calming. She had loved to breathe in the smell of the ancient stones, or catch at the long-faded aroma of incense. Unlike many other churches across the kingdom, St Peter's had not been stripped of its statues and relics.

Frances had always supposed that they had not been rich enough to attract the notice of King Henry's commissioners, and his daughter Elizabeth had not been so concerned with such outward shows of conformity. Although the form of service had changed over the years, Reverend Samuels had retained some of the old observances that he knew his parishioners drew comfort from. Frances hoped his successor would do the same.

Looking up at the high archway above the nave, she tried to order her thoughts by counting the Roman bricks that were nestled amongst those from more recent times. But the encounter with the Reverend Pritchard had left her feeling agitated. His brisk, austere manner seemed to have permeated the very fabric of this ancient building, rendering it suddenly cold and uninviting: a place of repentance, not of peace.

'In my sermon today, I will speak of a great evil in our midst,' the new priest began, jolting Frances from her thoughts. 'It is of the highest import, for it threatens not only our well-being here on earth, but our salvation in heaven.'

A hush descended as the shuffling and fidgeting ceased. Everyone was eager to hear how this new incumbent would make his mark. Frances, sitting directly in front of the pulpit, raised her eyes to the priest. Observing that he had secured a captive audience, the Reverend Pritchard indulged in a dramatic pause before continuing.

'I am appointed by King James himself,' he began, his shrill voice ringing out across the silent church, 'and as his servant, I must warn you all that the Devil is at work. He has enlisted an army of souls across the kingdom to carry out his despicable devices, all tending to the destruction of our sovereign Lord.'

With a flourish, he held up a copy of *Daemonologie*, the king's great treatise on witchcraft.

'His Majesty instructs you all to have vigilance. Each one of you must look about you. The Devil's slaves might be among us. Here, in this village. In this very church!'

There were audible intakes of breath and murmurings as the parishioners exchanged anxious glances. This was very different from the comforting homilies that they were used to in the Reverend Samuels's time.

'Satan's followers take many forms,' Pritchard continued. 'They might be widows, goodwives, or daughters. They might tend cattle, bake bread, or mend clothes. To the naked eye, they seem like any other of God's creatures. But be not fooled. They are consumed by evil. They have made a pact with the Devil. They are his servants, his subjects, his whores.'

Frances's eyes blazed as she looked up at the reverend. His arrogance astonished her. He was using this, his first sermon, to foster suspicion and fear among his flock, rather than offer reassurance in the wake of the queen's death.

'But the Devil is not so cunning as he believes. He has left certain marks on the bodies of those whom he has claimed as his own. He most commonly shows favour towards a particular type of woman. Sometimes she is poor. Often she is unmarried. She may also be skilled in the art of healing.'

Despite the cool of the old stone church, Frances felt her body prickle with a rising heat.

'It is the bounden duty of each one of you to be ever watchful,' he declared, making sure to cast his eyes across every member of the congregation. Some of them began to shift uncomfortably in their seats. Frances remained as still as one of the statues that filled the crypt below.

The rest of the sermon was mercifully brief, and, as soon as communion had been taken and the congregation dismissed, she hastened out of the church, ahead of the villagers, who were already talking animatedly about this unexpected introduction to their new priest. She knew that she could not keep her counsel if Pritchard waylaid her. By the time she reached the Godwins' cottage, she realised that she had broken into a run. Untying Hartshorn's reins with trembling hands, she swiftly mounted him and rode with all speed back to Longford.

CHAPTER 4

29 April

The lazy hum of bees was beginning to lull Frances to sleep as she lay outstretched, her hands behind her neck, on a patch of grass in the middle of the wilderness. She exhaled deeply and felt the troubles of the past few weeks melt into the grass beneath her. Even the Reverend Pritchard felt far away, his hellfire preaching drowned out by the whisper of the soft breeze.

She had been back at Longford for a month now, and every day had seen the chill of winter gradually surrender to the warmth of spring. Today was the first that she had felt the breath of approaching summer. Beside her was a copy of Thomas Elyot's celebrated treatise, *The Castle of Health*, which he had written for the old queen's father. Even though the author was not an authority on the plants and herbs that were the bedrock of Frances's art, she had learned a great deal about the healing properties of various foods, and of the importance of regular and prolonged sleep. She was only too glad to surrender to that now.

Stretching luxuriously, she felt the soft grass brush against the soles of her feet. Her red leather pantofles lay discarded some distance away, along with her linen coif. She had unpinned her hair from the intricately braided bun that Ellen had spent some considerable time on that morning, expertly weaving the long tresses between her nimble fingers, and it now hung loose about her shoulders. A gentle breeze blew a strand of it across her mouth, and she caught the scent of lavender and rosewater.

The tickle of a spider as it darted busily this way and that across her forearm made her itch to brush it away. But the longer it stayed, the more she delighted in its gossamer touch, imagining its tiny black legs picking their way between the fine hairs on her arm. She fancied that she might become invisible here, just one of a thousand creatures that inhabited the gardens surrounding the house.

'My lady!'

The voice was so at odds with her surroundings that for a moment Frances wondered if she had imagined it. But soon she heard brisk footsteps approaching through the grass. Sighing, she pulled herself up onto her elbows and shielded her eyes against the low sun. The wiry frame of Dymock gradually came into view.

'My lady, we have received word from the marchioness,' he panted, before coming to a halt in front of her. 'They will be at Longford the day after tomorrow.'

Frances's heart soared. Daily, she had looked for her parents' return, longing for their comforting presence.

'The house must be made ready,' she declared with a sudden resolve. 'Have you informed Mistress Dawson?'

'Yes, my lady, it is already in hand.' Frances thought she caught a hint of annoyance in his tone. Of all the servants at Longford, she knew the least about Dymock. Ever since his appointment three years before, upon the recommendation of one of her father's agents, he had kept himself apart from the rest of the household. Ellen had remarked upon the sparseness of his room, which had only a solitary cross on one wall and nothing pertaining to his comfort – or so the steward had told her. Although unfailingly courteous, Dymock's manner towards Frances had, she fancied, become rather cold since her return from court.

Pushing the thought to the back of her mind, she picked up her shoes and ran barefoot towards the house.

Frances rose early. She felt happier than she had in months, the prospect of seeing her parents again overshadowing the sorrow that had weighed upon her ever since the old queen's death. Dressing quickly, she hastened to the parlour, where a breakfast of manchet bread and cold meat had been laid out for her. She had always loved this cosy room, which overlooked the courtyard garden at the centre of the castle. One of the gardeners, a kindly old man named Bridges, was already at work trimming the low yew hedge that bordered the garden on all three sides. Frances felt the familiar sense of calm as she sat quietly observing him. Tearing off another piece of bread, she headed out into the garden.

'Good morning, Bridges.'

The old man stopped his work, and, turning, doffed his cap, his face crinkling into a smile.

'Ma'am.'

She breathed deeply next to the rectangular herb beds that ran alongside the hedge. The sharp, sweet fragrance of sage combined with the tang of chives and aromatic rosemary made a heady mixture. Master Gerard's own garden could surely not rival this.

'Did you sow the comfrey, Master Bridges?'

'Aye, my lady.'

'And the milk thistle?'

Bridges grinned. 'I can't fathom what you want with all these weeds, my lady.'

Frances returned his smile, but said nothing. They had had this conversation many times before, and it had become a kind of ritual. For all his gentle mockery, she knew that the old gardener liked to indulge her various whims, glad of the interest that she took in his work.

She wandered into the centre of the garden so that she might stand in the sunshine. Shading her eyes, Frances slowly turned around in order to gaze at each of the three walls that enclosed the garden. The grey stone was flecked with gold and interspersed at regular intervals with pale cream and black bricks, so that the whole had the appearance of a chessboard – a subtle reference to her father's crest.

Frances remembered that as a child she had been fascinated and perplexed in equal measure by the odd configuration of the castle, built as it was in a triangular formation. Most of the other gentry houses she knew were constructed around square court-yards in imitation of the royal palaces, so this design seemed both perverse and, at times, inconvenient.

The shrill sound of a horn shook Frances from her reverie. She ran back inside to the hall and gazed out at the hills that lay beyond the Longford estate, straining her eyes just as she had as a little girl watching for her parents' return. Soon, she knew, the train of wagons would come rumbling along the drive, laden with dozens of coffers and chests filled with her parents' clothes, tapes-tries, jewels, and other belongings. It was the same with every remove. Her mother's status as a marchioness demanded it, even if Helena herself would have been content with far less. Only a royal progress eclipsed such removes in scale and splendour.

Pausing to check her appearance in the looking glass, Frances hastened to the courtyard. The voice of the family's chamberlain, Sir Richard Weston, echoed around the walls as he arranged each member of the household in order of rank. Meanwhile, Mrs Lamport, the housekeeper, bustled about, red-faced, brushing down the skirts of the maids and giving a yawning groom a sharp tap on the back of his neck. Frances watched, amused, until the chaos had subsided, then took her place at the head of the entourage.

Looking through the archway of the courtyard, she could see her parents' coach, its gilded finials catching the sun so that it glittered like a jewel as it made its way slowly along the drive. She kept her eyes fixed upon it as if fearing that at any moment it might dissolve like an illusion. As she stared, the second carriage came into view, some distance behind that of the lord and lady, so that the coachman would not be engulfed in its dust. Frances imagined her two sisters in there, jostling and bickering. Elizabeth had turned twenty-five last month, and exalted in her status as the eldest of the Gorges children. Bridget was several years her junior, but consistently failed to show her the respect that Elizabeth felt was hers by right.

At last, both carriages rumbled slowly over the cobbled path that led under the large archway at the front of the house, and into the courtyard.

'My lady, the Marchioness of Northampton, and Sir Thomas Gorges,' announced Sir Richard, as if no one here knew them, Frances thought wryly. He opened the carriage door, and Frances's heart lurched with joy as she saw her mother gathering her skirts in preparation to alight from the carriage. The voluminous russet silk temporarily obscured the figure of her father, who was seated opposite his wife.

'Come now, Elin,' she heard her father chide softly, 'you are not under His Majesty's scrutiny now.'

He had always called her mother by her Swedish name, even though she was anxious to appear as English as all of the other ladies at court. Her dress was entirely in keeping with that of a home-grown peeress, and her flawless English was spoken with only a hint of an accent.

'My lady Mother.' Frances made a deep curtsey, her skirts brushing against the cobbles of the courtyard, then leaned forward to kiss her hand. Helena gently laid her other hand on her daughter's head. Frances caught the familiar scent of rose and chamomile. Even now, it had the same calming effect that it had had on her throughout her childhood, soothing away thoughts of malevolent sprites hovering just beyond her windowpane.

Frances saw her father's eyes sparkle with their accustomed affection and good humour as she greeted him. His neatly trimmed beard was flecked with grey – more so, she fancied, than when she had taken her leave of him at court.

'I trust you have kept the house well, Frances?' He smiled. 'I hope that you have not planted a herb garden in the gallery, nor given my study over to a distillery?'

She grinned. 'Not yet, Father. But if you had been away a day longer, I might have been able to execute my plans.'

Sir Thomas reached forward and stroked his daughter's cheek.

'Sister!' They turned to look at Elizabeth, who was alighting from the second carriage, with flame-haired Bridget following close behind. 'How we have missed you at court. Why, you have grown so flushed!'

'Good day, Elizabeth,' Frances replied evenly. 'And to you, Bridget.'

Her younger sister grinned mischievously. 'Did you miss us too, Fran?'

'Of course,' she replied with a smile. 'But I know His Majesty could hardly have spared you.'

'Indeed not,' cut in Elizabeth. 'He showed us great preferment, did he not Mama?'

'Yes,' agreed Helena distractedly. She was studying Frances closely.

'But he noted *your* absence,' Elizabeth crowed, her features suffused with a look of deep satisfaction.

'We are greatly fatigued from the journey,' their mother cut in. 'Let us go and take our rest before dinner.' She swept ahead of the group, then suddenly stopped and turned.

'Frances, I would be grateful if you could accompany me,' she said. 'Nobody has a steadier hand with a needle, and I fear one of my dresses will be quite ruined without your attention.'

Frances nodded her assent, and followed in her mother's wake. It took a moment for their eyes to adjust to the cool gloom of the reception hall, which was dominated by an ornate fireplace. With its Doric arches supported by half-naked mythical figures carved into the design, it had always reminded Frances of an ancient temple. As a child, she had been entranced to watch the figures as they seemed to move in the flickering light of the fire, their bodies weaving and swaying in a hypnotic dance.

Her mother's shoes tapped lightly against the polished mahogany as she began to mount the tightly twisting staircase. Frances followed closely behind, past the huge portraits of her ancestors that lined the walls. She drew a sort of comfort from the reminder that she was just one branch of the tree. Her bloodline had flowed through its ancient trunk for many hundreds of years and – God willing – would continue to give life to new shoots for many years to come. What she thought, felt, and feared was of little consequence, in the end.

At the first landing, the steps branched left and right. Helena took the latter, which led to her apartments. Her husband's, in a mirror image, were in the west turret of the house. Frances followed at a respectful distance. The gallery ahead was suffused with light, which streamed in through the long windows at either side, and at the far end. Even in winter, this part of the castle was noticeably warmer than anywhere else, and was a welcome refuge from the elements, but today the bright sunshine made it unbearably hot. Frances and her mother quickened their pace.

Passing through the doorway at the end of the gallery, their eyes had to become accustomed to the sudden gloom. It was mercifully cooler here, the thick tapestry curtains drawn across the small mullioned windows to preserve the privacy of Helena's apartments. The lavender that had been strewn on the rush matting released its potent scent as their soft leather soles pressed upon it.

When they reached the marchioness's privy closet, there was a bustle of activity as three of her ladies unpacked the coffers that were stacked precariously, one on top of the other. Each was covered with deep brown leather embossed with the Northampton crest in gold.

As Frances gazed around the room, her eyes feasted upon a riot of colour, the vivid silks, satins, and cloth of gold of her mother's dresses strewn across chairs and dressers, waiting to be brushed, wrapped in linen, and carefully placed into the huge wooden chests that lined the closet. There was a flash of blue as a string of sapphires caught the light, before one of the ladies carefully placed it inside the enamel cabinet that was set upon one of the dressers.

'You may leave us.'

The marchioness spoke softly, but with authority. Her ladies bobbed a curtsey and left the room quietly, their heads bowed.

Helena glanced around with a look of exasperation.

'Always such a trouble,' she said with a sigh. 'The packing and unpacking.'

'Your rank requires no less, Mama.'

Her mother smiled weakly. 'You are right, Frances. The late queen would have chided at such impatience. She always made much of exterior shows.'

She paused, all trace of her smile disappearing.

'But when it is for such a short time . . .'

Startled, Frances shot her mother an anxious look.

'Surely you have no plans to leave Longford just yet? The king cannot expect your presence at court again so soon.'

Helena reached out and stroked her daughter's cheek. Without answering, she scooped up the blue and gold brocade gown that lay across one of the chairs and placed it on top of another nearby. She gestured for Frances to come and sit on a cushion at her feet, as she had so many times as a child.

'My love, we can only stay until the sickness has left London. It arrived the day after His Majesty entered the city. Already it has claimed many hundreds of lives, the king's own attendants among them.'

Frances stared at her hands and fought to maintain her composure. She could not bear the thought of saying goodbye to her parents again so soon. With difficulty she swallowed, then remarked quietly: 'It does not augur well for the new reign.'

'Indeed. Already plenty of the court hanker after the days of our old queen – they, who were so quick to leave her side in order that they might hurry north to meet their king in waiting. They are just as quick to regret him now. People . . . people talk in whispers. They said that his accession was like a bolt of lightning, illuminating the kingdom in a brief, dazzling glow that seemed to leave it darker as soon as it had passed.'

'How was he received, upon his arrival in London?'

The marchioness paused before replying. 'As magnificently as might be expected,' she said at length. 'All those of rank flocked to London for the occasion. They were hard-pressed to find space in the palace. And the streets outside seemed paved with men, women, and children.'

'It must have pleased His Majesty to see so many loyal subjects come to pay him homage,' Frances remarked.

'Naturally,' her mother replied. 'But perhaps he has not been used to such ceremonies in his kingdom. They seemed to . . . tire him.'

The two women exchanged a look of mild amusement. Even in the old queen's time, Frances had heard that the King of Scots had little patience for the elaborate pageantry of court, preferring to spend time alone with his favourites.

Frances turned towards the window, and a flash of scarlet caught her eye. Rising, she crossed to the chest below it, over which was laid the most luxurious gown she had ever seen. The outer skirt and sleeves comprised at least two dozen ells of bright red velvet material, while the kirtle and bodice were fashioned from creamy ermine flecked with black. A long cloak that fastened to the collar of the gown was made from the same rich material. Frances could not resist reaching out to stroke the smooth, soft fur. Gathering it up in her arms, she was surprised at its weight. It would be stifling in the heat of summer.

'You will outshine all of the other ladies at the coronation in July, Mother,' she said wonderingly.

Helena waved away the compliment. 'I would be a good deal more grateful for such warmth on a winter's day.'

There was silence for a few moments, then Helena bade her daughter sit with her again, and clasped both of Frances's hands in her own.

'My daughter.' She pronounced the word as 'dotter,' a rare hint of her native tongue. 'You are my precious jewel. If only I could keep you as safe as these trifles—' she gestured to the coffers surrounding them, each secured with a brightly polished lock, the keys to which were only entrusted to her highest-ranking attendant.

Frances looked up into her mother's dark brown eyes. She had long since seen her fiftieth year, but with her pale skin, high cheekbones, and small rosebud mouth, she was still beautiful.

'Lady Mother?'

'Frances, you must know that the court – the kingdom – is greatly changed,' Helena began, her voice low. 'King James has no patience with the traditions upheld by the late queen. Already the court is beset with scandal and vice. It will bring shame upon the kingdom.' A scornful look crossed her face. 'Yet neither does he respect our former mistress's moderation in matters of religion, but insists upon the strict observance of the Protestant faith. He seems determined to bend his subjects to his will.'

Helena looked down at her hands for a moment, and when she raised her eyes to Frances again they were clouded with anxiety.

'He has declared a war on witches, Frances. He says that they are a canker in our midst, and that God has appointed him to destroy them all. He will not leave a stone unturned in his search for the "whores of Satan", as he calls them. Already Cecil is drafting a new Act against witchcraft. Any practice that is deemed to be sorcery will be punishable by death.' She paused, eyeing Frances closely. 'Even the arts of healing are under suspicion. There is to be no mercy.'

Frances looked doubtful. 'Surely the king does not mean to hunt down the wise women and cunning folk? His officials would have to scour every village in the kingdom, and to what purpose? Their skills have always been used for good, not evil.'

'All, Frances. Nobody is safe. Not even—' Her mother stopped abruptly, and Frances saw that her hands shook as she reached up to smooth her forehead, as if trying to press away the frown.

Frances felt her chest tighten. Deliberately, she slowed her breathing, as her mother had taught her. Panic is the enemy of reason. The court was far away, she told herself now. Here, at Longford, the world went otherwise.

'What proof can they find that such healing is harmful?' Frances demanded. 'Most of those who practise it do more good than apothecaries and physicians – and demand a lot less in return.'

'An accusation is enough to bring a witch to trial now,' her mother replied quietly. 'The authorities do not require further proof, beyond hearsay and rumour. A confession would be gratifying, of course, and no doubt King James intends to employ the means to wrest a few of those, as he has in Scotland.'

Frances suppressed a shudder. 'Surely you do not fear for me, Mother?'

'Cecil told you to have a care, Frances,' her mother replied. 'Now it is clear why. Every word he speaks is for a purpose.'

'But he knew that I was there to ease Her Majesty's suffering,' Frances protested. 'My herbs were to heal, not to conjure up the Devil.'

'Cecil knows only the king's truth now. And he is resolved to prove it. He will not rest until he has delivered a witch to his master, as a cat would kill a mouse for its keeper. If he can serve his own ends at the same time, then so much the better.'

'But what am I to Cecil?' Frances demanded scornfully. 'There must be many more people at court of whom he wishes to rid himself, and I am already out of the way here at Longford.'

'You know that he has long resented our family for the favour shown to us by her late Majesty, despite . . .' Helena's voice trailed off. After a pause, she reached out and grasped her daughter's hands again. 'We must keep you here, Frances, away from the vipers' nest of court.' Her face twisted with distaste.

'Nothing would give me greater pleasure,' Frances assured her.

'But you must understand, you will be alone here – the household and your personal attendants excepted, of course. Your sisters will accompany us to London – Lord knows, they hanker after returning,' Helena added. 'We must be seen to present ourselves to the king, or risk his displeasure.'

'I have been alone here these many weeks, Mother. And Longford is still standing, is it not?'

The marchioness returned her smile.

'I am sure you could manage ten such households, and still have time for those precious plants of yours,' she assured her. 'But even here, so far removed from the perils of court, you must look about you.'

Frances's expression darkened. 'I know that all too well.'

She regretted her words at once, but it was too late.

'What has happened?'

Frances hesitated. 'The Reverend Pritchard chose the evils of witchcraft as the subject for his first sermon,' she replied eventually, failing to keep the scorn from her voice. 'He seemed to disapprove of my attending the Godwin boy, who has sickened again, and warned his flock against healers and wise women. He would have done better to offer prayers for the late queen.'

Helena's brow was creased with concern. 'You take too many risks, Frances. You must put your own welfare ahead of those whom you think you help.'

'Forgive me, lady mother, but I *do* help them,' Frances urged. 'They have no other succour. The rantings of that cleric can hardly make any positive effect.'

Her mother shot her a warning look. Frances took a breath, then continued. 'I have done nothing against the laws of God or nature. I only use my medicines for good, Mother.'

'Would that you might not use them at all!' Helena burst out with a severity that surprised Frances, who nevertheless held her gaze steadily. Eventually, her mother gave a heavy sigh, and when she spoke again it was in a more resigned tone.

'It is because of me that you are in such danger, Frances,' Helena said quietly, her eyes brimming with tears. 'I, more than anyone, respect the skills of healers.' She paused, glancing up at the portrait of the Virgin Mary that hung on the wall opposite the window. 'When I was carrying your sister Elizabeth, I fell mortally sick with a fever. The queen sent her most trusted physicians to attend me, but it was all in vain. I continued to worsen. Then the queen's old nursemaid, Blanche, sent for a woman whom she knew to be skilled in the art of healing. Her tinctures broke the fever and saved my life – and that of my child.'

Frances stared at her mother and understanding suddenly dawned.

'And that is why you and my father have always encouraged my study of such arts, when I should have been spending my days with the needle or lute?'

Helena looked down at her hands.

'We have put you in danger, Frances. The old queen looked fondly upon wise women – and men,' she added, 'and refused to listen to Cecil and others of her council who spoke out against them. But they have been subject to the whims of the monarch many times before now. Hundreds have perished in the past on suspicion of using their skills to bring sickness and even death.' Her expression darkened. 'These are perilous times, Frances, and what was smiled upon in the last reign is condemned in the next.'

'So I must relinquish my healing? Turn my back on those who suffer?' Frances asked, her words clipped.

'If you do not, then your life here at Longford will be in as great a peril as if you were at court.'

Her mother had struck at the heart of her fear, and she knew it. Frances sighed, resigned.

'You know that I will do anything to stay at Longford, even if it means withholding my skills – for a time,' she added.

Helena nodded, satisfied. 'Safety will be your reward – and mine.'

CHAPTER 5

2 May

'What has happened to your hair, Frances?' Elizabeth demanded scornfully as soon as her sister walked into the parlour. 'You look as if you have been on the ducking stool!'

Bridget gave a giggle, but quickly stifled it when she saw her mother's face. Calmly, Frances took her place at the breakfast table. With Ellen's help, she had divested herself of her sodden riding gown and mud-stained boots, both of which now hung by the kitchen fire. A simple dress of pale blue silk had been hastily pulled over her head and laced up – a little too roughly, she fancied – and Ellen had tamed her tangled hair into a neat bun at the base of her neck. But there had been no time to dry it, and every now and then Frances felt a droplet of rainwater trickle down her back.

'My lady mother.' Frances inclined her head, then turned to the opposite end of the table. 'Father.'

She plucked a grape from the platter in front of her, then took a sip of ale. Slowly setting the glass down, she addressed her sister: 'I decided to take a ride before the weather turned.' She smiled. 'As you have observed, I was a little too late.'

Helena shot her a look of reproof. 'You should know better than to ride out into a storm, and without anyone to accompany you.'

'Our daughter was ever mistress of her fate, my love,' Sir Thomas cut in, smiling. 'That is no doubt why our late queen showed her such favour. She recognised a kindred spirit.'

Frances smiled ruefully at him.

'Well, that may have served in the last reign, but our new king would not take kindly to such waywardness in women,' her elder sister remarked. 'Lady Margaret writes that the queen is subject to his will in all matters – their daughter too.'

Frances saw the look of triumph in Elizabeth's eyes. She always loved to boast of her acquaintances at court, few though they were.

'Ah, but such great ladies have always found ways to trick their husbands into believing that they are compliant, when all the while it is they who wield the power,' her father observed, smiling at his wife.

Elizabeth opened her mouth to speak, but was interrupted by a sharp knock at the door. A moment later, Dymock walked in carrying a letter. He gave it to his mistress with a quick bow. Frances saw a fleeting look of concern cross her mother's face as she opened it. Glancing at the note, she could just discern the outline of a lion on the seal. Her scalp prickled.

Helena's eyes darted over the contents, which were evidently brief. Frances observed her closely, but her expression was impassive.

'The Earl of Northampton will dine with us this evening,' she announced at length. 'He has broken his journey in Salisbury, but will be with us by five o'clock.'

There was a brief silence. Frances's heart sank. Her uncle only ever made the journey to Longford in order to bend one or both of her parents to his will. He was not even a blood relative, but claimed kinship to Helena's first husband, and had always styled himself her brother. As a scion of the powerful Howard family, his word was law, as he saw it. Frances knew that her parents hated his visits just as much as she did.

'The earl must have followed in our wake,' Sir Thomas remarked evenly. 'We only saw him a few days ago at court.' Frances noticed the look that he exchanged with her mother.

'We are fortunate indeed that he has chosen to honour us with a visit when he must have more pressing business at St James's,' Helena replied.

Frances stared down at her plate, but her appetite had vanished. It had been many months since she had seen her uncle, but the memory of his visit remained all too strongly imprinted in her mind.

'How long will he stay?' she asked, careful to keep her tone neutral.

'He does not say,' her mother replied. 'But I doubt it will be for long. He will have much to occupy him, now that he is a member of the council.'

Frances looked up. 'Then he has succeeded, despite Cecil's opposition?'

Helena nodded. 'Our new king has no wish to make an enemy of the old noble families. The Earl of Nottingham has also found favour, though he is no more a friend to Cecil than my brother.'

Frances fell silent. Perhaps the king would prove more conciliatory than they had feared.

'We must make haste,' Elizabeth declared excitedly, interrupting her thoughts. 'My uncle will no doubt wish to discuss our marriage. We must have our best gowns prepared.'

'Lord Northampton will not be here for seven hours yet, sister. You might have a hundred gowns prepared in that time,' Frances observed sardonically.

'You would do well to make shift yourself,' Elizabeth retorted, looking her sister up and down. 'He will want to talk of your marriage too, even if there are fewer suitors for the second-born daughter.'

Before Frances could answer, Elizabeth stood up and gave a brief curtsey to her mother, then hastened from the room.

'If only that were true,' Frances said quietly to herself.

The fire crackled in the grate, its warmth releasing the scent of the fresh sprigs of rosemary and lavender that had been scattered across the floor. Frances and her sisters sat on a long, low mahogany bench, the seat covered with dark red velvet. Each of them wore their finest dresses, their hair beautifully coiffed, and their necks sparkling with jewels. Opposite them were their mother and father, seated next to each other. Helena's dress was of dark grey satin, shot through with a silver thread that caught the flickering light of the fire. Her back was straight, and her hands were clasped together on her lap. Nobody spoke.

After several minutes, a loud knock could be heard in the entrance hall beyond. Sir Thomas reached across and gave his wife's hand a reassuring squeeze, then rose to his feet. Another knock, and Dymock entered.

'The Earl of Northampton,' he announced, bowing low.

Frances's uncle swept past him. His imposing figure seemed to fill the room at once. He was dressed in a dark red doublet, slashed with gold silk, and Frances noticed that the fastenings were pulled taut across his stomach. He wore the white hose made fashionable by the men of court, but his red leather shoes, though pointed, had no heels. This latest embellishment must have been, literally, a step too far, she mused.

Frances and her sisters rose to their feet. Only their mother remained seated.

'My lord, we are greatly honoured by your visit,' her father said, giving a swift bow.

'Gorges,' the earl replied abruptly, then looked down at her mother, who proffered her hand. He kissed it briefly.

'Why are you not at court, sister?' he demanded without further ceremony.

Sir Thomas nodded to Dymock, who poured a glass of wine and offered it to the earl, then stood behind his chair. The rest of the company sat down.

'It is from Burgundy, my lord,' Sir Thomas remarked pleasantly. 'A particularly fine vintage.'

The earl grunted, and downed the contents of the glass. Frances noticed a droplet of the ruby liquid trickle from one corner of his mouth. He brushed it aside, then held out his glass for more.

'We will return to London as soon as the sickness has passed and we have put our estate in order, brother.' Helena spoke softly but with authority.

'What business can there be here of greater import than His Majesty's pleasure?' Northampton demanded, casting a scornful look around the room.

'It is our intention to leave the care of Longford in the hands of our daughter Frances, my lord,' she replied.

The earl swung to look at Frances, his eyes narrowing. She straightened her back and met his gaze. Her uncle had always been a thickset man, but she fancied he had grown heavier these past months, his complexion ruddier. The blond hair that now barely covered his scalp was flecked with white.

'Her?' he scoffed. 'What about your sons?'

'Theo and Edward are both completing their studies at Cambridge, my lord,' her mother cut in, 'and Robert and Thomas are staying in the household of the Earl of Derby.'

'That at least is good news,' the earl remarked. 'Lord Stanley will join me on His Majesty's council – God knows he's paid out enough for it. He will prove a useful ally against Cecil.' He took another drink, then looked back at Frances. 'But what does she know about running an estate? She is merely a girl.'

Frances felt herself redden, but remained silent.

'Our daughter knows Longford better than anyone,' her father replied a little too firmly. 'And she is quick to learn.'

'Have you no agent, man?' the earl continued, as if he hadn't spoken. 'This is not woman's work. Our new king would be shocked to hear of it.'

Frances imagined the look of triumph on her elder sister's face, but stared resolutely ahead.

'We trust Frances above any of our household,' her father insisted, though his voice lacked conviction. 'I am sure the king would understand that the bonds of family are stronger than any other.'

'With a whore for a mother?' the earl spat back. 'One who abandoned him when he was still in the cradle?' He glared at

Helena and her husband. 'You might have understood our new king better if you had troubled to pay your respects to him at Berwick, like sensible – and faithful – subjects.'

'Brother, you must know that my duties to Her late Majesty prevented our journeying north,' Helena replied sharply.

'So you tied yourself to a powerless old woman rather than show your obedience to your new sovereign?' he cried. Frances saw her mother's eyes widen briefly, but she remained silent. 'You have lived at court long enough to know where the path to advancement lies,' her uncle continued. 'You have brought disgrace upon our family, and if you do not soon return to court, it would be better that you remain for ever absent.'

'We will be there for the coronation, my lord,' her mother replied calmly.

'Along with half of London!' the earl retorted angrily, his colour rising even more. Frances noticed a small vein at his temple begin to throb. 'If you do not present yourself to King James before then, you will find yourselves at the back of a whole procession of supplicants for his favour. Your husband has already failed to secure a place on the council. There will only be scraps left for you both to scavenge by the time you reach him.' He took another long swig of wine. 'Do you not care for their fortune, either?' he demanded, gesturing towards Frances and her sisters, and spilling some of the contents of his glass. 'I have been working tirelessly to make them good marriages, but it will all be in vain if you do not show them at court.'

'We care deeply for all our children, my lord,' Helena countered, 'and will be taking Elizabeth and Bridget with us when we return to London.' Both girls sat up straight at the mention of their names, their eyes sparkling at the thought of being introduced to prospective suitors.

'They look well enough,' Northampton muttered, giving them a quick appraising stare. 'But you know this one is the real jewel in the family chest.'

Without warning, he grabbed Frances by the wrist and dragged her to her feet. 'She's a pale little creature,' he said, pinching her cheek between his finger and thumb. Frances winced and lowered her gaze, unable to bear the sight of her uncle assessing her as he would a horse that he planned to show off at the tiltyard. 'But she is the fairest of your daughters by far, and her beauty makes up for her being only the second-born. If we play it right, she will restore your family to favour.' His expression darkened. 'Had she not been so obstinate, she would already be married to a duke.'

Frances shuddered inwardly at the mention of the proposed betrothal to the aged Duke of Rutland. Her obstinacy had been rewarded, when, after several months of protracted negotiations, her prospective suitor had died. She glanced up at her parents, who seemed to have been struck mute. After an agonising pause, her father spoke.

'If you had three jewels, my lord, would you place them in the same casket,' he asked quietly, 'so that a thief might steal them all away at once?' The two men eyed each other intently. 'The court is a bountiful place, as you say,' Sir Thomas continued, 'but it is also a dangerous one. Though we may hope for peace and toleration, His Majesty has made no pronouncements yet. But it is no secret that he intends to purge England of witches, just as he has Scotland. Once this zealotry takes hold, there is no knowing where it will lead. You know that Frances is skilled in healing. She won favour with the late queen because of it, but it is more likely to earn her the censure of this new king. We will not risk her safety, nor that of our entire family, by bringing her too soon to court.'

The earl fell silent, considering.

'My niece would do well to desist from such practices at once,' he said at length. 'You have indulged her long enough with her plants and potions. The king will have her marked as a witch before she has even set foot in St James's, and Cecil will lose no opportunity to disgrace our family. He would have succeeded before now, were it not for the old queen. If my niece courts scandal, he will use it to oust me from the council.'

'Which is why we must keep her at Longford for now,' her father cut in. 'She will live quietly here, free from suspicion. And when the time is right, and memories have faded, we will bring her to court, where she might choose from a whole host of suitors.'

Frances's heart was pounding, but she could not help smiling at this last remark. Having married for love themselves, her parents were resolved that their daughters should do the same, no matter what the convention.

'Very well,' her uncle snapped. 'But when the time is right, a husband will be chosen for her. It is my will, and I am the head of the family. Even my cousin the queen knew her duty well enough in that regard.'

Frances sighed quietly. Her uncle would never let an opportunity pass to mention his distant cousin, Lady Parr, whose marriage to King Henry had gifted the earl his seniority in the family. If it had not been for his borrowed royal blood, her mother would have held sway and decided her own fate – and that of her children. As it was, she might hinder the earl only by proving slow to fall in with his schemes. But she could not hold back the tide for ever.

'Well then,' her father declared. 'It is decided. Shall we dine?'

He led the way into the dining room, where a splendid feast had been set out in the earl's honour. As Frances followed dutifully in his wake, she could not help hoping that he might choke on it.

CHAPTER 6

22 May

Frances thumbed idly through the pages of *The Gardener's Labyrinth*. It weighed heavily on her lap, its brown leather binding and gold lettering showing none of the wear and tear of the other gardening books in the library. Sighing, she closed the book and pressed her back against the cool stone of the window frame. Many times in the past she had occupied this seat in the library, which looked out over the River Avon. Even the noise of her siblings playing in the maze nearby, squealing with delight every time one of them found the other's hiding place, had never distracted her from the worlds into which she had escaped through her father's books.

Frances felt her eyelids grow heavy now. The rays of the afternoon sun still pierced the windowpanes, throwing diamond-shaped patterns across the polished oak floor and making the room unusually warm.

'Master Hill is as diverting as ever, I see?'

Her father's voice, soft though it was, jerked her back into consciousness. She smiled ruefully.

'I fear that I will never be worthy of his teachings, Father.'

'Is anyone, I wonder?' Sir Thomas asked, his eyes sparkling with mirth. 'He is surely an even greater oracle than your good uncle.'

Her smile faded as she remembered that evening three weeks before. Thankfully, the earl had left the following morning, eager to be back at court lest Cecil call a meeting of the council in his absence. Would that he might stay away for ever.

Frances watched her father as he walked over to the bookshelf containing his theological texts. He ran his hand along one of the rows as if looking for something in particular. She noticed that his expression had grown suddenly serious.

'What are you looking for, Father?'

At once, his features relaxed, and he shrugged his shoulders as if conceding defeat.

'Ah, it is nothing, my love. I was looking for a small jewel of a book – or rather, an author.'

He paused, noting his daughter's quizzical expression.

'But I can see that I have perplexed you as much as your Master Hill there,' he said, nodding to the book on her lap. 'I had not meant to play on words so dreadfully as he.'

Frances smiled as realisation dawned.

'Father Garnet was ever a favourite of yours. See, there it is,' she said, pointing to where the book was nestled between two larger volumes. Frowning, her father plucked it from the shelf and slid it into his pocket.

'I must find a safer home for this. We do not yet know if King James has the same taste in literature as his predecessor.'

'Surely he can take little interest in the libraries of his subjects, Father? Besides, the late queen had a good many Catholic texts in her privy chamber, even though she too was of the reformed faith.'

Her smile faded as she studied her father's face. He seemed to hesitate for a moment, then came to sit by her.

'I do not share the hopes held by others, Frances,' he said gravely. 'Until we know for certain that our new sovereign will be as tolerant as the last, we must act with caution.' Catching the alarm in his daughter's eyes, he forced a smile. 'So I shall confine my reading to the same dull texts as you favour,' he said, with something like his accustomed humour.

They sat in silence for a few moments, then Sir Thomas reached forward and squeezed his daughter's hand.

'My dear Fran. How I shall miss you when we leave.'

Frances looked up into his kind grey eyes. There were deep wrinkles at the corners, and his light brown hair was flecked with grey. But he was handsome, and his body still bore the strength of youth.

'Must you go so soon?'

He reached out to stroke her cheek, and smiled.

'I wish that it was otherwise, and we could live out our days happily here at Longford. But your uncle will not be denied – and neither will your sisters. They are most anxious to return to civilisation. Besides,' he added with a grin, 'the royal hose cannot look after themselves. Neither can the doublets, shirts, and linens.'

Frances did not return his smile. She knew that he was making light of it, but the long-awaited appointment by the new king had been little short of an insult, especially given her mother's status. They had heard of it from Cecil's hand two days before. It stung all the more because of the knowledge that her uncle had been right.

'Surely there are lesser officials who could take care of Richmond Palace? It is beneath your dignity, and that of my lady mother. The late queen charged you with defending the shores of her kingdom, yet now you are reduced to supervising the royal wardrobe. How will you bear it?'

'Ah, but you forget, daughter. The gardens, too, are to be given over to our care. And I hear they are in a sorry state, perpetually flooded at high tide. You above all others cannot wish us to neglect those sodden plants and hedgerows?'

His smile faded as he saw his daughter's stricken face.

'I know that we shall be leaving Longford in safe hands, my love. What you don't already know about the estate, you will soon learn. I will make sure of that. And I shall be happy to think of you here' – he glanced out at the gardens – 'with your cherished companions to keep you from loneliness.'

He stood silently for a few moments, clasping her hands. Then suddenly, as if remembering himself, he said: 'Well, now. We must not tarry here all afternoon. We have a visitor, after all.'

Frances jerked her head up in surprise.

'Someone here now? But I did not hear anyone arrive. Who is it?'

'Come now, Fran,' her father replied, enjoying her bemusement. 'The Reverend Pritchard will think us rude if we keep him waiting any longer. He must have been in the parlour for fifteen minutes already.'

Sir Thomas noticed his daughter's eyes widen, but his expression was unreadable as he held her gaze. Frances might have known that her mother would tell him everything she had confided. There were no secrets between them. Dutifully, she followed her father out of the library.

The parlour door was open, and as they approached Frances could hear the sound of footsteps pacing up and down. They stopped abruptly as she and her father entered the room.

'Lady Frances,' Pritchard said, inclining his head. 'My lord.' A deeper bow this time.

Sir Thomas nodded in greeting.

'I am glad to see you again, reverend.' Frances noticed the fleeting look of discomfiture on their visitor's face as her father spoke. 'How good of you to call on us, and on a Sunday too – your busiest day of the week. I often wonder what you clerics do on the other six days,' he added cheerfully.

Frances suppressed a smile. Before Pritchard could respond, Sir Thomas crossed to the largest chair by the fireplace and gestured for him to sit opposite. Frances moved to stand behind her father, her hands resting on the back of his chair.

'How may we be of assistance, reverend?' her father asked pleasantly.

Pritchard cleared his throat and straightened his back.

'Sir Thomas, I have been most anxious to call since you did me the honour of visiting the parsonage last Friday.'

'We are indebted to you, reverend. Especially on such a warm day.'

Frances saw Pritchard's eyes dart across to the decanter on the table next to the fireplace, but neither she nor her father made any move to offer him a glass.

'I know that the marchioness and your lordship will soon be departing for Richmond – much to my sorrow and that of my parishioners,' he said at length. 'And I wished to convey my heartfelt desire to be of service to your daughter, should she ever require it.'

Sir Thomas cast a sideways glance at Frances, who was watching the cleric uncertainly.

'I am sure my daughter is most grateful, reverend,' Sir Thomas replied affably. 'Was that the sole reason for your visit, or did you have something else to impart?'

Pritchard fidgeted in his chair again.

'My lord, your benevolence is well known throughout the parish. Indeed, barely a day has gone by since my arrival but that one of my flock praises your generosity and—'

'I am very grateful to you for relaying such heartening news, reverend,' Sir Thomas interrupted. 'Now, I am sure that Frances and I must not detain you any longer. You will have evensong to prepare for.'

'I trust that I might be assured of your lordship's beneficence towards myself also?' the reverend persisted. 'As you were kind enough to remind me at our last meeting, my tenure at Britford very much depends upon your continuing favour.'

Frances smiled, understanding suddenly dawning.

'Naturally,' replied her father. 'I am sure that if you follow the example set by your predecessor, there will be no need for any intervention on my part.'

He stood abruptly, signalling an end to their conference. 'I wish you well, reverend. Should I ask my chamberlain to escort you from the castle?'

'I thank you but no, your lordship,' Pritchard replied with a curt bow. 'I can easily find the way by which I arrived.'

As Frances watched him step briskly from the room, an angry red flush creeping up his neck, her mouth slowly lifted into a smile.

'Well then,' her father repeated with satisfaction. 'All is well.'

1604

CHAPTER 7

23 June

The warm, sweet scent of ripening wheat wafted on the breeze as Frances rode back through the parkland. Craning her neck from the saddle, she could just see the green stalks swaying gently. Although she enjoyed the long, warm days of summer, it was harvest time that she loved best, with all of the riches of nature on display, promising to reward and nurture the villagers during the long winter months ahead. She looked forward to watching the wheat being scythed and gathered around each field in neat stooks, which would then be set out to dry before being moved to the barns, safe from the elements and thieving hands. Despite the gloomy predictions of the astrologers and soothsayers, the rains had stayed away, and if the summer continued in this way, it would bring forth one of the most bountiful harvests for many years. Perhaps God was smiling on the new king after all, Frances mused. She wondered if the sun shone as brightly in London.

Although it had been more than a year since her parents and sisters had left for Richmond, the sadness of their parting still struck her keenly whenever she allowed herself to think of it. Closing her eyes, she could feel the warmth of her mother's hand as she had gently stroked her cheek, wiping away the tears that, despite her best efforts, Frances had not managed to suppress.

There had been letters, of course – precious missives that she had greedily devoured over and over until she could recite each one as she ground the seeds of valerian into a thick yellow paste, or made a salve of feverfew and cottonweed. She was glad that they contained little news of court, the king being content for her parents to remain for the most part at Richmond – much to her sisters' irritation, and that of her uncle. In the last letter, her father had spoken of a visit to Longford, before the onset of winter made the roads too treacherous. This alone made Frances impatient for summer to pass.

Yet for all that, she was grateful for the peace and beauty of Longford, and could not deny that she enjoyed being its sole mistress. Dymock excepted, all of the household servants treated her with as much reverence as if she were the marchioness herself. In the village, too, she was respected. Her first visit to St Peter's after that satisfying encounter with her father and the Reverend Pritchard had allayed any lingering fears that he might be tempted to make fresh trouble. His weekly sermons had settled down into a pattern of dreary homilies, irritatingly self-righteous, but uncontroversial at least.

She ducked as Hartshorn passed under the gate at the entrance to the drive, then paused for a moment while the horse dipped his head and tugged at some grass by the side of the path. In the distance, the castle seemed to have assumed an almost ethereal glow as the honey-coloured stone reflected the sunlight. Her mouth lifted into a slow smile, and she chided herself for having wished that things had been otherwise. For as long as she remained here at Longford, she could withstand the pain of separation.

'My lady!'

Dymock's voice rang out across the stables as Frances was unsaddling the horse.

'My Lord of Northampton is here, and demands your presence.'

Frances stopped what she was doing. She was aware that her breathing had quickened, and she could feel small beads of sweat forming on the back of her neck.

'Tell him I will be with him presently,' she replied at length, when she could trust her voice not to betray her.

Dymock hastened away, eager no doubt to curry favour with the earl, Frances reflected bitterly. A moment later, Ellen came bustling into the stables.

'My lady, nothing is made ready for the earl. His visit is most unexpected.' She eyed Frances closely.

Frances knew that Ellen loved to gossip, but she was in no mood to indulge her. Deliberately avoiding her old nurse's gaze, she calmly fetched water for Hartshorn and gently stroked his mane as he drank.

'I am sure it is no cause for concern, Ellen. Perhaps he wishes to convey a message from my lady mother.'

There was no time for further conjecture. The earl was not a patient man. Ignoring Ellen's pleas to straighten her hair and change out of her riding clothes, Frances walked determinedly towards the house.

'Good afternoon, niece,' he addressed her, unsmiling, as she entered the hall. The earl was seated in the best chair – usually reserved for her father alone. Frances paused to glance at the portraits of her parents that hung on either side of the fireplace, drawing strength from them as she had as a child when court business had taken them far from Longford.

She had always loved this room, with its large bay windows casting light across the bright marble floor and illuminating the intricate plasterwork of the ceiling. She and her sisters had spent many hours picking out the intertwined initials 'H&F' among the elaborate, twisting vines, ivy, and roses that the expert craftsmen had carved across the expanse of the ceiling. Her brothers had had little patience for such games, preferring to run amok through the long panelled corridors and sheltered courtyards beyond.

The chair creaked as her uncle shifted impatiently. Frances lowered her gaze and swept a deep curtsey.

'My lord, forgive me. I had not expected to see you.'

'I do not doubt it,' the earl replied, smirking. 'You must have thought to hide away here for the rest of the reign.'

'Longford is my home, Uncle,' she replied evenly.

'Not any more,' he retorted with obvious satisfaction.

Frances felt her chest contract.

'Don't trouble yourself. There is to be no talk of betrothal.' Her uncle often seemed to know what she was thinking, she noticed.

Frances tried to conceal her relief.

'At least – not yet,' he added, clearly enjoying her discomfiture. 'There is a fish swimming close to my hook, and with the right bait I should land him in time.'

He took a swig from the glass that had been placed on the table next to his chair.

'But Uncle, my parents wish me to choose a husband for myself, as you know. I cannot marry where there is no affection.'

'Affection?' her uncle sneered. 'What use is affection when marriages are made? I met my wife on the day of our betrothal. I cared nothing for her looks or accomplishments. Her dowry was handsome enough.'

'I hope she felt the same disinterest, Uncle,' Frances replied coldly. She had never met his wife, for she had died in childbed after only a few years of marriage. Their child – a boy – had only outlived her by a day. Frances knew that the lack of an heir born of his own blood had driven her uncle to direct all of his attention to the fate of her own family. She wondered if it was also to distance himself from his late brother, who had been executed for treason during the last reign.

'She would have been a fool not to – like that damned cousin of mine,' the earl snapped, jolting Frances back to the present. 'Paying court to your mother like a lovesick boy, when he was a man of fifty-two and she a girl of sixteen. She can have found no joy in the marriage bed, but no matter – she did not long endure it. My cousin was dead before the year was out.'

Frances could no longer keep her silence. 'My lord, you insult my lady mother. She was of noble birth, and a favourite of the queen. She had no need of the marquis's riches. She greatly esteemed him, and always talks of him in the most respectful terms. Would that you might pay her the same courtesy.'

Her uncle smirked. 'You will soon be stripped of your naivety at King James's court.'

Frances felt herself grow pale. 'I have no plans to visit it at present, my lord,' she replied carefully.

'You have no need of any,' the earl retorted. 'I have made them for you. The king has seen fit to appoint you to the household of the Princess Elizabeth. You are to return to court at once.'

Frances took in a sharp breath. Her uncle was right: she had thought herself safely forgotten in the tranquillity of Longford, many miles from London. Surely her elder sister, residing with her parents at Richmond, should have come to the king's notice instead? Discreetly, she lowered her hand onto the back of the chair facing her uncle and gripped it hard.

'There is no need to thank me,' the earl snarled. 'Although I went to a great deal of trouble on your behalf.'

Frances spoke at last: 'But it was agreed that I should remain here, to manage the household on my parents' behalf.'

'It is thanks to your parents that I was obliged to act. They should have heeded my advice and made themselves more pleasing to the king. Instead, they are as good as banished in Richmond, your sisters with them.'

Frances's eyes widened in horror. 'But he cannot so insult a lady of rank, and one whose family has always been loyal to the crown.'

'The king can slight whom he chooses. Besides, your mother is tainted by her association with the old queen. She should have deserted her like the rest of the court when it was clear that the old woman would not much longer draw breath.'

Frances bit back a retort, but her eyes blazed. Never had she despised her uncle more.

'It is well for you that I still enjoy His Majesty's favour,' he continued, 'and that I am not without friends on the council.

Even so, I had to pay handsomely for your appointment as a lady of the princess's bedchamber.' He eyed her closely. 'But you will repay my debt in full. Your parents have fallen foul of the king, and Cecil conspires endlessly against me. You must strengthen our hand by coming to court and marrying whomever I choose for you. Our family's reputation rests upon how well you perform.'

'But my lord, you agreed with my parents that the risk was too great. His Majesty's new Act against witchcraft has but lately been pronounced. The Reverend Pritchard made sure to read it out in full during his last sermon. My skills as a healer are well known at court, and Cecil will not miss an opportunity to cause trouble – as you yourself have pointed out.'

The earl grunted. 'Hang Cecil, the crooked devil! The king sneers at him, though he flatters and fawns. He has not the looks to retain favour for long, and there are many handsome boys to take his place. We need not fear him.'

'Surely His Majesty's favour is not decided by looks alone?' Frances replied scornfully. 'Besides, Cecil knows the workings of the council better than any. He is too useful to be so easily discarded.'

Her uncle took a long swig of wine and set the glass down so hard that Frances feared it would shatter.

'What do *you* know of the court?' he demanded. 'You have been absent from it for more than a year, and will find it much changed since that crooked old spinster sat on the throne. I will have no more debate. You must prepare to leave Longford tomorrow.'

Frances stared down at her hands. Her mind was racing. She could not leave Longford, and everything she held dear, to live in that vipers' nest, as her mother had called it. It was unthinkable. She would not do it. There would be ladies aplenty clamouring to take her place at court if she managed to stave off her uncle for long enough.

'My lord, I am greatly flattered,' she replied slowly so that she might keep her voice steady, 'but as you know, I am here at my mother's command.'

'And her word means more to you than the king's?'

'I serve His Majesty above all others, of course,' Frances replied calmly. 'Only God excepted.'

'Then you shall accompany me to Whitehall.'

There was a pause. Frances could just make out the soft ticking of her mother's silver-gilt clock, a New Year's gift from the late queen.

'My lord, I regret that I cannot leave Longford at present. Not without consent given by my lady mother's own hand.'

She noticed a muscle in her uncle's jaw twitch. There was a long pause, during which she held his cold gaze. Slowly, he rose from the chair. His lips lifted into a lazy smile that did not reach his eyes. He stood in front of her.

'So good to see a dutiful daughter,' he purred, and then, without warning, he struck Frances a stinging blow across the cheek, sending her stumbling to the ground.

'You may not refuse me.' His voice was as soft as velvet. 'I am the head of the family.'

CHAPTER 8

27 June

A wave of nausea swept over Frances as the stench of rotting meat filled the air, so different to the sweet scent of the forest and the cool waters of the Avon. Instead, she was surrounded by the noisy, fetid streets of London. She fumbled for her pomander, which she had filled with freshly picked lavender and rosemary from the courtyard garden at Longford. The fragrance was at once welcome and familiar.

Outside, the rain began to fall. Before long Frances could hear it drumming on the carriage roof. Within minutes, the road would be a treacherous, muddy mire. She heard the coachman crack his whip, and the carriage lurched forward, trying to beat the onset of the deluge.

It could be worse, she reflected. If her uncle had had his way, she would have been travelling with him, in his coach, but she had persuaded him to let her remain at Longford for a few days more, because she needed to set affairs in order there. Although this was true, what she had not admitted was that she had wanted to eke out some precious time in the castle and its parkland, to immerse herself in the familiar sights and smells as if she might capture them for ever in her senses.

At last, the city's western wall was in view. Progress from here would be slowed, she knew, not by the weather, but by the growing throng of people, carriages, workshops, stalls, and detritus that littered the streets of London. Soon, the cries of the market traders mingled with the clipping of horses' hooves, and the screams of children darting perilously between the carriages that trundled relentlessly on through the crowded streets.

For one brief, giddy moment Frances thought about calling for the coachman to stop the carriage so that she might escape. She imagined herself back in the wilderness of Longford, the late afternoon sun caressing her face as she lay listening to the soft rustling of the grass.

'Get out of it!'

The cry of the coachman jolted her back to the present. She opened her eyes and peered through the window, which was already splattered with the mud of the streets. A scrawny boy scuttled to safety on the other side of the track. His shirt, which was a dirty grey colour, was hanging out of his breeches, and his bare feet were caked in mud. Glancing over his shoulder, he made an obscene gesture at the coachman, who muttered a curse.

As they drew away from the city gate, the throng of travellers and tradespeople gradually began to disperse and was replaced by open fields on either side. To Frances's relief, the stench abated too, and as a gust of wind whipped across from the south, she caught the smell of the Thames. Frances knew that in the height of summer this, too, would normally have been rank enough to turn the strongest of stomachs, but because of the heavy rain that had fallen in the last few days it was mercifully fresher. A sudden break in the clouds threw a glimmer of sunlight onto the river in the distance, beyond the spires and rooftops, as it wound its way eastwards, past the great palaces of Whitehall and Greenwich, and out towards the sea. How she wished she might follow it.

The sun was sinking now as the carriage continued eastwards. The pleasant manors of Chelsea, with their gardens sweeping down towards the Thames, punctuated the view to the right. Before long, though, the houses became smaller and more numerous, the bustle of the approaching city invading the relative tranquillity of Chelsea and its immediate surrounds. The ancient church of St Giles in the Fields lay at the crossroads ahead, its squat tower rising above the copse of trees that shielded the main body of the church. The coachman pulled hard on the reins, and Frances felt the carriage lean sharply to the right as it followed the road south through the city.

Several men in court livery hastened alongside the carriage, weaving their way among the tradespeople and residents down towards the river, where they would catch one of the numerous barges to Whitehall Palace. They must be close now, Frances realised, her heart sinking. Her uncle had left strict orders that she should seek him out as soon as she arrived at the palace. He would make sure to present her to the king at the earliest opportunity, once he had assured himself that she was suitably attired – and, she assumed, compliant. Her heart quickened as she imagined being introduced to James – and his daughter – for the first time. For all her uncle's assurances, she would have preferred a position that would not attract so much attention.

Their progress slowed again, then after about half an hour of rumbling along at barely a walking pace, the carriage veered to the left, and there before them was the great gatehouse of Whitehall Palace, a huge red-brick edifice with four towers. Peering beyond it, Frances could see the unmistakable grandeur of the royal apartments and Great Hall. These had once formed part of Cardinal Wolsey's luxurious London residence, before his fall from grace, and she recalled how the older members of Elizabeth's court had still referred to it as York Place. Despite its rather haphazard appearance, there was no mistaking that this sprawling mass of buildings was a royal palace, so magnificent was the whole effect.

Her old nursemaid suddenly awoke, looking startled for a few moments until she realised that they had at last reached their destination. She rubbed her eyes and shifted uncomfortably in her seat.

'What a tiresome journey,' she grumbled. 'I feel bruised to my very bones.'

Frances looked at her with affection.

'It is a wonder that it did not interrupt your sleep,' she said.

They passed under the great gatehouse, and Frances noticed a high, neatly clipped hedge on the left. Behind it lay a lavish suite of apartments. She reached across to lower the window on that side, and the scent of roses filled the coach. She breathed deeply.

'Those are the queen's chambers,' remarked Ellen, assuming the role of guide. 'Not as grand as the king's, of course, but I have always thought them more pleasant.'

'And they must command a fine view of the river,' Frances observed.

The path widened out ahead into a square courtyard, large enough for carriages to turn around in after their passengers had alighted. Frances and Ellen were jolted as the coach drew to an abrupt halt. The finality of it struck Frances suddenly. She gazed up at the red-brick façade that towered over the courtyard. This was her life now. There would be no return to Longford – at least, not for many months, even years. Ellen was already busying herself with smoothing down her skirts and pinching her cheeks to take away the pallor of sleep. By contrast, Frances sat as still as a statue. She felt unable to move, even if she had wished to.

The sudden opening of the carriage door broke the spell. A yeoman of the guard stood to attention, his bright red livery bearing the initials 'JR.' He stared straight ahead, but held out his hand so that Frances might step down from the coach. She looked around the courtyard and saw numerous messengers, pages, and other members of the royal household scurrying this way and that, like so many ants, all intent upon their business.

'Lady Frances.'

She swung around to see a smartly dressed official in the deep scarlet livery of the king's household. She recognised the Lord Chamberlain at once, having encountered him many times in the late queen's presence chamber. He had cut short his famously long pointed beard so that he might mimic the closely cropped style favoured by the new king. Soon James would glance around his court as if looking in a mirror, Frances thought. The official bowed quickly, and clicked his heels together.

'Welcome to court, my lady. I trust your journey was not too uncomfortable?'

'Thank you, Lord Howard. All was well.'

Behind her, Ellen climbed gingerly down from the carriage, wincing at the stiffness in her joints. She bobbed an awkward curtsey to the official.

'My lady wishes to be shown to her apartments so that she might take her ease before dinner,' she said in the superior, clipped tone that Frances knew was a sign that her old nurse felt at a disadvantage.

Lord Howard sniffed. 'Of course,' he replied smoothly. As Lord Chamberlain, he was the most senior court official, and controlled everything that took place in the household above stairs – or *Domus Magnificence* as he preferred to call it. 'Wait here, please. I will summon an escort.'

Several minutes passed. Frances glanced around the courtyard. A series of large mullioned windows were set into the red-brick façade on each side of the quadrant. Through one of these, Frances could see a precarious stack of books, so high that they must have blocked out the light in the room beyond. She supposed the chambers might belong to the Lord Chamberlain and his staff.

The sound of rapid footsteps heralded his return. He looked a little flushed, Frances thought. In his wake was a boy of about twelve years old. He was tall and thin, with the awkward gait of a young colt. His doublet was of the deep blue worn by members of the queen's household. He did not look at Frances, but stood with his head lowered, fiddling with his cap.

'My lady, this page will escort you.'

Ellen stepped forward, ready to follow.

'No madam,' Lord Howard said firmly. 'You are to be taken to Lady Frances's apartments so that you may unpack her coffers.'

Ellen cast Frances an anxious look.

'But surely that is where my lady mistress is going to, Lord Howard?'

He gave a quick, tight smile.

'Lady Frances will be there presently. Now please,' he added, 'there must be no further delay.'

With that, he motioned to the page, who made a quick bow to Frances before walking off in the direction of the large doorway that led into the palace. Her uncle must have been informed of her arrival already, she reflected with a creeping sense of dread. She gave Ellen's hand a brief, reassuring squeeze, then followed in his wake.

As soon as they were out of sight, the boy quickened his pace so that Frances was obliged to gather up her skirts and take longer strides in order to keep up with him. Darting this way and that, the boy led her through a series of interconnecting chambers, each one gloomier than the last. She would have liked to take her time to look at the paintings and tapestries that hung on the walls. Even at a glance, she could see that they were exquisite. Most of the portraits were of the new king's ancestors, both in England and Scotland. She guessed they must have been procured from his native palaces.

A burst of sunlight momentarily dazzled Frances as the page opened a narrow door in the last chamber. It gave out into a small courtyard, which was paved with cobbles. A climbing rose covered the entire wall on the south side, and its sweet scent filled the air. Frances stood for a moment, steadying her breathing. She reached up to her neck, which felt clammy and warm.

The boy rapped sharply on the door, then hastened away before Frances had time to ask him where they were. It was opened by a young woman dressed in the fine but simple attire of a lower ranking privy chamber attendant.

'Lady Frances?'

She was flushed and agitated, and seemed close to tears. Frances nodded, smiling with an assurance that she did not feel.

'There is little time,' the woman said hurriedly. 'Come, my lady.'

Frances followed after her, taking care to close the door quietly first.

A strong smell of stale sweat hit her as Frances entered a small, stifling chamber. A large fire was roaring in the grate, and heavy curtains had been drawn across the window. Sitting on the bed, blocking Frances's view of its occupant, was a finely dressed lady. Her robe was of slate-grey satin, edged with white lace and pearls along the square neckline, and with stiffly padded sleeves that rose to a point at each shoulder. Her dark blonde hair had fallen loose about her shoulders, but she held herself erect.

Frances stepped forward and saw a woman lying on the bed. Her skin glistened with sweat, and strands of matted hair clung to her face, which was puce. Tossing from side to side, she made a low, keening sound that occasionally broke into an unbearable wailing.

'Hush, my dear, hush!' the lady urged, smoothing away a tendril of hair, and dabbing gently at her forehead with a silken cloth.

In her distraction, she had not been aware of Frances's arrival.

'Lady Frances is here, ma'am,' the attendant announced quietly.

The lady turned around and gave Frances a slow, appraising stare.

'Forgive this unexpected summons, but I understand you possess some skill in healing.'

She spoke with a soft, clipped accent that reminded Frances of her mother. The conversation at Longford came back to her. *You take too many risks.* Frances hesitated. Was this a trap? She glanced again at the woman on the bed. Her sickness was no pretence.

'Only modest skill, I fear, my lady, but whatever I can do, I will,' she replied after a pause. 'How long has she been in a fever?'

'Three nights and two days. She had attended me all evening and showed no sign of discomfort. But a servant awoke me that night to tell me she had sickened.' A haunted look crossed her face. 'I think it must be a judgement from God.'

'What has been done to ease her, my lady?'

'We did everything the physician instructed. She was bled several times, and has been given nothing to drink – though she did ask for it, at first.'

Frances bit back a scornful remark. She had seen too many victims of physicians' ministrations to hope that they might have worked a positive effect. Without hesitation, she strode over to the window, pulled back the curtains, and threw open the pane. She then grasped a ewer from a nearby table and poured its contents onto the fire. A sharp hiss rose from the embers, and smoke filled the room.

'What are you doing?' the lady demanded in alarm.

Not pausing to answer, Frances proceeded to pull the covers from the bed. Gently but swiftly, she peeled back the patient's nightgown, which was drenched with sweat. Her breath had the stale stench of decay. Rinsing a clean cloth, Frances applied it to the forehead of the woman, who had stopped tossing about and lay panting, her eyes still closed.

'I would be glad if you could bring me some hyssop, spurge, and hartshorn from the courtyard garden,' Frances said calmly, addressing the woman who had admitted her. 'With a mortar and pestle, and fresh water.' The servant eyed her uncertainly for a moment, then bustled away.

The minutes passed like hours as they waited for her return. The finely dressed lady began pacing the room. Frances stole a glance at her as she dabbed at the patient's face and neck. Her back was straight, and she held her head high. The expression on her face was impassive. Only the small, regular twitching of her jaw betrayed her distress.

'You are newly arrived at court, Lady Frances?' she asked in her clipped tone as she stared out of the window.

'Yes, my lady. I have not yet been to my chambers.'

'I am sorry for it. But Bea—' she paused. 'My servant's condition seemed such that delaying your attendance would have been unwise.'

'Of course, my lady,' Frances replied smoothly. 'Time is always of the greatest import in such cases.' She was about to ask how the lady knew of her skills as a healer, but something about her expression made her decide against it.

The lady resumed her pacing and said no more. Frances turned back to her patient, who seemed quieter now. She lifted one of her wrists and could feel only the faintest flicker.

At last the attendant returned with the items that had been requested. Frances leaped to her feet and began deftly to pick the tiny flowers and leaves from their stems before grinding them into a fine paste and mixing them with a little of the water.

As soon as the mixture was smooth, Frances carried it carefully over to the bedside. Gently tilting the beleaguered woman's head forward, she poured a spoonful of the tincture into her mouth. At once she fell into a paroxysm of coughing as it slipped down her throat. Fearing that she would vomit, Frances placed her hand on her chest to calm her. Soon the fit receded and her breath came more easily. After a few moments, she slipped into a deep sleep.

'What have you done? Is she—' the lady faltered, her face a pallid mask.

'She is sleeping now, my lady. The herbs will soon take effect,' Frances replied softly, then glanced at the clock on the fireplace. 'Forgive me, but I must attend my uncle – he will have expected my presence long before now.'

The lady hesitated, giving her a long and appraising stare.

'I will return as soon as I can,' Frances assured her. 'The maid will keep watch with you while I'm gone.'

At length the lady sighed, as if in defeat. 'Very well,' she conceded. 'But be sure to come back before dawn.'

CHAPTER 9

27 June

The same boy who had led Frances to the sick woman's chamber had been summoned to convey her to her uncle's apartments. They walked at a more leisurely pace this time, Frances trying to memorise the numerous twists and turns as they made their way from what she now realised had been a secluded part of the palace to the vast suite of public rooms.

Crossing the Great Hall, Frances paused and looked up in wonder at the huge vaulted ceiling, painted in dazzling blue with gold stars. Set amongst this celestial expanse was a host of playful cherubs, their skin soft pink and white. One clutched a harp, while another was puffing out his cheeks as he blew on a tiny trumpet. Looking closer, Frances could see small faces interspersed amongst the eaves. Although they stared down benignly, she knew that their presence was intended to remind the courtiers below that everything they said was seen and heard by the king.

The boy had already reached a doorway at the far end of the hall, and, turning back, gave a small cough that echoed around the walls. Reluctantly, Frances tore her gaze away from the ceiling and followed him. A series of long, dark corridors stretched into the distance, and as the boy picked up his pace, Frances guessed that they must be nearing her apartment. Rounding a corner, they almost collided with her uncle, who was marching purposefully in their direction.

'Damn you, boy!' he shouted, clipping the page around the ear. Before Frances could protest, he had scuttled away like a wounded dog.

'Uncle.' She gave a brief curtsey.

The earl gave his niece a long, penetrating stare, his mouth lifting into a slow, sardonic smile.

'How gracious of you to call on me, niece,' he purred. 'At last.'

'My lord, forgive me,' she said calmly. 'I was required to pay attendance upon a member of the household.'

'Indeed? It must have been a most urgent matter to keep you from your duty.'

Frances held his gaze but said nothing.

'Where is Ellen?' she asked after a few moments, deciding that it was safer to talk of other matters.

'Halfway back to Longford by now, I expect,' her uncle retorted, enjoying the look of dismay on her face. 'There are attendants enough at court. You have no need of her here.'

Frances knew it to be a punishment, but bit back a reply.

'I would advise you to go to your chamber and make shift,' he said, taking a long, deliberate look at her gown, which still bore the creases from the long journey. 'You will take dinner in the hall. But be sure to retire early,' he added with a smile. 'I have plans for you tomorrow.'

He turned on his heel and strutted towards the door of his apartment, slamming it shut behind him.

Frances stood for a few moments, staring after him. She had a sudden thought of running – out of the palace, out of London, to – where? If she returned to Longford, her uncle would have her brought back immediately. The thought of his fury made her shudder. She had already angered him enough.

Resigned, she went in search of someone who might direct her to her apartment. It was not long before she found another young page, hurrying about his business and clearly irked by the unwelcome interruption. A shilling from the purse that was tied to the waistband of her dress sweetened the task, however, and he took her back to the Lord Chamberlain's office, where she was directed to a part of the palace close to the riverside gateway.

Frances unlocked the panelled oak door, with apprehension. This was the room where she would spend most of what little leisure time was afforded her. It must be a haven, not a prison.

Entering, her spirits lifted. As lady of the bedchamber to the king's eldest daughter, she was afforded a comfortable room, large enough to accommodate a dressing table, armchair, and tester bed. The thick mahogany bedposts were carved with tiny putti bearing platters of fruit, and the embroidered green coverlet reminded Frances of the moss and lichen that carpeted the forest floor at Longford. The dark wooden floor contrasted with the pale yellow of the walls, which was like newly churned cream.

The room faced west, catching the warmth of the fading evening sunlight that glittered on the river below. Crossing to the window, Frances flung it open and closed her eyes to the warm, gentle breeze. Breathing in the sharp scent of rosemary and myrtle from the hedgerow that bordered the palace walls, she could almost imagine herself back in Wiltshire. She wondered how close she was to the princess's apartments.

Her eyes sprang open. The princess. She had barely had time to contemplate her position in the young girl's household. As lady of the bedchamber, she would be one of Elizabeth's closest attendants, yet she knew practically nothing about her. There had been precious few children at the old queen's court, and although she had experience enough of tending to her younger sisters, that hardly compared to serving a princess.

A knock at the door interrupted her thoughts.

'Lady Frances. Your uncle sent me.'

The dour-faced woman regarded Frances steadily.

'Thank you, Mistress—'

'Banks, my lady.'

'It is kind of you to attend me, but I have everything that I need at present.' Seeing the woman hesitate, Frances said quickly: 'I am tired from my journey, and would take some rest.'

Mrs Banks pursed her lips and made a slight curtsey.

'Very well. I will call upon you in the morning.' Taking her leave, she walked briskly back along the corridor.

Feeling suddenly exhausted, Frances lay on the bed, not troubling to undress. She knew that she would have to rise again in an hour for dinner. Her mind was full of the events of the day, but they gradually merged into a hazy confusion of thoughts as sleep overcame her.

She awoke with a jolt several hours later. Her heart pounding, she looked around her, confused that her chamber at Longford was so strangely altered. She gave a deep sigh as she realised where she was. Her uncle would be angry that she had missed dinner. Raising herself from the bed, she padded across to the ewer and splashed some water on her face, then pushed back the stray tendrils of hair that had escaped the bun at the base of her neck.

Stealing out of her room, she made her way silently through the maze of corridors and courtyards, hoping she remembered the way to the apartment that had formed her introduction to Whitehall. She whispered another prayer as she went. If her herbs had not done their work, then God must.

The first streaks of light were in the sky as she knocked softly on the door. It was opened by the same girl who had been in attendance the day before. Frances studied her face for any sign of emotion, good or bad. But she saw only fatigue.

Entering the gloomy chamber, Frances noticed the lady, dressed in a nightgown of russet silk, her skin even paler than it had been the night before. Frances nodded in greeting, then crossed over to the bed and placed one hand gently on the sick woman's forehead. With the other, she touched her neck, keeping her fingers there for a few seconds.

The lady was watching her intently, and Frances could sense that she was holding her breath.

'How is she?' It was barely a whisper.

'She is peaceful, madam,' Frances replied. Then, seeing her eyes widen in alarm, quickly added: 'The fever is passed, and all seems well. We must have patience.'

The lady slowly exhaled.

'If she were to die, I would be alone,' she said, almost to herself. 'My husband could not abide our friendship. He knew it gave me comfort.'

Frances looked away. She pitied the lady for her miserable marriage, which sounded to be like so many others among those of rank.

Just then, there was a movement from the bed. The patient sighed and her eyes fluttered open.

'Madam?' she whispered, her mouth parched dry.

'Bea.' The lady reached to grasp her hands in her own. Her attendant smiled weakly up at her.

'What they say of your skill is true, Lady Frances,' the lady said, turning to her. 'I am greatly indebted to you.'

Frances returned her smile. 'She is weak, and needs to rest,' she replied. 'As do you, madam.'

The lady looked into her eyes, her expression uncertain. She opened her mouth to speak, but after a pause gave a slight nod and turned back to the bed.

CHAPTER 10

6 July

'You must make haste, my lady. My Lord Northampton will brook no more delay.'

Mrs Banks bustled about her chamber, retrieving pins from the floor and tidying away discarded ribbons. With trembling fingers, Frances fiddled with the lace on her sleeves.

As she turned to go, she caught a glimpse of herself in the looking glass. She had never seen such an elaborate, ridiculous costume in her life. Her dress was a vision of orange-tawny and silver-green silk. It was bedecked with long ribbons of the same material that rippled as she made the slightest movement, giving the effect of gently undulating waves beneath her waist. Her hair was caught up in a silken rope, with tendrils straying down her neck. On her feet she wore pointed satin shoes of emerald green, and every inch of skin that showed above her gown was painted white to enhance her ethereal appearance.

Frances supposed that her uncle had cajoled, threatened, or bribed the Lord Chamberlain to award her a part in the masque that was to be performed before the king that evening. Such places were always highly sought after. She was to be 'Valencia', one of several sea nymphs who bewitched and seduced a hapless mariner.

The arduous task of dressing her in this sumptuous disguise, for which she had been obliged to seek the help of Mrs Banks, gave Frances a new sympathy for the late queen. It had taken Elizabeth's ladies two hours to sew her into her robes each morning, apply her make-up, and bedeck her with jewels. Then another two hours in the evening to strip her of this 'mask of youth,' as she called it. How had she borne it?

But there was no time for such reflections. Frances had already courted the displeasure of her uncle for failing to present herself as soon as she had arrived at court. She could not risk another transgression. With a final, dismayed glance in the mirror, she left her apartment and hastened through the corridors and chambers that led to the Banqueting House, where the masque was to be performed.

The shouts and squeals she heard as she approached signalled that the revelries were already under way. As the doors were thrown open, Frances stood for a moment, trying to make sense of the riot of colour and light. She had once before attended a masque in this hall, and still recalled the elegant interior, with its white marble columns interspersed with neatly hung tapestries. But that same hall was barely recognisable now. Scarlet swags of taffeta hung from the doorway, and over the great fireplace. The pillars were festooned with silk ribbons of purple, turquoise, and orange. Looking up, Frances saw an enormous chandelier, laden with hundreds of candles that threw a dazzling light across the crowds below.

A pile of velvet cushions was strewn in one corner of the room. Languishing on top was a woman, naked except for a trail of silk wound from her neck down to her chest, just covering her breasts, and then encircling her waist and ending at the top of her thighs. She wore a mask of dark green velvet edged with gold, and her luscious dark hair tumbled down over her shoulders. A seductive smile played about her scarlet lips as she sipped from a tumbler of Venetian glass. It took Frances a few moments to realise that she was looking at Lady Mary Howard, the scandal of the late queen's court, but evidently the darling of the present one. Her mother had been right. The king's puritanical views had no bearing on his court.

'La belle Marie!'

The shout could be heard above the cacophony, and the lady slowly turned her head towards it, smiling in recognition when she saw the figure of Richard Sackville approaching. Even from a distance, Frances recognised the attractive grandson of the late queen's Lord High Treasurer. She had been introduced to him once, and, although he had muttered the usual pleasantries of a seasoned courtier, she knew that he had barely noticed her, preferring to lavish all of his simpering attention on the aging queen. As he drew closer, she could see that his dark hair was slicked back from his face, and that he still had the elegant moustache and pointed beard that had been favoured in the late queen's day. Perhaps he judged that it suited him better than the new fashion, Frances thought. His ambition for preferment might be fierce, but it was exceeded by his vanity. Dressed for the impending masque, he wore a white silk doublet, embroidered with eyes, and, coiling around the neck, a golden serpent, its darting, scarlet tongue fashioned from silk ribbon. The earl's long legs were encased in white hose, and on his feet were long pointed shoes of scarlet damask.

As he strolled languidly towards the voluptuous young woman, he held her gaze unflinchingly, not heeding the greetings that were called to him on the way.

'Lady Mary.'

'My Lord Dorset.'

Frances watched, transfixed, as slowly he lowered himself onto the cushions and lay facing Lady Mary. He whispered something in her ear, and she threw back her head and laughed. When she stopped and turned to look at him once more, her face was much closer to his, her lips within tantalising reach. Frances saw his hand trace its way along the contours of Lady Mary's thigh, coming to rest at the end of the ribbon. Gently, he pulled, so that it came loose from her neck and began to unravel. Lady Mary's eyes never left his as her body was slowly exposed in all its glorious nakedness.

Frances felt her neck prickle with heat, and was aware that her breathing had quickened. Unthinking, she raised her hand to the base of her throat. It felt clammy beneath her fingertips as she slowly stroked her collarbone. She knew that she should be appalled, and yet she could not look away. As she stared at the seductive scene that was being played out in front of her, she inhaled the pungent smell of a hundred perfumes blended together in the heat of the hall, felt the press of bodies jostling against her, and the soft silk pulled tightly over her skin. She felt dizzy, as if her senses were being completely overwhelmed.

She might have remained there all night had it not been for the sudden, unwelcome arrival of her uncle.

'Ah, my dutiful niece!' he drawled sardonically.

'My lord.'

'Mrs Banks informed me that you had been made ready. You know the part that you are to play?'

For a moment, Frances was unsure whether he meant at court or in the masque. The latter was easy, if humiliating; the other, a different matter entirely.

'Yes, my lord. The Lord Chamberlain has been most instructive. We have been rehearsing all afternoon.'

'Good, good. Now turn around so that I can inspect your costume.'

Holding out her arms to either side, Frances rotated slowly, then gave an exaggerated curtsey. The sarcasm of the gesture was lost on her uncle.

'Hmm. Your costume becomes you well enough, niece. Let's hope that your acting skills are of the same standard.'

Gripping her by the wrist, he pulled her closer and hissed in her ear: 'I went to a great deal of trouble to get you this part. A *great* deal. This is your chance to come to the king's notice. If he likes you, and you serve his daughter well, he will make a good marriage for you. Far better than your mother made with that manservant.'

'I would rather he save himself the trouble!' Frances spat, her temper stirred by the slight to her father.

The earl smiled, but his grip on her wrist grew tighter, making her wince.

'If you defy me, you will suffer the consequences,' he growled. Pulling her suddenly even closer, his other hand seizing her throat, he whispered: 'I will take you as my whore.'

Frances felt as if she were choking as she looked up into his eyes, which glittered dangerously.

'My Lord Northampton.'

The voice was commanding, imperious. The earl released his hold at once as they both swung around to see who had spoken. In an instant, her uncle sank to his knees in humble supplication.

Frances gazed at the elegant lady. Her mind was a blur of confusion as she tried to make sense of what had just happened. The woman who stood before her now was the same one whose attendant she had treated. But what could she be to the earl, who was still prostrate at her feet?

The silence was broken by her uncle. 'Your Majesty!'

Comprehension suddenly dawned. Immediately, Frances lowered her eyes and made a deep curtsey, all the time hoping that the shock had not registered on her face. Focusing upon a small knot in the oak floorboards at her feet, she struggled to control her breathing. After a few moments, she dared to glance up at the woman whom she now knew to be the queen.

Anne's face was a mask of composure. She looked every inch the Danish princess whose portrait Frances had seen at Richmond, where it had been hung with unseemly haste before the old queen had even breathed her last. Those same small black eyes were staring out at Frances now. Striking rather than beautiful, her face was long and pale, and wore an expression of wry amusement. Her dark blonde hair, which had hung about her shoulders in ragged disarray when Frances had last seen her, was now sculpted into an extraordinarily high coif, and adorned with pearls. The queen's dazzling silver gown was flanked by a large, stiff collar of white lace, and the front of her dress swept down so low that it barely covered her bosom. She was just as exotic as a princess from across the seas, from the land of the Vikings, should be.

'Your Majesty, forgive me. I was just instructing my niece—' the earl spluttered.

'So I observed,' Anne cut in. 'I am still getting used to your English customs, and this manner you have of conversing with members of your family is most unusual.'

The earl reddened as he continued to kneel, staring intently at the floor. Frances shot the queen a look of gratitude, but Anne remained impervious.

'Well,' she said, after a long pause, 'we must prepare for the king.'

Staring straight ahead, she gathered up her skirts and strode forwards, stepping onto the earl's foot with the sharp heel of her shoe. He flinched, but remained kneeling. Frances thought she caught the glimmer of a smile on the queen's lips as she swept past.

A fanfare of trumpets rang out across the hall, and all eyes turned to the doorway where Frances stood. Suddenly realising she was in the way, she stepped aside and swept another deep curtsey as the king and his entourage passed. Still struggling to comprehend the enormity of what had just occurred with the queen, she nevertheless felt curious to meet her new sovereign, the first of the House of Stuart to rule England. She was surprised to see a diminutive man with an awkward gait. He walked with a pronounced limp, and his legs were bowed, as if he were sitting on an invisible horse. His left arm was in a sling – she knew he had suffered a fall on his journey south to claim his throne. As he came closer, Frances noticed that his skin was remarkably soft and white, and his beard so sparse as to be barely visible. Then she looked at his fingers, which flitted about his codpiece in a distracted manner. She was not the only one to notice this, and a wave of suppressed titters could be heard as he made his way through the room. The rumours about his unkingly habits had been true, Frances realised with dismay.

Lowering himself onto the throne beneath the canopy of crimson satin, bedecked with naked cherubs and clouds, that had been crafted for the occasion, James turned to greet his wife. Still staring straight ahead, Anne held out her hand. Her husband gave it the most fleeting of kisses, his lips barely touching the velvet of her glove. Frances had heard it whispered by one of the old queen's ladies that the King of Scots treated his consort more as an adornment than as a wife. He might beget heirs on her, but he took his pleasure elsewhere, in the beds of the pretty boys who surrounded him. Such talk was treason now, of course, but all the court knew of it.

'What manner of welcome is this? My mouth is parched!' James declared in an accent so strong that many of the assembled gathering looked about them in confusion. Thankfully, his page had already grown used to it, and scurried off to pour his master a large goblet of wine. Grabbing at it rather unceremoniously, James proceeded to drain its contents, some of them spilling down onto the silk doublet that covered his pot belly. Swiping his hand under his nose, he sniffed loudly and gave a spluttering cough.

'This cursed English rain is wetter than the Scottish. It has soaked my bones.'

A few of his courtiers laughed falteringly, uncertain whether he was joking. James stared at them with his bulbous eyes, a dribble of wine glistening on his chin. The laughter quickly subsided, and an uncomfortable silence followed.

The Lord Chamberlain motioned to Frances and her fellow revellers to take the stage. Quickly, she fell in line behind the principal performers as they mounted the temporary scaffold that had been festooned with swags of scarlet velvet braided with gold. All around the hall, the lights were extinguished so that only the stage was illuminated. Frances stumbled as she tried to find a position at the back. As soon as they were ready, Lord Howard gave the signal for the musicians to strike up the opening score. A sudden, thundering drum roll announced the start of the masque.

'Guards!'

There was a scramble of footsteps as the yeomen of the guard rushed forward and surrounded James. A groom quickly lit the sconce next to the throne, and all faces turned to see the king cowering underneath the canopy, a trembling hand on his sword.

'Calm yourself, husband. It is the striking of a drum, not of an assassin,' the queen muttered. Even at a distance, Frances caught the scorn in her voice. Recovering himself, James gave a loud, barking laugh. For a few moments, it rang out across a horribly silent hall, until the Lord Chamberlain took up the theme with a bellowing laugh, as mirthful as a lament. Urgently, he motioned for the players to ready themselves, and the masque began.

To Frances, it was an experience every bit as humiliating as she had feared. As she swayed and twirled with her fellow sea nymphs, entwining the sailor in their amorous embrace, she fervently wished herself back at Longford. Stealing a glance at the other ladies, their faces flushed and eyes sparkling, she wondered how they could delight in being part of such a spectacle. Why did they not share her resentment at being paraded in front of the braying men of the court in this way, like cattle at Salisbury market?

With a sudden rush of annoyance, Frances turned from them to peer out at the king, who was still illuminated by the hastily lit sconce. He was clearly revelling in the performance. Tapping his foot in time to the music, and laughing uproariously whenever there was even a hint of a jest – and sometimes when there was none – he was as transfixed as a child who had happened across a gathering of imps and fairies at play in the forest.

Frances forced her attention back to the masque, trying desperately to remember her steps. There had been one final, hasty rehearsal this afternoon. The smoke from the blazing sconces filled her nostrils, blending with the sweat from the dancers as they leaped and cavorted towards the crescendo. Her face burned, and the silk of her dress clung to her chest as she tried to keep pace. The king sat forward as a dozen men dressed as various fantastical sea creatures rushed onto the stage, his eyes roaming over this new source of interest with obvious excitement. Frances glanced at the queen, and caught her look of disdain. *So the gossips speak truth.*

One of her fellow nymphs jostled Frances out of her reverie as their frantic, seductive dance resumed. Stumbling, she felt herself fall, but was caught deftly by one of the new players, who guided her gently to the rear of the stage. Surprised, and deeply grateful, she mouthed her thanks as he looked at her, smiling. His eyes were dark brown, she noticed, and his mouth curved so appealingly that she could not help returning his smile.

Before she could say anything further, they were whisked along in the dazzling, swirling dance of the finale, and ended, breathless, to the rapturous applause of the king and his court.

Flushed with relief, and, despite herself, enjoying the adulation of the crowds, Frances stepped down from the stage and looked about her for – who? She realised she knew nothing about her rescuer, not even his name. But he was no longer among the players, and, as her eyes darted over the hundreds of jostling revellers, she was interrupted by the sudden, unwelcome presence of her uncle.

'You presented yourself tolerably well,' he said, his face severe. 'But you were too much in the background to attract the notice of the king.'

'I am sorry to have failed you, my lord.'

'No matter – you shall come with me now.'

Without waiting for a reply, he grabbed his niece's hand and pulled her into the throng. As she passed through the sweating, pawing, swaying crowds, Frances glanced over to the stage, and saw that some of the players had started to strip off their costumes and cavort almost naked in imitation of the masque. One of them, Lady Grisby, had already drunk so much wine that she was having trouble keeping her balance, and, lurching suddenly forward, vomited over the side of the stage.

Frances pressed forward to escape the unsightly mess, but found herself pushed up against a couple, their mouths pressed together as if they might devour each other. One of the woman's sleeves was hanging loose, exposing her creamy white shoulder, which glistened with sweat, and the man was pawing at the other as if trying to rip the entire bodice away. Frances smelt the stale tang of wine as she surged past them, her heart pounding.

The crowds were even more stifling now, as everyone jostled for an audience with the king. Her uncle used his bulk to force his way through, never releasing his grasp on Frances's wrist, so that she was pulled painfully, inexorably forward. At last they were standing before the throne. Sweating and red-faced, the earl panted his greeting.

'Your Majesty, may I present my niece, Lady Frances Gorges.'

James barely looked at Frances as she gave a low curtsey before him.

'You are welcome to court, Lady Frances,' he muttered distractedly, his eyes drawn to an attractive young actor, clad only in a sash, who was performing an elaborate dance for a loudly appreciative crowd of onlookers.

'Your Majesty has appointed my niece to the princess's household.'

The king turned to face Frances. 'Have I?' He scrutinised her closely now, taking in her gaudy costume and dishevelled hair. 'She is of good character?'

'Impeccable, sir,' Northampton cut in quickly, before Frances could answer. 'Her mother served the late queen.'

'Ha! That is hardly a recommendation. Tell me, Lady Frances, was she as ugly as my ambassadors reported? They said she had barely a tooth or a hair by the time she died.'

Frances felt her colour rise at the insult.

'The late queen was the very image of majesty, Your Grace. She—'

Swiftly, her uncle interrupted with protestations about not wishing to detain the king any longer, and proceeded to shove his niece roughly back into the crowd. But they had barely left the dais when they came face to face with Robert Cecil.

'Surely my lord is not leaving already?' he purred.

'I am afraid we must, my Lord Privy Seal,' the earl replied brusquely. 'My niece is greatly fatigued by this evening's revels.'

Cecil turned his piercing eyes on her. 'Ah, Lady Frances. What a pleasure it is to see you again. I thought you preferred to breathe the air of Wiltshire, rather than the stench of court.'

'Indeed I do, my lord,' she replied, before her uncle could stop her.

Cecil smiled at the earl's obvious irritation. 'It seems the court is not to your niece's liking. Perhaps she still hankers after that of the old queen?'

'She does not!' thundered the earl. 'She greatly reveres His Majesty, who, as you know, has singled her out to serve his daughter.'

'Of course. And we are as fortunate as the princess,' Cecil drawled. 'For we shall gaze upon Lady Frances very often now.' He paused, giving her a long, appraising stare. 'As often as we wish.'

Frances felt suddenly cold, despite the stifling heat of the room. Before she could answer, Cecil continued: 'When did you arrive?'

'Two nights ago, my lord.'

'Indeed? Here for such a brief time, and yet you have already met His Majesty, distinguished yourself in a masque . . .'

Another deliberate pause.

'And held a private audience with the queen.'

Staying just long enough to see Frances's eyes widen in shock, he turned on his heel.

CHAPTER 11

10 July

'The princess will see you now.'

Smoothing her skirts, Frances nodded at the young girl's attendant, and stepped forward into the royal bedchamber. The doorway was vast, with gilded beading lining the mahogany frame, and a red velvet canopy draped along the top. Her eyes drawn naturally upwards, Frances could not help but be impressed by the exquisite ceiling, with fat little cherubs playing happily among the benign white clouds that were flitting across a pale blue sky. The room below was dominated by an enormous red and gold satin canopy over a sumptuous bed, which was bedecked with silken cushions of the same vibrant colours.

It was a few moments before Frances noticed the small girl who was standing solemnly next to the bed, her hands clasped together and her small black eyes appraising her uncertainly. The lavishness of her surroundings made her appear all the more slight and delicate. Her hair was gloriously red, and, although it was pulled tightly back into a coif, a few unruly curls had escaped. With her pale face, and her chin narrowed to a perfect point, she appeared more like a doll than a child. The exquisitely fine dress that she wore was made from white-grey silk, with embroidered copper-coloured flowers that matched her hair, and her slender neck was encased in a stiff white lace collar. *A queen in miniature*, Frances thought.

She gave a low curtsey.

'My lady princess.'

A little giggle escaped the girl's mouth, and, looking anxiously across at her lady mistress, she immediately put up a hand to stop it.

'I am very pleased to make your acquaintance, Lady Frances,' she said, in clipped, rehearsed tones. And then, with eager curiosity: 'Is it true that you were the old queen's favourite?'

Frances smiled. 'I cannot claim that honour, Your Highness. But my lady mother was high in her favour.'

'They say that I look just like her,' the girl confided with a conspiratorial air, then frowned. 'But that makes Father angry.'

The princess glanced towards the window, where the tightly-clipped box hedges and pretty pink roses of her privy garden could be seen. Catching the longing in her gaze, Frances ventured: 'I have heard that your garden is the prettiest in all of London.'

'Oh yes!' Elizabeth cried, clapping her hands together. 'It is the sunniest place in the whole palace, the roses smell so sweet, and there is even a little maze – Mother told the gardeners to make me one. My brothers and I play in it for hours. Henry always finds his way out, of course, but it is so funny to see little Charles tottering about!'

Another glance at Lady Mar, who was frowning. She was a stout woman, with grey hair and small, piercing eyes. Frances felt them rest on herself now, and could almost sense the disapproval.

'Lady Frances . . . would you like to see it for yourself?' the princess asked, before the more senior of her attendants could stop her. 'I could show you the secret of escaping!'

'I would be delighted to, ma'am.'

Lady Mar began to voice an objection, but Elizabeth was already marching towards the door that opened out onto the courtyard. Frances gave a small curtsey to the older woman, then followed the girl. As she stepped outside, she felt the warmth of the sun like a balm on her skin, and turned her face upwards, her eyes closed in contentment. For the first time, she felt a glimmer of hope for her new life at court. She had only been there a week, yet it felt like a lifetime.

'Lady Mar is so dull,' the princess whispered, none too quietly. 'If she had her way, I would be cooped up in the school-room all day and all night, learning my Latin and reading my prayer book.'

'You must have worked hard at your studies, ma'am. You speak with greater eloquence than many ladies of my own age,' Frances remarked. The princess beamed with delight.

As they weaved their way in and out of the tiny paths of the maze, which only came up to Frances's waist, the young princess chattered happily about the antics of her adored elder brother, the exquisite dresses that her mother was forever ordering for her, the court occasions that she had been permitted to attend, and – above all – how much she preferred her life in England to the cold, dour existence she had endured in her father's draughty old Scottish palaces.

'My mother likes you very much,' she told Frances earnestly, after talking excitedly and without interruption for at least ten minutes. 'She says that I can trust you with anything.'

'I am greatly honoured, ma'am. Although I hope that you might form your own good opinion of me, in time,' Frances replied quietly. She wondered how the queen's attendant fared now. The fact that she had not been summoned back to her chambers gave her hope that she was recovered.

'I am sure I will,' the girl said with a lift of her chin. She fell silent for a few moments, then her face brightened as a thought occurred to her. 'My father says you are an excellent dancer.'

Frances laughed, surprised by the compliment. 'I think His Majesty must have mistaken me for another lady at court. He has only seen me perform in one masque – and very badly, I fear.'

'Oh no,' the princess insisted. 'My father knows a lot about dancing. He often watches me when I am practising my steps, and whips my ankles if any are out of place.'

It was said so guilelessly that it was clear she was not seeking pity. Before Frances could think of a response, Elizabeth begged her to teach her some English dances, and the two spent the next half an hour stepping, skipping, and twirling around the pretty little garden, until they were both quite out of breath. Frances felt more alive than she had for days.

Collapsing onto an ornate stone bench, they sat in happy, breathless silence for a few moments.

'Your Highness has been as excellently tutored in dancing as in language, etiquette, and no doubt many other accomplishments besides,' Frances observed with sincerity, as soon as she was more composed.

The young girl rolled her eyes. 'My dancing lessons are too short, and the rest too long. But my mother says that words hold more power than actions, so I must polish mine as often as possible.'

'You are blessed to have such a wise mother, ma'am – as is the kingdom,' Frances replied. She wondered if the queen had felt constrained by her own lack of words, as by so many other things, upon first arriving in her husband's strange domain.

She leaned forward and stroked the soft petals of a rose, then inhaled the scent on her fingers. Her new charge copied her, tugging a little too hard so that the petal came away in her hand.

'Oh. I didn't mean to do that.'

'Do not worry, ma'am,' Frances said brightly. 'If we pick a few more, I can make a syrup to revive you.'

The girl leaped to her feet immediately and began gathering the pink petals, holding up her skirts to catch them. The heady fragrance of the disturbed flowers filled the courtyard, and Frances was loath to follow the princess back inside.

Lady Mar frowned when she saw Elizabeth's dress bunched up to hold its precious cargo, her cheeks still flushed and her hair now a mass of escaped curls. Before she could voice her disapproval, however, a shout of 'Liz!' rang out from the corridors beyond, and a few seconds later, a young man stood at the doorway, a little older than the princess, but not much taller. He had the same thin face and pointed chin, and his skin was so pale as to be almost other-worldly.

'Harry!'

Elizabeth ran towards him, forgetting all about the rose petals, which scattered in her wake. She flung herself at him, reaching up to encircle his neck with her slender little arms.

'Where have you been? I have been looking for you for ever.'

'Who is this?' The young man brushed her question aside.

Frances paused from carefully gathering the strewn petals, and gave a low curtsey.

'Your Majesty.'

The boy lifted his chin slightly. Dressed in a long red velvet doublet with a purple cloak that was too large for his slight frame, he had a bejewelled black velvet cap to enhance his height, and wore a pair of white satin shoes so delicate that they would have befitted any lady at court.

'This is my new lady of the bedchamber,' Elizabeth announced with pride. 'Lady Frances Gorges.' She had been taught to pronounce the name perfectly, Frances noticed.

The prince sniffed. 'How many royal children have you attended before, Lady Frances?'

'Your sister will be the first, sir.'

'Indeed? Why then have you been appointed to serve the princess?'

Frances eyed him steadily. 'My family has served at court for many years. My lady mother and I attended the late queen, and my uncle, the Lord Northampton, is a member of His Majesty's council.'

'But what do you know of rhetoric? Of languages? And the scriptures?' he demanded. 'My sister will expect you to converse with her on all manner of subjects.'

'I was fortunate to receive an excellent education, Your Grace. My father believed that my sex should not be a barrier to learning.'

The princess glanced anxiously from her brother to her new attendant.

'Lady Frances has promised to make me some rose syrup, Henry. Will you stay for some?'

Her brother wrinkled his nose in distaste. 'Regretfully, no. Our father requires my attendance.' Drawing himself up to his full height, he added: 'No doubt he has matters of great import to discuss with me.'

With a stiff little bow to his sister, he walked briskly out of the chamber. The princess turned anxious eyes to Frances.

'Don't mind Henry.'

Frances grinned. 'I thought him the very image of a prince and heir.'

'Isn't he?' Elizabeth sighed. 'I wish I had his grace. I am forever stumbling and tripping about, or so my mother tells me.' Her face fell. 'I fear I must sometimes disappoint her.'

'A mother always wishes her daughter to grow in grace and accomplishments. My own mother used to chide me for spending too long out of doors and being late for my lessons.'

The princess's face brightened. 'I can't imagine you ever vexing your mother as I do. You are too perfect.'

Frances let out a bark of laughter. 'I am very far from that, ma'am.'

After her first audience with the princess, Frances retired to her own apartment. She knew that her leisure hours would be scarce, so she was resolved to treasure them. Sinking down onto the bed, her hand closed on the few rose petals that she had kept back when she and Elizabeth had made the syrup, intending to dry and press them in one of the many books that she had brought with her from home. She smiled at the thought of her young charge, who seemed a charming blend of innocence and curiosity; dutifulness and gaiety. She had warmed to her instantly. Elizabeth's speech was so polished that Frances looked forward to conversing with her on a whole manner of subjects – certainly more than most other ladies at court were capable of. If she must stay here, then to serve in this delightful young girl's household was surely one of the most pleasant ways to spend her hours.

A sharp rap at the door wrested Frances from her thoughts. Sighing heavily, she went to answer it.

'Well? Were you to the princess's liking?'

Her uncle was already striding into the room, casting his gaze over its contents. His eyes narrowed as they alighted on the pile of books that were stacked high on the dressing table.

'Why in God's name did you bring those? You would have been better advised to fill your coffers with clothes fit for a woman who needs a husband.'

'Her Highness seemed pleased with her new attendant,' Frances replied evenly.

'Good. Make sure she remains so.'

The earl sank down into the mahogany chair, which creaked in protest. His mouth curled into a sardonic smile. Frances knew that expression all too well.

'It seems you have won favour in other quarters too.'

'Oh?' Frances's fingers played distractedly with a solitary rose petal as she looked at her uncle, her face a mask of calm enquiry.

'Sir Thomas Tyringham was at the masque. He wishes to make your acquaintance.'

'I am surprised to have been singled out from that performance,' Frances remarked. 'It was hardly to my credit.'

'Well, it was enough to make him enquire after you. He sent a message to me this very afternoon, asking if he might become better acquainted with me and my niece.' He gave a smug smile. 'He has caught sight of my bait, it seems.'

Frances bristled. 'My lord, you have three nieces.'

'Don't trifle with me, girl. Sir Thomas was very clear that it was you he wished to meet.'

'Then I shall be delighted,' she said, with as much grace as she could muster.

'I shall return at five o'clock tomorrow.' The earl rose. Then, throwing a bundle that he had brought with him onto the bed, commanded: 'Wear this.'

CHAPTER 12

11 July

Frances looked at the bundle and sighed. It had lain untouched since her uncle had brought it to her the day before, and she had a momentary urge to throw it out of the window. At Longford, she was mistress of her own fate, but here she was to be dressed up like a painted doll and used by her uncle as he saw fit. In annoyance, she roughly pulled away the linen that had been folded carefully around the dress, then stared, momentarily transfixed. The skirt and bodice were crafted from gorgeous peacock blue satin, with silver embroidery around the low square neckline and cuffs. An underskirt of white and silver set off the dress to perfection. As Frances shook it out and held it up against her, a little velvet pouch fell to the ground. She was surprised to see that her uncle's attention to detail had extended to providing a string of pearls for her neck, and two delicate pearldrop earrings.

Frances could not help her eagerness to try the outfit on, though she felt angry with herself for it. Peeling off the tawny dress that she had worn to attend the princess – thinking as she did so that it appeared as a sparrow next to a bird of paradise – she gently pulled on the luxurious satin. She laced it up with deft fingers and turned to look at herself in the dressing-table mirror. Too small to capture the full length of the dress, the reflection still showed that the overall effect was stunning. Scooping up her hair and catching it with a delicate silver comb – a gift from the late queen – she carefully looped the pearls twice around her neck and clipped the earrings into place. Finally, she slipped on the grey satin shoes that served as her best, though they did not match the finery of the gown, and with a final glance in the mirror went to greet her uncle, punctual as ever.

'The dress suits you well.' His eyes roamed appreciatively over her body. 'My Lady Worcester assured me it would. She is a similar size to you.'

The earl enjoyed boasting about his various flirtations with the ladies of the court. His riches compensated for his advancing years, so he was never short of admirers.

'Come. We cannot be late.'

He thrust his arm at her so that she was obliged to place her hand on it and walk with him to the Great Hall. Although she had been at court for two weeks now, she had scarcely found her bearings in this ramshackle palace. As they made their way towards Sir Thomas's apartments, Frances noticed that the paintings lining the walls became more numerous; the tapestries finer. Rush matting lined the floors, and fresh lavender had been newly strewn along it, releasing its heady perfume as they walked.

Her uncle came to an abrupt halt outside a large oak door with a gently pitched arch above, into which were carved the intertwined roses of the House of Tudor. Traces of the red and white paint still remained, but old King Henry's successors had not cared to restore the decoration to its former vibrancy, and there was little hope that the new Stuart king would do so.

The earl knocked on the door, and as they waited for an answer, he pinched his niece's arm and hissed: 'Be sure to make a good impression. There will be no further disobedience in this matter.'

Frances continued to stare straight ahead.

'Of course, Uncle.'

A page wearing dark brown livery opened the door and bade them enter. The apartments within were richly but tastefully furnished. A series of anterooms gave way to a large hall with a fine plasterwork ceiling that reminded Frances of Longford. A huge fireplace dominated the left-hand side of the room, and, facing it, three large bay windows provided spectacular views of the river, as well as the mansions and churches on the opposite bank. At the far end of the chamber was a full-length portrait of the king in his coronation robes.

'There is much to admire in our king, is there not?'

A softly spoken voice cut through the silence. Frances and her uncle turned to see a smartly dressed young man with an expression of faint amusement on his face.

'A great deal,' the earl responded gravely. 'We are fortunate indeed.'

'Even more so because we are at last free of a woman's rule, eh?'

Sir Thomas seemed to direct the question at Frances, who remained silent. Although her uncle had told her that this latest suitor was of a similar age to herself, there were thin lines at the corners of his grey eyes. His light brown hair was clipped short, and, in contrast to most other men at court, he was clean-shaven. Neither did he favour the gaudy clothes of his peers, who seemed to Frances like so many prancing peacocks competing for the king's attention. Instead, he wore a dark grey doublet and black hose, which were finely made. But, though he dressed well, Frances knew enough of her uncle's taste in suitors to hope for anything good of this one.

'Forgive me. Lady Frances?' Their host smiled openly now, and, stepping forward, lightly kissed her hand.

'Sir Thomas.'

'What do *you* think of the painting?'

She considered for a moment. 'It is a fair likeness – or at least it may have been when it was painted.'

Sir Thomas laughed.

'You know it is tantamount to treason to note any sign of aging in your sovereign.'

'He is a man first, a king second.'

Frances heard her uncle's sharp intake of breath as she made the remark, knowing that decorum prevented his doing anything about it.

'Well, Lord Northampton,' Sir Thomas was clearly amused, 'you never told me that you harboured such an opinionated young lady in your family.' Before her uncle could answer, their host continued: 'In any case, I had little choice in the matter of decorating these rooms. The painting was already hung when I arrived, and it would hardly be politic to remove your king from his place of honour, would it?'

Frances could not help smiling – briefly – but had not forgiven his earlier remark.

'Shall we dine?'

Grateful for the distraction, the earl accepted the invitation at once and sat down opposite his host. Frances could not help but admire the display before them. The dark oak table was covered with a beautiful cream and red damask cloth, embroidered with leopards, unicorns, and bears – part of Sir Thomas's crest, she assumed. It was already laden with a variety of sweetmeats, breads, cheeses, fruit, and other delicacies, and from the serving room beyond Frances could smell that there were more treats to come.

As she took her place at the side of her uncle, she noticed that another setting had been laid next to Sir Thomas. Following her gaze, he said: 'Ah yes, we are expecting one more guest to complete our merry party. I trust you know Thomas Wintour, my lord?'

The earl grunted. 'He represented my opponent in a land dispute some years back. Cost me a fortune.' He took a swig of red wine from the fine glass goblet in front of him. 'So, he is back at court?'

'He arrived some three weeks ago, at the request of the queen. He is assisting her with a legal matter. You will be gratified to hear that his skills are as sharp as ever,' Sir Thomas remarked, grinning. 'I employed him myself to untangle a vexing matter of conveyance in Buckinghamshire. Almost before the ink was dry on his letter of appointment, he had worked the whole affair to my advantage. Not only did I gain in land, but in riches and reputation. I owe him a great deal.'

'I don't much care for his methods,' the earl muttered resentfully.

'Come now,' Sir Thomas cajoled. 'All's fair in love and law, eh?'

Frances saw her uncle's face grow red, a sure sign of danger. But their host seemed to care little for that, and smiled benignly from across the table.

'Thomas Wintour, my lord,' the groom announced, stepping into the room.

'Ah, Tom!' Sir Thomas exclaimed, leaping to his feet. 'We are pleased to see you indeed. Come, join us.'

Frances sighed quietly. Was there to be no variety in this monotonous charade? Even the names were the same. Reluctantly, the earl rose to his feet, obscuring his niece's view of the new guest.

'My Lord Northampton.'

Frances raised her eyes in curiosity, but she could see only the newcomer's arm, as he bowed low to her uncle.

'Wintour,' her uncle replied brusquely.

The young man moved forward to greet her.

'Lady Frances.'

With a jolt, she recognised her rescuer from the masque. She hoped the shock had not registered on her face, which felt suddenly warm. He was dressed very differently now, she noticed, with the same sober refinement as his patron, and his smiling eyes seemed to betray no hint that he knew who she was.

'Mr Wintour,' she said at last.

His lips brushed her hand, and he gave a solemn bow, holding her gaze.

'Well, do let us begin our feast,' Sir Thomas broke in affably.

'How pleasant it is to see you again, my Lord Northampton. I trust your coffers are recovered?' Wintour enquired pleasantly.

Frances smiled at her uncle's obvious irritation. Her prospects of enjoying the evening had greatly improved.

'My friend Tom is full of goodly works,' Sir Thomas said warmly. 'He is quite the rising star at Gray's Inn.'

'You are already a member, Mr Wintour?'

'Yes, my lady. I have been fortunate in my patron,' he replied, smiling at Sir Thomas. 'He encouraged me to exchange my sword for a pen, and was kind enough to recommend me to the queen, who is now my foremost client – if I can call Her Grace that. The military life was not conducive to peace and repose, such as I now find in my hours of study.'

'Nonsense, Tom! That sharp mind of yours opened more doors than my meagre recommendations.'

'Where did you serve?' the earl interrupted.

'In the Netherlands, on behalf of Her Majesty's allies.'

'The Dutch were always a drain on her coffers,' Northampton grumbled. 'It would have been better to leave them to face the Spanish alone.'

'And leave us prey to another Armada?' Wintour challenged. 'Our late queen was concerned only to defend our shores.'

The earl tutted. 'What would a woman know of war?' he demanded scornfully.

Frances opened her mouth to protest, but was interrupted by the appearance of four attendants, each bearing a dish that they set down in front of the diners. She looked down at the plate of glistening oysters.

'Please, begin,' their host encouraged.

The fresh, salty taste of the sea filled her mouth as Frances swallowed one of the oysters. She took a sip of wine, and began to relax. She took another. Although she had no intention of accepting her uncle's latest candidate, she might as well enjoy his hospitality. But she knew there would be a price to pay if she did not prove compliant. She shuddered inwardly as she remembered her uncle's threat. He would neither accept nor understand that she might wish to make her own choice. After all, he had been quick to set aside his Catholic faith when the wind turned in favour of the Protestants. It seemed to Frances that this was an age when people's consciences had to spin as easily as a weathervane.

'How did you enjoy the masque, my lady?' Wintour asked when they had finished their first course.

She hesitated, unsure how to respond with tact and truth.

'It was certainly a great spectacle,' she replied at last.

Sir Thomas and his companion eyed her steadily as she lowered her gaze. Her uncle, who was preoccupied with levering a piece of oyster from one of his teeth with a pick, seemed oblivious to the exchange.

'You should have taken part yourself, Tom,' Sir Thomas remarked. 'A lawyer is bound to be nimble-footed.'

Frances thought she caught a flash of conspiratorial smiles between Sir Thomas and his protégé.

'I fear that I would have followed the steps very badly, sir,' Wintour replied smoothly.

'Damned foolish nonsense, if you ask me!' the earl declared to nobody in particular. 'Of course, I paid handsomely to secure my niece a part, but that was only for the purpose of displaying her to the court.'

Frances felt her face flush.

'I trust it was worth the investment, Uncle.'

'Time will tell,' he replied, unperturbed. Then, raising a glass towards his host, added: 'Eh, Sir Thomas?'

'I very much hope so, my Lord Northampton.'

Frances took another long drink of wine, her hand trembling slightly as she clasped the glass a little too tightly. To be openly touted in this manner was intolerable.

'I fear the king will have no hunting tomorrow.'

Wintour directed their glances to the windows, from where they could see dark clouds gathering.

'My Lord Northampton says it always puts His Majesty in such a bad humour when he cannot join his horses and his hounds,' he continued. 'Still, there is enough within the court to occupy him at present. News of a fresh plot seems to break every day.'

'It gives people something to gossip about,' Sir Thomas remarked dismissively, 'besides the usual scandals of the court.'

'You have a low opinion of your fellow courtiers, sir,' Frances observed, coldly. She saw Wintour raise his head and stare at her.

'Not in the least,' Sir Thomas replied genially. 'Just of mankind in general.'

'The papists have been muttering ever since the king banished their priests from the kingdom,' her uncle cut in. 'And many are near penniless from paying so many fines for failing to attend the true church. They would do better to starve to death and remove their troublesome presence altogether.'

Frances stared at him, marvelling again at how swiftly he had turned his coat. But then, politics had always won out over principle where her uncle was concerned.

'You do not believe their complaints to be just, Lord Northampton?' Tom Wintour asked quietly.

'To hell with their complaints!' the earl retorted. 'They would be well advised to cease their endless babble.'

'Well, well,' Sir Thomas remarked. 'So long as all they do is talk, the king and his court can rest easy in their beds.' Turning to Wintour, he said brightly: 'Come now, Tom, you have told us nothing of your late travels. You were absent for nigh on three months. Did you sail to warmer climes to escape our English winter?'

Frances thought she saw Wintour's hand shake slightly as he took a sip of wine.

'Sadly not, Sir Thomas. The Flemish winter is just as unforgiving. But the company I kept provided ample warmth.'

'Ha!' the earl exclaimed. 'I have heard that there are as many bawdy houses as dwellings in Flanders. Little wonder that you found such diverting acquaintance.'

Frances closed her eyes.

'If that is true, my lord, then I must have overlooked them all,' Wintour replied evenly. 'My companions were men of great learning and respectability. They included two gentlemen from Spain, who will soon be arriving at court as guests of His Majesty.'

Frances saw her uncle's eyes narrow.

'What business have they here? Spain is full of papists, and their king is no friend of ours.'

'I am sure your lordship cannot expect a humble lawyer to be privy to such secrets,' Wintour replied with a smile.

'Then we must be patient, gentlemen,' Sir Thomas interjected. 'Time will tell. Now, please, eat before my cooks despair of our appetite.'

The rest of the meal was passed with studiedly polite topics of conversation, interspersed with the regular succession of dishes that were placed before them. Roasted capon, spiced ham, baked salmon, honeyed figs, and sugared almonds; all filled the room with heady aromas.

Frances ate sparingly; anger always suppressed her appetite. By contrast, her uncle was devouring the food as if he had been starved for a fortnight, stuffing forkfuls of roasted meat into his mouth, and washing them down with goblet after goblet of the fine Burgundy wine that his host had provided.

'The capon is not to your taste, my Lady Frances?' Sir Thomas asked, with what Frances could not decide was genuine concern or amusement. She was aware that he had been watching her intently for the past half an hour, and had found herself cringing under his gaze.

'Forgive me, sir. The food is excellent. I am a little tired.'

Sir Thomas smiled. 'I have no doubt that the young princess gives you little time for rest.'

Her uncle grunted. 'That girl is too much indulged if you ask me. Needs a firmer hand.'

'I understand that the princess is a very accomplished young woman, Lady Frances?' Wintour asked pleasantly.

'She is indeed. Her Highness already speaks several languages, and her knowledge of the scriptures is exemplary for a girl of her years.'

'Her father must have read them to her in the cradle,' Wintour observed, sardonically.

The company fell silent. Frances stole another glance at Sir Thomas's friend, and wondered why he suddenly seemed so angry.

'Well, gentlemen.' Sir Thomas eventually broke the silence. 'We must not keep Lady Frances from her bed.'

The earl rose first, his heavy chair scraping loudly across the oak floorboards.

'Sir Thomas, I would detain you for a few moments.' He gave his host a meaningful look. 'We have some business to discuss.'

'Then allow me to escort your niece back to her chambers, Lord Northampton,' Wintour cut in.

The earl's eyes narrowed as he turned to look at the young man. 'My niece knows the palace well enough by now, Wintour. There is no need to trouble yourself.'

'It would be a pleasure, my lord,' the young man countered swiftly. Without pausing for a further reply, he took Frances's hand and placed it gently on his arm.

'Sir Thomas.' He bowed. 'Your hospitality has been as excellent as ever.' Pausing, he added: 'And as you know, I am particularly grateful for the invitation on this occasion.'

Again, Frances thought she saw the briefest exchange of conspiratorial smiles. She bobbed a quick curtsey to her host, studiously avoiding her uncle's gaze, and walked out of the room with Wintour, her hand still on his arm.

As soon as the door was closed behind them, he let out a loud laugh. Surprised, Frances turned a quizzical look to him.

'I am sorry, Lady Frances,' her companion said, recovering himself. 'It is a fault of mine to react in this way to mirthless company. My schoolmaster quite despaired of me.'

Frances grinned. 'The conversation was not to your taste, then?'

'Far less than the dinner, I'm afraid. Sir Thomas is an excellent man, but he surrounds himself with fools.'

'Lord Northampton is my uncle, Mr Wintour.'

'And yet you share my view, I think?'

Frances resisted the temptation to agree, and they continued in silence for a few moments.

'I must ask your forgiveness, Lady Frances. Presumption is another of my faults. You are discovering them all in the course of one evening.'

As they rounded the corner into the long corridor that led to her chamber, they saw a small, slight figure walking towards them in the shadows ahead. The light from one of the sconces illuminated his face as he stepped forward.

'My Lord Privy Seal.' Wintour bowed low.

Frances maintained her composure, but every encounter with Cecil made her uncomfortable. He reminded her of a stoat eyeing its prey.

'Another client, Wintour? I hardly meet anyone these days who you haven't worked for.'

'We have been dining with Lord Northampton and Sir Thomas, my lord,' Wintour replied smoothly. 'Lady Frances's uncle is keen for her to make new acquaintance at court.'

Cecil smirked. 'Your uncle is most assiduous for your welfare, Lady Frances. He could not have introduced you to a more useful friend. Mr Wintour seems to specialise in helping ladies in distress. Tell me Wintour, how fare your efforts on behalf of Widow Bedwyn?'

Wintour smiled. 'Your Grace is well enough versed in the workings of the law to know that I am not at liberty to respond.'

The merest flicker of irritation crossed Cecil's features. He stared at Wintour for a few moments, before turning to Frances.

'I trust your room has everything for your comfort?'

'Yes, my lord. It is very well appointed.'

'Good, good. I thought you might appreciate its proximity to the herb garden.'

Frances held his gaze.

'Your lordship is most thoughtful.'

'Well.' Cecil sniffed. 'I fear that I have interrupted your discourse for too long. I will bid you goodnight.'

As he shifted his weight onto his right leg, Frances noticed him wince. Although he did his best to conceal it, she knew that his crooked back must give him pain, even in repose. With a brief, impatient bow, he took his leave.

Frances exhaled slowly as she and Wintour turned to go, but they had only walked a few steps when Cecil's voice rang out again.

'Oh, Lady Frances, I almost forgot! I had called to invite you to a most interesting spectacle tomorrow.'

'My lord?'

'I will not spoil the surprise. Believe me – it will be most diverting.'

'But my lady princess—'

'I have already spoken to the king. He has graciously agreed to release you from your duties tomorrow morning. He agrees with me that it will be most advantageous for your education.'

Smiling at her obvious discomfiture, he added: 'My page will call for you at six.'

CHAPTER 13

12 July

Frances stirred as her chamber slowly began to fill with light. She turned over, pulling the heavy covers tighter, and drawing her knees up to her chest. One side of her head pulsed with a dull ache that she knew would grow stronger as the day wore on. She closed her eyes again, willing sleep to overcome her, but her thoughts had already begun to intrude.

Tom Wintour was one of the most unusual men she had ever met. He had all the charm that could be expected of a gentleman at court, yet there seemed to be so much more hidden behind his easy smile and sharp wit. More than once, his eyes had seemed to blaze with something like anger, though there had been little enough to provoke him, she thought. When he had looked at her, there had been an intensity to his gaze that left her feeling discomforted. She would have liked to find out more about him, but she realised with a pang that this was unlikely, given her uncle's obvious disapproval. But then, if he was working for the queen, she might encounter him without the earl's knowledge, since her chambers were next to those of the princess.

Rolling over so that her back was to the window, she gave a groan as she remembered that Cecil's page would soon be calling for her. Again, she replayed the conversation with Cecil, just as she had when she had lain in bed last night, robbing her of sleep until the small hours. That he should single her out for such attention might have been a sign of favour. But she suspected that it was something very different.

As the light in her room turned to soft yellow, Frances got out of bed and drew back the curtains. There was little sign of life in the city below. Only a baker's cart, rumbling slowly along the cobbled streets of Whitehall, disturbed the repose. She opened the window a crack and breathed in the fresh morning air.

Walking over to her writing desk, Frances drew out the small prayer book from the pile of volumes that she had brought from Longford. She ran her fingers along its soft spine, the leather binding smooth and shiny from frequent use. The book had been a gift to her father from the late queen, a sign of forgiveness for marrying her favourite lady-in-waiting. One of Frances's earliest memories was of sitting on his knee as he read to her from it. Though incomprehensible to her then, the words had been as a gentle, melodic chant that had made her feel at peace. As she gazed now at the tiny lettering, interspersed with exquisite and still vibrant illuminations, she felt the tension ease out of her neck and shoulders, the pain in her head receding enough for her to focus on the words.

> *Blessed is the man who does not walk in the counsel of the wicked. The wicked . . . are like the chaff that the wind blows away.*

Feeling a sudden chill, she pulled her nightgown more tightly around her, then closed the book and rose to dress. Cecil had given no hint of what lay in store, so she was obliged to choose a gown that would serve her indoors or out, and be suitable for anything but royal company. She scraped her hair up and wound it tightly into a bun, fixing it into place with several pins. After lacing up her boots, which she judged would be appropriate for riding or walking, she paused for a brief look in the mirror, catching the anxiety in her eyes.

The sound of brisk footsteps along the corridor outside made her start. Grabbing her cloak as the sharp rapping sounded around the room, she went to unbolt the door.

'My lady Frances.'

Cecil's young page looked slightly flustered – from exertion or embarrassment, Frances could not tell. She gave him a smile of reassurance that did not quite reach her eyes, and followed him silently along the corridor.

'Might I enquire where we are going?' Frances asked.

Without turning, the boy answered: 'To the stables, my lady.' He said it in such a way that it was clear this was all the explanation she was going to get.

Frances quickened her pace to keep up with the wiry page. He wore the dark green velvet of the Cecil livery, with tiny gold coronets embroidered around the collar. He led her through the increasingly familiar halls and corridors, away from the river and towards the western side of the palace, close to the great abbey, which rose like an enchantment above the rooftops.

The chiming of the bells interrupted her thoughts. Four, five, six. Soon the whole palace would be awake. A hive of bees crawling, flying, and buzzing insistently around the king and his entourage, infinitely more hazardous than her father's hives at Longford.

As they rounded the corner, Frances saw the unmistakable figure of the Lord Privy Seal standing by the archway that led into the stables. His slightly stooped aspect and his habit of continually smoothing one hand over the other gave him a vaguely apologetic, almost guilty air.

'Ah, Lady Frances! Nocturnal creature that you are, I feared you might have overslept.'

'Not at all, my lord. I always rise early to attend my lady princess,' she replied, ignoring the jibe. 'I trust that Her Highness was content to spare me for the morning?'

'Of course. The young are fickle, Lady Frances. You must not be fooled into thinking that she has any particular attachment to you – especially not after so brief a time. The promise of sweet-meats was quite enough to banish you from her thoughts.'

At that moment a groom appeared, leading two fine horses – one white, and the other a glorious chestnut brown. The sound of the hooves on the stone cobbles echoed across the sleeping courtyard. Frances reached out to stroke the nose of the chestnut horse, which stood closest to her. It nudged her arm and smelt her fingers. She reached into her pocket and offered it the apple that she had brought, correctly assuming that whatever Cecil had planned for her did not involve a sumptuous breakfast.

'It seems you have chosen your horse – or vice versa.' He gestured to the groom, who led them over to the mounting block and tethered them to a post next to it. Frances and her companion watched in silence as he prepared the saddles. When they were ready, he bowed to Cecil, who climbed the steps and awkwardly swung his crooked body onto the white horse. Sensing its rider's disquiet, it whinnied and stamped.

Climbing onto her side-saddle with practised ease, Frances was grateful to enjoy a fleeting moment of superiority. Cecil gave a sharp tap of his heels, and his horse lurched forward. Jerking the reins, he called over his shoulder: 'We are riding westwards.'

Cecil's yeoman of the guard rode ahead of his master. Frances followed at a gentle trot. She imagined herself cantering across the softly rolling hills and barrows of Wiltshire. But the noises of the awakening city soon called her back to the present.

They had left the sprawling palace complex now. As they emerged from the royal mews, Frances noticed the beautiful but decaying statue that stood by its entrance. Set on a circular plinth of steps, a series of intricately carved arches rose up to the heavens. In the central arch was the statue of Edward I's beloved queen, Eleanor of Castile, looking down on the people below, her left hand raised in blessing. Although the years had worn away her features, her expression was unmistakably benign. Hers was an unearthly wisdom, a peace that could only be attained in heaven.

'There was a woman who knew how to behave!' Cecil called out across the cacophony of the streets.

'And whose husband showed her infinite love and respect,' Frances replied pleasantly.

Cecil turned back to the road ahead, his shoulders hunched forward. Frances looked around her. All London seemed to be preparing for the celebrations to mark the anniversary of the coronation. Even now, banners in the Stuart colours of red and blue were being hung from every house that lined the processional route from the Tower to the abbey.

At first, her companion followed the wide avenue that led from Whitehall, but after half a mile he suddenly veered off into the narrow streets of St Martin's parish. The timber-framed houses perched perilously on wooden struts, and the occupants of the upper chambers might easily have leaned out of their windows and shaken hands with their neighbours on the opposite side of the street. So little light penetrated the overhanging gables that lanterns still burned in the streets below, even though the sun had long since risen.

From time to time Frances glanced into the windows of the upper floors. Most were sparsely furnished, with one wooden bed and several makeshift ones scattered around. The pervasive smell of woodsmoke was not strong enough to conceal the stench from the filth-strewn cobbles beneath her horse's hooves, and she was grateful for the small bunch of lavender that she had tied to the inside of her bodice, just below her breastbone. The pungent, sweet aroma rose in waves from the growing warmth of her body as she bobbed gently up and down in the saddle.

At last, they emerged into the open fields of the old deer park belonging to Hyde Manor. Frances breathed in the clean, fresh smell of the grass, still wet with dew. The day was overcast, but it took a few moments for her eyes to become accustomed to the light after the claustrophobic gloom of the enclosed streets that they had just left behind. Cecil also seemed to relax, and he slowed his horse to a gentle trot so that Frances might draw up alongside him.

'King Henry had an excellent eye for acquisitions,' he remarked, his gaze sweeping across the parkland that surrounded them. 'The old cardinal knew that only too well. No sooner had the last brick been laid at Hampton Court than he was obliged to give it to his master.' He chuckled. 'Then Wolsey's arms were painted over with those of the king, the royal tapestries covered the walls, and it was as if the cardinal had never existed.'

Sensing that she was being bated, Frances remained silent.

'Of course,' Cecil drawled after a few moments, 'kings have always had the power to reduce their subjects to nothing; to erase them from history altogether. Just look at Our gracious Majesty. His own mother had her head struck off, and he barely raised a hand to stay the axe.'

A deliberate pause.

'But then, he had been raised to believe that she was a witch.'

Staring straight ahead, Frances kept her voice as even as possible.

'Is that so? I know little of the matter. I was a child when the Queen of Scots was executed.'

'Oh yes!' Cecil continued, warming to his theme. 'She was little better than a common harlot, bedding the man who murdered her husband and bearing his bastard twins. Happy for them that the mewling creatures scarcely lived long enough to draw breath.'

He smiled at Frances.

'Fancy having such a mother! Little wonder that he should grow up to believe that all women are Satan's whores.'

'His Majesty esteems his wife, and dotes upon his daughter,' Frances remarked carefully.

'Naturally,' Cecil agreed affably, as if they were discussing nothing of greater moment than the weather. 'But experience taught him to be wise in his choice. Not like old King Henry. He was led by lust into the snares of that great sorceress, Anne Boleyn.'

Frances bit her lip so tightly that she could taste the blood. Such an insult to the late queen's mother would have cost him his head while Elizabeth still breathed.

'We are blessed to have such a wise and prudent king,' she observed tightly.

'We are indeed. And we are about to witness just how wise and prudent he truly is.'

Frances had been so incensed by Cecil's taunts that she had momentarily abandoned her speculation about the purpose of their early-morning ride. As they neared the edge of the park, she noticed a steady stream of people walking briskly along the wide street that lay beyond. It was the same road along which she had travelled upon arriving in London a little over two weeks ago. The growing murmur of excitement was carried on the wind, and Frances's anger gave way to curiosity.

'Stay close to me,' Cecil commanded as they passed through the gates.

It was with some difficulty that Frances steered her horse, which was suddenly skittish with fear, through the growing throng of people.

'Make way for my Lord Privy Seal!' shouted Cecil's yeoman, who rode ahead of them. As word spread through the excited crowd, a path gradually opened up for them, enabling them to pick up their pace.

For a time, Frances was obliged to keep her gaze fixed upon the ground immediately in front of her, afraid lest her horse should trample one of the children who constantly darted across their path. But as the way gradually cleared, she was able to look further ahead.

What she saw made her sick with dread. About a quarter of a mile in the distance, almost shrouded by a cluster of elm trees, was a large mound to one side of the road. On top was a wooden platform onto which had been raised a set of gallows.

Silhouetted against the grey sky, Frances could clearly see, were six ropes suspended from the beam that ran the length of the platform. They swung gently, mesmerically, in the quickening breeze.

Frances felt the pulsing at the side of her head grow more intense as she stared, willing this to be a terrible dream. Her vision began to cloud, and she gripped the pommel of the saddle. As the reins went slack, her horse came to a sudden halt, prompting outraged cries from the crowds of people behind, who almost tumbled on top of one another. One man cursed loudly, and another shouted: 'Move on there!'

Automatically, Frances yanked the reins, and the horse lurched forward. By the time she reached Cecil, the crowds had grown so dense that they were obliged to dismount. Tying the reins to a nearby post, they travelled the remaining distance on foot.

Cecil's page had ridden ahead, and was waiting to escort them to the raised platform upon which sat about twenty finely dressed gentlemen. Frances recognised several members of the council among them. One by one, they noticed Cecil approaching and got to their feet. He nodded in greeting, and led Frances to the two vacant seats right at the front of the platform. She was grateful to sit down. Her legs felt weak, and she was nauseous from the constant, throbbing pain in her head.

She became aware of a growing cacophony among the general shouts and cheers. It was coming from the road along which she and Cecil had ridden a few moments before. Craning her neck, she could just make out the ears and mane of a carthorse as it plodded slowly through the crowds, pulling behind it a wagon in which sat a young woman.

Her head bowed to the taunts that rang out all around her, the prisoner stared intently at her hands, which were tightly bound together with a thick length of rope. A white linen hood covered her hair, and her dress was of coarse brown wool, with a white linen collar and cuffs. As she drew closer, Frances saw that her lips moved in a constant prayer that was drowned out by the jeers of the crowd. She could not have been much older than twenty, Frances guessed, but she bore herself with quiet dignity.

The wagon was drawn to a halt at the foot of the steps that led up to the gallows. One of the men who had been standing on the platform walked slowly down, raising his hands to whip up a fresh round of cheers from the crowd. Relishing the moment, he climbed into the wagon and roughly pulled the woman to her feet. As soon as he released his grip, she fell back onto the seat, prompting cries of 'Get up, witch!'

With considerable effort, she eventually raised herself onto her feet. Her legs were visibly trembling. Without warning, the man pushed her violently forward and, stumbling, she fell over the side of the wagon. Unable to stay herself with her hands, she landed hard, awkwardly, her face slapping against the dusty ground.

Frances felt a desperate urge to help her, but was tortured by the knowledge that she must remain in her seat, as implacable as the other spectators on the platform. As if sensing her unease, Cecil placed his hand on her wrist. He kept it there, slowly tightening his grip.

'Your potions cannot help her, Lady Frances,' he whispered, his breath hot against her ear.

Frances rounded on him. 'If she were really a witch, then she could surely help herself, my lord,' she muttered.

With slow, painful steps, the young woman mounted the scaffold. Whenever she paused to steady herself, her tormentor jabbed her in the back with his boot so that she stumbled forward once more. By the time that she reached the top of the steps, the crowds had fallen silent. Her head still bowed, she shuffled forward, and came to a halt a few feet in front of the platform. Slowly raising her eyes, she scanned the faces of the dignitaries seated in front of her, returning their affronted stares as if she were of equal rank and importance.

At length, her gaze alighted upon Frances. For a few moments, their eyes were locked together. Frances looked at the steady, knowing face of the accused. Was she already filled with the grace of heaven? The serenity of her expression suggested so, but there was also a glint of anger at a life snatched away.

As Frances returned her gaze, she had never felt so worthless. Cecil was right: all her powers of healing were as nothing now. She could only stare out helplessly, hoping to convey something of her sympathy, of her wretchedness at the knowledge of what lay ahead. *Please forgive me for watching this.* She thought she saw the smallest twitch of the woman's mouth into a quick, answering smile before she stared again at the floor, her back stooped in defeat. Frances imagined her bent over her pestle, grinding herbs into a paste for a salve, or mixing them with oil for a tincture. She wondered how many people had been glad of her ministrations, before this new king declared them to be the work of the Devil.

An anxious murmur ran through the crowd. In an instant, Cecil was on his feet.

'Good people!' he shouted across the throng, which extended as far as the eye could see. 'We are here to witness the just punishment of a despicable crime against His Majesty and all his subjects.'

He waited for the now excited murmur to die down.

'According to His Majesty's late Act against the practice of witchcraft, enchantment, and sorcery, any person who is found to have invoked or conjured wicked or evil spirits, or to have consulted or made a covenant with Satan or his followers, shall suffer pains of death.'

'Death!' he repeated again, louder this time. There was an answering cheer. A smile of satisfaction crossed Cecil's face as he looked around the crowd. He pointed towards the prisoner, who was still gazing down at the ground.

'This woman conspired against a noble family in the king's county of Suffolk. She made a pact with Satan to carry out his evil designs here on earth.'

A pause. Everyone had now fallen silent and was listening intently.

'Having lain with the Devil numerous times, she turned her lustful eyes upon the earl, her master, and did on sundry occasions commit unlawful and indecent acts to seduce him to her will.'

His eyes glinted as he slowly ran his tongue around his thin lips.

'On one such occasion she bewitched the earl so that he might copulate with her as if she had been a common beast of the field.'

There was a gratifying exclamation from the crowd. Frances noticed that the woman's hands were clenched tightly. She wondered what choice her master had given her in their affair. Many lords viewed their servingwomen as chattel, to be used as they saw fit, and then discarded when their desire was spent.

'Having thus ensnared him with her body, her spells and her potions,' he continued, casting a look at Frances, 'she so bewitched his mind and his body that he was unable to beget a child upon his wife, the countess.'

'Whore!' someone cried from the throng. There were answering shouts of 'Devil's slut!' and 'Witch!'

Cecil made no motion to silence them, but merely waited, a smile playing about his mouth.

'And so, thanks to the evil wiles of this whore of Satan, the earl's line will die with him. But, not content with this victory, she conspired to ruin his estate so that all his cattle fell prey to a strange disease, his crops were destroyed, and his orchards were washed away in a tempest.'

The cacophony of shouts and cries from the outraged crowd grew deafening. There was a stamping of feet so violent that the scaffold shook. Several people spat at the woman, who remained standing in front of the platform, her gaze fixed on the ground. Even when a stone was hurled, almost striking her eye, she barely flinched.

'His Majesty's Court of Assize heard of all these crimes – and more – committed by this lamentable creature here, who uttered not one word in her defence, and found her justly guilty.'

'Guilty!' he cried again, smiling at the answering cheers from the crowd. 'And so it was the pleasure of that court, and of the King's Majesty, that she should perish, as do all witches, and be hanged from the neck until she is dead!'

The near-hysterical shouts that his triumphant declaration sparked made Frances's head pound with a pain so intense that she had to dig her nails into her arms to keep from vomiting.

Cecil nodded to the hangman, who grabbed the woman by the arm and yanked her towards the row of nooses that still swung gently in the early-morning breeze. Choosing the one that hung at the centre, in full view of the crowd and assembled dignitaries, he dragged a tall wooden stool across and positioned it underneath. Holding it at the base, he motioned to the woman to climb on top of it.

Gathering up her skirts as best she could, she tentatively placed one foot on the supporting rung of the stool, testing its stability, then, crouching, manoeuvred both feet onto the stool. Agonisingly slowly, she straightened her shaking legs until she was standing straight, the stool wobbling precariously beneath her.

The hangman propped up a long ladder against the beam and climbed up it until he was level with the woman. Reaching forward, he grabbed the swinging noose and dropped it over her head.

There was a cheer from the crowds. Frances knew they sensed the impending kill, like her father's bloodhounds. She had seen them tear a fox to pieces once, and the memory made the bile rise in her throat, just as it had on that bright spring day fifteen years before.

The crowd had fallen into hushed anticipation.

'Lord God forgive me; Christ receive my soul,' the woman murmured quietly, her voice cracked and trembling.

Frances watched as a stream of urine ran down the woman's legs and dripped onto the dusty boards below.

Then again, more loudly, as if the words gave her confidence: 'Lord God forgive me; Christ receive my soul!'

Frances noticed that Cecil looked suddenly fearful, as if aware that this show of piety might invoke the sympathy of the crowd. He nodded quickly to the hangman, who gave one sharp, swift kick at the stool, sending it crashing away.

The woman dropped towards the floor, the rope tightening around her neck. Her body jerked and twisted as her still bound hands clawed desperately at the rope. Her eyes were screwed tightly shut, and her face was turning a dark red.

Frances's gaze was locked onto the suffocating girl, just as it had been on the fox as the breath was ripped from its body. The seconds passed like minutes; the minutes like hours. The woman's face turned from scarlet to purple.

The crowd was silent, and Frances knew the mood had changed.

'Pull on her ankles!' somebody shouted. Others took up the cry. Some people began to weep.

At last, the jerking grew softer, slower. The woman's face was now blue. Slowly, she opened her bulging eyes and turned them up to heaven. Her body grew still, swayed only by the wind as it blew gently across the mound. The only sound was the steady, rhythmic creaking of the beam overhead.

After a few moments, Cecil, his face grim, motioned to the hangman, whose expression was masked by the black hood that extended down to his shoulders. He mounted the ladder once more, and, coming face to face with the woman, reached out to touch her neck. Holding his fingers there for a few seconds, he then dropped them and gave the slightest nod to Cecil.

'So perish all witches!' the Lord Privy Seal cried, his voice not quite matching the earlier conviction of the words.

Turning, he held out his hand to Frances, who slowly stood up. She tasted bile in her mouth. Descending the steps, each one a trial, she reached the ground below and stumbled quickly towards the back of the scaffold. Free at last from the prying eyes of the crowd, of Cecil, of the dead woman, she fell to her knees and retched into the dust.

After several moments, she rose unsteadily to her feet. Turning, she saw Cecil.

'Have a care, my lady,' he whispered, leaning towards her. 'I am watching you.'

CHAPTER 14

13 July

'You are very quiet today, Lady Frances,' the princess remarked softly, her eyes wide with concern. 'I hope you are not ill? Lady Mar says the sickness has returned to London. You look very pale.'

Frances forced a smile. 'Forgive me, ma'am. I slept badly last night, that's all. I promise that I will be quite well by dinner time, and will seek amends by allowing you to vanquish me at the card table all evening.'

Elizabeth grinned. 'You know that I always win fairly. You have taught me well.' Her smile faded. 'But I think you should take some rest this afternoon. Lord Sackville promised to take me for a ride on the river if the weather is fine, and Lady Mar can accompany me.'

Frances hesitated. Much as she loved being in this charming girl's company, her bones ached with tiredness and she longed for the oblivion of sleep. Images of the wretched woman's face as the life was choked from her had plagued her all night.

'If Your Highness is sure that you can spare me, then I would be grateful for a little rest,' she said at last. 'But I promise to attend you as soon as you are returned. We can practise the steps for tonight's dances.'

'Then it is decided,' the princess declared with satisfaction, giving Frances's hand a little squeeze. 'Now go before Lady Mar comes back. You know she will not approve.'

Frances bobbed a curtsey and hastened from the room, casting one last, grateful smile over her shoulder at the child who sometimes seemed so wise for her age.

The sun cast long shadows across her chamber as Frances blinked the sleep from her eyes. She glanced across at the clock on the fireplace. Half past six. With alarm, she realised that she had slept through dinner. The princess must have given orders that she was not to be disturbed. Frances raised herself onto her elbows and looked towards the window, shielding her eyes against the sunlight. The evening's entertainments would be under way by now. She pictured Elizabeth being whirled about by Lord Sackville, or one of the other young courtiers eager to curry favour with the king by delighting his daughter. With luck, her absence would hardly be noticed, except by her uncle – and Cecil. She closed her eyes at the thought, suddenly desperate to escape their scrutiny, for one evening at least.

With an impulse, she flung back the covers and padded quickly over to the window. The river glinted gold and grey as it snaked its way through the muddle of buildings that clung to the riverside, as if trying to submerge themselves in its cool depths. Frances shifted her gaze to the waterside gate. Two palace guards were leaning at either side of it, staring nonchalantly out across the river. They would surely not deny her a brief stroll along its banks, given that she had evidently been released from her duties for the evening.

Pausing briefly to pin back the strands of hair that had worked loose while she slept, she let herself out of the room and walked briskly down the corridor, brushing out the creases from her skirts as she did so. She could just hear the distant thrum of music and the muffled shouts of the revellers. Her mouth twisted in distaste at the thought of another evening frittered away in wine and sin. What hopes there had been for this king, whose licentious habits made a mockery of his apparently staunch belief in the austere religion of the reformists. If he was a perfect model of a Protestant king, then she sympathised with those who sought refuge in the old religion, with its comforting rituals and devotions.

The shouts grew louder as she neared the Great Hall, but she veered off down a staircase that led to the kitchens. As she walked quickly along the gloomy corridors, which were still filled with the aroma of roasted meats, she was jostled by numerous servants, red-faced and sweating, who were so intent upon their business that they barely noticed her. Fearing that she may get lost, Frances tried to picture the layout of the rooms above. She must be directly underneath the Great Hall now, judging from the thunder of a thousand footsteps and the screams of drunken laughter. With a shudder, she forged ahead, the intense heat from the kitchens making her skin prickle as she rushed by. At last, the air grew cooler, and the gloom of the passageway began to lift. She must be close now, she judged, picking up her pace so that she was almost running by the time that she emerged into the courtyard.

Usually bustling with officials and servants, it was now deserted. Frances paused for a moment, shielding her eyes from the low sun as she glanced around. She breathed out slowly, her body sagging with relief at being alone. Yet as she stood looking out towards the river that glinted between the arched gateway, she had a creeping sensation of being watched. Her breathing quickened as she darted a quick glance over her shoulder. Nobody was there, and every window that looked out over the courtyard was black.

Pushing away the thought that Cecil was lurking behind one of them, she walked determinedly towards the guards. At the sound of her footsteps, they turned and stared.

'The princess has released me from my duties this evening, so I intend to take a short walk along the river.'

Frances addressed the older of the two men. He continued to stare, his eyes roaming over her body and a slow smile crossing his face. She swallowed back her distaste.

Glancing across at his companion, he gave a brief nod. Frances did not wait for any further assent, but walked briskly forward. As she drew level with the guards, the one she had addressed took a step forward so that she almost brushed against him. She caught the smell of stale sweat and tobacco as she passed.

A soft breeze blew from the river, inviting her to step closer. It was at a low ebb now, she noticed, as it flowed steadily eastwards towards the sea, exposing a wide stretch of sand and gravel along its banks. Frances stepped off the edge of the wooden platform and slipped off her shoes. She wriggled her toes and pressed the soles of her feet against the shingle, revelling in the touch of the cool stones. She took a step forward, wincing slightly as a tiny shard of gravel pricked the soft skin under her feet. As the sun sank lower, casting its rays across the river, the waters appeared as liquid gold. They lapped gently against the shore, enticing her to come closer. How she longed to submerge herself in their cooling depths, to wash away the stench of court, cleanse her mind of the terrible images that had filled it since the ride to Tyburn.

'Master Holbein himself could not have imagined such a composition.'

Frances turned so sharply at the sound of his voice that she almost stumbled. Tom Wintour stepped quickly forward and steadied her, his hand cupping her elbow. She felt the warmth of his touch through the sleeve of her dress as he held it there a little too long.

Flushed, Frances stepped quickly away. For a few moments, Wintour did not move, but stood there, his hand suspended where it had touched her. Her heart still hammered in her chest, though the shock of the sudden interruption had subsided. He returned her gaze with a mixture of admiration and amusement.

'Forgive me, Lady Frances. I should not have disturbed you.

You looked so serene, silhouetted against the river. I had to be sure that you were not one of the phantoms that are said to stalk this shore.'

Frances raised an eyebrow. 'I thought lawyers were too rational to believe in such things.'

'On the contrary. We spend so much time poring over insufferably long and dull texts that our minds eagerly latch onto anything that might offer entertainment.'

His brow was creased, but his eyes glinted as he looked at her.

Frances laughed. It was the first time in weeks, she realised, relishing the feeling of lightness and momentarily forgetting the cares that had weighed so heavily upon her since coming to court. She stole a glance at her companion. He was, she thought, a few years older than herself. Unlike most other men at court, he was clean-shaven. The determined set of his jaw contrasted with his full, smiling lips and large brown eyes that always seemed to shine with good humour. He was dressed in the same dark brown doublet and black hose that he had worn for Sir Thomas's dinner. The white linen shirt underneath was finely made, judging from the embroidered collar and cuffs that Frances could see protruding from it. His skills as a lawyer had clearly brought him some wealth, though, like his patron, he displayed it modestly.

'I looked for you at this evening's entertainments,' he said, after they had walked in silence for a few moments. His expression was suddenly serious. 'I was concerned that you might be unwell, or that Cecil's business had taken you away from court.'

An image of the woman's face flitted before her again. All trace of merriment left her, and she stared bleakly ahead, trying to focus upon a small barge as it was rowed eastwards. It was fading from sight when Frances finally spoke.

'The princess allowed me some rest as I had little sleep last night. I only intended to close my eyes for an hour, but when I woke I had missed dinner. I hope she will forgive me.'

'I am sure Her Highness would forgive you anything, Lady Frances,' Tom replied quietly. 'It is obvious to all how greatly she esteems you. And you have already influenced her studies. She speaks like a lady twice her age.'

Frances smiled briefly. 'I cannot take credit for that. Her language was already far advanced by the time I arrived at court.'

She fell silent again, and could feel his eyes upon her, though she continued to look out across the water. He moved closer, so that their arms almost touched. 'What did Cecil want with you?' he whispered, casting a glance over his shoulder.

Frances hesitated. Though she was drawn to this man, she knew precious little about him. For all she knew, he could be another of Cecil's spies. Yet there was something in his manner, in the intensity of his gaze, that made her trust him.

'He took me to Tyburn, to witness the hanging of a witch.'

The words sounded flat, but she swallowed hard to suppress the tears that threatened to betray her.

Wintour stopped and reached for her hand. She resisted at first, desperate to keep walking away from the palace, from Cecil, from the nightmare that she knew would always torment her. But his grip was tight, his hand warm and comforting. With a sigh she relented, and turned to face him. He did not let go of her hand as he spoke.

'The king will not stop until he has fulfilled God's will – as he sees it. And Cecil will do whatever is necessary to win favour, even though he can little believe that these poor wretches are guilty of the crimes that send them to the gallows.'

His eyes blazed as he spoke, and his grip on her hand had tightened. The surprise must have registered on her face, for his tone was softer when he continued.

'I am deeply sorry that you were witness to such a scene, my lady. I saw a burning once, in Flanders. The image haunts me still.'

Though he still gazed at her, she knew that his eyes saw something other than her own. At length, he blinked as if awakening from a trance. His eyes were now filled with concern, and he gently stroked her hand with his thumb as he looked at her. The movement was small, but Frances felt as if every nerve in her body had been awakened. She was only vaguely aware of holding her breath.

'Why should Cecil wish to show you such horrors?' he asked quietly. 'It is well known at court that he has no love for your family, but that seems little reason to torment you. He would do better to focus his efforts upon removing your uncle from the council.'

'Perhaps it was a warning.' Her words were barely a whisper. 'The old queen showed me preferment for my knowledge of plants and remedies. But such skills are no longer smiled upon. The woman whose death I witnessed yesterday was accused of using potions to seduce her master.' Her voice was bitter with disdain.

She bit her lip and fell silent, keeping her gaze fixed on the ground, but she knew that his eyes were on her. When he did not answer, she looked up and saw that he was staring at her intently. For a moment she feared that she had said too much. Her mother was always chiding her for her impetuous nature, and since coming to court she had understood why. Indiscretion could spell death.

Just then, the sun glinted off something in the distance, over Tom's shoulder. Frances turned to look, and recognised one of the gilded finials of the Tower of London. They had walked further than she realised. The sight of the imposing fortress filled her with a sudden foreboding. Catching the look on her face, Tom turned to see what had caused it. They both stood for a moment, looking at the huge keep, a potent symbol of royal authority. It dominated the landscape for miles around, dwarfing the spires of churches, and the patchwork of ramshackle houses that clung to the streets nearby.

'I should go,' Frances said briskly. She made to turn back towards the palace, but Tom tightened his grip on her hand again.

'Frances—' he said urgently, then shook his head in frustration at his transgression. 'Lady Frances – forgive me – please, do not go yet. What you told me . . . you can trust me, I will not—'

'I have already said too much,' she said, pulling her hand free and walking purposefully back in the direction of Whitehall, dipping her head to avoid the dazzle of the sinking sun. Wintour stood for a moment, watching her retreating figure, then ran to catch up. He was careful to keep a step behind her until at last she slackened her pace.

'Lady Frances,' he said, when he had caught his breath. She turned sharply at his words, but seeing his eyes glinting with their former good humour, she felt herself begin to relax.

'I came to find you this evening because I had something I wanted to give you,' he continued, reaching into the pocket of his doublet. Frances watched as he drew out a leather-bound book, its spine and cover exquisitely decorated with vine leaves picked out in gold leaf. They reflected the light of the fading sun as he handed it to her. She turned it over in her hands, transfixed by the beauty of the binding, and saw that the pages were so thin as to be almost transparent. There must be many hundreds of them, she guessed, as she carefully ran her fingers along their edges.

'It is a fine enough cover, I grant you,' Tom said, 'but the real joy of books lies within.' She could hear the smile in his voice, though she kept her eyes fixed on the beautiful volume. At length, she slowly opened the cover and carefully turned back the first few pages until she came to the frontispiece.

THE COUNTESS OF PEMBROKE'S ARCADIA

WRITTEN BY SIR PHILIP SIDNEY, KNIGHT

Her heart leaped as she read the words. Many times, her father had spoken of the celebrated soldier-poet of Elizabeth's court. His bravery in battle had been superseded only by his genius as a writer. During his short life he had penned numerous works in honour of the queen, his friends, and family. This one, dedicated to his beloved sister Mary, was said to be his greatest. When he was cut down in battle just before his thirty-second birthday, the kingdom had been plunged into mourning and the queen had ordered a funeral befitting a prince.

'Thank you,' Frances breathed, still gazing at the book. She longed to begin reading it straight away – she would do so as soon as she was back in her apartments.

'I am glad to see that it already brings you pleasure,' Tom replied softly. 'But there is something in particular that I think you will enjoy.'

Frances looked up at him. He was smiling even more broadly now, the lines at the corners of his eyes deepening. She had a sudden urge to reach out and touch his face, trace the outline of his sensuous lips, and feel the hair that curled at his nape.

'Oh?' she whispered at last, hoping that her eyes had not betrayed her.

He took a step closer and reached for the book, his hand brushing hers. As he began to leaf through its pages, she could feel his warm breath on her neck. She closed her eyes, willing the moment to last a little longer.

'Here,' he said, too soon. She opened her eyes to see his finger pointing to a finely drawn sketch of a castle. With its round towers and barley twist chimneys, it was like something from a fairy tale, but as she looked closer she noticed that it was built in a triangular formation, and that its brickwork resembled a chessboard. She gave a small gasp.

'Longford!'

Tom grinned. '*Amphialeus*, to be precise. But yes, Sir Philip was said to have modelled it upon your father's castle. They were great friends, I understand, and Sir Philip visited Longford many times when your parents were newly married. I have heard your father speak of it.'

'You know my father?' Frances looked at him in surprise.

'I had the honour of meeting him once or twice, when the queen's business took me to Richmond.' Though his smile had not faded, there was a new intensity in his eyes. 'Well, we must make haste,' he continued, before Frances could reply. 'But I shall sleep easier in my bed knowing that now you can gaze upon Longford as often as you wish.'

'Thank you, Mr Wintour,' Frances said earnestly.

'Tom – please,' he replied with a smile. 'If you and I are to be friends, then we must rid ourselves of unnecessary titles.'

He paused. They had reached the palace gates now. The same guards were there, still slumped against the archway. Tom flicked a glance at them, then looked back at Frances and held both of her hands in his.

'And please be assured, Frances, I *am* your friend.'

Frances looked up at him again, and saw the sincerity in his eyes.

'And I yours,' she replied quietly.

CHAPTER 15

25 July

Frances gazed up at the imposing edifice of the White Tower, shading her eyes as the hot July sun reflected off its façade. Up close, it was even more impressive than the glimpse that she and Tom had had of it as they strolled along the foreshore two weeks before. She tried to remember what her father had told her about its history, but her thoughts were drawn back again to that evening. Tom's smiling eyes as he gave her the book, the touch of his hand, the intensity of his gaze as they parted. Having neither seen nor heard from him since, her memory had tried to fill the void that his absence had brought, making her restless during the day, and depriving her of sleep at night. The precious book had been her only solace during the time she spent away from the princess. Already, she was on her second reading, having devoured it the first time, and was now savouring every beautifully composed sentence, the evocative descriptions taking her to lands that she could only dream of. And of course, that sketch of Longford. The book now fell open at the page, she had looked at it so often.

A shuffle of feet drew her attention back to the present. Glancing to her left, she saw her fellow courtiers standing in ranks, lining the inside of the western curtain wall of the Tower. They were here to join a procession marking the anniversary of the king's coronation. Most were grim-faced, Frances noticed. Over the past year, the joy that James's subjects had expressed at being free from fifty years of female rule had soon been replaced by mutterings about his strange habits and 'unkingly' nature. Already, they were looking back with longing to the reign of 'Good Queen Bess'. Frances gave a wry smile. The old queen had known the fickle nature of her people all too well. Little wonder that she had waited so long to name a successor. 'I am not so foolish as to hang a winding-sheet before my eyes,' she had scolded one persistent adviser.

For all his unpopularity, there was a palpable sense of anticipation for the arrival of the king. Frances felt it too, but not for the same reason. When the princess had told her, eyes wide with excitement, that Frances's parents were to attend, she had hardly dared believe it. Every time that there had been a masque or other great gathering at court, she had hoped to see them among the throng. But on each occasion she had been disappointed. Clearly, their presence was required at Richmond – or perhaps it was their absence from court that was required, she reflected bitterly. But even Cecil could not exclude the highest ranking peeress in the kingdom from the anniversary celebrations. She took a deep breath to steady her heart. It could not be long now.

Although it was not yet ten o'clock, the heat of the sun, trapped within the walls of the Tower, was growing so intense that Frances could see the faces of those who stood in line with her beginning to glisten. A bead of sweat was winding its way slowly down her neck, towards the apricot-coloured silk at the top of her bodice. The latter had been pulled even tighter than usual, so that she, like the other ladies present, could mimic the unfeasibly narrow-waisted gown that the queen had chosen to wear.

In the Longford woods there would be cool shade. Enchanter's nightshade, her favourite, would be in full bloom now, its tiny pink buds opening up into delicate white flowers that nestled amongst the roots and ferns of the forest floor. If she closed her eyes, she could almost smell their sweet scent and feel the velvety petals against her fingertips. It seemed strange to think of the flowers still blooming there, the river winding its way gently along the boundary of the estate, and the men who worked the fields preparing for harvest.

A blast of trumpets suddenly rang out across the courtyard, and all eyes turned towards the royal apartments that abutted the White Tower. Everyone seemed to be holding their breath as the echo slowly faded into silence. Several moments passed. Frances could feel a steady, rhythmic pulse at her temples. Her mouth was dry, and as she ran her tongue along her upper lip it felt parched and cracked. The base of her spine ached, as much from the restrictive clothing she wore as from the long hours of standing. She knew there would be many more hours to come.

At length, the large oak doors in the middle of the curtain wall were slowly pulled open by two yeomen of the guard, their halberds gleaming as they reflected the sun, momentarily blinding Frances and her companions as they stared towards them.

'Make way for the king!' one of them cried. Then both turned sharply to face each other, several feet apart, so that there was room for their royal master to pass. A muttering could be heard from inside the archway, then James emerged, red-faced and cursing.

'Damn ye, man, leave it!' he snapped at an attendant who was stooped behind him, rearranging the long train of his cloak. The man scurried away into the shadows.

As the king stepped into the blazing sunlight, Frances thought she heard a few sharp intakes of breath. He looked as if he had been dressed in several sets of clothes, one on top of the other. The white satin sleeves of his doublet were heavily padded, and the breeches even more so. The latter made the coat that he wore over them stick out so far that it resembled one of his wife's farthingales, and he was obliged to hold his arms out at his sides, like a bird about to take flight. His neck was obscured by an enormous white ruff, the numerous layers of which pressed tightly up against his chin. On his head was the golden crown that had been worn by kings of England for centuries, but even this had been padded out with red velvet on top, and a thick layer of ermine around the base. The only part of his body not to be encased in reams of suffocating material were his legs from the knee down, which appeared ridiculously thin in their white silk hose.

Frances felt an urge to laugh. The fashions that James had brought with him from Scotland had certainly drawn a sharp contrast to the elegant sophistication of the old queen's court, but this outfit was something else entirely. Then it dawned upon her. James was dressed not for fashion, but for safety. Even the sharpest assassin's rapier could not penetrate the thick layers of tightly-woven fabric.

Frances had heard it whispered many times that ever since he took the throne, the king had been jumping at his own shadow, and she had seen how he eyed his courtiers with a mixture of suspicion and disdain. Now he was more timorous than ever. Fear made him irritable, so that he lashed out at even those closest to him – most often the queen, who bore it all with a quiet, detached dignity that pained Frances to watch. The atmosphere at court had become as unbearably oppressive as the sultry July weather.

All humour had left Frances as she watched the king now, his usual awkward gait heightened by the cumbersome clothes into which he had been sewn. In his left hand he held a silk handkerchief, ready to hold to his nose as they made their way through the crowds that were lining the streets to Westminster. A case of the plague had been reported close to Greenwich the previous week, and there were now more across the city. James had been set upon issuing a decree ordering his new subjects to keep to their homes this day, and had only reluctantly been persuaded of the evils that would arise if he did so. God knew, there had been little enough cause for celebration so far in his reign.

On the king's feet were shimmering gold satin shoes, each narrowing to an uncomfortable-looking point that was decorated with a large white silk bow. That they were causing him pain was obvious from the halting manner of his steps as he made his way past the line of courtiers. He neither acknowledged nor looked at them, but stared grimly ahead towards the archway that led to the outer ward of the Tower, and along the riverside wall.

Just before he passed under it, James suddenly stopped and turned to the dozen or so dignitaries who were following him in a single, straight line. At their head was the Lord Privy Seal, dressed in the heavy robes of his office. His coat was fashioned from deep red velvet, over which was a cloak of the same material in black, lined with ivory silk. A stiffly starched ruff was around his neck, and the seal of office, its rubies glittering in the sunlight, was carefully placed around his shoulders. In his right hand he carried a long wooden staff. Frances noticed that he was leaning on it rather heavily.

'Why the devil do you follow at such a distance?' the king demanded.

'Forgive me, sire,' Cecil soothed. 'I did not wish to infringe upon your dignity.'

'To hell with it!' James shouted. 'You act like some simpering flower girl. Stand up straight, like the man you pretend to be.'

Frances saw Cecil's right eye twitch, and he quickly suppressed a wince as he drew himself up to his full height. His hands were clenched into tight fists, the knuckles showing white through the skin. Frances knew that after the torments he had inflicted on her, she should have enjoyed his humiliation. But she could feel only pity.

'God's wounds! Your back is as crooked as your advice,' the king cried out, loud enough for all to hear. Frances saw one of the pretty young men at the back of the entourage place a delicate gloved hand in front of his mouth, which had the intended effect of drawing attention to, rather than concealing, his amusement.

Suddenly, James reached forward and grabbed the staff from Cecil's hand.

'Here,' he declared. 'This will straighten it out.'

Before Cecil could do anything, his royal master had yanked him around so that his deformed back faced the crowd. Then, pulling on his minister's ruff so that there was a small gap between it and his neck, James took the staff and rammed it roughly down the length of Cecil's spine. The sniggering boy now let out a peal of high-pitched laughter as the hapless minister stood, his head as low as it could be without causing the ruff to dig into his neck even more. The staff was clearly visible through the back of his breeches, and it stuck out above Cecil's head. James took a step backwards to admire his handiwork, and Frances saw him exchange an amused look with his young favourite. She could sense that many of the onlookers were torn between flattering the king with laughter and not wishing to antagonise his chief minister. Cecil would not forget any who scorned him.

After a brief pause, James broke the tense silence. Sighing deeply, he motioned for one of his attendants to remove the staff from the Lord Privy Seal's back so that they might continue with the procession. As soon as the king and his immediate entourage had passed through the archway, Frances and her fellow courtiers fanned out into a long line, three people across, and followed in their wake.

She kept her head bowed for most of the slow walk along the southernmost wall of the fortress, grateful for the shade that this narrow walkway afforded, its towering ramparts on either side lined with dozens of yeoman warders. She knew from the previous day's rehearsal that the procession would come to a halt halfway along, so that the queen and her entourage, along with a group of high-ranking courtiers, could join it. Her heart leaped at the thought that her parents would be among the latter.

Already, James was drawing level with St Thomas's Tower. Frances glanced at that ominous watergate, under which so many prisoners had passed for the last time. She jumped as another blast of trumpets sounded, and the procession came to a standstill. A few moments passed before the queen emerged, bedecked in a gown of dark silver, embroidered with gold thread that caught the light as she moved. Large rubies had been sewn at intervals across the sleeves and bodice, and at her neck and wrists she wore several strings of soft white pearls. More pearls were studded across her dark blonde hair, which her ladies had fashioned into a stiff, high coiffure. Despite the intensity of the heat, Anne's complexion was characteristically pale, and her thin lips had been made bright red by the careful application of beeswax and cochineal.

Impressed though she was by this dazzling ensemble, Frances could not help feeling that there was something familiar about it. As Anne inclined her head to the dignitaries at the front of the procession, the sunlight reflected off the silver and gold thread of the bodice, and Frances had a sudden recollection of the old queen being carried on an elaborately decorated white sedan, so delicate that it resembled one of the sugar work sculptures of which she had been so fond. She remembered that there had been an ethereal quality to her late mistress that day, her skin made whiter still by the reflection of the silver dress that she had been wearing.

With a jolt, Frances realised it was the same dress that she was looking at now. She had heard the rumours among the queen's ladies that their mistress had visited the Great Wardrobe at the Tower, and had declared that nothing could surpass Elizabeth's robes. But she had not believed the reports that Anne had set her dressmakers to work at once in having some of these old robes altered so that she might wear them. Such thriftiness should have been commendable, yet there was something distasteful about it – as if Anne had stolen the clothes from the old queen's back. Frances pushed the thought away.

Anne's expression remained unchanged as she approached her husband. He stepped forward and kissed her on the mouth, the movement swift and awkward. Without speaking, he then resumed his former position at the head of the procession. His wife joined it a few paces behind. Their three children appeared from the shadows of the archway, Henry strutting out in front, and Elizabeth holding the chubby hand of her younger brother. Even with her assistance, Charles walked with such an unsteady, tumbling gait that Frances judged it would not be long before his lady mistress, Lady Carey, would step forward and carry him in her arms, as she had been appointed to do. The princess was then to walk alone, directly behind her elder brother, to reinforce her maturity. Royal childhood was all too brief, Frances reflected, as she looked at her young charge. The princess stole a glance in her direction, and they exchanged a quick, furtive smile.

A line of high-ranking ladies and gentlemen then emerged from underneath the archway to join the procession. Frances craned her neck, and her eyes darted this way and that. Her heart was beating so fast that she was sure it must be visible to the courtiers on either side of her. Then, at last, she saw her: a vision of elegance and nobility unparalleled in James's court. She was arrayed in the red velvet dress and ermine cloak that Frances had seen in her bedchamber at Longford the previous year. Her best robes. Frances was not sure if they were intended to flatter the king or uphold her dignity. On top of her head she wore a tiny gold coronet with a single pearl suspended from the front, just touching her forehead.

Frances's eyes filled with tears, but she hastily blinked them away, desperate not to miss a precious moment. Now her father emerged from the shadows, taking his place next to her mother, but a fraction behind, as was his custom. He was dressed in a dark grey doublet and matching hose, and Frances knew that his choice of such a sombre colour was deliberate, so that he should not deflect any attention from his wife. It reminded her of a ploy by the old queen, who had insisted that her ladies wear only black or white, so that the gorgeous colours of her own gowns were shown off to best effect.

Her parents were just a few feet away from her now. She could almost touch them, if she reached out. It took all of her resolve to keep her hands by her sides. But she would not divert her eyes, even if Cecil was watching her every move. She began to fear that they were unaware of her presence and would pass by unnoticing, but just as they had almost drawn level, her father suddenly glanced in her direction. His eyes were merry as he held her gaze, then he gave the slightest wink, before turning back to face the direction of the procession. Without moving her head, her mother shot her a brief look filled with affection – and, Frances thought, some anxiety – but her mouth remained expressionless. All too soon, they had passed, and Frances was left gazing in their wake. This encounter, as sweet as it was brief, may have to suffice for many more months to come, she realised with a pang.

When all of the dignitaries had assumed their places, the procession continued towards the westernmost tower that led out into the city. As the king passed under the gateway and the huge portcullis was raised, a sudden clap of thunder reverberated around the walls of the ancient fortress, closely followed by a flash of lightning.

Frances glanced up. With luck, the rain would soon come, and they would be obliged to pick up their pace so that this whole charade would be over more quickly. As they turned onto Eastcheap, there was a thunderous roar from the crowds that thronged each side of the street, pushing and jostling each other to get a view of their king. Frances kept her eyes fixed on the towering spire of St Paul's, the top of which was obscured by dark grey clouds, so that it seemed to pierce heaven itself. She knew that when they drew level with the cathedral, they would be almost halfway to the abbey.

The first, heavy drop of rain splashed onto the paving stones in front of her, quickly followed by another, which ran down the length of her spine. She drew her shoulders together, relishing the feel of the water, like an icy blade being drawn along her sun-baked skin. The drops were falling quickly now, and soon became a torrent. It was as if the heavens were weeping at the sight of this king, who was cowering beneath the small canopy that his attendants, blinded by the driving rain, struggled to hold aloft.

The plays and pageants that lined the route still continued, but James did not so much as glance in their direction. Instead, he stared doggedly ahead, his impatience and discomfort showing plainly on his face. The brightly painted flags and streamers that had been draped from every balcony soon hung limp and sodden, their colours dripping onto the pavement below.

The crowds quickly began to scatter, some running into nearby buildings, and others seeking shelter in the many taverns that lined the route of the procession. By the time that they reached the Temple Church, its ancient, honey-coloured stones washed a dull brown by the torrent, there were only a few hardy souls, hunched and sodden, to greet their king. Their frail cheers were drowned out by the rush of the water as it raced along the gutters, spilling their stinking detritus into the path of the courtiers. Frances watched, amused, as Lord Sackville grimaced at his shoes, the fine ivory satin now smeared with filth. She herself looked as if she had been plunged into the Thames. Her neatly plaited hair hung in sodden knots around her face, and her gown was so mud-spattered that she doubted Mrs Banks would ever be able to brush it clean. But she hardly cared. The cooling rains seemed to wash away the oppressive atmosphere – not to mention the heat – that had hung over the court these past few days. Even if it was a temporary blessing, she was grateful for it.

They had passed St Paul's now, and were trudging along Fleet Street. Frances looked across at the handsome red-brick gate-house to her right, its archway picked out in marble that had been washed so white that it glistened. A figure stood beneath it, his face obscured by the hood of his cloak. As she drew level with him, her heart gave a lurch.

Tom.

He pulled back his hood and smiled, then gave a small bow. He wore a plain black gown with a high collar and white ruff, together with a simple black hat, rising to a point in the centre. Lawyer's clothes. This must be the entrance of Gray's Inn, Frances realised. Suddenly conscious of her own rain-soaked appearance, she put a hand to her hair and pushed back one of the tendrils that clung damply to her cheek. She smiled ruefully and gave a shrug. His grin widened, making her feel warm despite the rain that coursed down her neck and seeped under her tightly laced bodice.

She tried to slow her pace, but was soon jostled by the line of courtiers behind her, impatient to be inside the shelter of the abbey. Reluctantly, she turned to face the road ahead, which was rapidly becoming a river. Just before they rounded the corner that led to the Strand, she turned, craning her neck towards the red-brick gatehouse. He had stepped out from under it now and was standing, perfectly still, his hood still pulled back. Though she could no longer make out his features, she knew that his eyes were fixed upon her.

Turning back towards Westminster, the spires of which were now just visible above the grand mansions that lined the Strand, her mouth lifted into a slow smile.

CHAPTER 16

28 July

The entertainments were already under way when Frances arrived at the Banqueting House with her young charge. Looking down, she saw that Elizabeth's eyes sparkled with excitement at being allowed to attend the evening reception, the lateness of the hour adding to the sense that she was, at last, being treated as an adult, rather than just the little sister of her revered brother, the prince and heir. This was the third night of revelry in succession, and Frances's heart sank to think that there were still another four to go. Perhaps, with all this magnificence, the king hoped to mask the disappointment of the anniversary parade itself.

By the time they had reached the abbey, the king had been in a foul temper. The inadequate canopy had offered little shelter, and he had trudged up the aisle of the ancient cathedral scowling, rain dripping onto his face from the ermine that fringed his crown. Even the ceremony of thanksgiving had seemed to irritate him, and he had obliged the archbishop to cut short his oratory. As if the tempest was not ominous enough, James's ungracious behaviour had surely set the seal on God's displeasure – and that of his subjects.

Looking around the ornate hall now, with its immensely high ceiling and lavishly decorated walls, Frances found it hard to believe that it was all just a temporary structure, put up by the old queen as part of a charade surrounding the negotiations for yet another potential marriage.

A heady smell of spiced wine filled the air. The princess breathed in deeply, and Frances had to smile at the look of sheer joy that suffused her delicate features. In the few short weeks since entering her service, she had developed a strong affection for the young girl, whose natural exuberance was infectious. It had proved a welcome diversion from the intrigue and suspicion that increasingly pervaded the court. Every day there were rumours of another conspiracy, and the king looked about him with narrowed eyes.

'Ma'am.' A page stepped forward with a silver tray laden with gold-rimmed crystal glasses. Elizabeth immediately took one and began devouring its contents.

'Slowly, my lady,' Frances cautioned. 'The wine is strong, and you need to preserve your nimble feet for the dancing.'

Elizabeth giggled, and handed her attendant the glass, which was less than half full.

'Come! I must greet the king and my lady mother.'

Together they advanced towards the throne. A path was rapidly cleared for them as they walked, the courtiers bowing low as the princess passed. She held her head high, inclining it slightly every now and then. As they came before the king and queen, sitting underneath the great canopy of state, Frances and the princess bowed low.

'Sweet Liz, come here.' The king beckoned to his daughter. Torn between the need to maintain her newly acquired maturity, and the desire to receive some rare fatherly affection, Elizabeth walked slowly forward. When she came within reach of the king, he grabbed at her and pulled her clumsily onto his knee. Frances saw her recoil slightly as he breathed close to her face, spittle falling on her pale cheek.

'Your mother is not in a good humour this evening, Lizzie,' he said, looking scornfully across at the queen. Stealing a glance,

Frances noticed that Anne appeared in some discomfort. Her face was waxy pale, and beads of sweat were forming at her temples. Every now and then her hands, which lay across her stomach, would press into it sharply.

'Mama.' Elizabeth jumped down from her father's knee and went to kneel for her mother's blessing. Anne tentatively withdrew one of her hands from her stomach and placed it briefly on her daughter's head.

'Lady Frances.' The queen nodded towards her. 'I trust you are well?'

'Very well, Your Majesty,' Frances replied quietly. 'Can I bring you something for your ease?'

Before Anne could reply, a cacophony of noise erupted to the right of the platform on which she sat.

'Stop it, Henry! Stop!'

The childish scream rang out across the hall, bringing the music and chatter to an abrupt halt. The infant Charles lay kicking at his elder brother's feet, as Henry pinned him down and forced a pointed ivory silk hat on to his head. The hat was so large that it completely engulfed Charles's head, and when he got to his feet, he stumbled forward, unable to see. Henry laughed uproariously.

'Behold, good subjects! The new Archbishop of Canterbury!' he called, collapsing into a fresh fit of laughter. As his infant brother staggered around on his thin, rickety legs, flailing wildly with his arms, the laughter spread across the room. Soon the whole court was in uproar.

Frances watched as the little prince tripped over an outstretched foot, prompting a fresh burst of hilarity. Even the queen, momentarily distracted from her discomfort, wore an expression of indulgent amusement. But her husband was glowering. He leaped to his feet, and, pushing back the courtiers who were too slow to react, he ran to his eldest son and dealt him a blow across the face so hard that the crack reverberated around the hall. Henry staggered back, holding his jaw. Slowly, James walked over to where his youngest son was on his hands and knees, sobbing. Gently but firmly, he wrested the mitre from his head. The little boy buried his face in his hands, as much to stay his tears as to hide himself from the eyes of the court.

'You young runt!' James shouted at Henry, and, without warning, flung his glass towards his son's head. The prince ducked just in time, and the goblet shattered onto the flagstones, its contents spilling over the onlookers nearby.

'No!' The cry came from the platform. All heads turned to see the queen, her face now ghastly white; sweat glistened across her face and neck. She took a painful step forward, and there was a collective gasp as those close to the throne saw the blood that was pooling at her feet.

'Lady Frances,' she whispered, swaying suddenly as if intoxicated. Frances rushed forward, and put her arm around the queen's shoulders as she fell into a faint.

'Help me, quickly,' Frances quietly urged the other ladies in attendance, who were standing nearby, aghast. Together, they half carried, half dragged the queen's limp body through the hall, towards the Great Watching Chamber that lay beyond. As she closed the door behind her, Frances caught a glimpse of Cecil staring after her, his expression thunderous. She knew she did not have much time.

Casting about the room, Frances saw a cluster of velvet cushions scattered around its perimeter. Gathering them up, she hurried back to the queen, who was still slumped in her ladies' arms. Lowering her gently onto the cushions, Frances commanded Lady Mar to loosen the queen's stays. She sent another for water and linens.

Holding Anne's limp wrist between her forefinger and thumb, Frances felt a faint pulse. The blood was still seeping from under the queen's skirts, staining her white stockings with bright, glistening red. When the woman returned with water, Frances gently cradled Anne's head and brought the goblet to her lips. Dribbling a small amount into her mouth, she closed it with her fingers and watched her throat. Seeing a small movement, Frances gradually administered another drop, and another.

Slowly, Anne opened her eyes. She stared at Frances in bemusement.

'He should not tease Charlie so,' she said. 'The boy has such a temper.'

A tear weaved slowly down the queen's cheek. Her face was still as white as the marble pillars that flanked the doorway of the hall.

'It would have been a winter baby, and Elizabeth did so want a little sister.'

'Your Majesty is still young. The princess might have a nursery full of sisters yet.'

The words sounded false, even to her own ears. The queen smiled bitterly, and slowly shook her head.

'The king will get no more children on me now. God knows he visits my bed seldom enough.'

Frances caught the look that Lady Mar exchanged with another of the ladies, but busied herself with wringing out the sodden sheets and rearranging the queen's skirts so that she might be conveyed with dignity to her privy apartments.

A rapping at the door reverberated around the lofty chamber. For a moment, nobody stirred. Frances looked at the queen, who gave the slightest nod. Rising to her feet, she crossed slowly to the door and opened it a crack.

'Lady Frances, I cannot permit you to detain the queen any longer. The king is growing impatient.'

'My Lord Cecil.'

Even through the narrow gap, Frances could see the irritation on his face.

'The queen needs rest. I would be obliged if you could instruct the Lord Chamberlain to bring her sedan so that she might be carried to her chamber.'

There was a moment's pause as he weighed the necessity of her request with the infringement of hierarchy that taking instructions from her represented.

'Very well, but I will also arrange for the queen's physician to attend her. She requires the ministrations of an expert, not the homespun remedies of a—' He paused. 'Of our resident wise woman.'

He turned on his heel and walked briskly away, the sound of his footsteps uneven as he moved with his usual awkward gait.

'My husband is not a patient man,' the queen observed softly. 'He despairs of the female sex altogether. But then, he has enough male companions to console him for our deceits and disappointments.'

Frances was glad when, at that moment, the Lord Chamberlain and his men arrived with the queen's sedan. Setting the elegant ivory silk chair down in front of her, they kept their eyes fixed straight ahead as the ladies lifted her into it. Frances saw Anne wince as she shifted in the chair, trying to find a position that she could endure for the short journey to her apartments. She wished that she would be allowed to accompany her, but Cecil had made it clear that her services had been superseded by those of the royal physician. He shot Frances a haughty, disapproving look as he followed the entourage that conveyed the queen out of the room.

Suddenly remembering that the princess would still be in the hall, Frances hastened to find her, ashamed that she had been so far from her thoughts. She arrived to find that most of the company had dispersed. Only James appeared unmoved by the event. He remained on his throne, flanked by the usual coterie of favourites. One of them lay reclined at his feet, and Frances noticed that he distractedly stroked James's silk-clad calves. The Prince of Wales was standing sullenly next to the platform, his arms crossed and his mouth set in a determined line. His younger brother had been taken to bed, and the crumpled bishop's hat lay discarded halfway across the hall.

Frances hoped to find Elizabeth and spirit her quietly away. Casting about the room, she caught a movement of pink satin from behind one of the pillars. She walked softly over to it, and, drawing closer, heard the muffled sound of sobbing. The princess was sitting at the base of the pillar, hugging her knees tightly, her face buried in them. The delicate satin of her dress was stained with tears.

Tracy Borman

Lowering herself next to the young girl, Frances gently put her arm around her shoulders and drew her close.

'Ma-Mama,' Elizabeth gasped in between sobs. 'I-is she dead?'

'No, my lady,' Frances soothed, wrapping both arms around her, and gently rocking her. 'Your mother will be well. She is resting now.'

The princess lifted up her red, swollen eyes. 'But there was so much blood. I felt sure that Mama must have been murdered.'

'Hush now.' Frances smoothed back the loose tendrils of hair from the girl's face. 'All will be well.' Knowing that she would not be so easily appeased, she added: 'Your mother was with child, but it was very early and it bled away.'

Elizabeth looked up at her wonderingly.

'I was to have a sister?'

Frances smiled. 'Or a brother, my lady.'

A look of sadness passed over the princess's face.

'I should have so liked a baby sister,' she said. Then, considering, asked: 'Might I still?'

Frances thought of the queen's words, and the finality with which she had spoken them. But she could not bear to deprive her young charge of all comfort, so she simply said: 'If God wills it.'

This was enough to pacify Elizabeth, whose eyes now sparkled with hope, as well as tears.

'Then I shall pray to Him every night that it may be so,' she said decisively.

Frances gently withdrew her arms from around the princess, and stood up. She reached forward and took Elizabeth's small hands in her own, pulling her to her feet.

'It is late. I must take you to bed, my lady.'

For once, her charge did not protest. Overcome with the sweet exhaustion that follows tears, she blinked slowly up at Frances, smiling.

'Lady Frances!'

The king's voice, thick with wine, rang out across the near-deserted hall. Frances closed her eyes briefly, then, turning, made a low curtsey towards the distant throne.

'You would do well to attend your proper duties, rather than usurping those of my physicians,' he drawled. 'My daughter should have been abed long before now.'

'Forgive me, sire.' Frances kept her gaze fixed on the ground. 'I wanted to ease the queen's distress.'

'I am sick to the stomach with meddling women!' he shouted suddenly, slamming his goblet down so that the contents splattered over his companions. Frances felt the princess's hand tighten around hers. She gently stroked it with her forefinger as she waited, not sure whether this was a dismissal. Several moments passed. A grunting noise made Frances look up sharply. She saw that the king's head had lolled forward onto his chest. He had fallen into a deep, wine-induced sleep. The young man who had been stroking his calves sniggered. Another reached forward and unlaced James's collar. Then they all settled down to sleep, like dogs at the feet of their master.

CHAPTER 17

30 July

A hammering on the door jolted Frances awake. It was pitch black. She wondered whether her heart had been pounding all night, or whether it was the unexpected knocking. She felt about for her cloak, and, wrapping it around herself, reached the door just as it was shaken by another volley. She could hear the sound of footsteps now, running in the direction of the Great Hall.

She opened the door to find Tom standing before her, his agitated face illuminated by the single candle that he carried in his trembling hand.

'Frances, you must come with me,' he urged, pulling her by the wrist. 'The court is in uproar.'

Without pausing for further explanation, he slammed the door shut behind them and raced down the hallway, still holding Frances tightly by the wrist. She had no time to absorb the shock of his sudden appearance as they ran along the gloomy corridor. At the end of it, she caught a glimpse of a small, slight figure loitering in a doorway, but Tom had pulled her around the corner before she could look back.

'Where are we going?' Frances demanded, trying to jerk herself free.

'To the princess,' Tom replied breathlessly, as they rounded the corner that led to the royal nursery.

Frances felt her chest tighten in panic.

The door to the princess's bedroom was already open when they reached it. Rushing in, Frances saw a bewildered-looking Lady Mar. Elizabeth's bed, the covers flung back, bore the imprint of her small body, but she was nowhere to be seen.

'Where is my lady princess?' Frances demanded urgently.

'Frances!' The high-pitched voice called out behind her, and she swung around to see Elizabeth hastening towards her from the little anteroom that led off from her bedchamber. She buried her face in Frances's skirts, hugging her legs tightly.

'Thank God she is safe,' Tom breathed, his shoulders sagging.

'Tell me now – what is happening?' Frances commanded, her heart still racing.

'Treason.' Lady Mar spoke the word with a kind of wonder.

'It is true,' Tom said gravely. 'A papist conspiracy has been uncovered. Cecil has issued orders for the entire palace to be searched, lest any conspirators remain in its midst.'

Frances fell silent, recalling the conversation at the dinner with Sir Thomas Tyringham. Her uncle's gloomy predictions had proved remarkably accurate.

'Who is behind it?' she asked at last.

'I don't know, everything is still in confusion. Lady Arbella was mentioned.'

Frances remembered the haughty young woman who had been summoned to court by the late queen towards the end of her reign. With the royal blood of the Tudors and Stuarts coursing through her veins, her very birth had been the result of a plot by those ambitious matriarchs, Bess of Hardwick and Lady Margaret Douglas, niece of Henry VIII, to produce a rival claimant to the throne. Elizabeth had eyed the flame-haired Lady Stuart with customary shrewdness, quickly concluding that this indulged and volatile young girl was not the stuff that queens were made of.

'Is she taken?' Frances imagined the proud young woman behind the dark walls of the Tower.

'I do not think so – at least, not yet,' Tom replied. 'She will no doubt insist upon her innocence, as she has before.'

'Was she going to kill my father?' the princess whispered, her eyes wide with fear.

In her eagerness to find out more, Frances had abandoned her customary discretion. Tom crouched down in front of Elizabeth and smiled his reassurance.

'No, my lady princess. Your father would have been safe, even if this had come to pass.' He looked up at Frances. 'I am not so sure about Cecil and his friends. They have many enemies in the kingdom.'

Elizabeth gave a scornful laugh. 'He is always such a bore – I have never seen him dance, not even once – and look at the horrible gift he gave me!'

Frances watched as the princess skipped over to her dresser and pulled out a small oblong box wrapped in velvet.

'I was showing my father the dance steps you taught me, Frances, when Cecil came in and gave it to me. He knelt as he did so, as if I was the queen! He said I might both play with it and learn from it,' the princess prattled on, oblivious to the silence into which her companions had fallen.

'Look!' She thrust the box at Tom, who slowly unwrapped it. When he saw its contents, he became unnaturally still.

'The Lord Privy Seal gave you this, my lady?' he asked quietly.

'Yes. Isn't it ghastly?' The princess was indignant.

Tom picked the small doll out of the box and held it so that Frances might see.

'Look how poorly she is dressed!' Elizabeth said scornfully. 'Her gown is of rough black cloth, and her hat is all bent at the top.'

Frances recoiled as if from a snake. She saw that lines had been painted on the small, pinched face, and the nose was so hooked that it almost met the chin. Black leather shoes with small holes pierced into them were forced onto the feet. Around the waist was tied a piece of rope from which were suspended a few tiny sprigs of thyme. Frances tasted the same bile that had filled her mouth at the hanging.

'And what is this?' The princess reached over and picked something else out of the box.

Tom took it from her. It was a small twig that had been sliced several times at the end and frayed to resemble a broom.

'It must be for the old lady to clean with,' he said with a small smile.

'What an ugly thing! It is not at all like my other dolls. They have pretty faces, and are dressed in gowns like my own. Why would he give me such a gift? He must hate me after all.'

'Impossible!' Tom cried with exaggerated indignation. 'A man would have to be blind or a simpleton not to worship the very ground that those pretty little shoes walk on,' he said with a wink. 'Besides, my Lord Privy Seal is not used to children.'

'But what did he mean by giving me such a horrible thing? I shall never play with it.'

'Perhaps he meant it as a servant to your other dolls,' Frances soothed. 'After all, there are so many of them, and they need a good deal of looking after.'

Elizabeth giggled, casting a glance at the pile of dolls that lay strewn across the far corner of her room, a mass of brightly coloured silk and shiny curls.

'They can be quite unruly!' she admitted.

'Well, let us put Master Cecil's kind gift away for now.' Frances took it deftly from Tom's hands. She walked briskly over to the mahogany dresser and pushed the box into one of the drawers, slamming it shut.

The sound of footsteps approaching made them turn. Tom walked towards the door, his body suddenly tense. Frances saw his features soften with relief as he recognised Cecil's men approaching.

'Here again, Wintour?' one of them asked. 'You are becoming quite a fixture in the princess's apartments.'

Frances looked across at her companion in surprise. When had he last visited? The princess had not mentioned it, and she herself was almost always in attendance.

Tom smiled with accustomed ease. 'I wanted to be sure that no harm had befallen her grace, but as you see, Lady Frances has her in safe keeping,' he replied smoothly. 'Are all the conspirators apprehended?'

The man nodded.

'They are already in the Tower. We do not believe that there are more, but we must remain vigilant. Papists are apt to crawl into all manner of mouse holes.'

Seeing the princess's distress at the thought of conspirators still at large in the palace, Frances cut in: 'Gentlemen, as the danger has passed, I think it is time that the princess returns to her bed.' Ignoring the beginnings of a protest from her young charge, she added firmly: 'She is greatly fatigued from the night's events.'

'I fear Lady Frances is right, sir,' Tom concurred with a placatory shrug.

Frances busied herself with smoothing down the sheets and snuffing out the candles. Elizabeth rubbed her eyes.

'I am not in the least bit tired,' the girl insisted, climbing into bed.

Tom arranged for one of Cecil's guards to remain behind and stand watch outside the princess's door. Frances thanked him, feeling both grateful and a little curious that he should be so solicitous of Elizabeth's welfare.

'You are quite safe now, Your Grace, so you must take your rest,' she said to the princess with a smile. 'I will attend you as usual in the morning.'

She bobbed a curtsey and left the room, Tom following close behind.

'Permit me to escort you to your chamber, Lady Frances.'

'Thank you, but there is no need,' she said, a little too abruptly. Tonight had made her painfully aware of how little she knew about him, despite the growing intimacy she was fool enough to believe they shared.

'Then allow me to do it for the pleasure of your company.'

Frances could think of no objection that would not sound churlish, so she nodded her acquiescence.

They walked on in a silence for a while, but she was intensely aware of his presence. He unnerved her in a way that she could not explain. Sometimes she thought it was irritation at his easy grace, which seemed to border on impertinence. At others, she felt there was something almost threatening about him. The intensity of his gaze was both disconcerting, and, she had to admit, disarming.

'You claim to desire my company, and yet we have not spoken one word since we left the princess,' she said at last, when he showed no inclination to speak.

'Do you think, then, that conversation is the essence of good company?'

'It is generally thought so.'

'Well, then, let us converse. There is, after all, a great deal that I wish to know about you.'

'And I about you,' she countered, a little defensively.

'Oh, I am singularly uninteresting,' he said airily. 'I am of good English stock, the son of a gentleman from Worcester. I have two brothers and two sisters of indeterminate talents. I fought for the old queen in the Netherlands, picked up as many languages as I did diseases, and returned to England in time for the new century. I have been working as a modest lawyer ever since.' He paused. 'I told you I was dull.'

Frances studied him for a few moments. His eyes glinted, and he was smiling pleasantly at her, but he seemed to be in earnest.

'Did the military life suit you well?' she asked eventually.

'Not in the least!' he replied jovially. 'We were as despised by our allies, the Dutch, as by our Spanish enemies. It is a wonder that they did not choose to fire upon us as well. Even the queen did not seem to have a high opinion of us – or at least, the tightening of her purse strings suggested so.'

'Her Majesty was ever of a frugal nature.' Frances smiled at the recollection. Her mother had always marvelled at the queen's ability to maintain a court worthy of Croesus, while keeping her coffers filled with gold. She had even been slow to pay the sailors who had repelled the mighty Armada. 'Her grandfather could not have counted his coins more carefully,' Helena had been fond of saying. And yet the old queen had been capable of acts of the most extraordinary generosity – as Frances and her family knew only too well. Longford had been built from the gold and silver recovered from a stricken Armada ship that the queen had granted to her father.

'And does the law keep you in better state?'

'You sound like your uncle,' he chided. 'He would be proud of the way you interrogate the prospects of potential suitors.'

Frances flushed. 'I assure you, my interest is entirely impersonal.'

'Forgive me, Frances. My father is forever chastising me for my impertinent jests. He says they will put an end to any hopes of advancement at court.'

'So long as the king and Master Cecil find you amusing, you need not worry,' Frances assured him. 'Although I cannot believe the Lord Privy Seal laughs at anything but other people's misfortunes.'

'How true,' Tom agreed. 'The finest comedy by Master Shakespeare did little more than raise a fleeting smile when it was performed at the old court, so I am told.'

Cecil's name seemed to interrupt the flow of conversation, and there was a pause before Tom asked: 'So how did you come to be here? You are surely too much a woman of reason to thrive in the snakepit of the court.'

'I had little choice in the matter. My uncle is determined that I should enhance my family's fortunes.'

'By finding a good husband?' His disconcerting eyes studied her intently.

'In part, yes,' she admitted. 'But also by proving a loyal servant.'

'Ah well, you have already succeeded in the latter. You are an excellent companion for the princess, and her mother also seems to be greatly in your debt.'

Frances stopped walking and looked at him. Had he, like Cecil, learned of her first encounter with the queen? He served her as a lawyer, but was evidently a confidant too. Those eavesdroppers in the Great Hall were right. There could be few secrets at court.

'How are you enjoying Sir Philip Sidney's worthy tome?' Tom asked at last.

Frances relaxed at once, her face lighting up with pleasure as she thought of the book that had been her unfailing companion during her leisure hours.

'It is a source of constant delight,' she enthused, her eyes sparkling. 'I am already on my third reading, but discover new enchantments each time. I will be forever in your debt, Mr –Tom.' The name sounded at once unfamiliar yet welcome on her lips.

He smiled warmly, as much at her obvious pleasure in his gift as at her use of his first name. But as he looked at her, she saw a shadow flicker across his eyes as a new thought occurred to him.

'If only all gifts were so well received,' he said gravely. 'What do you think of the doll?'

'A child's toy can surely hold little interest to you,' she replied lightly, resuming her walk.

'You know what it signifies,' he said, regarding her closely. 'Cecil does not deal in trifles.'

Frances held his gaze.

'If it was meant as a warning, then I shall try to heed it,' she said levelly. 'Whatever it means.'

They had reached the door of her apartment.

'Thank you for proving me right, Lady Frances,' Tom said softly.

Frances raised an enquiring eyebrow.

'Your company has given me as much pleasure as I anticipated. More, even.'

She smiled. 'I am glad you have had some small reward for your kindness.'

He did not return her smile, but regarded her gravely. He took a step closer. She could smell the woodsmoke from his cloak, and the warm scent of sandalwood on his skin. Again, that intense gaze. She was determined not to look away, though she felt her neck prickle with rising heat. Her smile faded as she struggled to keep her breathing slow.

Gently, his eyes never leaving hers, he reached for her hand and brought it slowly up to his lips. He held it there, so close to his mouth that she could feel his warm breath. Lowering his head, he planted a soft kiss on her fingertips.

'Frances,' he murmured, still holding her hand. Then, reluctantly, he released it. 'I must leave you to your rest.'

He gave a small bow.

She watched as he walked away, his slender form gradually merging with the gloom.

CHAPTER 18

17 August

Frances rose early, before the rest of the court began to stir. Even though it would be several hours before the sun reached her chamber, it already felt warm, and there was not a breath of air from the window, which had been opened wide all night. She padded over to it now and looked out across the Thames, which glistened in the early-morning light. The grey-blue sky seemed to hang low across the city, and the houses on the opposite bank appeared hazy. The tempest that had blighted the anniversary procession had given way to more hot and sultry weather, to which there seemed to be no end. Frances had found the court even more oppressive than usual. The very air seemed to entrap her.

She crossed to the wooden chest and pulled out a pale green cloak. Not troubling to change out of her shift, she wrapped the cloak around her and slipped on her pantofles. Carefully lifting the latch, she opened the door a crack and peered out. The passageway was empty. Her heart pounded as she slowly pushed the door closed, then, with a final glance over her shoulder, made her way along the corridor.

Padding silently down the narrow stairs that led to the privy garden, she felt a rush of anticipation. Serving the princess filled most of her hours, but she still missed the comforting ritual of preparing her salves and potions, even if she dare not risk putting them to use. Many times since her arrival at court, she had longed to visit the herb garden that lay beneath her window, to feel the velvety sage leaves between her fingertips, and pluck the tiny stems of rosemary. With luck, she could gather some herbs before the rest of the court was awake, and then lock them in the small casket that lay nestled among her books. As she reached the door at the foot of the stairs, she paused, her fingers suspended over the handle. Her mother would be angry if she knew that she was taking this risk. She shook the thought from her head and gently lifted the latch.

The familiar scent of myrtle reached her first as she entered the courtyard garden. She allowed herself to take a long breath, and closed her eyes as she turned her face up to the hazy sunlight. Then, reaching into the pocket of her cloak, she pulled out the tiny pair of silver shears that her father had given her two summers ago. 'It will be winter ere you will tame the ivy with these, Frances,' he had said, smiling, as she had unwrapped the precious gift. 'But patience was ever the gardener's friend.'

She walked over to the furthest quadrant, which was still in shade, and crouched down amongst the flowers and herbs, careful not to crush any underfoot. Working quickly and methodically, she deftly clipped stems of juniper, rosemary, lavender, and hartshorn, placing each one on her lap so that before long the skirt of her shift was filled with a heady mixture of scent and colour. Casting an anxious glance up at the windows overlooking the courtyard, she cut a few more stems, then gathered up her skirts and stole silently back inside.

'The whole court is talking of it,' Lady Mar announced breathlessly, without preamble, as she came bustling into the princess's bedchamber.

Frances and her charge were sitting in the window seat, reading a beautifully illuminated prayer book; Frances traced each line as

Elizabeth read the tiny script. Their heads jerked upwards, and Frances shot the older woman a disapproving look.

'The conspirators are apprehended, and there is no cause for further alarm, my lady,' she told her.

'No, not that,' Lady Mar said impatiently. 'There is a witch in our midst!'

Frances kept very still.

'A witch!' Elizabeth whispered, with a mixture of fear and wonder. 'I have read about them in my books. Father wrote one himself,' she added proudly. 'He says they almost drowned him and my mother when they were newly married.'

'What proof is there?' Frances cut in abruptly.

'The Lord Privy Seal himself has declared upon it,' Lady Mar replied haughtily. 'He brought the matter before the Privy Council early this morning, as they met to discuss the affair of Lady Stuart.'

'I saw a witch put to the flames once,' Elizabeth cut in.

Frances swung around to look at her.

Pleased that she had reclaimed her attention, the princess continued: 'Oh yes, she was such an old woman that her head was almost bald, and she could hardly stand. They had to tie her to the stake. And even though she was all skin and bone, as my father said, she burned so brightly!'

Frances stared at Elizabeth, whose sparkling eyes looked back steadily at her. She suddenly felt very alone.

Turning back to Lady Mar, she quietly repeated: 'What proof?'

'He says that the . . . indisposition of the queen was the result of a bewitchment. It is well known that witches always try to meddle with the bringing forth of children.' Lady Mar paused for effect. 'The king says that witchcraft is rife in his kingdom. His new laws will ensure that they are hunted down as they are in Scotland. Many more will be hanged like that miserable wretch at Tyburn.'

Frances felt her mouth go dry.

'Mama was bewitched?' The princess's eyes were wide with fright. Frances rounded on the older woman.

'Lady Mar, I would thank you not to terrify the princess with such ridiculous tales!' she scolded, her fear turning to anger.

The older lady lifted her chin and sniffed.

'The king would wish his daughter to know that the Devil is at work in his court,' she retorted. 'We must all be vigilant, Lady Frances.'

Bobbing a swift curtsey, the older woman swept out of the room. Before the princess could begin any wild speculations about who the witch might be, Frances cut in abruptly: 'Ma'am, I promised to call on the Lord Chamberlain to discuss the banquet in honour of your birthday.'

The princess clapped her hands together.

'Oh, we must have sweetmeats! And marchpane! And the master cook must craft an exotic bird or animal out of sugar, like he did for Henry's feast,' she said excitedly, her eyes sparkling as she imagined the array of delicious delicacies. She was still calling out suggestions as Frances made her curtsey and backed out of the room.

Closing the door of the bedchamber behind her, Frances paused for a few moments, catching her breath. Had Cecil or his spies seen her in the courtyard that morning? She was sure she had not been followed, and even if she had, she could reason that she was simply gathering a few sweet-smelling herbs for her chamber. She tried to push away the thought that hundreds of women had gone to the gallows for much less.

Gathering her skirts, she hastened from the room, brushing past the guards at the door beyond, who looked after her, surprised. She quickened her pace, taking long strides along the narrow corridors and through the succession of courtyards, the sun bursting onto her in quick, searing intervals. Courtiers looked after her as she hurried past, but she did not heed their curious stares. Several times, she thought she heard the light, rapid tap of footsteps behind her.

When at last she reached his apartment, she knocked quietly on the door and waited, panting, beads of sweat trickling down her neck and between her breasts. The heat was so intense now that it had penetrated the thick stone walls of the palace, and it felt like a furnace within.

Frances struggled for breath as she waited. After a few moments, the door opened, and Tom looked at her with a mixture of surprise and alarm. Without hesitating, he pulled her into the room and closed the door quickly behind her. Holding her by the hand, he gently guided her to a chair next to a desk, on which there was a large pile of papers.

'I am sorry,' Frances said, looking towards them. 'I disturbed you—'

'Hush,' he interrupted gently. 'Calm yourself. Here—' He handed her a glass of water. Frances gulped it down gratefully.

'You have heard Cecil's pronouncement,' he said quietly.

She nodded, not trusting herself to speak.

'Apparently he excelled himself in council, whipping the king up into a fury that some witch had murdered his unborn child. Already there are scores of lawyers at work drafting the new statute. I had to plead the pressure of the queen's business to avoid becoming involved myself.'

Frances looked up at him bleakly.

'Cecil's men are all over the palace,' Tom continued. 'They have been instructed to report anything unusual to their master. The king's guard are on alert too. What with this, and the late plot, everyone is jumping at their own shadow.'

'I must go back to Longford,' Frances said. 'I will be safe there.'

'If you leave now, it will be taken as an admission of guilt,' Tom replied quickly. 'You must stand firm. Cecil has you marked, but you enjoy the favour of the queen and her daughter.'

The reassurance sounded weak.

'You know that will count as nothing if Cecil persuades his master that I am the witch he seeks. The king has no love for his wife, and he will soon find another favourite for his daughter. I must leave. I can excuse my departure by some urgent business. My parents charged me with the care of their estate, after all.'

Tom fell silent. He walked over to the window and stared out at the river. His chamber, Frances noted, was a good deal smaller and less well-appointed than her own. There were no hangings on the walls, and the oak floorboards lay exposed at their feet. On his desk, next to the papers, was a half-eaten plum and a small goblet of water. He seemed to have few belongings. There was a prayer book on the small table next to his bed, and what looked like a chain or a necklace beside it. Frances's gaze was distracted from it when Tom spoke.

'If you go to Longford, Cecil's men will follow you there. He has heard of your fondness for the place – God knows, your uncle has complained of it often enough.'

He paused, watching her intently. 'I know you long to leave this place, but it is safer to stay and weather the storm. It need not be for long. The king is notoriously fickle. His obsession with witchcraft will be replaced with a fervour for hunting or jousting before the winter is upon us.'

'Cecil has greater patience,' Frances countered grimly.

Tom shrugged.

'He will soon have other matters to attend to. The king easily tires of state business, and gladly passes it to his chief minister. Cecil may not be a favourite, but there is nobody more able.'

Frances stared down at her hands. After a few moments, she gave a heavy sigh.

'You are right. I have no choice but to remain at court and counter whatever Cecil levels at me. Besides,' she added, lifting her eyes to Tom's, 'I am not entirely without friends here.'

'Lady Frances – Frances,' he said softly but earnestly, 'your welfare means a great deal to me.'

'I am greatly indebted to you,' she replied, holding his gaze.

He walked slowly over to where she was sitting and knelt down in front of her. His brown eyes regarded her uncertainly. Frances reached forward and touched his cheek, which felt warm against her palm. Immediately ashamed of her impulsiveness, she made as if to withdraw her hand, but Tom reached up and held it there. He leaned forward so that their faces almost touched.

'I will keep you safe,' he whispered.

Then, slowly, he kissed her. Frances tasted the sweet tang of summer plums on his lips.

CHAPTER 19

18 August

Frances looked out across the Thames, her eyes slowly adjusting to the gloom. It would not be light for another hour yet, although she fancied that the sky was already marked with the first wisps of dawn. Relishing the stillness, she watched the swollen waters of the river as it flowed westwards, hoping that it might carry her thoughts away. But again they were drawn back to the events of the day before, and she felt as if her heart was being squeezed. Terror at Cecil's witch hunt merged with the warmth of desire that seemed to pool in the pit of her stomach when she thought of Tom. An image of his face, close to hers, appeared so clearly that it was as if he were standing next to her now.

A sharp creak outside her door jolted her back to the present. She waited for the knock, but none came. It was far too early for Mrs Banks to attend her. She usually arrived, scowling, a little after six. After a pause, Frances padded silently over to the door. Turning the key slowly in the lock, cringing against the scraping noise that it made, she opened the door to see a boy standing before her. He made no attempt to move, but simply stared straight ahead, his face impassive.

'What is your business here?' Frances demanded, her voice low but urgent.

The boy smirked at her, but remained silent.

'Why are you following me?'

Still he said nothing, but the smile remained. He gave the slightest of bows, and sauntered away down the corridor, whistling tunelessly as he went.

Frances took her breakfast in the dining hall that morning, for once preferring the noise and clamour to the tranquillity of the princess's apartments. She welcomed the distraction of the endless chatter as her fellow courtiers tore chunks of bread and dipped them into their ale, or cut generous slabs of cheese and meat and devoured them as if they had not eaten for a week.

'The Lady Arbella is now thought to have conspired with witches,' she heard someone remark above the clamour.

'Aye,' their companion agreed. 'Master Cecil says it is certain that there is one amongst us – probably a whole coven.'

Frances busied herself with spreading butter on the warm bread roll from the basket that one of the red-faced kitchen attendants had just put on their table.

'He won't be satisfied until he's found her and burned her, like they do in his kingdom,' another retorted.

Rising, she walked over to the long table that ran along one side of the hall, and helped herself to some water from a large pewter jug.

'My lady.'

The voice came from close behind her, making her start. She turned to see a servingwoman whom she recognised from the queen's household. Her light brown hair was scraped back into an untidy bun at the base of her neck, and she wore a crisp white apron, the seams of which she fretted with her hands.

'I have need of your skills,' she said quietly.

Before she could say anything else, Frances guided her swiftly and discreetly to a corner of the room where they might not be so easily overheard.

'My sister's child is gravely ill, my lady,' the woman continued. 'He is but five weeks old, and was a lusty baby until now. They say the sickness is back.'

Frances looked at her steadily for several moments, considering whether this might be a trap set by Cecil and his men.

'I am sorry, madam, you are mistaken. I have no skills to help your nephew.'

'But my lady, I have heard say that your skills surpass those of any wise woman. I beg you to use them now so that you might save his young soul.'

Frances looked around the room, her eyes searching for the boy appointed to watch her. She shook her head, keeping her expression neutral.

'You are mistaken, madam,' she repeated carefully. 'Perhaps one of the court physicians can help?'

A look of scorn passed over the woman's face.

'Their potions and purges do more harm than good,' she said briskly. 'The boy needs succour from a healer. It is his only chance,' she added, her voice cracked.

'I am sorry,' Frances said sadly. 'I regret that I am unable to help.'

As she turned to go, the woman grasped her hands.

'Please, my lady. My sister's house is on Throgmorton Street, next to the old friary. It is not two miles from here.'

With that, she hastened away into the throng of courtiers. Frances watched until she disappeared from view. Then, as calmly as she could, she drank the contents of her cup, and walked slowly from the hall.

Frances retired early to her chamber that night. The princess had been tired from the ride through St James's Park that they had taken in the afternoon, so for once needed little persuasion to take her rest. Pushing away thoughts of the conversation in the dining hall, Frances tried to recall each species of flower that she had seen blooming in the park, and soon felt her eyelids begin to grow heavy. The trees of St James's slowly merged with the woods at Britford. It was autumn, and the leaves she kicked up danced like flames around her feet; reds, browns, yellows, and golds flickering in the sunlight. Then the colours seemed to be flickering up her skirt, and her dress was on fire. She started running, but the flames swept across the woodland floor.

Frances sat bolt upright in bed, suddenly awake. As the panic of the fire subsided, she heard the Reverend Samuels's voice as if he were in the room.

God wishes you to use your skill to help others, Frances. You must never deny Him.

Frances sat still, listening intently. A few moments passed, but all she could hear was the pounding of her heart. Her imagination was playing strange tricks tonight. Her breathing began to return to normal, but she knew that all hope of sleep was lost. Sighing, she got up and splashed some water from the ewer onto her face, then slowly wiped it dry with a linen cloth. She caught a glimpse of herself in the small looking glass. Her pallid skin appeared almost translucent in the gloom of her chamber, and there were dark shadows under her eyes.

It is his only chance. The words returned, unbidden, as Frances stared at her reflection.

She recalled her mother's face, flushed with anger, during their conversation at Longford. Though she knew that Helena only wanted to protect her, she still felt a prick of irritation. Her mother might be well-intentioned, but she did not appreciate how skilled her daughter was.

Seized with a sudden resolve, she got up and walked quickly over to her wardrobe. Her fingers felt for the plain, heavy gown that she wore for her woodland rambles at Longford. It had hung, unused, in her wardrobe ever since she had arrived at court. She pulled it on over her shift and hastily fumbled with the lacings. Scraping back her hair and knotting it tightly into a bun, she tucked it into the simple cap that she wore when making up her tinctures. She then wrapped her cloak tightly around her, pulling the hood down so that it obscured her face. Rifling through the small wooden chest that contained her precious herbs and potions, she selected a few and dropped them carefully into the leather purse that was concealed among her skirts.

She opened the door a crack and peered out. The corridor seemed empty. Walking silently along it, she quickened her pace as she progressed further through the palace. At length, she reached the heavy oak door that opened out onto the cobbled courtyard that bordered Whitehall. Two yeomen of the guard stood on either side of it, and as they saw Frances approach, they lowered their halberds so that they formed a cross in front of the doorway.

'What is your business?'

'Please, I must pass. My nephew lies grievously ill. I must attend him.'

'What is your name?'

Frances hesitated. She could reply falsely, but they might send for a clerk of the Lord Chamberlain if they doubted her. Giving her real name would mean that Cecil would almost certainly find out about her night-time excursion – if he had not already.

'Lady Frances Gorges,' she replied at last. 'I am lady of the bedchamber to the princess, and have Her Majesty the queen's sanction to make this visit.'

The guards exchanged glances. Eventually, one of them shrugged, and they raised their halberds to let her through.

The sound of the door swinging shut on its hinges reverberated around the courtyard. Pausing to take a few deep gasps of the chill night air, Frances darted furtive glances around her. She felt sure that eyes were looking out at her from the dark windows that lined the courtyard. But everywhere was silence.

Drawing her cloak more tightly around her, she walked through the gateway that led out onto Whitehall, and turned south towards the river. The bustle of London's main thoroughfare had subsided now, but a few boatmen still lined the banks, their small vessels lit by swaying lanterns. Frances chose the closest one, and instructed its owner to take her downriver, towards the Tower.

As they glided out into the dark waters of the Thames, Frances felt suddenly alone. The hunched form of the boatman was hardly discernible in the gloom, and the rhythmic splash of the oars set her nerves on edge. She knew Cecil's men might be waiting for her. But she also knew that the Reverend Samuels would have gone to the child, even if it had led him to the gallows.

At length, the imposing silhouette of the great Tower loomed into view. Frances looked up at the huge keep, glimmering white in the moonlight, its onion domes picked out against the dark sky. The oarsman steered the boat towards the mooring next to the watergate. Pressing a shilling into his leathery palm, Frances climbed out of the vessel and walked away from the river, towards Tower Hill. From there, he had told her, she would be able to see the ruins of the old friary, which was a short distance away.

The streets were eerily quiet as Frances made her way towards the skeletal arch. Once or twice she allowed herself a quick glance behind her, but there was nobody in sight. If he were following her, then Cecil's boy was more discreet than usual.

As she reached the friary, she could see a dwelling just beyond the old nave, at the corner of Throgmorton Street. Although the rest of the houses were in darkness, a light burned in an upstairs window. As she stood at the threshold, she hesitated for a moment, then knocked gently on the door.

Frances realised that she was holding her breath as she waited for an answer, straining her ears for any sound of movement. Eventually, she heard the creak of footsteps on the stairs, and a few moments later the door was opened just wide enough for a whey-faced man to peer outside.

'Who calls here?' he asked in a quiet, fearful voice.

'I am a friend of your wife's sister, sir,' Frances answered calmly. 'I have come to help your son.'

The man opened the door a fraction more and eyed Frances uncertainly. Just then, the woman from the queen's household came bustling down the stairs, and, seeing Frances, called: 'Let her in, John.'

Frances stepped into the parlour. The embers of a small fire glowed weakly in the grate, and the bitter smell of tallow filled the room. It was sparsely furnished, with a dark wooden table and chairs, and a gnarled old chest in one corner. A few rushes were scattered over the stone cobbles of the floor.

'You have come, my lady,' the woman said quietly. 'I did not expect you.'

Frances gave a quick, reassuring smile.

'Please, take me to your nephew.'

Following her upstairs, Frances felt the familiar pang of foreboding. No matter how many patients she had attended, she never enjoyed the comfort of complete faith in her healing. That power lay only with God.

In the far corner of the room, a woman – very like the one who had summoned her here – sat on a chair, a baby swaddled on her lap, rocking to and fro. She turned tear-stained eyes to Frances.

'Can you save him, my lady? My sister says you have great skill. Please save him.' She resumed her rocking. 'He will not even take my milk, though the Lord knows I have tried.'

Frances walked across the room, and laid her hand gently on the woman's shoulder to stay the rocking. Looking down at the little form that lay in his mother's arms, her heart sank. The infant's face, and the tiny fingers that poked out from the swaddling, were tinged with purple, as if Death had already marked the child for his own. Through the linen sheet that encased him, she could see the little chest rising and falling in a jerking movement. His lips were slightly apart, and there was a waxy sheen to his skin.

'I will do what I can to ease him,' Frances said quietly.

She untied the leather pouch from her skirts and took out a small phial filled with a tincture made from juniper, milk thistle, and hartshorn. Leaning forward, she gently took the baby from his mother's arms. He was as light and insubstantial as air – a little spirit already passing to the next world. Stroking his soft, downy head, she let a few tiny drops of the tincture fall between his lips. He wrinkled his nose in a feeble gesture of distaste, and looked up at Frances with dark blue eyes. She held him close to the warmth of her chest and closed her eyes, praying silently that God might spare him.

After a few moments, Frances felt the tiny form move slightly beneath her hands, then grow still. She opened her eyes and looked down at the little face, and knew that he had gone.

CHAPTER 20

19 August

'There is to be a play performed for my birthday!' Elizabeth burst out breathlessly as soon as Frances arrived in her chamber.

'Forgive me for being late, ma'am. I slept badly last night.'

The princess rattled on as if she hadn't spoken.

'It has been written specially by Master Shakespeare himself!' she exclaimed, clapping her hands with glee.

'Then you are greatly honoured, ma'am. He and his company performed before the old queen many times. She loved his plays the most.'

'Oh, my father cannot abide them!' The princess giggled. 'That's why he told Master Shakespeare that he must make it shorter than his others.'

Flinging open the oak chest that lay at the end of her bed, Elizabeth began rifling through its contents. Gorgeous blue silks, deep red and purple velvets, and silver satin gowns were thrown carelessly into a tumbling heap. A wisp of white silk jolted Frances back to the little house on Throgmorton Street. The baby had looked so peaceful, swaddled in his linen, pale as marble. She could almost feel him in her arms now. Then the image came, unbidden, of his mother gazing at her in dismay. And her sister, with a look of – what? Anger? Suspicion.

'I must wear something dazzling. None of these old rags will do,' Elizabeth said, with a flash of her father's notorious temper.

Frances, who had begun carefully refolding the gowns, shot her a look of admonishment.

'Your Highness has more beautiful dresses than any young woman in your father's kingdom. I am sure that we can find one to suit the occasion,' she said patiently.

'Lady Frances. I hoped to find you here.'

Neither of them had noticed the queen entering the room. Frances gave a low curtsey.

'Mama! Have you heard about the play?' Elizabeth cried exuberantly.

'Yes, my dear,' Anne replied calmly, surveying the chaos. 'And it looks as if you plan to have as many costume changes as the actors.'

Elizabeth giggled, then returned to her search.

'Lady Frances, I would speak with you in private,' the queen said quietly.

Frances bobbed another curtsey.

'Of course, ma'am.'

She followed Anne into the courtyard garden, keeping her eyes fixed upon the gorgeous orange satin of her royal mistress's gown. Evidently her lateness had already been reported.

'Your Majesty, forgive me—' Frances began.

'Allow me to speak frankly,' the queen interrupted in a low voice. 'I placed you in great danger as soon as you arrived at court.'

Frances looked up at once.

'It was not my intention. I was so concerned about Beatrice. But my Lord Privy Seal' – Anne's face creased into a look of distaste – 'he sees everything in this court.'

'Your Majesty must know that I was glad to be of assistance,' Frances replied.

Anne waved away her assurance.

'But the fact remains that thanks to involving you in this matter, and in such a way, I put your life at risk,' she said firmly. Eyeing

Frances carefully, she added: 'You must know what he suspects you of?'

Frances nodded slightly.

'Well, it is of no matter. I have spoken to my husband. He has agreed to call off his dog.'

Frances paused, unsure how to answer.

'I hope the price you had to pay was not too great, ma'am.'

The queen smiled fleetingly, but her eyes were grave.

'You have been here for so little time, yet already you have the measure of your king and his wife,' she replied. 'It was not so hard. Great witch hunter though he is, even he could see that persecuting a member of his own daughter's household was hardly conducive to harmony in his court. He will tell Cecil tomorrow, in council.'

'I am deeply indebted to you, ma'am.'

The queen nodded briskly, and walked back into the chamber. Frances could hear the princess immediately fire a volley of questions at her mother about the gown that might suit her best. She sank down on the stone bench, which was already warmed by the mid-morning sunshine. She had not anticipated that she would be so fortunate as to enjoy the queen's protection. Anne was as loyal and benevolent as her husband was intolerant and obsessive. Little wonder that theirs was an unhappy match.

Frances breathed in the sharp scent of the neatly trimmed myrtle that bordered the courtyard, mixed with the heady fragrance of the soft white peonies that had burst into bloom since she had last visited the garden. Despite the events of the previous night, she felt a greater sense of peace than she had since her arrival at court.

She lay down on the bench, her face pressed to the warm stone. Closing her eyes, she listened to the low humming of the bees as they flitted between the summer buds, and allowed sleep to overcome her.

* * *

A great company had gathered in the Banqueting House for the performance. The vast hall reverberated with nervous, excited chatter, as the courtiers exchanged exaggerated tales of plots and bewitchings. Lady Grimsby swore that she had seen a woman wearing a dark cloak stealing out of the queen's bedchamber the night before her miscarriage. Lord Stafford, meanwhile, attested that a strange potion had been discovered in a tiny glass phial underneath Her Majesty's pillow.

After her conversation with the queen, Frances had shared the princess's light-heartedness as they prepared for the performance. Elizabeth had been unable to keep still as she had been laced into her dress. The decision about what to wear had been solved that morning when a gift had arrived from her father. Fashioned from sumptuous gold and cream satin, studded with rubies, it was one of the most beautiful dresses that Frances had ever seen. The scarlet ribbon that Frances had chosen from the queen's tailor that afternoon matched the precious jewels perfectly, and set off the princess's red hair to dazzling effect. Elizabeth had insisted on wearing a heavy necklace of gold and pearls, with earrings of the same design, waving aside Frances's protests that they would cause her discomfort as the long evening of entertainments wore on. With her mother's sanction, she had been permitted to wear some powder on her face and neck, giving her pale skin an ethereal glow.

'I am eight years old, after all!' Elizabeth had insisted, in answer to Frances's disapproving look.

Frances had had little time to dress herself for the evening. She had returned to her apartment for no more than half an hour to put on the blue gown that her uncle had bought her. Sweeping her dark hair up into an elegant bun, and securing it into place with the jewelled pins that her mother had given her for her first audience with the old queen, she shot a cursory glance in the looking glass, before returning to the princess's chamber.

By the time she reached Elizabeth's apartments, the young girl was barely able to contain her excitement as she waited for her brother Henry to escort her to the Banqueting House. At length he arrived, gave his sister a formal greeting, and nodded curtly to Frances, who followed in their wake. He could not long resist the princess's infectious excitement, however, and soon their sprightly little legs carried them on apace.

A fanfare announced their arrival at the great door that led into the hall. Immediately, the chatter died out, and a respectful hush descended. The princess, her chin tilted upwards and her arm linked with that of her elder brother, strutted proudly through the throng of courtiers, all of whom bowed low as she passed. She nodded this way and that in greeting, her studied decorum soon giving way to irrepressible gaiety as she approached the raised dais at the end of the hall. The king and queen were already seated under the canopy. James beamed at his daughter as she mounted the steps and went to sit next to the queen, then he scowled as Henry took his place to the right of his father's throne.

Frances curtseyed to the royal party, then backed away into the crowd, resolving to take a seat at the rear of the hall. Despite succumbing to that brief, sweet sleep in the garden earlier, she was aching with fatigue. The hall was already stifling, the warm air of the summer evening mingling with the heat of the courtiers who had jostled their way in to see the performance. She would rather not risk falling asleep in full view of the court.

'Lady Frances.'

She knew the voice before she turned around to see Cecil standing there, an insipid smile playing about his mouth.

'Surely you are not leaving us?' He pretended concern.

'No, my lord. I am greatly looking forward to Master Shakespeare's performance,' she replied lightly. 'If you will excuse me, I must find a seat before the play begins.' She turned to go, but he grabbed her sleeve.

'No need,' he said smoothly. 'I know how fond you are of the theatre, having accompanied the late queen so often, so I took the liberty of reserving you a seat next to me.'

Before she could protest, he placed her hand firmly on his arm and led her to a row of seats at the front, on the opposite side of the stage to the royal platform. Several members of the king's council had already taken their places. Frances saw that her uncle was among them, and felt almost relieved. The earl failed to hide his surprise as she sat down next to Cecil, who was smiling and nodding benevolently to his fellow councillors.

'I trust the view is to your liking, Lady Frances?'

'Yes. I thank you, my lord,' she replied, staring straight ahead. A horribly familiar feeling swept over her as she recalled the platform at Tyburn.

'Oh, there is no need to thank me,' he said breezily. 'I was most desirous of the pleasure of your company. Besides,' he added, smirking, 'I am relying on you to explain the play's meaning to me.'

At that moment, the dozens of candles that had lit the stage in front of them were extinguished, and the hall was plunged into darkness. There were excited murmurs from the crowd as the silhouettes of three figures shuffled to the centre of the stage.

Suddenly a brazier sprang into flame, illuminating their faces. Each of the three women was cloaked in black, and stooped with age, their grey hair straggling beneath their hoods. Their faces had been painted with deep lines and warts, and plaster had been moulded to their noses and chins so that they appeared hooked. There were cries from the audience as the flames burned brighter, revealing every hideous detail of the hags.

'When shall we three meet again?' cried out the first in a high-pitched screech. 'In thunder, lightning or in rain?'

Frances felt as if she had slipped into a terrible dream. The witches danced before her, rubbing their hands together and forging their terrible schemes. Glancing past them, she saw King James sit forward, transfixed, his eyes alight with excitement. The queen looked on in dismay, and next to her, Elizabeth was staring wide-eyed at the players, one hand to her mouth.

Cecil sat as still and silent as a cat. Frances knew that his eyes were not upon the stage.

'Fair is foul, and foul is fair:
Hover through the fog and filthy air.'

The witches shrieked their pact in unison, and the stage was once more in darkness. With mounting horror, Frances watched the unravelling as Macbeth fell victim to the witches' curse, and descended into an orgy of evil, spurred on by his rapacious wife. She knew that Master Shakespeare had played to the king's natural misogyny as much as to his witch hunting fervour.

Every time the three hags appeared onstage, tempting the hapless Scottish lord with their prophecies of power, there were hisses and cries from the audience.

'The play is not to your liking, Lady Frances?' Cecil whispered, during a brief pause between scenes.

'On the contrary. It is most diverting.' She did not look at him as she spoke.

'I am so glad,' he retorted. 'It was I who commissioned it. I was very precise in my instructions to Master Shakespeare – I would not have wished the king to veer from his course.' She could hear the smile in his voice. 'Perhaps I should exchange politics for play-writing?'

Frances found it hard to believe that Master Shakespeare had made it a shorter play than his others. It seemed to last an eternity. Finally, though, it reached its terrible conclusion. Macbeth was slain, condemned to everlasting torment. The triumphant witches remained at liberty to inflict their evil designs on a world as helpless as a babe in arms.

As soon as the last line had been spoken, all of the sconces were relit, illuminating the faces of the audience. They sat in silence for several moments. Eventually, the king rose to his feet. All eyes turned to him, but his expression was unreadable. He looked as likely to admonish the players, who now shuffled their feet awkwardly onstage, as to burst into applause. At length, he spoke.

'Noble subjects, what you have witnessed here this evening was no fanciful tale; no mere figment of Master Shakespeare's imagination,' he said, nodding to the playwright, who was among the players onstage, looking even more apprehensive than the rest.

'We saw the havoc, the destruction wreaked by those three witches. With their spells and incantations, they brought down one king, and corrupted another, so that he too descended into hell.'

He scanned the faces of his courtiers, who were looking increasingly uncomfortable.

'And they were just three. Think, then, of how much greater the destruction, how much more potent the evil that thousands of witches across the globe – nay, even across England alone – might conjure up. For there are so many. They are in every town and every village.' He paused. 'They are even here in this court.'

There was a collective intake of breath, and a low murmur, as each courtier voiced their suspicions to their neighbour. Suddenly everyone was looking around the hall, as if expecting to find the witch sitting amongst them, bent over a cauldron and muttering a spell to seal their doom.

Frances could no longer maintain her composure. She too began scanning the room, hoping to see Tom's reassuring presence. But instead, her gaze alighted on the servingwoman from Throgmorton Street standing at the back of the hall. Staring back at Frances, she smiled grimly, and crossed her arms.

The loud rapping of a heavy staff on the wooden floorboards startled everyone into silence. The yeoman of the guard stepped back into his place behind the throne, and James continued to address his terrified subjects.

'God has appointed me to vanquish this evil, to rid my kingdom of witches. No parish, no dwelling, no chamber, will be left unsearched. My servants will be as a plague of locusts descending into every corner of the realm. There will be nowhere to hide. Those whores of Satan will be ripped from their lairs like a canker from the bark.'

He paused again, his eyes bright with righteous fervour. Frances stole a quick look towards the queen, who was struggling to conceal her dismay. Her daughter had moved to sit at her feet, and she stroked her soft hair distractedly, as if she were a lapdog.

'To strengthen my hand, God in his wisdom urged me to pass this new law. There is no punishment too severe for any woman – or man,' he added hastily, 'who is found guilty of practising or abetting witchcraft in all its forms. Sorcery, necromancy, fortune telling, healing . . . all are now punishable by death.'

The murmurs started up again, and there were many nods and looks of affirmation.

'God save Your Majesty!' one man called from the back of the room. It was echoed by several others.

James sat down, satisfied that he had filled all of those present with the same witch hunting zeal with which he himself was consumed. He smiled benevolently upon his court. He was a true king at last, appointed by God to do His will.

'Your Majesty.' Cecil walked over to the platform and slowly mounted the steps. Giving an exaggerated bow to the royal party, he turned to address the hall.

The courtiers, grave-faced, fell silent once more. All eyes turned expectantly to the Lord Privy Seal, who was clearly savouring the moment.

'The evil that we have seen played out in this evening's performance is indeed a most grave threat to His Majesty's kingdom. It is the responsibility of all of us, the king's subjects, to maintain the utmost vigilance.'

He narrowed his eyes as he surveyed the crowd. Some of the courtiers shifted uncomfortably in their seats. Frances held her breath. The palms of her hands felt clammy, but she kept them perfectly still, clasped together on her lap.

'That is why I have paid particular care to this matter,' Cecil continued. 'To ensure the safety of Their Majesties and their children, as well as of all of you, I have had men appointed to watch everything and everyone within the sphere of this court. Nothing has escaped their notice.'

His eyes, which had continued to scan the now fearful faces of the audience, suddenly rested upon Frances. Her scalp prickled and her heart thudded painfully in her chest. She felt as if she were playing an unwitting part in a macabre performance that was about to reach its terrible denouement.

'I am pleased to announce that they have succeeded. You may rest easy in your beds tonight, for the witch is apprehended.'

There was an audible intake of breath. He paused, gratified.

'Imagine my shock at discovering that the queen had been cherishing a serpent in her bosom.'

'Lady Beatrice,' the king muttered, loud enough for Cecil to hear.

Anne jolted forward on her throne, but James grabbed her arm and kept his hand clamped across it so that she was unable to move. The queen looked about in panic, as if seeking her favourite attendant.

'No, sir.' The Lord Privy Seal spoke calmly, as if placating a child. 'Though the Lady Ruthven is here at court, certainly.' He paused, noting with satisfaction the fury that had suffused James's face. 'But her only crime is in flouting Your Majesty's orders. She has attended the queen these several months, despite her banishment from court.'

Seeing that James was about to speak, and, not wishing to divert attention from the matter at hand, he continued smoothly: 'We will deal with that another time. For now, we must eradicate the evil in our midst. It is an evil that goes to the heart of Your Majesty's court.'

Without warning, Cecil stepped forward and grabbed Frances by the wrist, yanking her to her feet.

'Here, sir, is the canker in your court!'

As Cecil spun her around so that she faced the court, Frances saw the looks first of shock, and then fear, directed towards her. Her uncle was regarding her with a mixture of dismay and repulsion, his face a deep scarlet and beads of sweat popping up on his brow. She turned away from him, her gaze desperately scanning the crowds again. If she could see Tom, even at a distance, she could face whatever lay ahead. But the only faces she saw were those of hostile courtiers, recoiling from her in disgust. Behind her, she could hear the stifled sobs of the princess. She longed to comfort her, to tell her that this was nothing but a macabre encore to the play. But Cecil still held her in a vice-like grip, his cold fingers bruising the soft flesh of her arm. Her breathing had become shallow, and she felt light-headed, almost calm, as if she had already slipped into another world.

'I have ample proof that Lady Frances has practised witchcraft since the day of her arrival at court, intent upon nothing less than the destruction of Your Majesty and all your family.'

The crowd descended into an excited babble, and there were cries of 'Kill the witch!' and 'Hang her!'

The courtiers in front of Frances turned to a blur, and as the darkness advanced and she slipped from consciousness, the last thing she saw was Cecil's face. He leaned forward so that his mouth was almost touching her ear.

'I have given the king his witch,' he whispered.

CHAPTER 21

22 August

Frances shivered. She pulled her cloak more tightly around her, and drew her knees up to her chest. The cold seemed to seep through the thick stone walls, which were impervious to the seasons. It could be the winter sun that shone so brightly through the casement window, for all she knew. Yet, her lodgings were more comfortable than she had dared hope, and certainly better than the dark cell she had imagined as the barge had conveyed her along the Thames to the Tower. Her rank counted for something, she supposed, even if it could not protect her from an accusation of witchcraft.

Word would have reached her parents by now, she knew. Frances closed her eyes against the thought. And her uncle – the look of dismay and revulsion on his face had haunted her ever since that night. It was as if, at a stroke, she had deliberately destroyed her family's fortunes. Even now, he must be desperately trying to claw back favour with the king. Or had Cecil, ever with an eye to an opportunity, used her disgrace to have him thrown out of court?

She shook her head, trying to dispel the same thoughts that had filled her mind for the past three days. Sleep had all but evaded her, and whenever she had slipped into unconsciousness, she had been plagued by such terrible visions of torture that they were still before her when she awoke. If only she had been given time to gather some possessions before being brought here, she would have taken the little casket of dried lavender that she kept by her bed. Its soothing scent always lulled her to sleep. But then, it would merely serve to condemn her further – that, and the copy of Master Gerard's book, which she longed for now. The only book that she had been allowed was the tiny prayer book that hung from her girdle. She had tried to read it several times, but the words seemed suddenly empty of meaning. God had surely forsaken her.

The loud cawing of a raven suddenly broke the silence, echoing around the walls of the Tower. Frances crossed to the window and looked out across the lawn that lay between her lodgings and the chapel. The bird cocked its head, as if listening. Frances prised open her window a crack. The raven caught the movement at once, and with a swift, jerking movement, looked up to where she stood. Frances smiled and made a clicking sound with her tongue, overcome with a sudden desire to keep the bird in sight. Its sleek black feathers glinted in the sunlight, and its sharp beak remained tightly closed. Frances knew that it could snap off her finger like a twig from a branch. The raven stood quite still now, looking towards her as she gazed upon it.

The striking of the chapel bell broke the silence. Startled, the bird hopped quickly out of sight. Frances cast a resentful look towards the bell tower, which was perched precariously at one end of the chapel roof. As if to reinforce the fortress's ominous reputation, the chapel had been named in honour of Saint Peter 'ad Vincula.' Frances had enough grasp of Latin to know that this referred to his suffering 'in chains' as a prisoner of Herod Agrippa. The side of the chapel was dominated by four huge windows that almost stretched from floor to ceiling. Frances shuddered at the thought of the headless traitors whose remains lay buried under the flagstones within.

A movement to her left drew her eyes away from the chapel. Stepping briskly out of his apartments in the handsome timber-framed building at the corner of the green was the tall, gaunt figure of Sir Richard Berkeley, lieutenant of the Tower. Her heart quickened as she realised that he was heading in the direction of her lodgings. For three days, she had received neither visitor nor message, only the stale bread, cheese, and watery ale that were left outside a small serving hatch next to her door. Her anxiety and exhaustion had mounted with every passing hour – which was no doubt Cecil's intention, she realised. It was no wonder that scores of women before her had needed little persuasion to sign the confessions that had been thrust at them, attesting to all manner of wicked sorcery and conjurations. Even death would be a merciful release from the agonisingly long hours of waiting and uncertainty. She had a sudden recollection of the woman's face as she hung, gasping for breath, from the gallows at Tyburn. Her blood ran cold.

After a few moments, she heard his steps, slow and uneven, as he mounted the narrow staircase that led to her chamber. There was a pause, then Frances jumped at the loud scraping of the iron bolt as it was slid back.

'My Lady Frances.'

The lieutenant made a deep bow as he addressed her. His voice was soft and melodic, with a faint West Country burr. Frances curtseyed in greeting, and lowered her gaze.

'I trust you are comfortable, my lady?' he asked, flushing slightly at the banality of the question.

'I thank you, yes, Sir Richard.'

She looked up and saw that he was studying her closely.

'Forgive me, my lady, but you are very pale, and I have heard report that most of your food has been sent back untouched.'

Frances eyed him steadily. 'I do not find my place of residence to be conducive to either sleep or appetite.'

The old man's brow furrowed, and he fiddled distractedly with the keys in his hand. Frances noticed that the joints of his fingers were swollen. A paste of ginger and meadow saffron would ease the pain that they must give him.

'Lady Frances—' He hesitated, as if struggling to find the right words. Frances diverted her gaze, hoping that it might ease his discomfiture. After a long pause, he continued: 'The king is intent upon ridding this kingdom of the evils of witchcraft. He has been appointed by God for the task, and will not rest until it is done. In this, he has been assisted by the Lord Privy Seal, who has been working tirelessly to uncover any signs of the Devil's work in His Majesty's court – as you know,' he added, eyeing her closely.

Frances continued to study her hands, which felt cold and clammy. She pressed them into her lap.

Sir Richard sighed, and when he spoke again it was in a gentler tone.

'My lady, you must be aware how much my Lord Cecil needed to be seen to act. Your arrest was proof of that. It has demonstrated his commitment to the cause that the king holds dearest.'

Frances looked up quickly, her heart surging with unexpected hope.

'So I am already made an example of?' she urged. 'My arrest is enough to prove Cecil's loyalty?'

Her mind was racing. She had seen members of the court used in this way before, even in the old queen's day. They would be publicly shamed, as she had been, then held prisoner long enough for the news to be carried to all corners of the kingdom. After a time, the queen would pardon them, thus proving her mercy and forbearance. Before long, the scapegoat would be permitted back to court. It had been this way with Sir Walter Raleigh numerous times: he would be so familiar with his lodgings by now that they must seem like a second home.

'My lady—'

Upon seeing Sir Richard's expression, her face, which had been flushed with relief, instantly paled.

'Your interrogation will begin on the morrow. The king himself will superintend the proceedings.'

Frances stared at him in horror.

'The king?' Her voice was barely a whisper.

The lieutenant slowly inclined his head, then continued quietly: 'The gravity of the case, and your ladyship's status, has incited His Majesty to take a closer interest than is customary. He wishes to ensure that justice is served.'

The walls seemed to be closing in on Frances as she struggled to make sense of Sir Richard's words. The hope that had flared within her for a brief, giddy moment had been replaced by a cold, clawing fear. She knew that hers was not the only interrogation that James had attended. News of Agnes Sampson's ordeal at the King of Scots' palace of Holyrood had reached the court in London several years before. Frances felt her temples begin to pulse. The old woman's head had been shaved so that the rope would cut more deeply into the skin as it was pulled tight around her skull. All the while, James had looked on in 'great delight,' the old queen's envoy had reported. When at last Agnes had confessed, she had been hauled to a scaffold and strangled to death in front of a large crowd. Her broken remains had then been reduced to ashes in a huge pyre, choking the onlookers as a fierce wind whipped them across the courtyard.

Frances swallowed hard. She felt as though a piece of flint had been jammed into her throat, stopping her breath. The air seemed suddenly stale, and she fancied that it filled her lungs with the putrid stench of decay. In desperation, she cast about the room for something to calm her thoughts. At length, her gaze rested upon a Bible that lay on a small shelf above the window. She had not noticed it before. The black leather binding was frayed, and the lettering on the spine had long since been worn away. She imagined all the fingers that had leafed through its contents, searching anxiously for words that might bring comfort.

The Lord Himself goes before you and will be with you.

The verse came suddenly and with such clarity that Frances wondered if it had been spoken out loud.

He will never leave you nor forsake you.

She felt her breathing begin to slow as she repeated the words to herself. Her mother had quoted them many times to her at Longford, whenever something had troubled her. How trivial such things must have been, she realised now. Her life had been an unbroken sequence of pleasure and comfort, with nothing more troubling than a dropped stitch or a lost trinket to disturb her repose. If only she had known then that this had been so. She might have taken greater delight in every moment.

'I thank you, Sir Richard,' she said at last. 'I know that you have taken great pains in delivering these tidings.'

The old man eyed her with a mixture of sadness and admiration.

'Is there anything I can have sent for your comfort, my lady?'

Frances smiled briefly and shook her head.

'I require only my solitude.'

Sir Richard gave a low bow and walked slowly from the room. Frances heard the bolt slide back into place, its echo sounding long after the old man's steps as he made his way down the stairs and out into the bright expanse of the courtyard.

CHAPTER 22

23 August

Early the following morning, Frances was taken from her lodgings to the Beauchamp Tower. Sir Richard had dispatched one of the yeoman warders to escort her the short distance across the green. As they descended the steps that led into the tower, Frances paused to glance up at its imposing façade. There were just three small windows on the upper floors, and the only other source of light for those within were the arrow slits that had been chiselled into the thick stone.

The warder took a moment to search through the large ring of keys that hung from his belt. His thickset frame blocked out what little light penetrated through to the entrance, so having found the right key, he was obliged to run his fingers along the smooth oak door until he found the lock. The doorway was smaller than the others that Frances had encountered in this vast fortress, and she had to duck her head as she followed her guardian through it.

Once inside, an even lower doorway led through to a dark passageway. The warder gestured for Frances to go before him. She hesitated, struggling to see anything in the gloom. Reaching out her hand, she felt a wall on her left and edged her way along it, her fingers brushing the cold, damp stone. After a few moments, her eyes began to adjust to the darkness, and she could just make out a spiral staircase ahead.

'Up to the first floor,' the warder directed abruptly.

The staircase was so narrow that Frances was obliged to gather in her skirts so that they did not snag against the nails that she could feel jutting out at intervals along the wall. The steps were uneven, and once or twice she stumbled, her hands flailing desperately in search of something to steady herself. When at last she reached the small platform at the top of stairs, she paused and waited for the guard. Her breath came quickly, and her forehead prickled with sweat, despite the chill.

Brushing past her, the warder strode towards a large dark mass at the end of a short passageway, which Frances assumed was a door. He rapped sharply on it with his staff, and there was an answering call from within. Frances had no time to register the familiar voice because in the next moment the guard had flung open the door and thrust her forward.

The blaze of light from within the chamber temporarily blinded Frances, and she stood blinking for several moments. Dozens of candles had been lit in sconces around the walls, and a fire roared in the grate. Silhouetted against the glare, Frances could see, were two figures – one tall and well-built, the other short and stooped.

Cecil.

'Lady Frances,' he drawled. 'Who would have thought that we would meet in such a place?'

Frances was thankful that she could not see his smug smile. She made a slight curtsey.

'My Lord Cecil.'

'Baron, if you please,' he replied with a smile. 'His gracious Majesty has seen fit to reward me for my late efforts.'

He seemed to be waiting for her to congratulate him. When she remained silent, he continued: 'You have been comfortably housed, I hope? Lord Thomas tells me your lodgings are almost as spacious as those you occupy at Whitehall.' He gestured towards his companion, whom Frances now recognised as Thomas Sackville.

'You are fortunate, Lady Frances,' Cecil continued. 'The Tower is so stuffed full of traitors at this time that most new arrivals are hard-pressed to find lodgings.' His gaze intensified. 'Lady Frances, you know why you have been brought here. You have contravened His Majesty's laws governing the practice of witchcraft and sorcery. Masquerading as one who is skilled in the art of healing, you have used your potions to cause calamity, sickness, and death.'

'No!' Frances cried. Cecil pretended surprise at this uncharacteristic outburst, then his mouth twisted into a slow smile of satisfaction.

'We have ample testimony from one whose family has suffered at your hands,' he continued. 'Mistress Kynvett attests that you put her young nephew to death with your foul practices. You have attended several ladies from the queen's household since your arrival at court. It is a mercy that they still draw breath. We know there are others. Your father's servant, Dymock, has been most forthcoming about your pastimes at Longford.'

Frances struggled to control her breathing. Rage surged within her. How could Cecil stand there so calmly and speak such despicable lies? He must know that his allegations were preposterous. Yes, of course he knew. But that counted for nothing. He had given the king a witch, as he himself had whispered to her on that dreadful night. The truth had no place in his schemes.

'What proof can you have, my lord?' She kept her voice low.

'Mistress Knyvett's testimony is enough to condemn you,' he replied smoothly. 'But there is much more besides. Your night-time rambles have been well observed by my – by the officers of the court. And I myself have seen you dabbling with your tinctures and potions, even at the bedside of the old queen as she lay dying. Who is to say that you did not hasten her end?'

Frances stared at him, her eyes blazing.

'You accuse me of murdering my sovereign, our anointed queen?' Her jaw was so tightly clenched that the words came out in a low murmur.

'Speak up, woman!'

Frances turned quickly towards the corner of the room by the fireplace, which had been obscured from view by Cecil and his companion. They stepped aside now and made a slow bow. Frances squinted into the gloom, and could see a figure seated there, shrouded in a dark cloak. As he struggled to his feet, cursing, she took a sharp breath.

'Your Majesty.' She made a deep curtsey, her heart pounding painfully in her chest.

'I'll have none of your womanly tricks and wiles,' he drawled, spittle flying from his mouth. 'You whores of Satan are forever mumbling curses and spells under your breath. Speak the truth now. What did you do to that boy?'

Frances's mind was a blur, and she struggled to form any words in her defence. Averting her eyes from the king, who was staring at her intently, she cast about the room for something to calm her thoughts. An inscription carved into the stonework above the fireplace caught her attention. She peered closely at the spidery letters, which were illuminated by the flickering fire below.

Quanto plus afflictionis pro Christo in hoc seculo,
tanto plus gloriae cum Christo in futuro.

Frances repeated the words slowly to herself, deciphering the meaning of each in turn.

The more affliction we endure for Christ in this world, the more glory we shall have with Christ in the world to come.

As she looked closer, she saw that a name had been chiselled underneath.

Arundel

A chill ran through her. The earl had been imprisoned here as a suspected traitor during the later years of Elizabeth's reign, and had eked out the rest of his miserable days in this dark fortress. She pictured the young man now, carefully working each letter into the hard stone. Glancing around, she realised that the walls were covered with such etchings, some so elaborate that they might be mistaken for decoration. How many hands had toiled over them, desperate to leave behind a trace of themselves before leaving this world for ever? Frances felt strangely comforted by the thought that she was not the first to experience the terror of being brought here a prisoner. She drew in her breath.

'Your Grace, I have only ever used my skills to bring healing and relief,' she began, making sure to speak clearly and slowly. 'The child was close to death when I reached him. My tincture could work no effect.'

'Mistress Kynvett tells a very different story,' Cecil cut in. 'She attests that you overheard her speaking of her poor nephew at table, and persuaded her that you could help him. She denied you, knowing His Majesty's strictures against the arts you practise, but you were so insistent that at length she agreed.'

Frances opened her mouth to protest, but he continued: 'Upon reaching their dwelling, you gained admittance on the pretence of being a friend of Mistress Kynvett, and before she was able to act, you had poured your poison down the infant's throat.'

'She does not speak truth.' Frances's voice trembled with a mixture of fury and fear.

'Will the woman swear to it at the Assizes?' The king, ignoring her, directed his question at Cecil.

'She will derive great satisfaction from doing so, Your Grace.'

Frances recalled the look of hatred on the woman's face when she had seen her at the play. She had no doubt convinced herself of Frances's guilt. Better to blame her for the boy's death than accept the cruel randomness of sickness and disease.

'And what of Lady Ruthven?' James asked with a sneer. 'Pity you did not succeed with her too.'

Frances hesitated. If she told the truth about how she had been summoned to attend the woman, she would betray the queen.

Even though Cecil had already told James of the affair, she had no wish to bring her royal mistress further trouble.

'I believe that my herbs hastened God's work. Lady Ruthven recovered swiftly, once the fever had broken.'

'News of your talents evidently preceded you, Lady Frances,' Cecil remarked with a smile. 'You had barely set foot in court before you were spirited away to the lady's chamber. It must have been a very well-informed person who knew of your coming.'

Frances did not answer. Her face was impassive.

'I will not suffer obstinacy, Lady Frances.' The king's voice was dangerously low as he walked slowly towards her, his eyes locked upon hers. She could smell the stale aroma of wine on his breath, and noticed a thin trail of saliva working its way down one side of his mouth. Without warning, he suddenly grabbed her chin and yanked back her head so hard that she thought her neck might break.

'Would that you were in Scotland,' he whispered, his wet mouth brushing against her ear. 'We know how to deal with witches there.'

Her neck throbbed with pain, and her chin felt already bruised, but Frances kept as still as she could. She felt like one of her father's lambs, its fleece snagged by a nail in the fence. She knew that the more she struggled, the worse the pain would become.

The king's breathing grew more rapid as he tightened his grip. 'I wonder which would make you squeak out your story? The rack, perhaps . . . or maybe the Scavenger's Daughter.' He reached forward and gripped the back of her skull with his other hand. She flinched involuntarily, sending a sharp pain down her neck and spine. 'Ah no, I have it,' he continued. 'The Scold's Bridle. That will wrest any thoughts of witchcraft from your pretty head.'

Frances closed her eyes. *Think of the pain to lessen its power*, she had heard the Reverend Samuels tell his patients time and again. She did so now, the thought of her old mentor providing as much comfort as his advice.

At length, the king sighed, and released her so roughly that she stumbled backwards. Lord Sackville stepped forward to steady her, but a look from Cecil made him stop abruptly. Frances glanced longingly towards the chair by the fire. She felt suddenly weak, as if all the tendons in her body had been snapped, and she had been left as limp as a ragdoll. Is this what it feels like after the rack, she wondered?

'Pity that you Englishmen have no stomach for such devices,' James observed, shooting a scornful look at his two ministers. 'They would save a great deal of time and trouble.'

'Begging Your Grace's pardon,' Cecil replied, 'but your fortress here contains an extensive collection of such instruments, all of which have hastened many a confession over the years.' Registering the confusion on the king's face, he added: 'Torture might contravene our laws, but what is written in the statute book is not always practised in the privacy of Your Grace's domain.'

The king let out a bark of laughter.

'I am glad of it, my little beagle.'

Frances saw Cecil wince slightly at this new nickname. She wondered if James intended it more as a compliment than an insult. After all, he was fonder of hounds than humans, it was said.

'How am I to fulfil my promise to God and root out witches from my new kingdom while the law ties one hand behind my back?' he continued. His smile faded as he looked back at Frances. 'So, Lady Frances. Now that you know the pleasures that might await you here, will you loosen your tongue, or shall we do it for you?'

'I have never practised anything against the laws of this kingdom, Your Grace,' Frances said quietly. 'My family has always been loyal to the crown.'

'The old crown, perhaps,' Cecil interrupted.

The King took a deep swig of his wine, then flung the rest into the grate, which hissed and spat. 'But what of Lady Ruthven?' he persisted, his gaze now fixed again on Frances. 'Who commanded you to attend her?'

'That was not told to me when I was summoned to her chamber,' she replied truthfully.

'And you remain in ignorance?' the king demanded.

After a pause, Frances inclined her head slightly. She noticed the king's neck begin to redden.

'Well, 'tis no matter,' he declared. 'Mistress Knyvett's accusation is sufficient to bring you to trial.' He fell silent for a moment, considering. 'Of course – if we could find another sign that you are a witch, it would make the outcome even more certain.'

Frances felt her scalp prickle.

'It is well known that to seal the pact with his whore, the Devil will suck upon a part of her body until he has left a mark. Being cunning, he usually selects a part that is hidden.'

He paused, scrutinising the faces of his advisers for any sign of distaste or disbelief. Both men remained impassive, although Frances saw a muscle in Lord Sackville's jaw begin to twitch.

'The mark might resemble a spot or a teat,' James continued. 'It can easily be mistaken for a natural blemish on the skin by all but those who are expert in finding it. The only way to be certain is to prick every mark on the body with a needle. If there are any that emit neither blood nor pain, it is the Devil's Mark.'

Frances winced involuntarily as she imagined the sharp needle piercing every inch of her body. She closed her eyes, but could not shut out the image of the needle as it broke each fresh piece of skin. Lord knows, there would be sufficient marks to stab on her own body. She had inherited her mother's pale, freckled skin. The thought of her mother made her heart lurch with longing and shame. What disgrace had she visited upon her family? They would surely never recover from it.

Tears pricked Frances's eyes, and she opened them so that she might blink them away. With a jolt, she realised that the king was staring directly at her, his own eyes glinting with excitement.

'You are fortunate indeed, my Lord Cecil,' he said, without shifting his gaze. 'For when I first heard the rumour that there was a witch in our midst, I sent for John Balfour from Scotland. He is highly skilled at finding the Devil's Mark, and has sent many witches to the flames.'

Frances fixed her gaze on the floor.

'I will have him brought here as soon as he arrives.' He paused, looking at the darkening sky. 'Although if the weather breaks, it could take several more days. Let us leave Lady Frances to her reflections until then.'

He made as if to leave, but then stopped, remembering something.

'Tell Sir Richard that she is not to be taken back to her chambers,' he commanded Cecil. 'She shall be kept here, with two guards to keep watch that she does not sleep. Mark me, Cecil,' he said, grabbing his chief minister's arm and drawing him close. Though he spoke in a low murmur, Frances still caught his words. 'It is the surest way of bringing a confession.'

CHAPTER 23

30 August

She no longer knew if she was awake or asleep as she paced slowly about the chamber, her feet dragging along the flagstones as she was supported on either side by a yeoman warder. Her guards must have changed places numerous times, she supposed, but she could not distinguish their faces from the men who had preceded them. Perhaps they were the same ones who had begun this relentless sequence of walking, standing, and sitting, all the time suspended between one world and the next, or so it seemed.

Amidst the haze of her thoughts, Frances clung to the words that the king had spoken before leaving the chamber – when? One, two days before? A week? She must not betray the queen, or herself, by confessing to her supposed crimes, no matter that she might then at last be permitted to slip into the sweet abyss of sleep. Perhaps she need not worry. The few words that she had spoken during the past hours, asking for water, or rest, had required such an effort that they had sounded slurred to her ears, as if she were intoxicated from the Burgundy wine that flowed freely at court. Though she smiled inwardly at the thought, her lips remained downturned, her facial muscles too slack to muster any expression.

As she lapsed into a doze, she heard voices in the distance. At least, they seemed far away, but she could hear one of the warders reply and they had now stopped their relentless pacing. He stepped forward to admit the visitors, and Frances stumbled sideways, then slumped to the floor before the other guard could catch her.

'This is John Balfour, gentlemen,' the king announced proudly.

'God give you good day.' Frances caught the Scottish drawl, and tried to place the name, which she thought she had heard before somewhere.

'You will leave us.' Cecil this time.

She sensed the guards hesitate, then the brisk clipping of their footsteps as they retreated from the room.

The next thing that Frances was aware of was water being thrown over her face. The shock jolted her awake, and she shivered as she felt the ice cold droplets weave their way down her neck. Someone dragged her to her feet. Glancing down, she saw that the hands that held her in a vice-like grip were large and coarse, the fingernails caked with grime.

'Don't ye worry, I will soon prick her awake,' the man scoffed, his voice as rough as his hands. The king gave an answering bark of laughter.

Frances was now fully awake, fear igniting every nerve in her exhausted body. A woman stepped forward from the shadows. Her brown woollen dress was frayed at the hem, and a few wisps of dark grey hair escaped from the dirty white cap that covered her head. She looked at Frances and grinned, showing teeth that were black and uneven.

'Remove her outer clothes,' Balfour commanded.

Frances recoiled in horror.

'I forbid it,' she cried, her eyes darting from Balfour to the woman, who was now advancing towards her. 'Your Grace, you cannot allow this,' she said, turning to the king. 'I am the daughter of a marchioness. I will not be treated like a common whore.'

The king's eyes glinted.

'Ah, but you are a whore of Satan, and as such shall you be handled.'

Frances struggled for breath as the room began to spin. Balfour pushed her roughly down onto a chair and motioned for the woman to bring her water.

'You wouldn't want to miss the pretty dance that my lad here will lead you on,' he grinned, patting a scabbard that hung from his belt.

Frances took a sip of the water, which tasted bitter. She held it to her nose. The scent of eucalyptus was overpowering – she wondered that she had not smelt it before. There was something else that she could not quite discern.

'You have an excellent collection of herbs, Lady Frances,' Cecil remarked, smiling. 'I spent a very instructive morning in your apartments, with Master Gerard for company. He extols the reviving properties of eucalyptus and chervil.'

His smile broadened as he caught the flash of fury in Frances's eyes.

'Those are my private effects.'

'Regrettably they are now the property of His Majesty, as are any effects belonging to suspected felons and traitors,' Cecil replied affably. 'Little matter, though. Even if you are found innocent of witchcraft, you can still have no use for such things. They will be burned as soon as your case has been heard.'

Frances dug her fingernails into her palms so sharply that tears pricked at her eyes. She did not speak, but stared directly at Cecil, her eyes blazing.

James shifted impatiently in his seat. 'Come now, man,' he barked, gesturing at Balfour. 'She is recovered enough for you to start your work.'

Her fear had been obscured by anger, but at the king's words it returned with such a surge that it felt as if her heart were being squeezed by a fist. Instinctively, she wrapped her arms around herself, gripping her shoulders tightly. With a swift, practised movement, Balfour stepped forward and prised her fingers away, while the woman began to unlace her gown at the back, pushing Frances forward in the chair as she did so. Her fingers worked so deftly that soon the bodice fell away and she was able to begin on the sleeves and petticoat. She would have made an excellent lady's maid, Frances thought bitterly. When the woman's nimble fingers had finished their work, she dragged Frances to standing so that she might step out of the clothes that lay crumpled at her feet. Only a thin linen shift now covered her body.

Frances stared straight ahead, and kept perfectly still. She could no longer distinguish fury from fear. Her senses were so heightened that she seemed to hear the king's breath as it was drawn into his chest and out again. It seemed to quicken as she listened. The next sound was the soft pat of a leather sole on the flagstones, as Balfour moved slowly towards her, stealthy as an executioner. With mounting terror, she thought of how the old queen's mother must have felt as she waited, blindfolded, while the expert swordsman slipped off his shoes and padded silently around the scaffold, a short distance from where Frances now stood. Had Anne heard the sharp whisper of the sword as it sliced through the air, before the darkness engulfed her?

The sudden grip of a hand on her neck made Frances flinch. She stood, panting, waiting for his next move. There was a rasp of metal against leather, then Frances caught a flash of silver reflected on the wall in front of her. She could feel the warmth of his body behind her, and inhaled the acrid stench of stale sweat.

'My blade will have much to do with this one.' Frances could hear the smile in his voice. 'The Devil favours fair-skinned women, for he can conceal his mark amongst their many blemishes.'

He walked slowly around her, his eyes moving constantly over her body. Stopping in front of her, he brought his blade up to her face. It was like a needle that had been fashioned for a giant. Perfectly cylindrical, it tapered down to a point that looked sharp enough to spear a pip from an apple. Frances swallowed hard. It felt as if the blade was in her throat. Cecil made a small cough, prompting.

'Where should we begin?' Balfour seemed to be directing the question at her. He pressed the blade against her collarbone.

'Here?' Maintaining the pressure, he moved it up to her chin. 'Or here?'

Without warning, he suddenly jabbed the pricker into a small mole on the side of Frances's face. She cried out in pain and shock. A warm trickle of blood made its way down her cheek. Balfour smirked.

'We must find one that does not bleed.'

The second prick was at the back of her neck. Frances bit her lip and tried not to flinch. Another jab, and another. Still she made no sound. Her shift was now clinging to her back, with sweat or blood she could not tell. All of her senses were centred on where the pain would find her next.

Balfour paced slowly around until he faced her again. He pointed the blade at the middle of her chest. Pinching her shift between his fingers, he speared it with the jabber, then ripped it open so that her chest was exposed down to her navel. Frances drew a sharp breath. It took all of her resolve to continue staring straight ahead. He proceeded to pierce the soft flesh of her belly several times in quick succession. She closed her eyes and remembered when, as a child, she had disturbed a wasps' nest, and they had swarmed around her, their stings raining down on her like thorns. Her father had heard her screams and hastened to her rescue, batting away the angry wasps as he carried her to the house. Her skin had been covered in bright red welts for the rest of the summer, much to her sister Elizabeth's amusement.

There would be no rescuer now, Frances knew. The King of England would not be denied his pleasure – nor Cecil, for that matter. John Balfour was breathing hard now as he trailed his fingers up her abdomen, feeling for any bumps or marks on her skin. He lingered over her breasts, jabbing once or twice, but more gently than before. Frances felt her neck prickle with heat, and she closed her eyes more tightly still, as if to shut out the humiliation.

Balfour cleared his throat, then called for the woman to bring him a cup of ale. Frances heard the liquid being poured into one of the goblets that stood on a table by the window. Balfour gulped it down and swiped his hand across his chin.

'The Devil has hidden his mark well, Your Grace,' he said. Frances caught the anticipation in his tone.

There was a long pause.

'Then you must search harder.'

CHAPTER 24

31 August

The baying of the crowds grew louder as the hangman stalked around the wooden scaffold, raising his arms now and then to whip up an even greater cacophony. Frances stared bleakly at the spectators who were jostling for a view. Their mouths moved with jeers and chants, but she could not distinguish any of them. She looked up and saw storm clouds gathering. A cold wind suddenly whipped around the enclosure. Frances reached behind to draw her cloak more tightly around her, but her fingers grasped only the gauzy linen of her shift. Horrified, she looked down and saw that it was soaked with blood.

The cawing of a raven pierced her ears. She looked around for the bird, hoping it was the same one she had seen a few days before, but she could not see it anywhere. The raven's cry persisted. Gradually, the crowds fell silent, listening. With a sudden impulse, Frances swung around to look behind her. The raven was sitting on the long coil of rope that would soon be placed around her neck. It cocked its head and blinked at her, then opened its beak and began cawing so loudly that Frances pressed her hands over her ears. She tried to scream so that she might drown out the noise, which seemed as a death knell, but she could make no sound.

She awoke then, sweating and breathless. The scaffold and crowds had disappeared, and she was alone in her chamber. A movement at the window caught her eye, and she turned to see the raven sitting on the sill. It jerked its head and seemed to stare directly at her. After a few moments, it hopped out of sight. Soon, its cawing echoed around the empty courtyard.

Frances lay staring out of the window. The sun had already sunk low in the sky, which was tinged with pink and gold. She had no idea how long she had slept. Time had long since ceased to hold any meaning for her. She might have been here for a week or a year. It was all the same. Her life at court seemed a distant memory; Longford a once cherished dream, now long since faded.

After a while, her limbs grew stiff, and she rolled over onto her back. A shard of pain pierced through her, and she drew in a sharp breath. She held it until the stinging had dulled to a throb, then slowly exhaled. Gingerly, she ran her fingers along the top of her thighs. The space between was still sticky with blood, but the flow seemed to have abated. She resolved to stay still for as long as possible. Her body was covered in sores, and even the slightest movement triggered a fresh wave of pain. The witch pricker had been thorough in his work.

An image came suddenly, of his hands pawing at her shift as she lay on the floor, the cold stone pressing into her back. The blade was smooth as he ran it across her thighs, pausing now and then to probe a freckle or other blemish with his rough fingertips. And then the shock of searing pain deep within her. Darkness had followed.

She screwed her eyes shut, and tried to obliterate the terrible memories, but it was as if they had been seared into her mind with hot irons. She knew they would never leave her. The tears ran freely now, stinging the wounds on her face and neck as they coursed down. Her sobs turned to howls as she lay like an animal snared by a trap in the woods of Longford, unable to move for fear of sparking a new bout of agony. After a while, exhaustion overcame her, and she began to doze, her chest heaving now and then with a sob, before settling into a steadier rhythm.

When she next awoke it was morning. Clouds filled the sky, so she could not judge the hour. But the smell of freshly baked bread came from the hatch in her door. Her stomach made a low growl, and she felt suddenly ravenous. Easing herself slowly and painfully out of bed, she edged over to the hatch and pulled it aside. The plate was more plentifully laden than the last time she had eaten in her chambers. Along with fresh white bread, there were generous slabs of cheese and ham, a pat of butter, and a trencher filled with ale. She carried it carefully over to the table by the window, and lowered herself down onto the wooden chair, wincing as she did so. She then devoured the food, stuffing large pieces of it into her mouth as if it might be taken away at any moment, and pausing only to take gulps of the ale.

When she had finished, she felt tired again, but her desire to wash was stronger than the temptation to climb back into bed straight away. A large ewer of water had been placed on the table, with a quantity of fresh linen cloths. If only she had her cabinet of herbs, she thought. She could make up a tincture of wound-wort and comfrey to dress her wounds. *Would that you might not use them at all!* Her mother's voice suddenly sounded in her ears. Frances swallowed back angry tears as she realised that she should have heeded the advice. Her remedies had caused a great deal more harm than good. She had been a fool.

Having soaked the first cloth in water, she gently dabbed at any sores she could reach. The water had taken on a pink hue by the time she had finished. She had deliberately omitted the part of her body that most needed cleansing because she knew that the water would be too soiled with blood to be used on anything else. But she began dabbing at the top of her thighs now with a new cloth, turning it over and over with each application, before plunging it into the ewer. At once, the water began to turn a deep red, and Frances had to wring out the cloth quickly so that it might be at least partially cleansed before she applied it to her wounds again. When she brought it back to the bowl, she saw that a small area of the cloth was drenched with fresh blood.

With the remaining cloth and the belt from her gown – which she noticed had been folded neatly in the corner of the room – she fashioned a rudimentary girdle such as she wore during her monthly courses. She then put on the fresh linen shift that lay on top of the pile of clothes, and was about to lower herself into bed when she noticed that a small piece of paper had been pushed underneath the door. She padded across the oak floorboards and stooped slowly to pick it up.

Lady Frances Gorges

The hand was elegant, but understated, without the flourishes that were now fashionable among members of the court, for whom letter writing was more an art form than a means of communication. She turned it over. The seal, which had been broken, bore the letter 'W.' Frances felt her heart quicken. With trembling fingers, she unfolded the paper.

Dearest Frances,
  My friends and I are working day and night for your release.
You cannot be kept there without charge, and what proof can
they have? You have done no wrong. Your uncle also labours on
your behalf, taking advantage of Cecil's frequent absences of
late. Take courage – it cannot be long.
  Your loving friend,
  TW

Her mind racing, Frances read the note over and over again. What could he possibly do to help her, without endangering himself? He might easily be implicated for conspiring with a known witch. The penalty for that was almost as severe as for sorcery. And who were the friends that he spoke of? Sir Tyringham?

She hardly thought so. What surprised her most, though, was the reference to her uncle. She had assumed that the earl had altogether disowned her, humiliated by the shame that she had brought upon the family. The notion that he was trying to exonerate her was difficult to comprehend.

Turning the letter over distractedly, she noted the postscript.

My lady princess is ailing. She pines for your presence almost as much as I, and has eaten little since you were taken. Lady Mar says she is often awoken by the child's night terrors.

Frances felt a wave of grief for the young girl. She was a slight child, and could ill afford to forgo any meals. Then another thought intruded. If the princess did not improve, the finger of blame would soon point at her favourite lady-in-waiting. No doubt Lady Mar had already been filling the princess's mind with tales of her wickedness, conjuring up images of evil spells and potions concocted late at night in her apartments. Frances felt her heart contract with fear.

She looked again at the letter, and saw that in one corner a tiny inscription had been written in a different hand: *23 Aug*. The same day that she had been taken to the Beauchamp Tower. How many days had passed since then?

A soft knocking at the door interrupted her thoughts. Frances quickly tucked the note into the top of her bodice. Sir Richard Berkeley entered at her call. He gave a deep bow, then looked at her with a mixture of pity and shame.

'I am sorry for what you have suffered, Lady Frances,' he said after a pause, then lowered his gaze. 'I fear it has been brutal.'

Before she could answer, he continued: 'There is a visitor from court to see you. Should you require any assistance from me, just send word.'

Frances felt a jolt of apprehension as he backed hastily away, leaving the door ajar. A few moments later, she heard the tread of a different foot, and Thomas Sackville walked into the room. He gave a brisk bow and motioned for Frances to remain seated, for which she was grateful. His eyes alighted on the ewer filled with bloodied water, and then darted quickly back to her, taking in the wounds that were visible on her face and neck. He looked moment-arily ashamed, and hesitated before speaking. Frances waited, careful to keep her expression impassive despite the rapid hammer-ing in her chest.

'My lady, I am to accompany you back to court.'

The words were so unexpected that Frances could not mask her surprise. Her mind was racing, but before she could respond he continued: 'You are required to attend my lady princess without delay. She is gravely ill.'

Frances reeled, as much from the news of her young mistress as the notion that she – a suspected witch – should now be called upon to try to save her.

'But Sir Thomas,' she said at last, 'you must know of what I have been accused? How then can I be asked to attend the princess?'

Lord Sackville shifted uncomfortably. The lines in his brow grew deeper as he struggled to form an answer.

'His Majesty – that is, Their Majesties – have seen fit to pardon you for your supposed offences. His Grace informed the council that no proof of witchcraft was found, despite' – he hesitated again, unable to meet her gaze – 'despite a thorough investigation.'

Frances stared at him as she fought to control her churning emotions. Was this, too, a trap? But the king had made it clear that Mistress Knyvett's accusation was enough to bring her to trial, even though Balfour's blade had not provided any further proof. What would be served by testing her again? Besides, the princess's life was surely too precious to be toyed with. They must be desperate if they had summoned her.

'His Majesty's officers were indeed most thorough,' Frances replied quietly after a long pause, her voice as cold as ice. She continued to look at him until he at last lifted his eyes to hers. An image of the princess came into her mind, her small, slender frame racked by fever. She took a breath, then rose slowly to her feet.

'Well then, Sir Thomas, we must make haste.'

CHAPTER 25

1 September

The rain was falling steadily by the time Lord Sackville's barge reached the watergate. Frances welcomed its cleansing coolness and turned her face up so that she might catch more of the drops. For all her anxiety about the princess, she was sorry that the journey was over. She had relished the feeling of freedom as they glided along the vast grey waters of the Thames, putting an ever greater distance between themselves and the Tower. There was a sharp jolt as they butted up against the landing stage, where an attendant was waiting to tether their barge and escort them into the palace. His cloak was clinging to his shoulders, and droplets of water fell steadily from his cap. He must have been waiting there for some time. Frances noticed the panic in his eyes as she took his arm and climbed out of the barge. It reminded her of the boy who had rushed her to Lady Beatrice's apartments upon her first arrival at James's court, although that now seemed like a lifetime ago. More than ever, she wished that she had been allowed to remain at Longford.

Walking briskly alongside Lord Sackville, but not taking the arm that he had proffered, Frances passed under the gateway and into the courtyard. It was the usual hive of activity, but she fancied that there was a more subdued air than usual.

Just before they passed under the archway that led through into the first series of courtier lodgings, a small movement caught Frances's eye. Looking up, she saw a familiar figure watching her from one of the windows. His features were partially obscured by the leadwork, but she could see his dark eyes staring down at her. Her heart contracted.

Tom.

Suddenly conscious of the marks on her face and neck, she drew up the hood of her cloak, but kept her gaze fixed on him. Even at this distance, she could see dark shadows under his eyes. Her mouth lifted into a small smile. He did not return it.

The scraping of Lord Sackville's boot on the cobbles made her turn away abruptly. She had momentarily forgotten the cause of their haste, and, ashamed, walked on quickly without looking back at the window.

As they made their way through the succession of familiar rooms and passages, Frances felt as if she were looking at them through a dirty window. The gilding, tapestries, and other decorations seemed to have lost all of their lustre, and appeared as drab and lifeless as a tree in winter. She sensed that even when the candles were ablaze in their sconces, their light would not bring everything to life as it once had, but rather show it up as a hopeless façade, devoid of any true beauty. Even the lingering scent of beeswax and rush matting, which before had suggested warmth and comfort, now smelt stale and sickly.

Every courtier or attendant they passed bowed low to Lord Sackville, then their eyes flickered across to Frances. In one court-yard, a cluster of ladies who had been talking animatedly suddenly fell silent as they approached. Frances continued to stare straight ahead, but she could feel their eyes upon her. So this was to be her life now. She had heard it said that those who stood accused of witchcraft were damned, whether or not they went to the scaffold. Now she understood why.

At last they reached the entrance to the princess's apartments. The guards immediately raised their halberds so that they might pass through. Lady Mar was sitting in the antechamber, but leaped to her feet when she saw them approach.

'My Lord,' she said, dropping a deep curtsey.

Straightening, she regarded Frances coldly.

'Lady Mar,' Frances said, holding her gaze until she received a curt nod in reply. 'How fares the princess?'

'Worse. Her fever is still high, and she has taken no food or water for three days now.'

Frances frowned as she unlaced her cloak and handed it to the older woman, giving her no time to protest as she swept past and into the young girl's bedroom. Lord Sackville followed in her wake, closing the door behind them.

The curtains had been drawn across the window, and a solitary candle burned in the sconce above the fireplace. Frances had to stare for several moments before she could make out the small form that lay as still as a statue on the bed. The heavy coverlets that had been placed over her did not move. Frances walked slowly towards the head of the bed. She held her breath as she leaned forward and placed her hand on Elizabeth's forehead. It was icy cold, but when Frances drew her hand away it was covered with beads of sweat. The girl's skin had the pallor of wax, and her lips, which were parted slightly, were tinged with blue. Frances held her hand in front of them for a few moments, but could feel no warmth. Panic began to rise in her chest, and she cast an anxious look at Lord Sackville, who still stood uncertainly by the door.

Just then, a small sound came from the bed. It was so quiet that Frances wondered if she had imagined it. She listened intently, her eyes fixed on the girl's face. After a few moments, she heard it again, more distinct this time – a dry, clicking sound that seemed to come from Elizabeth's throat. Quickly, Frances reached for the small tumbler on the cabinet next to the bed and, cradling the princess's head, poured a few drops into her mouth. Elizabeth started to splutter at once, coughing and rasping as if she were being choked. Alarmed, Frances lifted her forward so that she was almost sitting. She was as light as a bird, and Frances could feel her ribs through the linen robe that she wore. The coughing fit grew more intense so that her whole body jerked with each fresh onslaught. All of a sudden, she started to retch, and, before Frances could fetch the ewer from the cabinet by the fireplace, she vomited over the bedclothes, the black bile soaking into the soft satin.

'Tell Lady Mar to bring a fresh gown and sheets,' Frances commanded Lord Sackville. 'And go to Lord Cecil. He must come without delay.'

The man hastened from the room, and Frances could hear the urgency in his voice as he issued her directions to Lady Mar.

The princess now lay limp in her arms, her wasted body exhausted from the coughing fit. Frances smoothed the damp tendrils of hair back from her forehead and rocked her very gently back and forth, caring nothing for the bitter stench that rose up from her gown. The girl's thin arms were marked with angry red blisters. Frances felt a surge of fury. The physicians' leeches had sapped her of blood, weakening her still further.

'Hush now, my lady,' she said softly, though the child did not stir, and seemed insensible of her presence.

The sound of brisk footsteps heralded Lady Mar's arrival. She entered the chamber bearing the linens that Frances had requested, and as she set them down on the bed her nose wrinkled. She glanced quickly at the princess, then turned and walked quickly from the room.

The princess did not awaken as Frances gently pulled the gown over her head and dabbed at her chest with a dampened linen cloth. She looked so frail that Frances's eyes filled with tears. Without pausing, she removed the stained coverlet and bundled it up with the gown, then fetched the fresh linens. As she eased the girl's small body into her new nightgown, it reminded her of the hours she had spent dressing her ragdolls as a child, pushing their pliant limbs into the tiny outfits that her mother had sewn.

Laying Elizabeth down so that she could smooth out the exquis-itely embroidered nightgown, she noticed a red lesion on her neck, smaller than those left by the leeches. Her heart contracted in fear. Working quickly, she searched the rest of the girl's body, running her fingers along her skin to feel for any bumps. She could find none. Perhaps she was mistaken. The Reverend Samuels had cautioned her against reaching any hasty conclusions, urging her to be guided only by the symptoms that she observed. The thought was a comforting one, but Frances could not quite push away the horrible sense of foreboding.

A quiet tap at the door disturbed her thoughts. Cecil entered at her call. He looked altogether different to the last time she had seen him. He appeared almost humble as he stood there, and he seemed to be waiting for something. At length, he broke the silence.

'His Majesty is grateful for your attendance, Lady Frances. My lady princess has been ailing these past ten days, and even the king's own physicians have been unable to determine the cause, or to bring her relief.'

A scornful look crossed Frances's face, but she said nothing.

Cecil's eyes flicked to the wounds that marked her cheeks and neck. They had not yet begun to heal, and sometimes when Frances moved her head too quickly or brushed against them, they bled afresh.

'I hope you have recovered from your ordeal.'

When Frances remained silent, he continued, his words coming more hurriedly: 'It was unfortunate, but I am sure you must acknowledge the necessity of being thorough in our investigations when witchcraft is suspected.'

'You were most thorough,' she replied drily. Cecil blanched as she held his gaze.

'Mr Balfour has examined many suspected witches in this way,' he added, without conviction. 'It is the only way to ensure that justice is served.'

Frances eyed him coldly.

'I did not request your presence so that you might defend your actions, and those of your king.'

Cecil raised his eyebrow at the last two words, but said nothing.

'If I am to help the princess, then I must have my cabinet of herbs, as well as my books – that is, if you have not already consigned them to the flames.'

'I will have them brought here directly,' he replied. Frances hid the relief that flooded through her.

Cecil paused.

'Will she recover?'

Frances turned to look at Elizabeth, who still lay insensible.

'Her fever has broken, but until I find out what ails Her Grace, I cannot be certain,' Frances replied, her voice softer now. The young girl seemed so fragile as she lay there, as if hovering on the edge of life. Then Frances's heart hardened as she looked back at Cecil.

'How can I be sure that this is not a trap?' she demanded. 'Why would you have me released so suddenly and brought here, when you had seemed intent upon seeing me hang like that poor wretch at Tyburn?'

Cecil's eyes widened for a moment, then he recovered himself.

'You are not here at my command, but at the king's,' he replied quietly. 'Their Majesties are naturally concerned for their daughter. When the royal physicians could work no effect, the queen persuaded His Highness to release you, knowing your skill in these matters.'

Frances searched his face for any trace of insincerity. He regarded her steadily.

'And what if I cannot help her?' she persisted. 'Will I then be blamed for her sickness?'

'You have my assurance that you will be free from all censure,' Cecil replied.

Frances let out a humourless laugh. 'Forgive me if I do not set much store by your assurances, Lord Cecil.'

'Then I shall give you that of a higher authority,' he countered. 'I will have a writ signed by the king and the council, attesting that you have been placed here at His Majesty's command, and that, even if you fail, you shall escape any reprisals.'

The princess groaned quietly, the noise catching in her throat. Frances glanced anxiously towards her.

'So be it,' she declared. 'I will employ all of my skills to help her, and will remain in this chamber day and night. Her Grace must not be left unattended.'

She saw relief flash across Cecil's face. He gave a swift bow, then hastened from the room.

CHAPTER 26

3 September

Frances worked quickly and silently, plucking the bright green leaves from the pennyroyal, and grinding them into a paste with the fern-like stems of tansy and a few drops of almond oil to bind and sweeten the mixture. She set aside the soft purple and bright yellow flowers from the plants so that she could make another tincture with them later. They were more potent, and she hoped they would not be needed, but she knew that she must be prepared.

The princess had not woken since Frances's arrival, but she seemed to find no peace in slumber, and often cried out when troubled by dreams. The fever had not returned, but her breathing had become more laboured, as if her throat were slowly contracting. Frances herself had slept little. There was a small pallet bed for her use, but she preferred to take her rest in the chair next to Elizabeth's bed.

The air was fresh after two days of rain, so Frances had opened the small casement window that looked out over the courtyard garden. A gentle breeze now blew the heavy curtains out a fraction, and a pale light stole into the room. She crossed to the window, and pulled back the heavy fabric. Soon, it would be bright enough to carry out a careful examination of the princess – the first of several that day. Even now, Frances thought she looked a little paler than the day before, but she hoped that her colour might return with the gathering light.

Crossing over to the cabinet, Frances soaked one of the fresh linen cloths in the ewer, and rubbed it over her face and neck. The cool water was reviving, and her aching neck and shoulders were eased by the pressure of her fingers. She breathed deeply, and felt her body sag as she exhaled. But then she tensed as a droplet of water ran over a wound at the back of her neck. She saw again the glint of the blade as it hovered near her skin. The terror of not knowing where it would strike next had almost been worse than the pain when it found its mark. She shook her head as if to expel the memory, then dried herself briskly and re-laced her gown.

As Frances looked towards the bed, a shard of light suddenly illuminated the princess's face, giving it an almost ethereal glow. Frances felt a rush of affection for the young girl, mixed with fear that she might never wake from her slumber. As she approached, she noticed what appeared to be a small lump on Elizabeth's upper lip. Her heart quickened as she leaned over to look at it more closely. Gently, she ran her finger over it, and felt a hard bump that was warm to the touch. She tried to still her breathing as she slowly pulled open the princess's mouth, but could not help exclaiming in horror when she saw that it was filled with the same red lumps. They were scattered like tiny toadstools over her tongue, and covered the back of her throat.

Smallpox. It was the word that she had not dared to utter during her conversation with Cecil, or even to acknowledge to herself. Yet it had lingered like a dark shadow at the back of her mind, prompting her to prepare the herbs that Gerard recommended for its treatment. Even he did not speak of a cure; only temporary relief. For most, there was none. The lesions would grow larger, until they engulfed the mouth, tongue, and throat, choking the victim slowly to death. The few who did survive would be disfigured with pockmarks left by the hideous lesions. Only a handful could hope to emerge unscathed.

The old queen had almost died from the disease early in her reign. Frances had seen her scars, which had hardly faded with time, and still covered her wasted face and neck in old age. Little wonder that she had forced her ladies to apply ever more layers of the thick white paste until her face appeared as flawless as a statue. The queen's attendants had been less fortunate. Her faithful nurse had died within days of catching the infection, and another had been left so hideously disfigured that even her husband shrank from her, and she had been obliged to hide her face with a mask for the rest of her days.

Tears filled Frances's eyes as she looked at the girl. She could not bear the thought of losing her. God knew she had found little enough to love at this court, but her affection for the princess was strong and abiding. Frances realised that though Elizabeth lay still, a fierce battle raged inside her. She must help her to win it, even though she would risk her own life in doing so.

Thinking quickly now, she hastened from the room. Lady Mar was startled from her slumber as Frances burst into the antechamber.

'Nobody must enter the princess's bedchamber,' Frances commanded.

The older woman narrowed her eyes, and was about to protest, but Frances continued: 'It is smallpox.'

At once, Lady Mar shrank from Frances. Her face was deathly pale, and she glanced quickly towards the outer door as if contemplating escape.

'You must alert Lord Cecil so that he might inform Their Majesties. None must be admitted to these apartments. Any victuals must be left outside the presence chamber door so that you can bring them in here and signal for me to collect them.' She caught the look of horror that flashed across Lady Mar's face. Before she could object, Frances went on: 'The contagion may already have spread to these apartments. If you venture beyond these doors, then you will put countless more at risk. Your only contact with the court must be by messenger, and he must stay on the other side of the door.'

The woman seemed dumbstruck. Her eyes were filled with fear, but as she continued to stare at Frances, they gradually resumed their customary coldness. Drawing herself up, she spoke at last. 'I am not accustomed to taking my orders from a lady of the bedchamber.' Her voice was as cold as her eyes. 'But since the Lord Privy Seal advised me to defer to you while the princess remains ill, I have little choice. Even if it means putting my life in the hands of a—' Seeing Frances's expression, she went no further.

'Thank you, Lady Mar.'

Frances woke with a start, her heart racing. She listened for the sound again, but for a few moments all she could hear was the pulsing in her ears. The room was in darkness, and Frances stretched her hand over to the bed, feeling for the small form that lay quietly there. She gently turned the princess's cool hand so that she might feel for a pulse, and in so doing brushed against the pustules that engulfed her hands and feet, as well as the whole of her face and neck. It pained Frances to think of how the princess would recoil if she saw her reflection now. Vanity had certainly been a failing in the young girl, but it was surely not one that deserved such a punishment.

There it was again. A quiet tap-tapping. Frances turned to the source of the noise, which she soon realised was the window. Her heartbeat pulsed in her ears as she slowly raised herself from the bed and padded over to it. Drawing back the curtain just enough to peer out, she was startled to see a man staring back at her.

'Tom.'

The princess stirred, and Frances silently chided herself. He put a finger to his lips, then motioned for her to open the door to the courtyard. With trembling fingers, she fumbled for the keys that hung from her belt, and, finding the smallest, slid it quietly into the lock. Every movement seemed to echo around the room. Frances looked anxiously towards the door that led to the ante-chamber, imagining Lady Mar pressing her ear to it, poised to raise the alarm. She held her breath for a couple of moments, then slipped noiselessly out into the courtyard.

Tom grabbed her wrist and pulled her towards him. The urgency of his embrace shocked her, but after a few breaths she seemed to sink into him, pressing herself against his chest and inhaling the warm scent of him. Remembering herself, Frances suddenly pushed him away and took a few paces backwards.

'You must not come near me. The risk of infection is too great,' she urged.

She felt suddenly cold as she stood apart from him. Her hands twitched to touch him, but she let them fall back to her sides. With an impatient gesture, he stepped towards her and took her hands in his.

'I care nothing for that,' he said earnestly, tightening his grip so that she could not pull away. He stared deep into her eyes, and, as she looked back at him, she tried desperately to steady her heart, which was pounding painfully in her chest. After a few moments, he moved his gaze from her eyes to the rest of her face and then down to her neck. She noticed him wince slightly when he saw each wound, as if he too felt the sharpness of the blade that had made them. His expression darkened.

'How does the princess fare?' he said at last, his voice low.

'The smallpox has ravaged her body, but her breathing is a little steadier, I think,' she replied quietly.

'Will she live?'

Frances fell silent, considering.

'I believe so, please God,' she whispered.

'And you? Have you any signs of the contagion?'

His brow creased with concern as he waited for her to answer.

'None.' She looked down at her arms and smiled. 'Though it might be difficult to tell for certain, at present.'

He did not return her smile.

'He is no true king who can sanction such barbarity.'

The severity of his tone surprised her. She motioned for him to be quiet, his anger having apparently overwhelmed any sense of caution. His breathing was rapid, and his eyes blazed as he looked at her. When he spoke again, his voice was dangerously low.

'I will see him burn in hell. And his pestilent advisers with him. God will wreak His vengeance on this evil.' He was breathing quickly now. 'Mark me, Frances. *I* will have my vengeance too.'

After a few moments, his grip loosened and the fury left his eyes, replaced by concern. Frances took a step back.

'Please – you must not put yourself at risk,' she urged.

Tom moved forward and took her hands in his, gently this time.

'My life would be as nothing without you, Frances,' he said softly, reaching to stroke a lock of hair that had escaped from her loose braid. He kept his hand there, gently cupping her cheek. She turned her head to kiss it, and closed her eyes. He slowly withdrew his hand, and she felt his breath on her face as he moved closer, then the warmth of his lips as they closed over hers. His body was pressed against her now, and she reached to stroke the hair that curled at his nape, drawing him forward as she opened her mouth. Their kiss became deeper, more urgent, desire flaring inside her as she ran her hands down his back, feeling the warm curve of his spine. A growing, rhythmic pulse seemed to spread over her whole body, pooling in her stomach.

All of a sudden, Tom pulled away. He was breathing hard, and his eyes blazed as he looked at her. Frances tried to catch her own breath as she stared back at him. Her mouth felt bruised, and her body still pulsed with longing. For a few moments, neither spoke, then Tom slowly took a step towards her.

'I love you, Frances,' he said quietly. 'I have thought of nothing but you since the night of the masque. When we are apart, I am restless and distracted. You even invade my dreams.' He gave a rueful smile, but it quickly faded. 'I want only to be with you, to protect you.' Frances saw pain flit across his face. 'If only I had done so better.'

She returned his gaze steadily, though tears pricked her eyes. After a pause, she reached for his hand and lifted it to her lips.

When she looked at him again, she saw her own longing reflected in his eyes.

'I love you too,' she said at last.

Tom's mouth lifted into a slow smile. Frances laughed, unable to contain the joy that surged within her. 'I love you,' she said again, relishing the sound of the words on her lips. They stood staring at each other, fingers interlaced, and then Tom bent to kiss her again, more gently this time.

'Frances!'

The princess's voice rang out across the courtyard. With a start, Frances turned towards the chamber, hope and fear surging within her. She hastened towards the door, but Tom stepped in front of her before she reached it, blocking her path. When she began to protest, he placed his fingers gently on her mouth.

'You must trust me, Frances,' he said earnestly. The intensity of his gaze unnerved her after their joyful professions of love. 'I will never forsake you.'

Slowly, he removed his hand and pressed it to his own lips. A moment later, he was gone.

CHAPTER 27

9 September

The princess set her looking glass down with a sigh. Her tears sprang afresh. Frances regarded her sadly, full of pity that they could not wash away the unsightly red marks that the smallpox had left behind. God knew the poor girl had wept enough of them since she had first seen her reflection.

'They will fade in time, Your Grace,' she said gently. 'And your face is not greatly marked.'

'Great enough!' Elizabeth exclaimed. 'You would not think so if you had been made as ugly.'

'My tincture will soon start to do its work, my lady. I have had Lady Mar bring fresh rosewater and honey, and I have a good quantity of dried mistletoe stems from the woods at Longford. When ground together, they make a powerful restorative.' She did not add that she had used them to treat her own wounds, which were now so faint as to escape notice.

Elizabeth fell silent. When she spoke again, it was with a hint of her former humour.

'I wonder that Lady Mar should take orders from you.'

Frances grinned.

'She carries them out briskly, if not gladly,' she conceded. 'But your lady mother has been most insistent that I am to be given whatever I judge necessary for your recovery.'

'When will she come to see me?' the princess asked, her eyes wide with hope.

'Soon, my lady. When the sores have begun to fade, we can be sure that the contagion has departed.'

Elizabeth sighed again. 'I am now more like to die from boredom than the smallpox,' she said peevishly.

Frances carefully placed the satin gloves that she had been refolding back into the coffer and covered them with the embroidered linen overcloth.

'I doubt that you have missed anything of note beyond these chambers, my lady,' she said with a smile. 'Though I have been absent too, I wager that I could tell you the subjects of conversation, the fawnings and flatterings, the deliberate slights . . . even the hour at which the Earl of Shrewsbury started dozing into his claret.'

The princess giggled. 'How rude you are about my father's court, Frances,' she chided, then paused, considering. 'I am minded to send you out into it as a punishment.'

'I thank Your Grace, but I am very well contented here.'

Frances turned back to the chest and pulled out another coffer. Its contents were as neatly packed as the rest, but she enjoyed the task of reordering them. Some contained items that she had never seen before: pale cream sleeves edged with delicate lace, a large sapphire set in a gold ring studded all around with diamonds, and a pair of exquisite yellow satin shoes decorated with a perfect ivory bow.

'Even so,' Elizabeth continued slyly after a pause, 'I would like to send my mother a token, to assure her that I am well.'

'I am sure that Lady Mar—'

'No, Frances, you must deliver it. She will trust no other. Besides,' she continued, anticipating Frances's next objection, 'you would have been covered in sores by now if you had caught the sickness. There is no reason for us both to remain prisoners here.'

Frances kept perfectly still, her hand resting on the smooth silk ribbon that was tied around the end of the coffer key.

'As Your Highness wills it,' she said quietly.

A sudden hush descended as Frances walked slowly down the length of the hall. Keeping her back straight, she stared directly ahead towards the red velvet canopy above the raised dais at the far end. The smell of roasted meat filled the air, and the candles that blazed in the sconces along the walls bathed the room in a soft golden light.

When she came within a few steps of the king and queen, she stopped, and, lowering her gaze, gave a deep curtsey.

'Lady Frances, it is a relief and a pleasure to see you,' Anne said in a voice that rang out across the hall. 'I was glad to receive notice that you would be attending us. How fares our daughter?'

'The princess is recovering well, Your Grace,' Frances replied steadily. She caught the look that Anne gave her husband, prompting. He took a swig from the glass in front of him, some of its contents dribbling down his chin as he did so, reminding Frances of the last time she had seen him. She swallowed back her revulsion.

'We are greatly indebted to you, Lady Frances,' he said at last. Frances looked directly at him now, searching for any signs of contrition. His face remained impassive, but his eyes darted this way and that. 'Your loyalty to our daughter is commendable. But for you, she would surely have perished.'

'I was glad to put my skills to good effect, Your Grace,' Frances replied evenly, though the words stuck in her throat. She took a breath. 'Those same skills that were lately condemned as the work of the Devil.'

Her eyes blazed with sudden fury, and she was aware of a collective intake of breath around the room. The muttering grew steadily louder. James looked anxiously about him, then motioned to the yeomen of the guard, who were stationed next to the dais.

They rapped their staffs sharply against the stone floor, the sound echoing across the crowded hall. At once, everyone fell silent again.

'It is true that you were wrongfully accused,' James began. 'But I was misled by certain members of my council.'

He shot a sideways look at Cecil, whom Frances now noticed at one end of the table, several places away from his accustomed position next to the king and his family. He was staring resolutely ahead.

'Even so, we must all remain vigilant,' the king continued, his voice growing more assured. 'God has set me on the throne to rid this kingdom of Satan and his followers. They are all about us, even now casting their wicked schemes to bring chaos and destruction to this realm.'

Frances's chest rose and fell rapidly as she struggled to regain her composure. She clenched her hands tightly by her sides, and stared at the king, her eyes glinting.

'Lady Frances, I believe you have a message from my daughter?' The queen's voice cut across the silence. Frances turned to look at her. The fury that had surged through her veins abated when she saw the expression on Anne's face, urging her not to spark her husband's anger.

'Yes, ma'am.' She stepped forward and handed her the note. Before Anne opened it, she signalled to the minstrels who stood watching from the gallery above the entrance to the hall. They struck up a lively tune, and gradually the conversations started up again on each table, so that before long there was as great a cacophony as there had been before Frances's arrival. Taking the opportunity to slip away unnoticed, Frances bobbed another curtsey and walked purposefully away. As she neared the large oak door at the end of the room, she heard footsteps hastening after her. She turned to see her uncle approaching, his face puce. With a sinking heart, she slowed her pace as she left the room.

Hearing the door close, she stopped.

'Good evening, my lord.' She spoke without turning around. In the silence that followed, she could hear him breathing heavily. When he had composed himself, he walked around to face her.

'Niece.'

His eyes scanned her face briefly before taking in her slender frame.

'You have grown thin,' he remarked with obvious disapproval. 'People will mistake you for a scullion, rather than the daughter of a marchioness.'

'Forgive me, Uncle, but I have not been housed in the most comfortable lodgings of late,' she retorted.

His expression darkened, and she waited for the chastisement that she knew would follow. What she had suffered would matter little to him. Her arrest had almost cost him his position on the council.

'That wretch will pay for what he has done,' he growled.

His words were so at odds with what she had expected that she did not know how to respond.

'His schemes have nearly brought us to ruin,' he continued. 'Were it not for the regard that the queen bears towards you, we would all be in the Tower. Thank God you justified her faith by saving that impudent minx, her daughter.'

Frances chose to ignore the insult to her mistress. 'I thank the Lord that she is out of danger.'

Her uncle grunted. 'A few pockmarks might teach her some humility at last.'

Before Frances could answer, he continued in a low voice, leaning closer: 'You will find the court greatly changed. The king no longer trusts Cecil – if he ever did. Your release has made a mockery of his campaign to rid the kingdom of witches.'

She eyed him doubtfully. 'Cecil is too useful to be out of favour for long,' she observed. 'Besides, he is always at his most dangerous when under attack.'

'That is true enough,' the earl replied. 'But there is another to take his place. The Earl of Northumberland is newly arrived at court. Already he has the ear of the king, for all that he is a closet papist.'

'And a traitor,' Frances cut in. 'He almost lost his head for joining Lord Brooke's conspiracy.'

'If a monarch chose to expel all those families who have been accused of treachery, their court would be much depleted,' the earl grumbled. 'Besides, a traitor in the old reign is a favourite in the next – particularly if his looks please the king. Mark me, Frances, you must seek Northumberland's good opinion.' He paused, considering. 'Pity he already has a wife – although they are not well matched.'

'The sister of the traitor Essex, I believe,' Frances observed coldly.

'Your brush with the Tower has sparked your interest in treason, it seems, niece,' her uncle replied sardonically.

Anger flared anew as she stared back at him. 'Not at all, my lord,' she replied tersely. 'Though what I have suffered would be enough to make anyone question their loyalty.'

He eyed her closely for a few moments, then sighed impatiently.

'Just be sure to court the earl's good graces.'

'I will certainly show him every courtesy, if ever I have the opportunity,' Frances replied evenly. 'But for now, I must return to my mistress. Already I have been absent for too long.'

She made a quick curtsey, and turned to go, but her uncle grabbed her elbow.

'That young churl Wintour has been making a nuisance of himself,' he said. Frances felt her pulse quicken. With an effort, she slowed her breathing so that her face might not betray her.

'The lawyer?' she asked, with an attempt at nonchalance.

'He will bring you no good, Frances,' her uncle warned. 'Sir Tyringham excepted, his associates are hotheads and villains. I have it on good authority.'

'What is this to me?' she asked lightly.

His eyes searched hers for a few moments, then he sighed and released his grip.

'Keep away from him.'

She watched as he strode briskly away, and continued standing there long after the door had closed behind him.

1605

CHAPTER 28

23 January

The leaves crackled underfoot as Frances and Tom picked their way through the woods that lay on the edge of the park. A hard frost covered the ground and clung to the branches of the trees. As Frances paused and glanced back towards Hampton Court, she was transfixed by the beauty of the wintry scene. The vast expanse of grass leading up to the palace had turned from green to silver, and the low hedges that surrounded the gardens glittered in the gathering light. The sun was still low in the soft golden sky, which Frances knew would soon turn to dazzling blue.

She caught a movement just on the edge of her vision. She held her breath and placed a finger to her lips. Tom kept perfectly still, but his eyes darted anxiously around before catching what Frances was gazing at. At the edge of the forest, just before it gave way to the rolling hills that stretched out into the distance, a stag stalked slowly into view. It stopped suddenly and sniffed the air, its head held high. Frances could see the breath plume from its nostrils. As she watched, a beam of sunlight broke through, silhouetting the beast against the horizon so that its antlers became indistinguishable from the branches overhead. She looked towards Tom and smiled. Her eyes glinted with tears.

When Frances turned back, the stag had vanished. For a moment, she wondered if she had imagined it. She gazed at the horizon, shielding her eyes against the sun's rays, which were creeping ever further into the forest. Everything was as still and hushed as a painting.

'He would not have evaded King Henry so easily,' Tom remarked softly.

Frances smiled.

'I am surprised that anyone would wish to hunt such a beast.' Her expression darkened. 'I hope that he is a long way from here before the king begins the day's chase.'

'They say he is more interested in hunting stags than witches these days,' Tom observed. 'But then, kings are fickle in their passions.'

He glanced towards Hampton Court. The sun was now high enough to catch the gilded weathervanes that nestled amongst the mass of chimneys.

'I wish that Cecil were so fickle,' Frances replied drily. 'He still watches me closely.'

'You mean the Earl of Salisbury, of course,' Tom corrected her. 'We must not forget the honour that the king bestowed upon him.'

Frances grimaced.

'It seems his efforts to win back favour have succeeded, for all the slights and insults he has suffered these past few months.'

'Ah, but he has none of the wizardry of his rival,' Tom replied with a grin.

Frances smiled. Despite his Catholic sympathies, Northumberland was still a rising star at court, and had recently been appointed to the Privy Council. The task of courting his favour had been a good deal more pleasant than Frances had anticipated. The earl was a learned man, and his library at Tynemouth Castle boasted ten times as many books as her father's at Longford. Many of them related to science and astrology, and his passion for alchemy had earned him the nickname of 'The Wizard Earl.'

Frances knew that every conversation she had with Northumberland was observed by Cecil. A witch conspiring with a wizard was too delicious a prospect to ignore, particularly when the latter was his chief rival. But she cared little for that. Being the subject of constant scrutiny, by Cecil and most of the court, had made her almost immune to their stares and whispers.

Tom walked over to where she was standing and slipped his hand around her waist. She reached up to touch his cheek. The hairs tickled her palm. She had not thought he would bow to court fashion, but she had to admit that the growing beard suited him.

'My lady princess will soon be demanding my presence – and yours,' she added with a smile.

'I shall be delighted to attend you both.' He paused and looked thoughtful. 'She has grown greatly in strength and courage since her illness, I think?'

Frances nodded.

'Her Grace is quite the little woman now. She has learned to be thankful for her survival, rather than lamenting the price that she paid for it. And she has devoted many more hours to her studies than she did before.'

'She will soon make a fine queen,' Tom observed quietly.

Frances laughed. 'I would not wish away her childhood so quickly.'

Tom did not smile, but fell to brooding. She had known him to withdraw into himself like this many times during the past few months, and although she did not understand the cause, she had learned to accept it.

The cawing of a crow broke the silence. Frances made as if to move away, but Tom drew her back, encircling her waist with both of his arms. She tilted her face upwards and closed her eyes as he kissed her, his lips warm despite the chill of the frosty morning air.

'You know I am bound to you, heart and soul,' he whispered, nuzzling her ear. Frances felt the familiar surge of desire, and pressed her body against his.

'As I am to you,' she replied softly, lacing her fingers into his hair, pulling him down to kiss her once more.

At length, Tom drew back, his expression suddenly grave.

'I never intended to ...' He paused, as if struggling to find the right words. 'That is, I can offer you little. You are the daughter of a marchioness, and I a humble lawyer. Your uncle has made it clear that there are many gentlemen at court whom he considers more suited to his expectations—'

'But not to mine,' Frances cut in quickly. They had talked about this many times, yet still Tom seemed ill at ease whenever the prospect of their future was raised.

'I care nothing for their fortune,' she continued. 'My mother married for love – in the end – and I intend to do the same.'

She planted a firm kiss on Tom's lips as if to settle the matter, but his brow was still creased into a frown.

'I have hopes of greater advancement, Frances,' he said earnestly. 'If my plans come to fruition, then I may at last be deserving of your love.' He fell silent again, his gaze fixed upon the ground. 'If they do not,' he added quietly, lifting his eyes to hers again, 'then I will be utterly undone. I pray to God that I do not bring you down with me.'

Frances felt a stab of fear at his words. His absences from court sometimes stretched to several weeks together. He had always been vague about the reason, referring only to a complicated case that required all of his labours. When he returned, at times he seemed troubled, at others almost joyful, as if the outcome was at last assured. She assumed it must be a case of the utmost secrecy, perhaps involving a powerful patron at court whose fortune would rise or fall on the result – and Tom's with it.

'I wish you would trust me enough to share your burdens,' Frances said as she took his hand. Many times, she had urged him to confide in her, but he had always gently resisted.

His eyes clouded with the familiar look of regret. 'I do trust you, Frances,' he assured her earnestly, lowering his head to kiss her fingers. 'I ask only that you trust me in return.'

* * *

The Great Hall was festooned with branches of holly and ferns, and a large fire crackled in the hearth that was set in front of the dais. Frances watched as the smoke curled upwards towards the small vent that had been cut into the ornate oak ceiling, cleverly concealed by the hammer beams that surrounded it. The exquisite tapestries that lined the walls were illuminated by the sconces above, the flickering flames picking out the shimmering gold and silver thread worked by the Flemish weavers many decades before. As a girl, she had listened, enthralled, as her mother had relayed the story that they told. 'Here, God appears to Abraham – see how he kneels in humble supplication. And here, Abraham offers up his only son Isaac as a sacrifice.' Frances had been entranced by the figure of the angel as it swooped down to stay Abraham's dagger, which was suspended above his son's bared chest. She looked at it again now, the silver-gilt of the wings a little faded, she thought. The king had been as neglectful of his predecessor's treasures as he was of his subjects.

A trumpeter in the minstrels' gallery above heralded the arrival of the king and his guests. At once, a hush descended among the assembled courtiers, who bowed low. The sound of muttered cursing could be heard, followed by a loud admonishment to an unfortunate page, who had failed to avert his curious gaze. The scraping back of the king's chair and the heavy sigh that followed signalled an end to their obeisance, and, as the minstrels began to play, everyone took their seats for the feast.

Frances looked across to the king's table. She had been seated close to the dais, on the same side of the hall as the princess so that she could undertake any command swiftly and discreetly. Elizabeth caught her eye and smiled, and Frances inclined her head. She noted with satisfaction that the girl's face, which bore only a few faded marks from her illness, had a healthy glow, and that her eyes shone brightly. The country air suited her well. Glancing across, she saw that at the opposite end of the table sat Prince Henry, scowling and sullen as usual, and next to him the four-year-old Charles, who had lost much of the plumpness of infancy. Their mother was dressed in a gown of russet silk fringed with silver lace. Frances noticed that the stays had been loosened again. It would be a spring baby. The princess had been overjoyed at the news, certain that she would have a sister at last. Frances had hidden her surprise. She had heard that the king had not visited his wife's bed for many months.

'His Majesty seems out of humour, my lord,' her uncle said in a low voice.

She had been too lost in thought to notice the Earl of Northumberland take his seat. He bowed his head in greeting, and she returned his smile.

'He has been denied the hunt today,' the earl replied. 'The council had much business to discuss in preparation for Parliament. It will be convened in two weeks' time.'

Her uncle grunted.

'He devotes more time to his hounds than his councillors,' he said, pausing to spear a large piece of beef from one of the plates in front of them. 'The people mutter greatly against it, especially as he is a foreigner.'

Frances darted a quick glance towards Cecil, who was seated several places away from them, and seemed to be listening. She touched her uncle's hand briefly, and nodded in Cecil's direction.

'His Majesty is intent upon uniting his two kingdoms,' Northumberland said in a low voice. 'There will be much debate about it in Parliament, judging from the objections that were raised in council.'

'That will never be passed,' her uncle replied. 'The Scots have long been our enemy, and no Englishman will ever be bound to them. Parliament has already thrown out that scheme once.'

'The king claims that God forged the two countries into a single island, by nature indivisible, and that we must now be united in law,' Northumberland countered. 'He will not let it rest.'

'Then he will turn even those of the true faith against him, as well as the Catholics,' her uncle muttered. 'God knows there are already enough plots simmering in the kingdom.'

ut as it is not you who have wronged me, my
ll not allow it.'

ing registered on the queen's face, and her features

given in apology, Lady Frances,' she said, her voice
othing could erase the stain upon my husband's
at he did to you, and I would not so insult you as to
forgiveness.'

out and gently lowered Frances's hand so that the
d on her lap once more. 'It is a recognition of the
you are held. An assurance for your future, not an
past.'

ere alight with sincerity. Frances held her gaze for
stared down again at the deed. If she was patient,
give her what she had wished for after all. The
ar exceed her salary in the princess's household,
tantalising prospect of independence, the ability
choices, free from the overweening influence of
mained silent, considering.

eason for which it is given, then I thank you, Your
t last.

led graciously and inclined her head.

you must speak of it to no one – not even those
e said, her eyes searching Frances's face. 'The
ing of it, and I would not wish him to.' She
d quietly: 'I hope that it brings you comfort and
ncertain times.'

ould answer, Anne stood up, signalling an end
. Frances rose to her feet and swept a deep curt-
wly from the room, the deed clasped tightly in

At that moment a server appeared and set down half a dozen fresh dishes before them. Frances breathed in the aroma of salmon roasted with onions, ginger, and wine, and of freshly baked manchet bread.

'Lady Frances?'

The Earl of Northumberland was looking at her expectantly.

'Forgive me, my lord. I was quite lost in thought,' she said, shaking her head.

'I was merely asking your opinion of the princess. Is she growing into a young lady of discernment?'

Frances's expression softened.

'Her Grace excels in learning and accomplishments, my lord,' she replied with a smile. 'I doubt not that she will prove a jewel in the Stuart crown, greatly beloved by all.'

Northumberland eyed her closely.

'What of her vanity? Lady Mar says she is too fond of her dresses and her looking glass.'

Frances bristled.

'The vanity of the young can hardly be condemned, my lord – particularly one who is surrounded by flatterers and luxury. The princess is a credit to the kingdom, and will only become more so as the years pass.'

She caught a fleeting look of triumph on the earl's face that left her feeling strangely unsettled.

'I hope very much that you are right, Lady Frances,' he replied quietly.

All of a sudden, he and her uncle scrambled to their feet. Frances turned to see the queen standing before them. She rose to curtsey.

'Lady Frances, I would be grateful for a moment of your time.'

Frances stole a glance at Anne, but her expression was as unreadable as usual.

'Of course, Your Grace.' She bowed her head, and, not pausing to look back at her dining companions, followed in the queen's wake.

The fact that there were no other ladies in attendance heightened Frances's curiosity. Perhaps, after all, she was to be released from her duties – discreetly so as to avoid any scandal. She had fulfilled her obligation by nursing the princess back to full health, but the stain of witchcraft still hung about her, and she saw the looks that Anne's ladies gave her whenever the princess visited her chambers. She had even caught the queen herself observing her with something like suspicion on occasion.

As they made their way along the corridors that led from the Great Hall to the queen's private apartments, Frances allowed the notion of her release to take hold in her mind, imagining a life free from the contagion of the court. Her first thought was of returning to Longford, but the idea of being there alone did not hold the appeal that it once had. She smiled at the realisation that she could no longer imagine life without Tom. She was his, heart and soul. Though they had not yet spoken of a betrothal, she had come to hope that the increasingly long hours that he spent at Gray's Inn were aimed at enhancing his means. Her thoughts raced on. He could go with her. A lawyer with his skill and connections would easily find work in Salisbury. He might also help to run the estate.

By the time that they arrived at the door to Anne's apartments, Frances's heart was racing with anticipation. The queen gestured for her to take a seat by the fire, opposite her own. She then crossed to her writing desk and unlocked one of the drawers with a small key that she drew out of her pocket. Frances craned her neck to see as she lifted out a small black casket and took something from it. As she came to sit opposite her, Frances saw that she held a folded parchment.

'Lady Frances, you have been poorly treated by my husband and his court,' she began without preamble. 'For all the love you bear my daughter, I know that you wish to be free of it.'

Frances's heart leaped. She glanced at the document on Anne's lap. The queen seemed to hesitate before continuing.

'We are greatly indebted
performed. Were it not for
perished.'

Frances waited. If Anne
then she had no need. Being
reward that she could wish
of reassurance, but the que

'This is a deed for s
Greenwich,' she said, har
has been transferred to y
from it as soon as the cu
year's time. It will provid
should you wish it.'

This was so unexpect
to speak. She gazed d
queen's seal. As she ra
struggled to hide her d
one of the richest man
courtiers would have
compared to her freed
but the Latin danced b
at the top of the docu
was signed 'Anna Reg

As she carefully re
of anger. Is this wha
that she had suffere
after? A piece of lan
pense. It was not ev
torture. The king h
that had followed.

Frances met the

'Thank you, Yo
holding out the de

Anne looked m
to take the deed

beneficence,
conscience wi
Understand
relaxed.
'This is not
softer now. 'N
honour for wh
try to buy your
She reached
document reste
esteem in which
apology for the
Anne's eyes
a moment, then
then this would
income would f
offering her the
to make her own
her uncle. She re
'If that is the r
Grace,' she said
The queen sm
'I am glad. But
closest to you,' s
king knows noth
paused, then adde
security in these u
Before Frances
to their conferenc
sey. She walked sl
her hand.

28 January

Frances traced the intricate stonework between the panes of glass, running her fingers along the small diamond shapes. The fire that had been lit in the small grate had long since burned out, and the air was chill, so that her breath misted the panes when she leaned against them.

Time seemed to pass more slowly here at Hampton Court, away from the noise and bustle of Whitehall, where every courtyard and corridor seemed crowded with people. In place of the shrill laughter and simpering flattery, she could hear the cawing of rooks, and the gentle lapping of the river against its banks. She felt, if not contented, then more settled than she had since returning to court. The deed that lay safely locked away in the casket next to her bed gave her greater hope for the future than she had felt for many months. She longed to speak of it to Tom, to begin making plans, but she would keep her promise to the queen.

Although impatient for freedom, she had to acknowledge that her life at court had become easier of late. Her duties were less burdensome than they had been before her arrest. As the princess's acknowledged favourite, she was no longer required to perform the numerous domestic tasks allotted to a lady of the bedchamber. Most of her time was spent conversing or reading with her young mistress, who was now so accomplished that Frances often had to remind herself she was still a child. It had also become their custom to go riding every afternoon, or, when the weather prevented them, to play bowls and tennis indoors. The king delighted in watching his daughter on these occasions, shouting encouragement from the galleries.

Only Tom's absences, which had grown even more frequent lately, disturbed her repose. He had left for Gray's Inn soon after their early-morning walk in the woods, taking advantage of the rising tide and a waiting barge. Although he spoke little of what had occupied his time when he was away, he never tired of listening to Frances talk about how she had filled her hours – of how the princess progressed in her study, the latest gowns for which she had been measured, and the subjects of her endless chatter. Frances pushed away the familiar unease she felt whenever she reflected upon the one-sided nature of these exchanges. It was at odds with the growing intimacy between them.

She glanced down at the privy garden, with its perfectly symmetrical swirls of hedges that encircled the small ornate fountain at the centre. She caught a peal of giggles, followed by the flash of a scarlet cloak. The princess was out walking ahead of her usual hour. Before Frances could begin to speculate about the reason, the queen came into view. She was following her daughter at a more sedate pace, looking on indulgently as Elizabeth darted this way and that, plucking sprigs of holly and kneeling to smell the heads of the roses, hoping to catch at their soft scent even though the petals had long since fallen away.

Now and then, the queen laid her hand on her belly. Frances could see her brows furrow as she did so. But she had none of the pallor of her last pregnancy, and the child appeared to be growing well. Her confinement would be in a little over two months' time. It would be her eighth. Frances wondered if the fear of what lay ahead diminished each time, or if the certainty of it made it all the greater.

At that moment a server appeared and set down half a dozen fresh dishes before them. Frances breathed in the aroma of salmon roasted with onions, ginger, and wine, and of freshly baked manchet bread.

'Lady Frances?'

The Earl of Northumberland was looking at her expectantly.

'Forgive me, my lord. I was quite lost in thought,' she said, shaking her head.

'I was merely asking your opinion of the princess. Is she growing into a young lady of discernment?'

Frances's expression softened.

'Her Grace excels in learning and accomplishments, my lord,' she replied with a smile. 'I doubt not that she will prove a jewel in the Stuart crown, greatly beloved by all.'

Northumberland eyed her closely.

'What of her vanity? Lady Mar says she is too fond of her dresses and her looking glass.'

Frances bristled.

'The vanity of the young can hardly be condemned, my lord – particularly one who is surrounded by flatterers and luxury. The princess is a credit to the kingdom, and will only become more so as the years pass.'

She caught a fleeting look of triumph on the earl's face that left her feeling strangely unsettled.

'I hope very much that you are right, Lady Frances,' he replied quietly.

All of a sudden, he and her uncle scrambled to their feet. Frances turned to see the queen standing before them. She rose to curtsey.

'Lady Frances, I would be grateful for a moment of your time.'

Frances stole a glance at Anne, but her expression was as unreadable as usual.

'Of course, Your Grace.' She bowed her head, and, not pausing to look back at her dining companions, followed in the queen's wake.

The fact that there were no other ladies in attendance heightened Frances's curiosity. Perhaps, after all, she was to be released from her duties – discreetly so as to avoid any scandal. She had fulfilled her obligation by nursing the princess back to full health, but the stain of witchcraft still hung about her, and she saw the looks that Anne's ladies gave her whenever the princess visited her chambers. She had even caught the queen herself observing her with something like suspicion on occasion.

As they made their way along the corridors that led from the Great Hall to the queen's private apartments, Frances allowed the notion of her release to take hold in her mind, imagining a life free from the contagion of the court. Her first thought was of returning to Longford, but the idea of being there alone did not hold the appeal that it once had. She smiled at the realisation that she could no longer imagine life without Tom. She was his, heart and soul. Though they had not yet spoken of a betrothal, she had come to hope that the increasingly long hours that he spent at Gray's Inn were aimed at enhancing his means. Her thoughts raced on. He could go with her. A lawyer with his skill and connections would easily find work in Salisbury. He might also help to run the estate.

By the time that they arrived at the door to Anne's apartments, Frances's heart was racing with anticipation. The queen gestured for her to take a seat by the fire, opposite her own. She then crossed to her writing desk and unlocked one of the drawers with a small key that she drew out of her pocket. Frances craned her neck to see as she lifted out a small black casket and took something from it. As she came to sit opposite her, Frances saw that she held a folded parchment.

'Lady Frances, you have been poorly treated by my husband and his court,' she began without preamble. 'For all the love you bear my daughter, I know that you wish to be free of it.'

Frances's heart leaped. She glanced at the document on Anne's lap. The queen seemed to hesitate before continuing.

'We are greatly indebted to you for the service that you have performed. Were it not for you, our daughter would surely have perished.'

Frances waited. If Anne was struggling with her conscience, then she had no need. Being released from service was the greatest reward that she could wish for. She was going to offer some words of reassurance, but the queen began to speak again.

'This is a deed for some land that lies in the manor of Greenwich,' she said, handing Frances the document. 'The title has been transferred to your name, and you may draw interest from it as soon as the current lease has expired in a little over a year's time. It will provide you with the means to leave this court, should you wish it.'

This was so unexpected that for a moment Frances was unable to speak. She gazed down at the parchment, which bore the queen's seal. As she ran her fingers over the smooth wax, she struggled to hide her disappointment. Though the land, lying in one of the richest manors in England, was a prize that her fellow courtiers would have fought bitterly for, it was as nothing compared to her freedom. She broke the seal and began to read, but the Latin danced before her eyes. Her name was in large script at the top of the document, an elegant flourish beneath the 'F.' It was signed 'Anna Regina', and dated three days earlier.

As she carefully refolded the document, she felt a sudden stab of anger. Is this what her ordeal was worth? The terror and pain that she had suffered in the Tower, the sullying of her name ever after? A piece of land, no matter how valuable, was a poor recompense. It was not even in the name of he who had sanctioned her torture. The king had shown precious little remorse in the months that had followed.

Frances met the queen's gaze at last, her eyes cold.

'Thank you, Your Grace, but I cannot accept,' she said firmly, holding out the document.

Anne looked momentarily surprised. When she made no move to take the deed, Frances continued: 'I am grateful for your beneficence, but as it is not you who have wronged me, my conscience will not allow it.'

Understanding registered on the queen's face, and her features relaxed.

'This is not given in apology, Lady Frances,' she said, her voice softer now. 'Nothing could erase the stain upon my husband's honour for what he did to you, and I would not so insult you as to try to buy your forgiveness.'

She reached out and gently lowered Frances's hand so that the document rested on her lap once more. 'It is a recognition of the esteem in which you are held. An assurance for your future, not an apology for the past.'

Anne's eyes were alight with sincerity. Frances held her gaze for a moment, then stared down again at the deed. If she was patient, then this would give her what she had wished for after all. The income would far exceed her salary in the princess's household, offering her the tantalising prospect of independence, the ability to make her own choices, free from the overweening influence of her uncle. She remained silent, considering.

'If that is the reason for which it is given, then I thank you, Your Grace,' she said at last.

The queen smiled graciously and inclined her head.

'I am glad. But you must speak of it to no one – not even those closest to you,' she said, her eyes searching Frances's face. 'The king knows nothing of it, and I would not wish him to.' She paused, then added quietly: 'I hope that it brings you comfort and security in these uncertain times.'

Before Frances could answer, Anne stood up, signalling an end to their conference. Frances rose to her feet and swept a deep curtsey. She walked slowly from the room, the deed clasped tightly in her hand.

28 January

Frances traced the intricate stonework between the panes of glass, running her fingers along the small diamond shapes. The fire that had been lit in the small grate had long since burned out, and the air was chill, so that her breath misted the panes when she leaned against them.

Time seemed to pass more slowly here at Hampton Court, away from the noise and bustle of Whitehall, where every court-yard and corridor seemed crowded with people. In place of the shrill laughter and simpering flattery, she could hear the cawing of rooks, and the gentle lapping of the river against its banks. She felt, if not contented, then more settled than she had since returning to court. The deed that lay safely locked away in the casket next to her bed gave her greater hope for the future than she had felt for many months. She longed to speak of it to Tom, to begin making plans, but she would keep her promise to the queen.

Although impatient for freedom, she had to acknowledge that her life at court had become easier of late. Her duties were less burdensome than they had been before her arrest. As the princess's acknowledged favourite, she was no longer required to perform the numerous domestic tasks allotted to a lady of the bedchamber. Most of her time was spent conversing or reading with her young mistress, who was now so accomplished that Frances often had to remind herself she was still a child. It had also become their custom to go riding every afternoon, or, when the weather prevented them, to play bowls and tennis indoors. The king delighted in watching his daughter on these occasions, shouting encouragement from the galleries.

Only Tom's absences, which had grown even more frequent lately, disturbed her repose. He had left for Gray's Inn soon after their early-morning walk in the woods, taking advantage of the rising tide and a waiting barge. Although he spoke little of what had occupied his time when he was away, he never tired of listening to Frances talk about how she had filled her hours – of how the princess progressed in her study, the latest gowns for which she had been measured, and the subjects of her endless chatter. Frances pushed away the familiar unease she felt whenever she reflected upon the one-sided nature of these exchanges. It was at odds with the growing intimacy between them.

She glanced down at the privy garden, with its perfectly symmetrical swirls of hedges that encircled the small ornate fountain at the centre. She caught a peal of giggles, followed by the flash of a scarlet cloak. The princess was out walking ahead of her usual hour. Before Frances could begin to speculate about the reason, the queen came into view. She was following her daughter at a more sedate pace, looking on indulgently as Elizabeth darted this way and that, plucking sprigs of holly and kneeling to smell the heads of the roses, hoping to catch at their soft scent even though the petals had long since fallen away.

Now and then, the queen laid her hand on her belly. Frances could see her brows furrow as she did so. But she had none of the pallor of her last pregnancy, and the child appeared to be growing well. Her confinement would be in a little over two months' time. It would be her eighth. Frances wondered if the fear of what lay ahead diminished each time, or if the certainty of it made it all the greater.

Anne was turning now, as if watching someone approaching. A few moments later, Tom appeared. Frances blinked in surprise. But there he was, bowing low before the queen and her daughter. He stepped back then and gestured towards two men who had followed in his wake. Both were dressed in extremely fine clothes, which even from a distance Frances could see were richly embroidered. The smaller man gave a sweeping bow, pulling off his hat with a flourish as he did so. Like the other, he had a beard that was trimmed down to a point, but his moustache was much more ostentatious and curled around at both ends. Frances judged that he was about the same age as Tom. His companion appeared a little older, and was much taller. As he knelt to make his obeisance, she peered closer. There was something familiar about him, yet she was sure they had never met.

Though she strained to listen, Frances could not make out their conversation. Now and then, there was a peal of laughter from the princess, who evidently delighted in their attentions. The small man talked the most, and wore an expression of smug amusement that Frances found irksome. She knew that she should not be so quick to judge, and that the real reason for her irritation was Tom's failure to tell her of their arrival – or his, for that matter.

With a sudden impulse, she pulled on her cloak and strode out of the room. As she descended the stairs that led down to the princess's apartments, she experienced the same sense of anticipation she always felt at seeing Tom. The realisation made her more irritated still, so that by the time she reached the door that led out into the garden, she did not pause to compose herself, but wrenched it open with such force that it slammed back against the wall. The assembled company turned around to look at her.

Seeing the queen's shocked expression, Frances flushed and dipped a curtsey, trying to steady her breathing as she did so. She was aware that Anne was observing her closely.

'Forgive me, Your Grace. I had not thought to find you here,' she said at length. 'Or my lady princess.'

Elizabeth giggled.

'I persuaded Mama to let me come outside,' she told Frances. 'It is too beautiful to be cooped up in my chambers, even with Master Homer for company.'

She looked across at the three gentlemen and grinned.

'I hope our company has provided some compensation for his loss, Your Highness,' the smaller man remarked, his voice as smooth as silk, 'though clearly you have not often neglected your studies. You speak with greater eloquence than everyone else here.'

The princess flushed with delight at the compliment.

'Forgive me – I have not yet made your acquaintance,' Frances cut in.

He gave a curt bow.

'Sir Everard Digby, my lady,' he said without looking at her. His smile had become fixed.

The name was instantly familiar, but Frances could not remember where she had heard it. She shot a cold look at Tom, then glanced at his other companion.

'This is Thomas Percy, Lady Frances.'

So that was why she thought she recognised him. Now that she was able to study him closely, she saw the same long nose and dark eyes as the Earl of Northumberland. He had mentioned a cousin whom he had appointed to manage his estates at Alnwick during his prolonged visits to court.

'We are truly blessed, Frances, are we not?' the princess observed gleefully. 'Mr Wintour has come back already, and he has brought us two new friends. I think the hours here at Hampton Court will begin to pass by much more quickly now.'

Sir Everard made another elaborate bow.

'We have been most desirous to gain an audience with Your Grace, but had not dared to hope that it would be so soon after our arrival.'

'Fortune has indeed smiled upon you, Sir Everard,' Frances cut in. 'Will you be staying long?'

The question was directed as much at Tom as at his companions.

'Alas, no,' Percy replied. 'We have important business to attend to in London, before Parliament is convened. But we will go to it with a lighter heart now that we have met Your Grace.'

The colour rose to the princess's cheeks again, and she made a pretty curtsey.

'Well, gentlemen,' the queen said, before her daughter could engage in any more flattery, 'the princess must return to her schoolroom, and I to attend His Majesty. We bid you good day.'

All three men bowed low, and Sir Everard stepped forward to kiss her hand, before paying the same reverence to the princess. Elizabeth looked at him regretfully.

'You will visit us again before you leave?' she asked hopefully.

Before he could reply, there was the sound of footsteps crunching on the gravel, and Cecil appeared from a gateway in the wall that bordered the garden. Frances wondered how long he had been standing there.

'Your Highnesses,' he said with a bow. 'Gentlemen.'

His presence was like a sudden chill on a summer's day. The queen kept her expression neutral, but Frances noticed Tom scowl. Both of his companions straightened their backs and gave a stiff bow.

'What a merry little party,' Cecil remarked with a smile. 'Would I were so at liberty to enjoy the delights of this place. I have been confined to the gloom of the council chamber these past three hours.'

'No doubt there was much business to divert you, my Lord Salisbury,' the queen replied evenly, 'with the next Parliament being so close at hand.'

Cecil gave an exaggerated sigh and shook his head.

'Ah, then you have not heard, Your Grace,' he said. 'Parliament has been threatened by a great catastrophe.'

Frances caught the look that Tom exchanged with his companions. Cecil eyed them closely before continuing. 'There have been reports of plague in the city,' he explained, then glanced down at the queen's stomach. 'Of course, Your Highness will not want to take any risks at such a time.'

'There is always talk of plague, Lord Salisbury,' Anne replied dismissively. 'How can you be certain that it is true?'

'My agent informs me that it has reached as far as Cheapside, and this chill wind blows it westward, towards Whitehall. It is a blessing that Your Majesties are so far out of its reach. I would urge you to remain so.'

'There was no sign of it yesterday,' Tom cut in.

'You were at Whitehall?' Cecil asked, raising an eyebrow.

'Not in the palace, but close by,' Tom muttered, not meeting Cecil's eye.

Frances shot him a questioning look. Gray's Inn was almost two miles from Whitehall.

'What of Parliament?' Tom continued. The urgency in his voice surprised her.

'The king, in his wisdom, has ordered that it be postponed.'

There was silence. Frances looked at the sullen faces of Tom and his companions, then at Cecil, who was smiling as pleasantly as if he had just announced that a new masque was to be performed at court. A sudden wind whipped up from the river. The queen pulled her cloak tightly around her, and drew the princess to her.

'You must excuse us, gentlemen,' she said. 'My daughter and I have tarried too long outside. We might be safe from the plague, but I have no wish to catch a chill.'

She inclined her head and walked swiftly away, gripping the princess's hand firmly. Frances cast a final glance at Tom, but he seemed lost in thought, and hardly noticed when she made a brief curtsey, then turned to follow in her young mistress's wake.

Frances gave a little yelp as she pierced her finger with the needle for the third time in as many minutes. She sucked it for a few moments until the blood had stopped, then continued with the embroidery. It was a small coverlet of intricate design, with roses and pomegranates intertwined with an elaborate vine. She intended it as a gift for the queen, to dress one of the cradles that had already been prepared in her confinement chamber. But she lacked the same leisure for embroidery that she had enjoyed at Longford, and she held out little hope of completing it in time, even though there were still two months before Anne would take her leave of the court.

With a sigh, she set down her work, consoling herself with the thought that the light was rapidly fading in any case. She looked over at Elizabeth, who was still persevering with her own needle-work. The girl's brow was furrowed in concentration as she jabbed inexpertly at the fine cloth that was stretched over the frame.

'Will it please you to stay here a few more weeks, my lady?' she asked softly.

'Of course,' the princess replied without looking up. A smile played about her lips. 'There is plenty to keep me busy, and no lack of company.'

'How did you like your new acquaintances?' Frances could not resist asking.

The princess put down her needle. Her face was flushed with excitement.

'Very well! Sir Everard was so charming – and he has such a handsome face, don't you think?' Before Frances could reply, she added: 'But Percy is a bit of a bore. He always looks so serious, and I swear he did not speak three words together. I wonder that Tom could have such a friend.'

Frances fell silent.

'It is not always the clock that ticks the loudest that works the best,' she observed quietly.

'I fancy Percy does not tick at all!' Elizabeth retorted.

Frances laughed, in spite of herself.

'Sir Everard said that I am a young lady of great promise,' the princess continued. 'He thinks that I could rule a kingdom one day, if I set my mind to it. Oh, do not look so grave, Frances,' she added impatiently. 'The English love queens, thanks to your former mistress. I even have the same name!'

'I do not doubt the truth of what you say, my lady,' Frances countered. 'But I would caution against believing the words of flatterers so readily. They usually cloak their own greed and ambition.'

Elizabeth fell silent and bent her head to her work once more. Frances knew better than to press the point. The princess had inherited her father's stubbornness, and would not be moved when she had fixed upon an opinion. Frances suspected that there was more to this than her belief in female sovereignty. Sir Everard's flattery had hit its mark.

There was a knock on the door, and Lady Mar entered. As usual, she had not waited for a reply. The princess looked up expectantly.

'Mr Wintour is here, Your Grace,' she announced with a look of obvious disapproval. 'I told him you would soon be dressing for dinner, but he begged for a few moments of your time.'

'Of course, Lady Mar – show him in directly,' Elizabeth commanded. Her spirits had visibly lifted again.

Tom strode into the room a few moments later. He looked quickly at Frances, before sinking to one knee and kissing the princess's hand.

'Your Grace, forgive me. I do not wish to intrude upon your repose, but I have a favour to ask of you.'

'Whatever it is, I am sure I shall say yes, Tom. You have kept me so well entertained in this place – Frances too,' she added, looking across at her companion. 'I have seen how she looks for you, just as I do.'

Frances shot her a disapproving look, but Tom laughed.

'I am delighted to have served such a purpose,' he declared. His smile faded. 'But I fear that what I ask might not be agreeable to you because it involves depriving you of Lady Frances's presence – only for a day or so,' he added quickly. 'I have a cousin who is staying in lodgings close to Whitehall. As children we were as close as brothers, and we have remained so ever since – though I see him all too seldom now. I have just received news that he is gravely ill. None of the ministrations of his doctors has worked any effect. He needs the help of a skilled herbalist,' he said, look-ing across at Frances.

'Are there no other healers in London?' the princess demanded. 'Surely you don't need to rob me of my favourite attendant?'

'Your Highness must believe that I would not ask such a favour if I had any other means to assist my cousin.'

Frances noticed that Tom's hands shook as he held them by his sides.

'What ails your cousin, Mr Wintour?' she asked quietly.

'He has a fever, my lady, and such pains in his bones as he can barely stand.'

Elizabeth recoiled. 'It is not the plague, I hope? Salisbury said that it is spreading.'

'No, my lady,' Tom replied quickly. 'I have seen such cases before, and this is quite different. Besides, my Lord Salisbury is ill-informed about the contagion. It is still contained within the eastern parts of the city.'

The princess fell silent. Frances recognised the sulky expression on her face all too well. She hesitated, then went to sit at Elizabeth's feet.

'Mr Wintour, you must understand that I cannot abandon my mistress. She has great need of me, for she is still of tender years. You cannot expect her to release a close attendant with as little thought as if she had been a young woman already.'

Tom caught her eye, and his mouth twitched with a smile.

The princess bristled with indignation. 'I am perfectly capable of doing without you for a day or so, Frances. I am in my ninth year, after all.'

'Then you will grant my request, Your Highness?' Tom asked, his eyes glinting.

Elizabeth paused as she pretended to deliberate.

'Very well, Mr Wintour,' she replied. 'But if you see any sign of the plague, you must both return at once. I would not risk the life of a lady of the bedchamber, even though I might easily find another to replace her,' she added petulantly.

Frances smiled as she bowed her head.

'I will be forever indebted to you, Your Highness,' Tom said as he knelt for the princess's blessing. 'God shall reward you for your kindness and wisdom.'

He turned to look at Frances.

'I will have a barge waiting by the watergate at dawn.'

Her eyes widened in surprise. 'We must depart so soon?'

Tom nodded briskly. 'I fear that my cousin might not survive if we tarry longer.'

Frances looked at her mistress, who gave a curt nod of acquiescence.

'Then I shall see you in the morning, Mr Wintour.'

CHAPTER 30

29 January

As she neared the watergate, Frances could make out Tom's silhouette against the pale grey sky. He wore a cloak and hat, and she could hear the tap of his leather soles as he paced backwards and forwards along the wooden landing stage. Hearing her own soft tread as she mounted the steps, he swung around and held out his hand to help her up. Even through her gloves she could feel that his fingers were icy cold.

'Thank you, Frances,' he said earnestly, pressing her hand to his lips.

They climbed into the waiting barge, and the boatman swiftly untethered it and pushed the vessel away from the landing stage with one of the oars.

'Have you had any further word from your cousin?' Frances asked, as the boatman found his course and settled into more rhythmic rowing.

Tom glanced quickly at the man, then shook his head and drew his cloak more tightly around himself. He did not meet her eye. His agitation made Frances uneasy, but she decided not to break the silence any more. She watched as he rocked slowly back and forth, his eyes fixed upon the horizon.

At her feet lay a small leather bag containing enough linens for two days, together with a wooden casket with the herbs and tinctures that she had selected for her task. Yarrow and elder-flower for the fever, meadow saffron and valerian for the aching limbs. She also had a small vial of ginger and briar leaves mixed with white wine, in case Tom was wrong about the plague. Though if he was, she knew that her herbs could offer little protection.

Her thoughts turned back to the night before. After dinner, she had sought an audience with the queen so that she might secure her permission for the leave of absence. As a servant of the princess, she did not require it, but she desired it all the same. Though Frances had spent the dinner rehearsing her reasons, the queen needed no persuasion. As soon as Frances had mentioned Tom's name, Anne had given her assent, telling her that she must remain with his cousin until she was certain that he was out of danger. She had not realised that Tom was so highly regarded by their queen. Or perhaps Anne was doing this for her. Frances knew that she was still thankful to her for saving her daughter's life, as she saw it, and that she had deeply regretted not being able to prevent her terrible ordeal in the Tower. And if the princess had caught the looks that passed between Frances and Tom, then the queen was sure to have done so too. Anne might not have been blessed with marital harmony, but she was by no means embittered against those who sought it for themselves.

Though the tide was in their favour, it seemed to take an agonis-ingly long time to reach the city. As they slowly rounded each bend in the snaking river, Frances expected to see the houses grow more dense along its banks, or the distant towers of Westminster and St Paul's come slowly into view. But for mile upon mile there were only fields stretching out on either side of them, interspersed with the dark silhouette of woodland.

Her mind raced ahead. She did not know what to expect when they arrived. Tom had spoken only vaguely of the whereabouts of his cousin's lodgings, and she knew nothing of the man himself – not even his name, she realised. As she looked at Tom now, still staring resolutely ahead, she felt a surge of unease. Although his haste the night before might have prevented his revealing any more details of his cousin's situation, she could not account for his reticence now. He certainly did not lack the time to tell her about him – how old he was, for instance, or why he had chosen to visit London when the court was not in residence. Or why two men who were as close as brothers had seen each other so seldom.

By the time they finally reached the city, Frances's disquiet had turned to dread. She had a strong instinct to remain in the boat and command the oarsman to return her at once to Hampton Court. But she knew that was ridiculous. Lack of sleep the night before had left her unsettled and fearful, that was all. She glanced at Tom, and felt the familiar surge of joy to be in his presence, even if he was so distant and distracted. But her smile faded as he turned to her and she saw that his eyes, too, were filled with fear.

The oarsman drew level with the landing stage that lay close to the Palace of Westminster. Tom pressed some coins into his hand, then climbed from the boat and turned to help Frances. She followed him up the narrow stone steps, through the doorway at the top, and out into a small courtyard. It was surrounded on all sides by gabled houses, which she assumed were used by the officials of Parliament. Above the rooftops, Frances glimpsed the spires of St Stephen's Chapel.

They crossed the courtyard towards an archway in the corner. This led into a dark passageway that smelt strongly of woodsmoke. There were neither doors nor windows, and the cobbles underfoot were uneven, so that from time to time Frances had to reach out and steady herself against the damp walls. At length, they emerged into another courtyard, much grander than the last, with a long gallery on its west side, and large timber-framed lodgings on the east. Directly in front of them loomed the old palace, with its huge arched windows and high pointed roof. Frances knew that they were only looking at a fraction of it, and that it spanned several other courtyards besides.

They walked under the wooden portico that had been built along the side of the palace and led out into the street. Frances was relieved to pause for a moment and take in the expanse of the garden that separated the old palace from its neighbour, Whitehall. It was intersected by a series of neatly kept gravel paths, lined with small trees in round wooden tubs that were still painted in the Tudor colours of green and white.

'Frances—'

Tom had that hunted look again as he motioned for her to keep pace with him. Regretfully, she followed as he left the gardens and led her into the street that ran parallel with the north side of the old palace. The bell of St Stephen's chimed eleven o'clock, but the streets were almost deserted. Fear of the plague, combined with the postponement of Parliament, had no doubt caused many to keep to their homes, or flee the city altogether.

Tom's pace slowed as he neared a house on the north side of the street. Glancing quickly from side to side, he pulled Frances gently behind him as he ducked into a passageway that ran alongside it. After a few paces, he turned left, and descended a long flight of stone steps that seemed to lead underneath the house. Frances wondered what sort of lodging his cousin occupied. If the air was as chill and dank inside as it was in the stairwell, little wonder his condition had deteriorated so quickly.

Tom knocked quietly on the door at the bottom of the stairs. Frances could hear footsteps advancing, but then stop abruptly.

'Who goes there?' a voice from within called.

'Tom Wintour – and a friend,' he replied, shooting a sideways glance at Frances. He squeezed her hand as they heard a bolt slide back. A moment later, the door was opened a crack. Frances could not see who was on the other side, but he was evidently satisfied, because he swung it quickly open and ushered them both inside.

Frances had visited chambers inhabited by the sick many times during her life. Though the symptoms varied, there was always a faintly stale, dank aroma She inhaled deeply now, but could catch only woodsmoke and something deeper, richer: tobacco. Perhaps this masked any odours of sickness, she reasoned.

She was suddenly conscious that the man who had let them in was staring intently at her with his small dark eyes. He was frowning so deeply that his brows seemed knotted together, and his lips were pressed into a thin line. Frances looked across at Tom, who was leaning against the fireplace and staring down at the dying embers. To the left of him was a door that led through into another chamber. Frances could hear no sound within it. Were they too late?

'You are sure she can be trusted?' the man asked, not taking his eyes off her.

'Quite sure. You know what she has suffered,' Tom answered in a low voice.

'Please, Lady Frances—' The man gestured to a chair next to the fire.

Frances hesitated, then sat down, clasping her hands in her lap.

'Where is your cousin?'

The words came out as barely a whisper.

'Here.'

She swung around as the other man spoke, her heart pounding in her chest.

'But—' she began, then paused as she tried to calm her thoughts. She felt as she had when, as a child, her father and elder brother had spun a complex riddle and refused to give her the answer.

'You are recovered, then?' she asked doubtfully, knowing that he could not have been so ill one day, and show no signs of it the next.

The man's eyes flicked towards Tom, who gave a slight shrug.

'I had to give her a reason – and the princess too. She would not have come otherwise.'

Frances felt panic rise in her chest. She thought suddenly of Balfour circling her, blade in hand, as she stood trembling in that other dark chamber. Catching the fear in her eyes, Tom placed his hand gently on her shoulder.

'Why am I here?' she whispered.

Tom looked across at his companion, who gave a curt nod. He sank down into the chair opposite Frances and clasped both of her hands in his.

'Our king is a tyrant,' he began. 'He promised freedom of worship for Catholics, but now persecutes us more ruthlessly than ever the late queen did. He has banished Catholic priests from the realm, and will not rest until he sees all those of the true faith perish on the scaffold – or worse.'

His eyes blazed as he looked at Frances. She tried to still her breathing. *Us?*

'Already he has shown his perverted bloodlust by sending thousands of women to the flames on suspicion of witchcraft. God knows, you have suffered by this, Frances,' he added when he saw her grow pale. 'He says that he is appointed by God to root out this evil, but he serves only Satan. The Bible tells us we must be ever watchful, for the Devil prowls around like a lion, seeking someone to devour. He and his minions will stop at nothing until they have all England at their mercy.'

He paused, his breathing rapid and his face aglow. He gripped her hands tightly, but they had grown cold.

'Why have you brought me here?' she asked quietly.

The other man stepped forward, but it was Tom who spoke.

'This is Robert Catesby, my cousin.'

Frances knew the name at once. He had been among the conspirators who, with Essex, had plotted rebellion against the late queen. Although their leader had vowed that they planned only to rid her of her evil ministers, Catesby was a notorious zealot, and made no secret of his desire to see a Catholic monarch on the throne. After his arrest, it was discovered that he had even written to the King of Spain, inviting him to invade. The discovery had so unsettled the old queen that she had slept with a sword under her bed ever after, and her screams had often pierced the privy chamber as she awoke, trembling and covered in sweat, tormented by terrifying dreams.

As Frances stared at him now, she wondered again why he had not gone to the block like the rest. Elizabeth had levied a weighty fine, which his cousin Sir Thomas Tresham had helped him to settle, and he had been pardoned. Now he had enlisted another cousin to fight for his cause.

'I know that my name might not be welcome to you, Lady Frances,' he said, noticing her expression, 'but I assure you that I am a true and loyal subject to the House of Stuart.'

Seeing Frances's scornful expression, he continued: 'Not to every branch of it, I admit – particularly those that are rotten to the core. But the queen is of the true faith, and her daughter shows great promise.'

Frances started at the mention of the princess. How could he hope to ensnare her in his schemes?

'We have resolved upon a plan to root out the canker that lies in the heart of this kingdom,' Tom cut in. 'It is not enough to rid the people of their king,' he continued, warming to his theme, 'we must strike against the contagion that surrounds him.'

'The disease is so rife that it requires a sharp remedy,' Catesby observed darkly.

Frances felt her scalp prickle. She did not want to hear more, but she knew that she had already heard too much to be allowed to leave.

'There is a network of tunnels underneath the old palace,' Tom continued. 'One of them leads directly to the cellar of this lodging. For almost a year now, we have been amassing enough gunpowder to destroy the whole of Parliament when it next meets. The king and his government will be reduced to ashes with a single spark.'

The walls seemed to be closing in as Frances listened to his words. He was as a stranger to her now. Everything that had passed between them had been as insubstantial as a dream.

'We have been gathering supporters, too, and a great protector,' Catesby added. 'The tendrils of this plot reach to the very heart of the court.'

He glanced at Tom, who was staring intently at Frances.

'You mean to murder the entire royal family?' she whispered.

'No,' Tom cut in quickly. 'Not all. The queen has already proven her loyalty. She will support our cause.'

Frances thought back to the previous day. She had supposed that the queen had happened upon Tom and his companions by chance as she strolled through the gardens with the princess. Now she was not so sure. Were Sir Everard and Thomas Percy involved too? She wondered how she could have been so blind.

'And the princess?' Frances demanded.

There was a pause. Tom looked across at Catesby, who inclined his head.

'We mean to put Her Grace on the throne.'

Frances stared.

'*Elizabeth*?' she asked at last, her mind reeling.

Tom nodded slowly. He did not take his eyes off her.

'She is but eight years old.' The words were all that Frances could form from the many other thoughts that were racing around her mind.

'The princess is advanced for her years. Already she has won the love of the people through her regal bearing and presence. She has the popular touch that her father so notably lacks,' Tom added, with a sneer.

'And what of her brothers? They stand before her in the succession. Do you plan to destroy them too?'

This time it was Catesby who spoke.

'Prince Henry is a preening fool. He will grow up to become a greater tyrant even than his father.' He spat into the fire. 'By the time that Parliament sits, the prince will have reached his eleventh year – old enough to attend. We hear that he has already petitioned his father to that end.'

'And Prince Charles?' Frances asked. 'He is barely able to walk, though he is four years old. Would you have his nurse-maids carry him to Westminster so that he might accompany his brother?'

'The boy is weak and will not grow to manhood. We need not concern ourselves with him.'

Frances fell silent again as she tried to order her thoughts. The only sound was the fire crackling in the grate.

'Why choose the princess above her mother? The queen is well able to govern, and, like her daughter, has the love of the people. If, as you say, she is of the Catholic faith, then there can surely be nobody better to serve your purpose.'

'We would appoint a regent until the princess reaches adulthood,' Catesby said with a trace of impatience. 'A Catholic husband would then be found for her.'

Frances gave a cynical smile.

'So Elizabeth would be little more than a puppet queen. With you and your friends pulling the strings.'

She turned her cold gaze to Tom.

'Now I understand the part that I am to play – indeed, the part that I have unknowingly played all along. I am your means of access to the princess. You courted me so that I might lead you to the prize you sought.'

Tom opened his mouth to speak, but Catesby cut in.

'You will continue to play your part.'

His stare was cold and appraising.

'And if I do not?'

'Then I will have you put to death.'

It was as if he had thrust a blade into her chest. She made to leap from her chair, but Tom gripped both of her wrists. His eyes blazed with what she thought was fear, but she no longer trusted her judgement. How could she have been so foolish as to believe he loved her? He had played her false from their first meeting, and she had been as easily beguiled as the princess by the flatterers who surrounded her. Tears pricked her eyes, but she blinked them angrily away.

After a few moments, Frances let her limbs go weak and sank back into the chair. Tom relaxed his grip, but continued to gaze intently at her.

'What would you have me do?' Her voice was flat, resigned.

'The princess and her household will soon move north, to Coombe Abbey, where she will live as a guest of Lord Harington,'

Catesby replied. 'The queen has persuaded her husband that Elizabeth's studies will be better advanced there, away from the distractions of court and the constant threat of disease. You shall accompany her, of course.'

Frances had heard Lord Harington boast of his Warwickshire estate to the late queen. He had been richly rewarded for his part in conveying the condemned Queen of Scots to Fotheringhay, and by the time of Elizabeth's death he was one of the wealthiest men at court. But, like so many others, Harington had found less favour in the new reign. Frances supposed he had retreated to his estates when it became clear that there were no further pickings to be had in James's court.

'When the time is ripe, Sir Everard will pay a visit to the abbey, and, at our signal, take the princess into his custody. You will make sure that she is compliant.'

Frances stared at him.

'I am to be Her Highness's gaoler?' she demanded.

'Merely her – companion,' Catesby retorted, with a sardonic smile. 'You shall be richly rewarded for your pains, when she wears the crown of England.'

'I want no reward at your hands,' Frances spat back.

Tom looked anxiously at his cousin, then turned back to Frances.

'In doing this service, you will be furthering the interests of God and all His faithful subjects,' he urged, his voice soft and coaxing. 'Surely you can feel no allegiance to a king who hunts down innocent women to fulfil his own perverted desires?'

Frances felt a surge of fury that he should use her suffering to justify his treason.

'When will we leave for Warwickshire?' she asked in a low voice.

'Within a week,' Catesby replied. 'Harington has already set his house in order.'

'He knows of the plot?'

Catesby raised his chin. 'He is a good Catholic. When the time comes, he will act according to his conscience.'

'And in the meantime, I am to return to Hampton Court?' Frances asked.

'Yes – without delay,' Tom replied. 'You shall tell the princess that my cousin was not as sick as I feared.' He glanced at Catesby. 'As soon as you are safely on your way, we will leave London. You can excuse my absence on account of needing to help my cousin put his estate in order.'

Frances nodded mutely.

Catesby walked slowly over to where she was sitting. He stood staring at her, his eyes as cold as ice.

'So, Lady Frances,' he said at last. His voice was low and menacing. 'Will you do as we ask?'

Frances looked from him to Tom. Her heart was pounding painfully in her chest, and her palms had grown clammy. She did not speak, but after a long pause gave a slight nod. A slow smile of satisfaction crossed Catesby's face, and she heard Tom exhale quietly.

Frances stood up briskly and reached for her cloak. She could not bear to look at either of them.

'I will accompany you to the riverside,' Tom said.

She did not reply, but walked to the door and waited. More than anything, she wanted to be away from this place, away from the horrors that she had heard. She wanted to be away from Tom, too, she realised. She had to stop herself from recoiling as he reached for her hand and gently placed it on his arm. Catesby held open the door as they passed through, and watched after them, his eyes narrowed.

Neither she nor Tom spoke as they made their way back through the streets of Westminster. She was hardly aware of her surroundings, and walked as if in a trance, her mind filled with these revelations and betrayals. The bell of St Stephen's began to chime for midday. Had they really been in that place for only an hour? It could have been decades, for all the changes it had wrought in her. She no longer knew what was truth and what was artifice.

As they descended the steps that led down to the landing stage, a sharp wind suddenly whipped up from the river. It brought Frances back to herself. She drew in her cloak against the chill. To her relief, a boat was tethered to the mooring. She had no wish to delay their parting. Tom took her hand as she stepped into it, and continued to grip it tightly after she had sat down. He looked at her with eyes that seemed filled with sorrow. Her own were utterly devoid of emotion.

'I will send word as soon as I am able,' he said, still clasping her hand.

She nodded briefly and made to withdraw her hand, but he pressed it to his chest. She felt the rapid pounding of his heart as he gazed at her, his eyes imploring now.

'Frances . . .' he began. His mouth moved as if trying to form the words that would restore her faith, her love.

At length, the boatman gave an impatient sigh and began to untether the vessel. Reluctantly, Tom released his grip and straightened himself.

'Take the lady to Hampton Court, please.'

The boatman nodded and pushed away from the mooring. Frances smiled briefly, then turned to look straight ahead as she was rowed steadily westward. When they reached the first turn of the river, she allowed herself to look back. She could just make out Tom's silhouette as he stood, stock-still, watching after her.

Turning back to the boatman, she commanded: 'Take me to Richmond.'

CHAPTER 31

29 January

The light was fading as they approached the meadows that surrounded Richmond. Ahead, Frances could see the turrets of the palace silhouetted against the sky, which had now turned to deep pink, interspersed with strips of gold. It had been a little under two years since she had last been here. How much had changed since then. If she had only known when she had attended the dying queen what would become of her in the next reign she would have – what? Defied her uncle? Escaped to the Continent? She felt her thoughts turn bitter. Everything seemed loaded against her. There was little choice for any woman but to bend herself to the will of men.

Her gaze still fixed upon the palace, Frances calculated that she had three days at most before the princess would begin pressing for her return from Westminster. Word of her absence was unlikely to reach Tom or his cousin in the meantime. She exhaled deeply. The rhythmic motion of the oars had helped to order her thoughts, and she had drawn comfort from the fact that they were taking her ever further from London. And from Tom. For all she knew he could be following in her wake, sent to spy on her by his distrustful cousin. But she sensed that he was not. He would probably be many miles away by now. They had passed only a handful of other boats during the long journey from Westminster.

Frances had long since learned to live on her wits and make her own choices – so far as the limitations of her position at court allowed. She had grown to trust her instincts, for they had often been proven right. Now, though, her faith had been shattered. She had been shown to be hopelessly naive. Not only had Tom concealed his true intentions – and faith – from her, he had spun an illusion of their relationship that was as false as a court masque. The realisation left her feeling utterly incapable of forming a plan for what she must do. To collude with this monstrous plot was unthinkable, but she knew that Catesby's threat had been made in earnest. More than ever, she longed to escape home to Longford. She did not belong anywhere else. But she knew that the plot would follow her there, forever tainting the idyll with its wickedness.

'Think only of the present time,' the Reverend Samuels had counselled her, when, as a young girl, she had been impatient for more knowledge, for greater skill, and for independence to act as she saw fit. The thought comforted her now, though she knew that little else would. The strength of Tom's faith had driven him to conspire the death of the king, and many others besides. Her own seemed suddenly weak by comparison, like the late queen's habit of adding water to her wine in order to reduce its strength. The Protestant beliefs to which Frances and her family adhered would satisfy neither the king nor those who clung to the old ways.

As they neared the watergate, Frances looked across at the neatly manicured lawn that swept down from the formal gardens to the riverside. She smiled as she imagined her father directing the gardeners to add his own touches to the old queen's design. He had often told her that it was better to enhance nature than to order it. As she looked more closely, she noticed that the rigidly clipped hedges and precise symmetry of the knot gardens had been softened by the planting of yew trees along the wall that bordered them. Already she fancied there was something of Longford here.

Stepping onto the landing stage, she paused for a moment to stretch out her aching limbs. She felt suddenly ravenous as she realised that she had eaten nothing since the small manchet loaf that she had taken with her for the journey to Westminster.

As she walked towards the gatehouse, an elderly guard appeared, lifting his lantern into the gathering gloom.

'I am Lady Frances Gorges,' she said at once, to allay his fears.

He stooped to bow.

'The Lord and Lady Marchioness are not expecting you, my lady,' he said in a querulous voice.

'No – I will not be staying for long. There is no need to make any preparations. Please—' She gestured for him to go back inside so that she could make her own way to the palace.

The old man hesitated, then shuffled gratefully back into his lodgings, where she could see a small fire flickering in the grate. She picked her way along the gravel path that led to a large, ornate stone doorway. As a child, she had fancied that it must have once been a giant's castle. She smiled at the recollection now as she rapped on the heavy oak door.

It was soon opened by a groom, who showed her into the entrance hall. Glancing at the small gold clock on the fireplace, she realised that it was dinnertime. As she waited, Frances looked up at the walls, which were hung with tapestries and paintings that her parents had brought with them from Longford. She breathed deeply, trying to catch at the familiar scent of her beloved home.

The sound of hurried footsteps echoed through the hall. Frances turned to see her mother hastening towards her. Her face was filled with anxiety mingled with joy, and her eyes brimmed with tears as she took Frances in her arms and held her tightly.

'My daughter,' Helena whispered, holding Frances at arm's length so that she could look at her. 'But you have grown pale – and thin,' she observed, her brow furrowed.

Before she could question her daughter further, her husband stepped lightly into the hall. He wore the same relaxed smile that

Frances remembered, and as he leaned forward to kiss her cheek, it was as if he had been expecting her visit. She had always marvelled at his ability to greet the many ebbs and flows of a courtier's life in the same sanguine manner.

'Well, Frances,' he said softly. 'This is an unexpected delight.'

She smiled ruefully, and squeezed his hand.

'Forgive me Father – Mother. I did not have time to send word of my visit. I was sent on an errand to Westminster, which did not take as long as I expected, so I seized the opportunity to see you. I will not be looked for at Hampton Court for another two days yet.'

'We are glad you are here, Frances,' her mother said. 'We have been so worried . . .' Her voice trailed off as she stroked her daughter's cheek. Frances felt her own eyes begin to fill with tears, but she blinked them away. She had no wish to talk about the Tower, though she knew that occupied their thoughts. The events of today had made that seem of little consequence.

'Well now, we are poor hosts, Elin,' Sir Thomas cut in. 'Our daughter must be in need of refreshment after her long journey. We had just sat down to dinner. Please – come and join us. You will make our feast a good deal merrier.'

Frances smiled gratefully, and followed her parents as they made their way towards the dining room.

The winter sun was already shining brightly by the time that Frances awoke the next day. She had slept more soundly than she could remember since leaving Longford. Her eyelids had begun to grow heavy soon after dinner, and when her mother had urged her towards bed, she had put up little resistance. A fire had been made ready in her bedchamber, and she could still feel the warmth from the dying embers as she lay blinking the sleep from her eyes.

The knowledge that she could only stay at Richmond until the following day made her resolve to relish every moment of the visit. If she had not been so tired, she would have stayed up long into the night talking with her parents, or simply enjoying the comfort of their presence. They must have long since breakfasted, she realised, as she crossed over to the dresser and splashed water onto her face. She noticed that the clothes that she had left discarded on the oak chest had been taken away, and fresh ones left in their place. Perhaps they belonged to her sister Elizabeth. She could not help feeling relieved that both she and Bridget were staying with friends of their mother in Hertfordshire. She had no wish to answer a barrage of questions about her life at court, or suffer the snide remarks that she knew Elizabeth could never resist levelling at anyone who made her jealous – though God knew she had little enough to envy.

After dressing, she went downstairs to find her parents. The dining room was empty, but in the place where she had sat last night there was a plate covered over with muslin. She lifted it to find a generous portion of smoked herrings, eggs, and bread. A little dish of butter had been placed next to it, along with a jug of wine. Just the sight of the food made Frances hungry, and she sat down to eat.

The sunlight streamed in, filling the room with warmth. As she looked out, Frances saw the familiar figure of her father strolling through the gardens. He paused every now and then, as if contemplating a new scheme for planting, once the frosts had receded and the soil was more yielding.

Tearing off another piece of bread, Frances rose from the table and made her way through to the hall, where she found her cloak hanging in a tall cupboard, next to those of her parents. It was almost as if she had been living here for as long as they had. With a pang, she thought of the following day, when she must once more bid farewell, not knowing when – or if – she would return. Quickening her step, she pulled on her cloak and went out into the gardens. As the heavy door closed behind her, she saw her father turn and smile.

'Good morning, my love,' he said, then added, with a hint of his accustomed mischief, 'at least, I think it is still just morning.'

Frances grinned.

'Forgive me, Father. I had not thought to stay abed as late as this.'

He squeezed her hand. 'You must have needed your rest,' he said.

She was aware that he was watching her intently. His smile faded, and he fell silent for a few moments.

'Why are you here, Frances?' he asked gently.

She sighed and looked at the ground. Her eyes pricked with tears, but she waited until she was more composed before answering.

'I am sorry, Father. I should not have brought my troubles upon you, but I knew of nowhere else to go. The thought of returning to my duties so soon after—' She raised her eyes to her father's, searching them for permission to go on. He remained as calm as ever, but she knew that he was waiting for the truth. She hesitated. If she told him what had passed at Westminster, she would be placing him in as great a danger as she was herself. But she could think of no other way to explain why she had not returned at once to court.

'These are troubled times, Frances,' he said, as if reading her thoughts. 'The king does not enjoy the love of all his subjects. Those of the Catholic faith had hoped for more freedom, but they have suffered even greater persecution than in the last reign. And they are not alone.'

He studied Frances closely, and she saw that his eyes were filled with anguish.

'Did you suffer greatly, Fran?' he asked softly, clasping her hands in his. They felt warm and comforting, and for a moment she was unable to speak.

'Not so much as other women, I fear,' she said at last. 'They did not find what they were looking for, but if it had not been for the princess falling ill, they might have continued their search.'

Sir Thomas gripped her hands more tightly, and closed his eyes. When he opened them again, they blazed with fury.

'Your mother and I came to the Tower as soon as we heard of your arrest. But Lord Berkeley would allow no one to attend you. He was under strict orders from Cecil, though he appeared to regret them. The lieutenant is a good man,' he added, when he saw the look of scorn on his daughter's face. 'We petitioned him daily, but it was no use. Then, on our last visit, we were told that you had left for court.'

'The king was glad enough to recall me when he thought I could be of use to him – or rather, his daughter,' Frances replied bitterly.

'I wish that he and the contagion that surrounds him might be swept away,' Sir Thomas retorted, his voice tight with fury. Frances started at his words, which struck her as being so like those she had heard in Westminster the day before. She had never seen her father like this. He had always remained so calm and accepting, even when provoked.

'There are those in this kingdom who work to that end,' he continued in a low voice. 'Godspeed their endeavours, for it is His will that they might succeed.'

Frances's heart was pounding as she returned his gaze.

'Of whom do you speak, Father?'

'I think you know, Frances.'

She had to remind herself to breathe. Everything around her seemed to fade so that she could see only her father, his eyes blazing into hers as if they sought her very soul. She had that same feeling of having stepped out of the world she knew and into a terrible vision, where nothing was as it should be.

'Then you are part of this too?' she whispered at last. 'And a Catholic?'

Her eyes searched his as she stared, willing him to deny it. But after what seemed like an endless pause, he slowly inclined his head. Frances felt as if her breath had been stopped.

'But you raised us in the reformed faith,' she said, her voice faltering. 'We attended St Peter's, denied the miracle of the sacrament, repeated the words set down in the new prayer book. Was it all a lie?'

'We were fortunate in our priest,' her father replied quietly. 'The Reverend Samuels respected the traditions of the old faith, while upholding the new. Your mother and I could not have borne to see our children raised without any of the comforts of our religion, even though for your safety we had to be seen to conform.'

Frances continued to stare at him.

'Then my mother, too, is a papist?'

She was gratified to see her father flinch at the word.

'Our faith was one of the many things that bound your mother and me together, Frances. As a favourite of the queen, she had to practise discretion at court, as well as at Longford, but in the privacy of our chapel, we could worship as our consciences dictated.'

Frances had a sudden recollection of the chapel in her father's apartments at Longford, the exquisitely carved altarpiece lit by the candles that blazed in the golden sconces on either side. Before he had left Longford almost two years before, he had ordered that it be stripped of its treasures, a copy of the authorised Bible placed on the altar. She had been too blind to realise the significance.

'We Catholics are used to finding ways to express our beliefs,' her father continued. 'Even through bricks and mortar.'

Frances gave him a quizzical look, curiosity making her temporarily forget the shock that coursed through her.

'You have often wondered why Longford was built to such an unusual design, around a triangular courtyard rather than the square variety favoured by most. It is because those three walls represent the Holy Trinity. Whenever we look upon them, we are reminded of our faith,' her father explained with a small smile.

Frances fell silent. Though she felt foolish at being so easily duped all these years, even by the bricks that surrounded her, she could not help but admire her parents' ingenuity.

'I would never have spoken to you of such things if I had not been certain that you were party to them already,' he continued. 'Tell me I am not wrong, Frances?'

Slowly, she shook her head, and lowered her gaze to the ground.

'No, Father,' she whispered. 'But I have only just discovered them – even though I have known one of those involved since coming to court. I grew to trust him, to—'

Tears were streaming down her face now. Sir Thomas drew her to him. She resisted at first, but the familiar comfort of his embrace soon overcame her. She sank against him, and he wrapped his cloak around her so that it covered them both. For several minutes, neither spoke as Frances gave vent to the grief that had been welling inside her ever since she had learned of Tom's betrayal.

'One of your earliest letters mentioned Tom Wintour,' her father said at last. She could feel his warm breath on her hair. 'He is a man of great courage, as well as faith, and would venture his life in this cause.'

Frances drew away from him.

'Would that he had as much honesty.' She saw her father's eyes widen at the bitterness in her voice. 'He has played me false for many months,' she continued. 'I had thought him a dear friend, when in truth I hardly knew him.'

'The truth carries great danger, Frances,' her father replied quietly. 'He was trying to protect you – as I have been. I wanted you to remain at Longford, safe from all harm.' A shadow crossed his face. 'But your uncle would not veer from his course. He will stop at nothing to restore the family's position – though God knows we seek no favour at this king's hands.'

'But why put me in danger now, when I suspected nothing of this plot?'

'Because the time is drawing near when we must act, Frances. As soon as the plague has receded, Parliament will be convened. But before that, the princess must be taken from London, to ensure her safety – and those who attend her,' he added, looking at Frances closely.

She nodded.

'I am to accompany Her Highness to Coombe Abbey before the week is out. We will be guests of Lord Harington.'

'Good, good,' Sir Thomas remarked. 'Sir John will ensure that you are comfortably housed. I believe he can be trusted to play his part.'

'And what of my part, Father?' Frances demanded. 'Though I have as much cause as any to revile the king and his court, I did not choose to become involved in this conspiracy. Am I to be as great a puppet as the princess?'

'You must only continue to do your duty and attend her.' He held her face in his hands and looked at her imploringly. 'Mind me, Frances. Speak of this to nobody. Commit nothing to paper. If this plot should fail, you must be free from suspicion.'

'And you, Father?' she asked softly, her brow creased with concern.

Sir Thomas smiled.

'Nobody will think to come looking in this backwater. I am quite safe – your mother too.' His face clouded over again. 'She knows nothing of this, Frances. Neither must she.'

Frances nodded, but continued to look at him uncertainly. 'Richmond is not so very far from court, Father. And our family is already marked out for being of the old faith. You are in as great a danger as I – if not more so.'

He held her gaze as he reached out to take her hands in his. 'I have weathered greater storms than this, Frances. Although we enjoyed the late queen's favour, there were those about her who were bent on destroying every Catholic in the kingdom. I have learned the art of discretion. If any of Cecil's men paid us a visit here, they would not find so much as an Agnus Dei to support their suspicions.' He squeezed her hands. 'You must have no fear for me, or your mother. I will keep us both safe, Frances.'

He paused, his gaze intensifying.

'Will you do your part, Fran? Without the princess, our cause is surely lost.'

She closed her eyes as she tried to make sense of everything she had heard in the last few minutes, the last day. Though she was still reeling from her father's revelations, she felt a sudden surge of bitterness that this weak and perverted king should dictate the consciences of his subjects, deprive them of the comforts of their faith. It would have been better for England if he had never come to the throne.

Or that he might be removed from it.

Her eyes snapped open. Was this plot really so wicked? Her heart quickened in time with her thoughts. God could surely not approve of such a cruel and twisted ruler, one who persecuted his subjects at every turn. A vivid image of the witch pricker's blade suddenly filled her mind, the sharp point piercing her skin, a thick droplet of blood weaving its way down her chest. Wincing, she turned her thoughts to the tempest that had been visited upon the anniversary procession, the failed harvests that had followed in its wake, the thousands of pour souls who had perished in the plague. God had surely shown His displeasure already.

'I will, Father,' she said at last.

Her voice sounded different to her ears, as if a stranger had spoken those words. She saw her father's shoulders sag, and his eyes glistened as he looked back at her.

Raising her gaze to the leaden sky, Frances shivered, suddenly aware of the cold. Her leather soles offered little protection against the frosty ground, and her borrowed clothes, though fine, were not made to keep out the winter chill.

'Come, my love,' her father said. 'Your mother will be angry with me for keeping you from her, and even more so if you have caught a chill.'

He held out his arm, and Frances threaded hers through it. As they walked slowly back towards the house, she hardly noticed as the first flakes of snow began to fall.

CHAPTER 32

5 February

Frances watched as the last of the wagons was loaded with the princess's belongings. Though nothing could eclipse the scale and splendour of the late queen's removes, she was still surprised by the quantity of furniture, hangings, clothes, and other accoutrements deemed necessary for her mistress's comfort during her stay at Coombe Abbey. The preparations had already been underway by the time that Frances had returned to Hampton Court, and her absence had been barely remarked upon in the frenzy of packing Elizabeth's belongings, and planning the journey ahead.

'We are to stay first at Windsor, and then Oxford,' the princess told her excitedly as they sat in the carriage, swathed in furs. It was for good reason that most removes were made in summer, although the frosts had made the ground so hard that the roads might be more passable. 'We will also visit Chastleton and Stratford before we get to Coombe. Sir Everard says that the people will flock to see me, and that our way will be lit by beacons and bonfires.'

Elizabeth's face was aglow as she imagined the adoration with which she would be greeted.

'I hope he is right, Your Grace,' Frances replied. 'Though you must not think badly of those who choose to stay in the warmth of their homes. This winter is the coldest we have had in many years.'

The princess seemed too distracted to pay attention to her words. She was fumbling about for her satin purse, which lay buried beneath the furs.

'There it is!' she cried in triumph, and took out a small folded note. 'I was going to send this to Sir Everard when we arrive in Warwickshire, but I have a mind to give it to him straight away, lest he thinks me ungrateful for all the care he has shown during these preparations for our journey. Frances – will you take it to him?'

'Now, Your Highness?' she asked in surprise. 'But we are almost ready to leave.'

'It will only take a moment, Frances. He was so distressed at our parting that I would like to offer him some cheer.'

She was already peeling the furs back from Frances's lap as she spoke. With a sigh, Frances took the note and disembarked from the carriage. She walked briskly along the path that led back to the gatehouse, and asked the porter to direct her to Sir Everard's lodgings. To her relief, they were a short distance away in Base Court. Frances wondered briefly how Sir Everard had been able to secure accommodation in the quarter that was usually reserved for the most highly favoured of the king's guests, especially when he had arrived so long after the rest of the court.

Frances passed under an archway in the middle of the west range of lodgings, and walked along to the end of the corridor, as directed by the porter. A soft light spilled under the door of Sir Everard's rooms, and, as she drew closer, she could hear low voices. She slowed her step and padded quietly towards the sound, heart thumping.

'Everything is made ready, my lord.' Sir Everard's voice, though soft, was clearly discernible.

'Good.'

There was something familiar about the second, though it was so quiet that Frances had to strain to hear.

'And in Westminster?' Sir Everard asked.

There was a long pause. Frances could not be sure if she had missed the reply. She leaned closer so that her face was pressed against the door. The movement caused a floorboard to creak. She stepped backwards and held her breath. She could hear the sound of a chair scraping across the floor, followed by a scuffle of footsteps. Quickly, she knocked on the door before those within could accuse her of loitering there. It was opened a crack. Sir Everard peered out into the gloom.

'Ah, Lady Frances,' he said, his features relaxing. 'What a pleasant surprise. I had thought you and the princess were already departed for Windsor.'

He made no move to open the door any further.

'Forgive the intrusion, Sir Everard,' Frances replied, 'but the princess was most desirous that you should have this note, before we leave the palace.'

She saw a flash of a smile, and as he reached to take the paper from her hand, the door drifted open a little. Before he could slide his foot across to stop it, Frances darted a furtive look inside the chamber. A large parchment was spread out on the table. It seemed to be a plan of some sort, but the contents were obscured from view. Aside from that, she could see two goblets in the centre of the table, and a candle with smoke rising the wick, as if it had just been snuffed out. Though she strained to hear, there was no sound within the chamber. Whoever was hiding there must be used to concealment, she realised.

'Her Highness is most kind to think of me at such a time. Please convey my deepest thanks, Lady Frances.'

He showed no inclination to open the note, but swept a low bow, as if to bring their conference to an end. As he did so, Frances caught the scent of something familiar. Ambergris and cloves. Her scalp prickled. She inhaled again, quietly, trying to recall where she had smelt it before.

Sir Everard gave a small cough. Frances eyed him closely for a moment, stole one last glance over his shoulder, then bobbed a curtsey and walked quickly back along the corridor. She could feel him watching her all the way.

'What did he say?' Elizabeth demanded, as soon as Frances stepped back into the carriage. 'He must have been heartened by my words. How did he reply?'

'He did not open the note in my presence, Your Highness,' Frances answered quietly.

'Oh. Indeed?' The princess looked crestfallen.

'No doubt he wished to do so in private, so that he might savour its contents,' Frances soothed.

Elizabeth brightened a little.

'Perhaps you are right, Frances.' She leaned forward and lowered the glass pane. An icy breeze whipped through the carriage as the princess peered out towards the palace, no doubt hoping to see Sir Everard hurrying towards her, Frances mused, drawing up her furs so that they covered her shoulders. She saw Elizabeth shudder, but the girl continued to look out of the window until their carriage lurched forward, signalling that their long journey had begun.

Frances felt her eyes grow heavy again as the carriage jolted along the narrow track. They had been travelling for five days now, and though they had taken frequent rests, and had been comfortably housed in the various estates selected in advance by the Lord Chamberlain's staff, the journey had been wearisome. Elizabeth had soon tired of it, the novelty of the remove worn thin by the cold and discomfort that it entailed. Neither had there been any sign of the crowds that Sir Everard had promised. A cluster of people from the locality had stood shivering by the gatehouse of each estate, cheering feebly as they passed, and then scurrying home to the comfort of their meagre stoves.

The train of wagons bearing the princess's belongings and those of her attendants was now far ahead of them, having made fewer stops so that the contents could be unpacked at the abbey ready for Elizabeth's arrival. The thought of her bed being made ready with the coverlet that she had brought from Longford was a great solace to Frances as she shifted uncomfortably in her seat. Though it afforded less warmth than the furs inside the carriage, she longed for its familiar scent of lavender and rose oil, and to run her fingers along the delicate embroidery of its borders. She must seek what comfort she could during the days and weeks ahead. Since that meeting in Westminster, everything had seemed so fraught with danger and uncertainty. And, though the princess was being conveyed to Coombe for her safety, Frances could not shake off the feeling that they were riding towards the heart of the coming storm.

The sun was beginning to sink towards the horizon as the carriage reached the brow of a hill. The coachman drew it to a stop so that the horses could take some water after the long climb. Elizabeth reached down and pulled out a rolled-up parchment that she had tucked under her seat. It was the itinerary for their journey, with a beautifully drawn map to indicate the name of each stopping place, together with the towns that they would pass on the way. She rubbed the windowpane, and squinted out against the dazzling rays of the sun, then consulted her map again.

'That must be Stow – see there, to the west,' she said, pointing her finger at a large steeple on the horizon. 'Chastleton must be very close by now, thank goodness. How my bones ache!'

Frances rubbed her neck and smiled.

'I will also be glad of a rest, ma'am. I hope this host is as welcoming as the others.'

The princess studied the itinerary again.

'Do you know Robert Catesby?'

Frances started, her heart suddenly racing. She forced herself to take a breath before replying.

'Only by name, Your Highness,' she replied at last. She studied the princess's face for any sign of suspicion, but the girl seemed entirely at ease. 'Why do you ask?'

'Because he is our host, of course,' Elizabeth retorted with a laugh. 'Really, Frances, I think we have been on the road for too long. It has quite dulled your wits.'

Frances reeled. She had not supposed Catesby to be a man of such means that he could host a royal visit. These occasions were enough to bankrupt all but the richest of landlords. She looked down at his estate. The parkland seemed well kept, though not extensive, and the house itself was more of a manor than the grand residences that they had been used to. It was an odd choice for their stay, especially when there must be other, larger houses nearby. She fell silent, considering who might have directed that it be included. Catesby had hinted that some 'great protector' was involved in their schemes. That he had secured a visit from the princess made Frances think this was more than just a boast.

CHAPTER 33

10 February

They passed the remainder of the journey to Chastleton in silence, Frances lost in thought, and the princess busily pinching her cheeks and smoothing down stray hairs as she glanced in the small looking glass that she had brought along for the purpose. As soon as the carriage had drawn to a stop, a smartly dressed groom opened the door and made a deep bow, then held out his hand so that the princess might climb down. Frances followed close behind.

They walked towards the house, their path lit by braziers on either side. The warmth was so welcome that Frances was tempted to tarry for a while, but the princess walked briskly on, eager to meet their new host. A torch blazed on either side of the doorway, illuminating the soft yellow brickwork. The few windows were small, and the walls were thick and solidly built, dating back to a time when even manor houses were fashioned more for defence than for comfort.

The figure of a man was silhouetted in the doorway. Any hope that it might have been another of the same name was dashed. Frances recognised his small, slender frame and proud bearing at once.

'Your Grace,' he said, his voice as smooth as silk. 'It is a great honour to receive you in my humble home.'

He knelt to kiss the princess's ring. Frances caught her pleasure at his exaggerated deference.

'We are delighted to make your acquaintance, Mr Catesby,' she trilled. 'And thankful to break our long journey in your home.'

Catesby bowed again, then motioned for the princess to proceed into the house. Frances made to follow, but he stepped briskly in front of her so that she was obliged to fall in behind. She kept her gaze fixed on his boots as she followed in his wake, anger mingling with apprehension.

In the dining chamber, a rich feast had been laid out on the long table, and a fire roared in the grate. The smell of roasted meats filled the air, and, despite herself, Frances felt a pang of hunger. The princess took her seat at the head of the table, and Frances sat on the chair to her right. Catesby remained standing, and gave a small cough.

'Your Highness, with your permission, I would very much like to introduce you to some acquaintances. Some of them will be known to you already, but others are most desirous to meet you.'

Elizabeth's face glowed at the compliment.

'Please, Mr Catesby, show them in,' she said in her most imperious tone.

Catesby nodded to one of the attendants, who left to fetch the guests. Frances held her breath as they heard footsteps approaching. They stopped on the other side of the doorway so that their host could introduce them one by one. Catesby was determined to display as great a ceremony as might be found at court, it seemed. But then she wondered if there were other motives behind these careful introductions. He might wish to ensure that Elizabeth remembered their names so that she would not be alarmed when they met again.

'Francis Tresham, Your Highness,' Catesby announced as a small, stout man entered the room. He was in his mid-thirties, Frances judged, and his hair was flecked with grey at the temples. As he stepped forward to kiss the princess's hand, she noticed that his own trembled slightly.

Tresham was followed by two brothers, Jack and Christopher Wright, and a tall, thickset man named John Grant. Frances took a sip of wine and breathed deeply. She looked up as the next man entered, and her heart began to race again. He was of medium build, and had an open, honest face – not quite handsome, but pleasant nonetheless. He had blond hair, and a neatly trimmed beard, and his large brown eyes were grave. Even though they had never met, Frances knew him before Catesby had made the introduction.

'Robert Wintour, Your Highness.'

The princess regarded him closely as he knelt for her blessing. 'Are you Tom's cousin? I cannot think you are brothers, though you look alike, for he would surely have mentioned you.'

'I did not wish to try your patience with such inconsequential matters.'

Frances turned at his voice. He was standing in the doorway, hat in hand. He swept a bow to the princess, a playful smile on his lips. As he straightened, Frances noticed him wince slightly. He looked tired, and, though smartly dressed, there was something dishevelled about his appearance. She wondered how many days' riding it had taken to reach Chastleton from wherever he had been hiding.

'Tom!' the princess exclaimed with obvious delight. 'How we have missed you. Have we not, Frances?'

Frances nodded mutely and forced a smile. Though she avoided looking at him, she could feel his eyes on her.

'Come, Kit,' he said to the younger Wright, 'you would not deprive me of a seat close to the princess?'

To Frances's dismay, the young man, who seemed somewhat in awe of Tom, hastened to his feet and moved to a place at the far end of the table. Tom grinned at him, and took his seat next to Frances. She was so distracted that she had not noticed there was another guest waiting to be presented.

'Your Highness, our merry company is completed by this gentleman,' Catesby announced. All eyes turned to the man standing awkwardly at the doorway, fumbling with his hat. Of a similar age to the rest, he had jet-black hair that touched his shoulders, and a long pointed beard. He appeared lithe and strong, and, for all his uncertainty, he held himself erect, like a soldier. Frances wondered if he had seen service with Tom in the Netherlands.

'Please—' the princess said, gesturing for him to make his obeisance.

His eyes darted this way and that as he walked briskly forward.

'Guido Fawkes, Your Highness,' he said as he knelt before her. His voice was gruffer than Frances had expected, and he spoke with a strong Yorkshire accent. After he had taken the last vacant seat, Catesby gave a cough, and the company fell silent.

'Your Highness, I cannot let a morsel of this humble feast pass my lips until I have thanked God for your presence here in my home and amongst my friends, whom you will soon realise are your most devoted subjects.'

Elizabeth inclined her head.

'Lord God, we humbly offer our heartfelt thanks for delivering Her most gracious Highness the Princess Elizabeth to us this night,' Catesby began. 'I pray that we may serve her for the rest of our lives, and that she – and You – will look kindly upon our endeavours.'

Frances felt her palms grow damp as she pressed them together.

'Amen,' the company proclaimed in unison. To Frances, it sounded like a battle cry.

Elizabeth was beaming as they began their feast. She talked animatedly throughout, turning from Catesby to Tom, revelling in their attentions and those of their companions, who were clearly astonished by her conversational abilities. As Frances watched them, she felt as if she was looking at a once beautiful painting that had been stripped of its dazzling oils to reveal a roughly drawn tableau of flattery and deceit. Every word they spoke carried another meaning for her from the one that the princess heard. Glancing at Tom, who seemed rapt by a story that Elizabeth was telling, she chided herself for having been as easily taken in as an eight-year-old child.

Frances remained silent during the meal that followed. She kept her eyes on her plate, though she ate little of the succession of dishes that were set down before them. She was glad that the conversation centred around the princess, who was growing increasingly animated, laughing uproariously at every new jest. As Frances picked at a piece of prune tart, she was suddenly aware that Tom was watching her. She took a sip of wine, then turned to say something to the princess, but the girl was now deep in discussion with Catesby.

'You must not think that it was all artifice.'

Frances did not look at him, but he spoke so quietly that she was obliged to incline her head towards him.

'Please, Frances,' he said, when she did not answer. He reached for her hand under the table, and she felt the familiar warmth of his palm as it closed over her fingers. She lowered her eyes for a moment, then snatched her hand away. The movement caught Catesby's attention. He darted a look at Tom, and his smile became fixed as the princess continued to regale him with her story.

'We cannot talk here,' Tom whispered. 'Meet me in the knot garden when the princess has retired.'

Frances glanced across at Catesby. He was talking animatedly again, and Elizabeth was listening and laughing, her eyes sparkling. For a moment, Frances imagined her seated on a throne, her small frame dwarfed by its high back and ornate canopy, a crown being slowly lowered onto her head. She felt an unexpected surge of excitement.

'I will make no promises,' she replied quietly.

She passed the rest of the meal in silence. When at last the spiced wine had been served and the wafers had been eaten, Catesby stood to make a final toast to the princess. Her cheeks were flushed, Frances noticed, and she giggled as the company raised their glasses in sombre reverence. She would take little coaxing to sleep tonight.

At the conclusion of the toast, Elizabeth got to her feet a little unsteadily. Frances moved swiftly to her side, and discreetly placed the girl's hand on her arm so that she could guide her from the room with as much dignity as possible. Each man bowed low as they passed, and the princess beamed with delight.

An attendant showed them to the princess's room, which was beautifully furnished, with a large tester bed and fine tapestries. Two bay windows looked out over the formal gardens at the front of the house. Elizabeth's coffers had already been unpacked, Frances noticed, and when the attendant had left, she fetched her nightclothes from the wardrobe. The princess sank down onto the bed.

'What a fine host Mr Catesby is,' she said, rubbing her eyes.

'He is very attentive, my lady,' Frances agreed, as she unlaced her mistress's gown with deft fingers. Elizabeth was like a ragdoll now, and her arms flopped back to her sides after Frances had pulled her shift over her head. She worked quickly and silently so that the girl was soon tucked up under the soft covers of the bed. She was already asleep by the time Frances had finished folding her clothes into the empty coffers. Frances padded silently over to the bed and looked at her for a moment. The princess's expression was so peaceful as she lay there, her tiny frame swathed in the rich coverlet. She was a child once more. Frances bent to kiss her smooth forehead. It seemed almost impossible that such murderous schemes were taking shape around this innocent girl.

'God keep you safe,' Frances whispered, then stole silently out of the room.

As she closed the door carefully behind her, she hesitated. Her own room was just along the corridor. She could go straight to it now and enjoy the solitude and rest that she had been craving ever since their arrival. She crossed to the small window that looked out over the privy gardens at the back of the house. They were swathed in light from the moon, its silvery rays picking out the dark hedgerows and neat gravel paths.

Suddenly, she saw him. He was standing underneath an archway, and was so still that he could have been mistaken for one of the statues that were situated around the grounds. She held her breath and stepped back into the shadows. Every nerve in her body seemed to prickle as she stood there, paralysed by indecision. Her instinct was to go to him, but fear prevented her – fear not of his actions but of her own, she realised. A few more moments passed. The ticking of the large clock at the end of the hallway seemed to taunt her. With a sudden impulse, she drew on her cloak and ran silently along the corridor and down the stairs.

The click of the latch as she let herself out seemed to echo around the garden. She stood still, listening, and gathered her cloak against the biting chill of the night air. After a pause, she thought she heard a sound like the scraping of a boot on gravel, but then the garden fell silent once more. She walked across the grass towards the marble archway, which seemed to glimmer with an ethereal light. Her heartbeat sounded in her ears as she drew close to it. But he was no longer there. She took a small step forward. Beyond the archway was a series of hedges, which she supposed was a maze. The hedges were so tall and close together that the moonlight illuminated only their uppermost branches; the path that threaded between them was shrouded in darkness.

Frances looked behind her, but the garden was empty, the house silent. Turning back towards the maze, she took another step forward, reaching out to either side of her so that the hedges might guide her. This was madness, she chided herself. She might get lost in here, and have to wait until dawn to find her way out, by which time the princess might have been taken far away by Catesby and his men. She hesitated, then drew in a breath and moved deeper into the labyrinth. The darkness enfolded her, and she felt as if she were moving in a dream. As she took a few tentative steps, the sharp scent of yew filled her nostrils and her fingertips were pricked and scratched by the neatly clipped branches. He could not be in here, she reasoned, as she moved further into the maze. He must have moved to a different part of the garden, or abandoned the idea of meeting altogether. She looked over her shoulder, and realised that she would not be able to find her way back now. There was no choice but to go on.

As she turned back into the gloom, she caught the familiar scent. He was here. She stood still and listened, not sure if the sound of breathing was her own. Tentatively, she reached out her hands, but felt only the prickle of the hedges on either side of her. She took a step forward and gasped as a cold hand suddenly grasped her wrist. His other hand stopped her mouth from making another sound. Slowly, he released his grip, and Frances let out a long breath.

'Forgive me. We must not be discovered,' he whispered. She could feel his warm breath on her face.

'What do you want of me?' Frances demanded.

He placed a finger to her mouth and held it there. She could feel that his face was very close to hers now.

'Your forgiveness,' he answered quietly. 'I did not wish to deceive you. If I had told you of the plot sooner, I would have placed you in great danger – especially as Cecil was already watching you. I had to wait until it was certain that you would leave court with the princess.'

'And now I am meekly to play my part by keeping the princess safe and compliant while you murder her father and brother?'

Tom fell silent.

'I will not force you to act against your will – or your conscience,' he said at last. 'But you must see how diseased this realm has become since the old queen's death. You have more cause than most to despise this king. Would that we had blown him back to his Scottish mountains before he had fixed his evil gaze upon you.'

She could feel his breath come quickly now, and he grasped both of her hands in his own. It was a few moments before he was able to speak again.

'Frances.' His voice was softer now. 'I know that you no longer trust me, but I beg you to see me as you once did, for you were not deceived. I love you as truly now as I did at the beginning.'

'That I do not doubt,' Frances replied bitterly.

Tom sighed, and scuffed the ground with his boot.

'I know you think that I have played you false, but I swear on my life that the only artifice was in concealing the plot from you.' He paused. 'I admit that I sought you out because of your position in the princess's household, but the more I came to know you, the more I craved your company for its own sake. You must believe me.'

He reached out and stroked her cheek. Frances closed her eyes and fought to steady her breathing. Reluctantly, she pulled away.

'I have lived too long at court to know truth from falsehood,' she said at last. 'I see how you and your companions beguile the princess with your honeyed words. How much easier it must be to seduce a lowly attendant.'

Tom did not answer. The bitterness of her words seemed to hang in the air as they stood in silence. Her eyes had become accustomed to the gloom, and she could see the outline of his face, but sensed rather than observed its pained expression. After a long pause, she sighed heavily.

'I will not betray you,' she said slowly. 'You speak truth about the king, and I hold no loyalty towards him after what he has done to me – and to many others besides. But my first duty is to the princess. If I believe her to be in danger, then I must act as my conscience dictates.'

Tom inclined his head.

'I can ask no more of you than that,' he said softly. He reached out for her again, but she drew back. She knew that if he touched her, she would not have the strength to resist him. With every fibre of her being, she longed to step forward and feel his arms encircle her, to stay here for ever locked in his embrace, hidden from the world beyond.

The sudden hooting of an owl as it flew overhead broke the enchantment. Startled, Frances turned to go.

'I may not see you for many weeks now,' Tom said.

She stopped, but did not turn around.

'I must leave before dawn – some of the others too. Parliament is likely to be convened any day now, so we will return to London. Catesby will follow as soon as the princess has departed.'

Frances nodded, but was unable to answer.

'God keep you safe,' he whispered, echoing the words she had spoken at the princess's bedside that night. Frances felt her heart lurch. Although he had seemed a stranger to her since that day at Westminster, now she felt a whisper of their former intimacy.

'And you,' she mouthed silently, then slipped away into the darkness.

CHAPTER 34

26 March

'She has marks all over her body, my lord. The Devil had easy work in concealing his.' His spittle flew into her face as he spoke.

'Then you must work all the harder to find it, Master Balfour.'

With a cry, Frances jolted awake. She sat up, and, with trembling hands, rubbed her eyes. Her skin was damp and hot, and her linen shift clung to her body. The smell was still in her nostrils, but she knew that when she breathed in again it would be gone, fading back into her subconscious with the rest of the dream.

Ambergris.

The sweet, cloying scent would have been overpowering had it not been mixed with the sharp tang of cloves. It was typical of the man who wore it that he should pay close attention to such trivial details as scent. Nothing escaped his notice.

Cecil.

The realisation smote her like a blow to the stomach. He had been Sir Everard's confidant on the day they had left Hampton Court. Her mind raced back to the dark corridor where she had stood, straining to listen. Closing her eyes, she imagined the door being opened by Sir Everard, the warm rush from the fire within, the scent of ambergris carried in its wake.

Her eyes sprang open. How could she not have recognised it before? She knew of no one else at court who wore the same fragrance. Yet he must do so sparingly, she realised, as she only recalled smelling it once before. The terror of that occasion must have caused her mind to bury the recollection.

She threw the covers off, and ran over to the dresser. Pulling out one drawer after another, she found her writing case at last. Her hands fumbled over the small wooden stopper on the inkpot. When at last she had released it, she jabbed her quill into the pot and began to write.

Thomas Wintour, Gray's Inn, London

Her usual neat script was reduced to a hasty scrawl, and she paused briefly to study it, fearing that the letter would not reach its destination. But there was no time to begin again, so she continued:

> *You must come to Coombe Abbey as soon as this letter reaches you. You are in great danger.*
> *F*

Frances folded the parchment and crossed to the fire so that she could melt the wax in the embers. Pressing her ring into the deep red liquid, she laid it on the dresser to set while she pulled on a simple woollen gown that required little lacing, and slipped her bare feet into her leather shoes. Twisting her hair up into a coif, she pinned it quickly into place, and drew on her cloak.

She picked up the letter and lightly prodded the seal, which was still warm. No matter – it would be set by the time she put it in the hands of the steward. She quietly let herself out of the room, and ran on tiptoe down the stairs to the entrance hall. The pale light of dawn was beginning to cast shadows on the pillars and flagstones, and Frances could just make out the door that led down into the servants' quarters. It gave an ominous creak as she pulled it open, and she held her breath as she listened for any movement above. Satisfied that the rest of the household was still asleep, she continued down the dark stone stairs.

At the bottom was a large parlour. In contrast to the upper quarters of the abbey, it was a hive of quiet activity, as the servants bustled this way and that, stoking up fires and ovens, kneading bread, filling ewers, and making myriad other preparations for the day ahead. They barely noticed her as she slipped into the room. She guessed that she must look like one of them in her simple apparel.

Having asked one of the servingwomen for directions to the steward's room, Frances made her way there. She knocked lightly on the door, and opened it, not pausing for an answer. A young man sat at a desk, writing entries in an account book. He looked up in surprise as she entered, and scrambled to his feet.

'Ma'am.'

'I apologise for troubling you at such an early hour, Mr Carter, but I have a letter that needs sending to London without delay.'

The man's eyes darted to the parchment in her hand. They narrowed briefly, but then he bowed and took it from her.

'Of course, my lady. I will see that it is dispatched.'

Frances hesitated, but decided not to press the point. She had clearly aroused enough suspicion already. Forcing a smile, she nodded her thanks and walked briskly out of the room.

Mounting the stairs back up to the entrance hall, she turned her thoughts to what else she could do. The note seemed so insubstantial. Would it be enough to make Tom abandon whatever he was engaged in and leave at once for Warwickshire? It might not even reach him. She had not seen nor heard from him since their clandestine meeting at Chastleton. Parliament had been postponed yet again, so he and his friends might have left the city – even the country, for all she knew. With a pang, she recalled the last words he had spoken to her. They seemed to take on an air of finality now. Pushing the thought away, she closed the heavy oak door behind her as quietly as she could, and began to climb the stairs back to her room.

'You are abroad early, Lady Frances.'

She froze. Turning, she saw Lord Harington step slowly from the shadows, leaning heavily on his stick.

'Good day, my lord. Forgive me – I hope I did not disturb your rest?'

He gave a weak smile of reassurance, but continued to regard her closely.

'One of the many trials of old age is to rob a man of sleep during night-time hours. Only when the sun is high in the sky, and the rest of the household is full of cheer and chatter, do I feel my eyes grow heavy. I fear I have been poor company for your mistress.'

'Not at all, my lord,' Frances said, returning his smile. 'You have been a most convivial and generous host. Her Grace and I have almost forgotten the diversions of the court, so richly have we been entertained here at Coombe.'

Harington waved away her compliment.

'It is nothing – to me, at least, if not to my cofferer,' he admitted ruefully. 'I am heartened that you and your mistress have not found life here too dull. There is a good deal less to converse about so far from London, where every day there is a new play to admire, a new fashion to emulate . . .' He trailed off as if losing his train of thought. Frances was just about to speak, when he continued: 'Or a new plot to uncover, eh, Lady Frances?'

His dark eyes seemed to bore into her very soul as they stood in silence for a few moments. Though Catesby had inferred that their host was privy to his conspiracy, she had not spoken of it since their arrival at Coombe. She had come to hope that he knew nothing about it, or of her own involvement.

The old man moved a few steps closer, and Frances noticed him wince every time his weight fell onto his right leg. A tincture of willow bark and dandelion would ease the pain from his swollen joints, but she knew better now than to offer her skills.

'There has always been talk of plotters and rebels, even in the late queen's time,' she replied at last.

Harington's eyes wrinkled in amusement, and he nodded.

'I know that better than most, having taken the most danger-ous of them to her death,' he said, with a hint of his accustomed pride. He paused. 'Lady Frances, if ever you require assistance, you must tell me. I think you know that I can be trusted.'

She inclined her head.

'Thank you, Lord Harington.' She hesitated, then bobbed a quick curtsey, and began to climb the stairs. 'Pray excuse me, but the princess will be awake by now, so I must attend her.'

With every step she took, she could feel his eyes upon her back.

'I have a fancy to ride this afternoon, Frances,' the princess announced as they were eating breakfast.

Frances looked out at the gathering clouds and frowned.

'That might not be wise, Your Highness. Perhaps we could ride tomorrow, if the weather has improved?'

Elizabeth raised her chin and clenched her small hands into fists.

'Nonsense!' she declared. 'The wind will soon blow those clouds away, and we will not feel the cold when we are riding. Besides,' she added with an impish grin, 'you have my permission to wrap me in my warmest cloak, if it will serve to brighten your face.'

Frances sighed quietly. She knew it was pointless to raise any further objection. Her mistress turned to their host.

'Lord Harington, will you accompany us?'

'I fear that I would only hinder your progress, Your Highness,' he said with a regretful shake of his head. 'I require the comforts of a carriage these days.'

The princess looked crestfallen. Frances knew that she craved the company of gentlemen, and that even the aged baron would suffice if there was nobody younger to take his place.

'But might I suggest a destination for your ride?' he continued. 'I believe you are acquainted with Robert Catesby, Your Highness? His estate is only fifteen miles from here. It is a very pleasant ride – even in inclement weather,' he added, shooting a look at Frances.

Elizabeth brightened immediately.

'What an excellent idea!' she declared, clapping her small hands together. 'Catesby told me about Ashby St Ledgers when we met at Chastleton. It is one of the oldest houses in the kingdom. It will provide a history lesson, as well as fresh air, Frances,' she persisted.

Frances felt a twinge of foreboding, but knew that the princess would not be persuaded against the idea.

'I will prepare your riding clothes, Your Highness.'

Elizabeth crammed another piece of herring into her mouth and drained the contents of her glass, then bade Lord Harington farewell.

The horses were already prepared by the time that Frances and her mistress arrived at the stables. She could not fault their host's efficiency, although she wondered at its cause. Ignoring the groom's proffered hand, Elizabeth climbed the mounting block and jumped lightly onto the side-saddle. With a sharp tap of her heels, she cantered off down the drive, Frances following close behind. By the time they reached the cobbled bridge that led out into the parkland, she had caught up with her mistress, and they rode on side by side.

The wind whipped around them as they cantered across the gently undulating fields that lay beyond the abbey. The cold air made Frances's eyes water and her cheeks sting, but she felt the familiar surge of excitement as her horse broke into a gallop. Elizabeth cried out in delight as she too gathered speed, and together they raced along the ridgeway that followed the line of the hills south-eastward towards Ashby St Ledgers.

By the time that the tall stone chimneys of the house came into view on the horizon, the sky had become leaden, and the first drops of rain had begun to fall. Frances dug her heels into her horse's flank, and it lurched forward again, lowering its head to gather more speed. The rain was falling faster now, and before long it had become a torrent, almost blinding Frances as they raced towards the gatehouse. She was relieved to see a light blazing in the window of the lodge, and as they approached, a porter emerged, scowling at the unexpected visitors who had brought him out in such weather.

'The master only arrived yesterday. The house is not made ready for visitors,' he said gruffly as he helped them from their mounts.

'The princess intends only a brief visit,' Frances replied.

The man looked stricken, and stumbled into an awkward bow.

'Forgive me, Your Highness. I did not know—'

Elizabeth waved away his apology. Handing him her reins, she strode purposefully towards the house, drawing up the hood of her cloak against the driving rain. A housekeeper was waiting by the door, and ushered them into a parlour, where a fire roared in the grate. She seemed a good deal less surprised to see them, Frances thought, as she helped the princess out of her cloak and hung it over a chair close to the fire with her own.

Elizabeth glanced around the room. Dark oak panelling lined the walls, which were bare of pictures or hangings. There was just one small window, and it was set so high into the wall that it afforded a view only of the sky, which was still leaden.

'It is rather a gloomy place, is it not Frances? I had expected Mr Catesby to have better taste.'

'Perhaps he spends little time here,' Frances replied quietly. 'Chastleton is more spacious, and only a day's ride away.'

'You are quite right, Lady Frances – as ever.'

They both swung around in surprise. Catesby was leaning against the doorframe, an expression of wry amusement on his face. The princess had the good grace to blush, but quickly recovered herself.

'Do you creep up on all your guests like that, Catesby?' she demanded.

His grin widened, and he swept an elaborate bow.

'Forgive me, Your Highness, but the sight of you standing in my humble parlour was so bewitching that I was loath to disturb you, lest you should fade away like a dream.'

Elizabeth smiled broadly, immediately placated.

'But you are right, Your Highness,' he continued. 'It is altogether too gloomy in here. Please – join me in the hall. A mutual acquaintance is waiting to pay his respects to you.'

Frances's heart began to pound. She had only sent the note two days before, so he could not have acted upon it already. But if chance had brought him here, she might seize the opportunity to talk to him, to warn him.

The princess sprang up, delighted at the prospect of a surprise. Catesby led them back into the entrance hall and across to a large doorway. Frances heard a chair being pulled back, and she held her breath as they entered the hall.

Sir Everard's face was swathed in smiles as he stood there waiting to greet them. Frances felt her heart lurch with disappointment and alarm. She tried desperately to gather her thoughts. Could she trust Catesby with her secret instead? No. For all she knew, he was in league with Cecil too. But she also knew that her instinctive dislike of him might have more to do with the part that he had played in deceiving her.

Her mind still racing, she lowered her gaze as Sir Everard walked towards them, and hardly heard the greeting that he exchanged with the princess.

'Fortune smiles upon us, does it not Catesby?' he said, when they were all seated. 'We had planned to seek Lord Harington's permission to visit you at Coombe, yet here you are now.'

A sudden flash of lightning illuminated the room, followed by a low rumble of thunder.

'What a tempest you have travelled through, Your Highness,' Catesby remarked, his face a mask of concern. 'You cannot think of returning today?'

'The storm will pass soon enough,' Frances cut in. 'And it is but a short ride back to the abbey.'

Elizabeth's face fell.

'Well, we shall at least stay to dine with you,' she said, shooting a peevish look at Frances. 'Now, tell me, what news do you have of court?'

Tracy Borman

'The king your father is in excellent health and spirits, thanks to the many opportunities he has taken to hunt of late,' Sir Everard reported. 'I believe that even now he is engaged in the chase at Oatlands.'

'Is the court not in London? We had heard that Parliament would soon be convened,' Frances interrupted briskly.

'Alas no, Lady Frances. Every day seems to bring a fresh reason for postponement. Though the plague has abated, the king does not seem minded to return to London quite yet.'

'And my mother?' the princess asked. 'I trust she is well?'

Frances noticed the anxiety on the girl's face. The queen would be in her confinement now, and her daughter still had nightmares about the baby that had bled away.

'Very well, Your Highness. She spends most of her time at Greenwich, and seems to take great delight in it – though of course she misses you greatly. The princes offer some consolation for your absence, but she must soon bid them farewell too as she enters her confinement,' Sir Everard replied with a sad smile.

Elizabeth bit her lip and looked down at her hands.

'But how much sweeter the reunion will be for these long weeks of separation,' Catesby observed. 'When the queen next sees you, she will be so proud of what you have become.'

Frances caught the look that the two men exchanged.

'Does my Lord Salisbury also reside at Oatlands?' She directed the question at Sir Everard, and watched closely as he considered his reply.

'I am not privy to the Earl of Salisbury's movements, Lady Frances,' he said airily. 'Though I do not believe he is with the king at present.'

'Perhaps he is at Whitehall, making plans for Parliament – and all that will follow?' Frances persisted.

Catesby shifted in his seat.

'I did not realise you took such a close interest in the earl's business, Lady Frances,' Sir Everard replied smoothly. 'He would be most flattered, I'm sure.'

She looked at him coldly.

'No more than you do, Sir Everard.'

The silence was broken by a clap of thunder, much louder this time. Catesby placed a reassuring hand on the princess's shoulder.

'The storm is drawing closer, Your Grace,' he said quietly. 'But we will keep you safe.'

CHAPTER 35

12 April

Frances turned her face up to the sun and felt the first warm breath of spring. The rain had finally cleared, and it was a glorious day. As she and the princess strolled by the river that ran along the edge of Lord Harington's estate, she felt the familiar contentment at being surrounded by nature. The monks had chosen the site well all those centuries ago. As well as the practical advantages of its position at the top of a valley, with fresh water in plentiful supply and woodlands on either side, there was a tranquillity about it that cannot have failed to inspire their devotions. She breathed deeply and pushed away the fears that played constantly on her mind so that she could enjoy a fleeting moment of peace.

Elizabeth occasionally stooped down and plucked a blade of grass, idly braiding them together as they walked. She seemed to be thriving in this rural idyll, Frances thought, as she looked fondly down at her. She had grown tall these past weeks, her irrepressible energy tempered by elegance. Even now, when she was at leisure away from the prying eyes of the court, she walked with an unmistakably regal bearing. Catesby was right. Elizabeth would make a fine queen.

Once it had taken hold, the notion had filled Frances with a growing anticipation – even impatience – to see this promising young girl crowned in place of her father. Her initial horror upon discovering the plot had had more to do with Tom's betrayal, she realised, than the scheme itself. The shock of her father's revelations had also abated, and she had spent many hours reflecting upon the clues to his faith that had existed at Longford, if only she had looked for them.

Though she flinched from the idea of the bloodshed that she knew the plot would lead to, it was surely a lesser evil than allowing this devil of a king to torture and murder hundreds more in the name of God. And if Tom and his companions succeeded, then she might serve Elizabeth as queen in a court free from the debauchery and repression into which it had fallen.

'What do you think of Sir Everard?' Elizabeth asked as she studied her braiding, a slow flush creeping across her cheeks.

The mention of his name jolted Frances from her reverie. The plotters did not yet know there was an informant in their midst. Sir Everard was no doubt keeping Cecil abreast of their every move, yet she had apparently been unable to get word to Tom – her note had gone unanswered. The reminder of her powerlessness smote her like a blow, and for a moment she was unable to answer the princess.

'He seems a charming young gentleman – though I hardly know him, Your Grace,' she replied at length. The princess did not catch the coldness in her voice.

'Lord Harington tells me that he has a wife, and that they have been married for ten years, though he is but twenty-four years old. I wonder why he never brings her to court?'

'Many wives are content to live in the peace of their estates, away from the vanity and backbiting of court,' Frances remarked, with more bitterness than she intended.

Elizabeth jerked her head up in surprise.

'You cannot mean that, Frances? You, who have lived so many of your days at court? All of life is there. The revels, the feasting, the dancing . . . I could not wish myself anywhere else.'

Frances bit her lip. She had already said too much, and could not expect a girl of eight to share her cynicism. She had been about the same age when her mother had first introduced her to the old queen's court. It was as if she had been transported into a magical world, with tapestries that glittered like jewels, and dazzling gowns that dripped with diamonds and pearls.

'Forgive me, Your Highness,' she said at last. 'I was raised in the countryside, far from court, and still feel most at home there.'

Elizabeth smiled, and they lapsed back into silence. When they reached the bridge at the top of the driveway, they both paused at the sound of horses' hooves. Frances shielded her eyes as she peered into the distance. She could just make out the figure of a horseman riding along the driveway, a small cloud of dust following in his wake. Instinctively, she put her arm around the princess's shoulders, but the girl sprang free and began to stride along the drive, eager to find out the identity of this unexpected visitor.

As he drew close, Frances saw that he was wearing the queen's livery. She felt a mixture of relief and apprehension. His breeches and cloak were splattered with mud, and the hair that showed under his cap was damp with sweat. Quickly, he dismounted and knelt before the princess.

'Your Highness,' he said, removing his cap.

Frances noticed that Elizabeth's hands trembled as she bade him stand.

'I bring joyous news,' he continued breathlessly. 'The queen your mother is delivered of a fair daughter. Both are well.'

The princess's face lit up at once.

'A sister!' she exclaimed, clasping her hands together and turning gleeful eyes to Frances. 'God has answered my prayers.'

Frances's heart swelled to see the girl so happy, and she uttered a silent prayer of thanks for the queen's safe delivery.

'You are to return to London for the christening, Your Highness. I am to accompany you – and Lady Frances, of course,' he added, with a brief bow to her attendant.

Elizabeth looked set to burst with joy as she reached out and clasped her hands. Frances forced a smile.

'It is wonderful news indeed, Your Highness,' she said quietly. Then, turning to the messenger: 'Are we to remain in London for long after the christening?'

'I do not know, my lady. My orders were only to convey you there without delay.'

'Of course we shall stay!' the princess exclaimed. 'You heard Sir Everard say how much Mama has missed me, and I have had the same from her own hand. I wager that once we are back at court, she will not want to part with me again.'

Frances did not reply, but thanked the messenger, and invited him to take some refreshment in the house. The princess was already walking briskly back along the drive by the time he had untethered his horse. With a sigh, Frances gathered up her skirts and followed in her wake.

The Thames snaked into the distance, its waters reflecting the slate grey sky. People had gathered along the banks at the sight of the royal barge as it made its way from Westminster, and every now and then there was a cry of 'God save Your Highness!' The princess beamed with delight and gave a graceful wave each time. But something about their manner made Frances feel uneasy. Their faces seemed watchful, almost suspicious, as they called their greeting, and few smiled. She pushed away the thought as she turned to Elizabeth, who was craning her neck for a glimpse of Greenwich Palace.

Frances was looking over to the opposite bank as they passed the great mansions that lined the Strand. Just north of them was Gray's Inn. Was Tom there now, forging his plans, or meeting his fellow conspirators in its cloistered chambers? She supposed he had done so many times before. She still felt a stab of bitterness at the thought of how easily he had deceived her, how she had willingly believed that his legal affairs necessitated such frequent absences.

'Shall we be there before dinner, do you suppose, Frances?' the princess asked eagerly, interrupting her thoughts. 'I do so long for some sweetmeats, or perhaps a little marchpane.'

Frances tore her gaze from the north shore and forced a smile.

'I am sure we will not go hungry to our beds, Your Highness,' she soothed. 'Look – there to the right, you can just glimpse the flags on top of the gatehouse.'

As the barge drew level with the landing stage, Frances glanced across to the palace. It was the first time she had visited Greenwich in springtime. The old queen had rarely stayed there, except to mark the traditional Christmas celebrations. Though it matched the splendour of Whitehall or Hampton Court, it had a more pleasant, tranquil aspect. The fact that it was separated from London by fields and pastureland added to its appeal, in Frances's opinion.

A page was waiting to escort them to the palace, and as they walked along the drive, Elizabeth's eyes darted this way and that, eager to see – and be seen by – some of the dignitaries of court. But the palace was strangely quiet, and though the windows to either side of them showed no sign of life within, Frances had the uncomfortable sensation of being watched.

The same quietness pervaded the interior of the palace as they progressed through the sequence of rooms that led to the queen's privy chamber. Two yeomen stood guard at the door to the presence chamber, their halberds crossed in front of it. They made no motion to lift them as she and the princess approached, but instead stared grimly ahead. Only when they were within a few feet of the door did they give a curt bow and step aside to allow them admittance.

The presence chamber was empty, save for a servingwoman, who sat quietly by the window with her embroidery. She hastened to her feet as they entered, and swept a deep curtsey to the princess, then went to summon an attendant in the adjoining room to escort them. As the door was opened into the queen's bedchamber, Frances and Elizabeth paused for a moment on the threshold so that their eyes might become accustomed to the gloom. The windows had been covered with heavy tapestries, and Frances noticed that even the keyholes had been stuffed with pieces of material to prevent any light from piercing the chamber. A fire blazed in the grate, though the weather was mild, so that the room felt uncomfortably warm and oppressive.

'Come, my daughter.'

The disembodied voice of the queen carried softly across the room. Peering into the gloom, Frances saw the outline of a familiar figure seated on a large chair in a far corner. Gingerly, Elizabeth picked her way across to her mother, then knelt for her blessing.

'I am glad to see you, Elizabeth,' she said tenderly. 'And you too, Lady Frances. I trust the journey was not too tiresome?'

'Not at all, lady Mother,' the princess said earnestly. 'I have been so impatient to see you – and to meet my sister.'

'I am sure she is just as eager to meet you, Elizabeth.' There was a smile in her voice. 'Though she is sleeping at present – which is a mercy.'

The princess looked quickly around the room.

'Why is it so dark in here, Mother? I cannot see the cradle.'

'You must understand that this is the first royal birth in England for many years, Elizabeth. I have to be seen to observe all of the traditions associated with a queen's confinement.' She sighed. 'Though quite why Lady Beaufort should have decreed that daylight is harmful to the child, I cannot understand. I have almost forgotten what the world outside looks like. And the heat . . .' Her voice trailed off. 'Well,' she continued after a pause, 'I have been delivered of a healthy child, so perhaps after all there is wisdom in these traditions.'

'And a girl, too!' the princess exclaimed delightedly. 'How I have longed for a sister, Mama.'

'I am glad of it, for your sake,' the queen replied. 'Would that everyone shared your joy. The king and his people looked for a prince, born on English soil.'

The bitterness in her voice was unmistakable. Elizabeth fell silent.

'Well, now,' Anne said at last, her tone brighter. 'You must tell me how you like Coombe Abbey. I have never visited, but Lord Harington has boasted of its beauty many times.'

'It is pretty enough, and there is excellent parkland for riding,' the princess replied without enthusiasm. 'But I do not like to live so far from court – or from you, Mama.'

Anne smiled.

'The court is not so gay as it once was, Elizabeth,' she remarked. 'The king rarely frequents it, and London has hardly been free of the plague for two weeks together, so that most of the nobles choose to live at their country estates.'

Frances wondered if that was the only reason why the city seemed so quiet.

'They will return for the christening, though, Your Highness?' she asked.

The queen shook her head.

'Not in great numbers, Lady Frances. The king prefers to be surrounded only by his family and his favourites these days. He grows impatient of crowds – and fearful,' she added quietly.

They looked at each other steadily. The princess moved to a seat close to her mother.

'Well, I am pleased to be here nonetheless,' she said, in a subdued voice.

The queen reached out and patted her hand. They fell into silence, but it was soon broken by a thin, high wail coming from the adjoining room. The princess sprang to her feet at once.

'She is awake!' she proclaimed joyfully.

Anne smiled indulgently.

'Tell the wet nurse to bring the child in here,' she said to the attendant. The woman bobbed a quick curtsey and left the room. A moment later, she reappeared with a small, plump lady of about Frances's age. She was wearing a simple grey gown, which was drawn tight around her large belly. In her arms, the tiny princess writhed and snuffled. The queen held out her arms, and the nurse carefully handed her the baby.

The fire that blazed in the grate illuminated the tiny princess. 'Oh, she is beautiful,' Elizabeth said wonderingly, as she gently drew back the richly embroidered shawl in which the child was swathed. 'What shall she be called?'

'The king wishes to wait until the christening before deciding,' her mother replied.

Frances caught the note of irritation in her voice, but Elizabeth was too enraptured by her new sister to notice. Forcing a smile, Anne motioned for her elder daughter to sit down so that she might hold her little sister. Taking the tiny, snuffling bundle, she cradled her with the same exaggerated care that she reserved for her favourite dolls, rocking her gently, and stroking the few wisps of downy red hair that had escaped from under the shawl. Frances looked down on the two sisters and smiled.

'She looks very like you, I think, Your Grace,' she said to the princess.

Elizabeth beamed.

'I believe you are right, Lady Frances,' she said proudly. 'And I will make sure to keep my gowns in good order so that she might wear them when she is old enough.'

The baby started to writhe, and gave a little cry. The queen nodded to the wet nurse, who stepped forward. Elizabeth looked up at her regretfully.

'You may accompany Mrs Bedwyn to the nursery, Elizabeth,' her mother said kindly. 'You can see that your sister is properly attended to.'

The princess beamed at her mother, then, standing up carefully, carried the mewling baby slowly out of the room. Anne motioned to her attendant, who followed them, closing the door behind her.

'Please – sit, Lady Frances,' she said, her face suddenly grave. 'I am glad you have come.'

Frances inclined her head. 'It is a great honour to attend the princess's christening, Your Grace. We had not expected it, being so far from court.'

A shadow crossed Anne's face, and she seemed to hesitate before replying.

'The king wished to arrange it as soon as possible, but I begged that we delay it so that the princess could attend.'

'She was delighted to receive the summons, Your Grace,' Frances assured her.

'It was not for her that I willed it,' Anne said, looking down at her hands. 'But for you.'

Frances felt her pulse quicken. She waited for her to go on.

'These are dangerous times, Frances. Every day there is talk of a fresh plot against the king. The people of England have not taken him to their hearts. They despise the Scots even more than those from across the seas,' she gave a rueful smile, 'but my husband has intensified their hatred by persecuting those of the old faith. He does not understand the wisdom of the old queen's moderation, but instead allows himself to be manipulated by those who would see the kingdom torn apart by civil war.'

Her eyes blazed as she looked at Frances, who struggled to maintain her composure.

'The Earl of Salisbury has drafted a series of laws for the next Parliament, which will further curtail their liberties, making them even more desperate. The king is too obsessed with his hunting and his favourites to see how he is played.' She smiled bitterly. 'God knows his head is easily enough turned.'

Frances ran her tongue along her lips, which felt suddenly dry.

'If he continues in this way, the kingdom will come to ruin. Something must be done to remedy the situation.' Anne paused. 'You know, I think, that a means has been found to rid England of the evil in her midst?'

The heat in the room seemed suddenly unbearable. Frances felt her scalp prickle with sweat. 'I have heard rumours of a plot,' she replied cautiously.

'I think you know that they are more than rumours. Do not speak—' Anne held up her hand. 'Words have become as dangerous as actions. Only listen. If this plot succeeds, it is imperative that you keep the princess safe. You must not leave her for a single moment of the day – or night. Upon her life rests the future of the kingdom. Of us all.'

Anne's eyes seemed to bore into her soul. Frances stared back at her. Was she the protector of whom Catesby had spoken? It had long been rumoured that the queen had secretly converted to the Catholic faith. But surely she could not countenance the murder of her husband, of her sons? It was too shocking to bear credence. And yet, as she gazed into Anne's eyes, so full of bitterness and anger, Frances felt a creeping sense of certainty.

'You would not betray those whom you love, I think?' Anne persisted, when it was clear that Frances was not going to answer.

Frances felt a sudden surge of anger. 'It is I who have been betrayed,' she retorted, her voice filled with bitterness. Her chest rose and fell rapidly, and the colour had risen to her cheeks, but she pressed her lips together to stop the words tumbling from her mouth.

Anne regarded her steadily for a few moments before speaking again.

'Things are not always as they appear, Lady Frances,' she said quietly. 'Sometimes what we believed to be true proves false, does it not?'

Frances did not reply. An image of Sir Everard flitted before her. Did Anne know that he had betrayed them? She dare not speak of it here – words carried danger, it was true. Then she thought of Tom, the imploring look on his face as the boatman rowed her away from the landing stage at Westminster. Her eyes welled with tears as she held the queen's gaze. She brushed them away impatiently.

'But sometimes we find that our instincts were right.'

Frances's brow creased in confusion as she waited for Anne to explain.

'You were not mistaken in believing that Tom Wintour loved you,' she said quietly. 'It was always my plan that he should win your friendship and trust, so that you could be relied upon to play your part when the time came. What I had not foreseen was the love that would grow between you.' She looked away, shamefaced. 'I admit that when I first began to suspect the strength of your feelings for each other, I was glad of it, believing that it would make you even more inclined to do as he asked. But then he begged me to release you from our plans, insisting that he could not hazard your life, even if it meant we would fail.'

She looked back at Frances, her expression bleak.

'I refused,' she said quietly. 'I knew that my daughter loved you above all others, that there was no one else in her household whom she would trust enough to obey when the time came. When Tom persisted, I threatened to have the charges against you resurrected – God knows, Cecil would have been glad enough to oblige.'

Frances stared at her, as if trying to recognise a stranger. Anne looked down at her hands again.

'I did not intend to carry out my threat,' she mumbled, almost to herself, 'but I had to make Tom see reason, to stop everything for which we had striven from crumbling into dust.' She took a deep breath. 'At length Tom relented, but only on condition that he could reveal our schemes to you immediately, rather than waiting until the last moment, as we had always planned. Then you would at least have the freedom of choice.'

Frances let out a scornful laugh.

'Freedom to choose between a traitor and a tyrant?' she spat. 'I would sooner choose between the Devil and Hades.'

'Few of us enjoy any better choices,' Anne replied, her expression hardening. 'Do you think that I would hazard the lives of my sons if the alternative were not so abhorrent? You do not know the torments that I have suffered at the hands of my husband. He will bring this kingdom to ruin with his heresy, his depravity. Though he masquerades as God's anointed king, it is the Devil whom he serves.'

Her eyes were blazing now. Frances felt her own anger begin to recede as she was confronted by the force of Anne's bile against the man that she, too, had come to despise. She saw the queen's chest rise and fall in rapid, jerking movements as she struggled to regain her composure. At length, she sighed, her expression softening.

'Tom's love for you is true,' she said earnestly. 'I know that you may no longer trust my word, but I have proof.'

She stood up and walked over to the finely carved oak cabinet in the far corner of the room. Unlocking it, she drew out the same casket that Frances recognised from her apartments at Hampton Court. She rifled through its contents for a few moments, then drew out a folded parchment. Frances took it from her. It was not sealed, so she opened it straight away, impatient to see what it contained.

The style resembled the deed that the queen had presented to her three months ago. It was written in Latin, and as Frances studied it she realised that it related to the same land that she had been gifted. She looked up at the queen for an explanation.

'This is the deed that transferred the land in Greenwich that I gave you from the original owner to myself,' Anne said. 'They wanted you to believe that it came from me.'

Frances stared at her for a few moments, then looked back at the document. Whoever had signed it was her benefactor. She directed her gaze to the bottom of the page. Her hands began to tremble as she gazed at the signature.

Thomas Wintour

'He invested his inheritance, and everything for which he has laboured in this land,' Anne said quietly. 'He gave up his own future so that yours might be assured, whatever happens.'

The letters began to blur as Frances stared at them. A tear weaved its way slowly down her cheek.

'Why didn't he tell me?' she whispered.

'He wanted to leave nothing behind that would tie your name to his, if our schemes should fail,' Anne replied, placing her hand lightly on Frances's shoulder. 'I should have destroyed this before now,' she continued.

She reached to take the parchment, but Frances pulled it away from her. After a pause, she raised it to her lips and pressed them to his name, then handed it reluctantly to the queen. Anne placed it gently in the grate. Soon, the flames licked at its edges, and they began to curl up. The two women watched as the fire took hold, its greedy fingers turning the words to blackened soot. Frances kept her eyes fixed on Tom's signature. A few seconds later, it too was engulfed by flames. She gave a small shudder.

'Was I right to trust you with this knowledge, Frances?' the queen asked quietly.

Frances could feel her eyes upon her, but she continued to stare into the grate.

'I will do my duty, Your Grace,' she said at last.

CHAPTER 36

5 May

Elizabeth shifted impatiently in her seat as the organist played another long refrain, the notes echoing around the vaulted ceiling. Frances gently laid her hand on the girl's arm. The ceremony had barely started: she would need greater patience for the many observances to come. The princess sighed heavily and stopped fidgeting.

Frances knew that she, too, would need to learn greater patience. They had been in London for more than a week now, yet she had been denied any opportunity to leave the confines of Greenwich Palace. She was desperate to see Tom, to tell him what she knew, that she would continue to play her part, that she loved him still. Gray's Inn was six miles away, but it might as well have been a hundred. The princess, overcome with excitement about the impending christening, had demanded her presence every time she had visited her baby sister or gone out riding in the park. Worse still, the shortage of accommodation in the palace, with so many guests gathered in readiness for the event, meant that Frances was obliged to sleep on a pallet bed in her young mistress's bedchamber. She felt almost as much a prisoner here as she had in the Tower.

All of the guests were now seated. Glancing over to her right, Frances saw a haughty-looking woman dressed in black, with an ostentatious silver collar. Her hair was dark red, and her small, piercing black eyes stared straight ahead. Arbella Stuart. Frances had been surprised at the announcement that she was to be one of the godparents. Perhaps the king wished to keep her close. Whenever a rumour of a new conspiracy began to circulate, her name was whispered in connection with it. Though nothing had ever been proven against her, Frances still found her presence unnerving.

A few rows behind, Frances recognised the familiar figure of her uncle. He must have arrived late, for she had not noticed him among the dignitaries who had assembled outside the chapel to greet Princess Elizabeth. Next to him was the Earl of Northumberland, his tall frame visible among all of the other guests. His long brown beard was flecked with grey, Frances noticed, and his face was grave as he dipped his head to hear what her uncle was saying.

At that moment, the doors of the chapel were flung open, and a flourish of trumpets heralded the arrival of the christening procession. All of the guests got to their feet and bowed low as the king swept past. Glancing up, Frances saw that his limp was more pronounced than before, and his purple silk doublet was pulled tightly across his stomach.

In his wake came the tiny princess, carried by a noblewoman, and flanked by two lines of gentlemen who held a scarlet canopy above the baby's head. She was swathed in purple velvet, embroidered with gold thread and furred with ermine, and her long train was held aloft by several more ladies. Elizabeth craned her neck so that she might catch a glimpse of her little sister.

Directly behind the canopy was the queen, her hand resting lightly on the arm of her brother, who had travelled from Denmark to stand as godfather to his new niece. His hair was white-blond, like his sister's, and he had the same high forehead and long nose. Frances wondered if he had made the arduous journey for any other reason. He had not been present for the other christenings, even that of his eldest nephew Henry. She shook her head to dispel the thought. She must not see traitors everywhere.

Last of all came Cecil. He was dressed in the deep scarlet and grey robes of office, a long black velvet cloak covering his hunched back. For all his finery, he seemed to have shrunk into himself somehow, Frances thought. His skin was pallid, and there were dark shadows under his eyes, which caught hers briefly as he walked past. Frances turned to face the altar.

'The grace of our Lord Jesus Christ, the love of God, and the fellowship of the Holy Spirit be with you all,' the archbishop pronounced when the members of the procession were seated.

During the long ceremony that followed, the sound of rustling and sighing could often be heard. The king had no more patience for such matters than his daughter. Frances looked across to Anne, who, by contrast, was as still as a statue, her face a perfect mask of composure.

At last came the moment of baptism. The godparents stood solemnly around the font as the archbishop prepared to anoint the baby. But just as he had gathered a handful of water, a loud crack of cannon fire reverberated around the chapel.

'Treason!' James cried as he leaped to his feet in terror. A moment later, his guards rushed forward to shield him, as they had on the night of the masque. But this time, his alarm was shared by the rest of the congregation, all of whom were scrambling for cover. Frances pulled the princess down to the floor and wrapped her arms around her trembling body, her own heart hammering painfully in her chest. A second volley sounded out, prompting cries of alarm among the cowering guests. The baby princess began to wail.

Amidst the cacophony, Frances could make out an insistent voice calling for calm. At length, the cries receded, and the voice could be heard more clearly. It was Cecil's.

'Your Majesties, my Lord Archbishop, do not be afraid,' he said now.

Frances peered above the top of the pew and saw him standing at the altar, his face even whiter than before.

'It is the cannon of the Tower firing a salute in the princess's honour. They are before their time, that is all,' he said soothingly.

There was a pause, then the king pushed his guards aside.

'God's wounds! Can ye not even arrange a christening?' he shouted at Cecil. 'Little wonder my kingdom is falling into ruins. I am minded to strip you of your titles, you undeserving wretch.'

Cecil bowed his head meekly.

'I have always served you to the utmost of my abilities, Your Grace,' he said quietly.

The king gave a scornful bark of laughter.

'Well those abilities are lacking, Salisbury. Thanks to you, this land is crawling with plotters and papists, all intent upon my destruction. And you stand by like a simpering girl and do nothing – nothing!' he screamed suddenly, making Cecil jump in fright.

Without warning, he dealt a stinging blow across his minister's cheek, sending him sprawling to the ground. Frances watched with mounting pity as Cecil fumbled about for the staff that had been knocked from his hands. She glanced across at the other members of the council, hoping that one of them might come to his aid. But they all stared straight ahead, except her uncle, who was watching his rival with barely concealed delight.

Just as Cecil's fingers were about to close over his staff, the king kicked it away, and it fell clattering down the altar steps.

'Get up, you miserable dog,' he sneered. Then, turning to the archbishop, who was regarding him in wide-eyed horror, the king commanded him to resume the proceedings. The congregation slowly took their seats again, and Frances gently helped the princess to hers. The girl's face was ghostly white. Frances reached across to still her trembling hands.

As soon as the ceremony was concluded, the king stalked out of the chapel without waiting for the procession to reassemble.

His guards followed quickly behind. After the princess had been carried back down the aisle, the rest of the guests filed quietly out into the bright May sunshine.

The banquet that followed was a sombre affair. When the last of the dishes had been cleared, the Lord Chamberlain marched up to the dais and bowed low as he presented the king with a small wooden casket. All eyes turned to the monarch as he swayed uncertainly to his feet.

'I present these jewels to the queen in return for the one that she has given me,' he declared, holding the casket aloft.

Frances watched as Anne gave a thin smile and inclined her head in thanks. The king remained standing.

'England has a new heir,' he declared loudly. 'And so God shows His favour to the House of Stuart. He rewards us for our endeavours in driving heretics and dissenters from this land.' He paused, his eyes scanning the room. 'But I will not rest until every last papist is discovered and punished with the utmost vigour and severity. Yea, even if their contagion strikes to the heart of our court.'

He turned to look at his wife and children. Frances noticed Prince Henry turn pale, though he held his head aloft. His brother Charles seemed to cower in his seat.

'Hear me now – if my sons were to become espoused to the cause of heresy, I would disown them and leave my throne to the Princess Elizabeth.'

There was a collective gasp, followed by murmurs of surprise. Frances felt her pulse quicken. She looked across at the queen, whose expression remained inscrutable. Elizabeth's face, by contrast, had become flushed, and her eyes sparkled with excitement.

The king stared out at his court for a few more moments, then sat down heavily, motioning for a page to fill his glass. Frances looked down at her plate. To either side of her, courtiers were speculating about the reason behind the king's unexpected outburst. Not wishing to be drawn into their conversations, she reached for one of the wafers that had been set down before them, and broke it into small pieces on her plate. She proceeded to eat each one slowly, though she felt she might choke.

As soon as the banquet was over, she slipped out of the hall and made her way to the gardens. The princess would not require her attendance until later that afternoon. More than anything, Frances craved solitude.

But to her dismay, when she emerged from the palace, she saw that a small crowd had gathered at the gates, hoping to catch a glimpse of the king and his new daughter. Frances could feel their eyes upon her as she walked briskly along the drive. To reach the gardens, she had no choice but to push her way through them. The only other way was to go back through the palace and out of the north gate, but she did not want to risk being accosted by her uncle.

With a deep breath, she motioned for the yeoman who stood guard by the gate to let her pass. The people at the front eyed her curiously, but bowed their heads and stepped aside so as not to hinder her progress. She smiled her thanks, and walked on, her head bowed.

When she was almost clear of the crowds, she felt a hand brush against hers. Looking up, her breath caught in her throat.

'Tom.'

He smiled, but said nothing. Falling into step by her side, he gently steered her towards the path that ran alongside the river. They walked on in silence until the crowds had receded. Frances stared resolutely ahead, though her mind was racing.

'Forgive me. I had to see you,' he said, as he slowed his pace.

She reached for his hand and pressed it to her lips. He stopped and turned to look at her, his eyes filled with confusion and hope.

'I know now that you spoke the truth, that you did not deceive me – in your love, at least,' she said, the words tumbling from her mouth.

She glanced around quickly to be sure they were not overheard.

'The queen told me everything,' she continued in a whisper. 'Do not be angry – she was right to do so. I am sorry I doubted you. I thought the love you professed was part of the deceit, but now I know the lengths to which you went to protect me. I will never again forsake you – or your cause.'

She bent her head to kiss his hands again. He gave a deep, shuddering sigh, then gently tilted her chin up and kissed her. His lips felt dry, but Frances pressed her own against them, savouring their warmth. When at last they drew back, Tom cradled her head against his chest. She felt the rapid beat of his heart as he held her so tightly that she thought her breath would be squeezed from her body. She longed to stay like this, forever in his embrace, but all too soon her thoughts invaded.

'Did you receive my note?' she asked, drawing away so that she could look at him.

'Yes.' He hesitated. 'But I could not come to you. I have placed you in too much danger already, Frances. Cecil's spies are everywhere. My coming to Coombe without an invitation from the princess would have prompted fresh suspicion.'

'It is you who is in danger,' she said quietly. 'Cecil knows of the plot already. Sir Everard is conspiring with him. I overheard them in his chambers, before we left Hampton Court.'

She saw his eyes widen briefly.

'You are sure it was Cecil?' he asked, after a pause.

Frances nodded. 'I have no doubt.'

'But Sir Everard is a man of the court, he might have been conversing on other matters.'

She did not reply, but continued to hold his gaze. Distractedly, he ran his hand through his hair and bit his lip.

'If this is true, then we are undone,' he said at last.

'Not if you act quickly, and only with those who you know can be trusted. Catesby was with Sir Everard in Warwickshire. Is he in league with Cecil too?'

Tom shook his head firmly. 'Robin is truer to our cause than any of us. He would rather die than betray us. He despises the king for persecuting those of our faith, and will not rest until he has rid this diseased country of the canker in its breast.'

Frances studied him carefully. Did he speak the truth, or was he so blinded by love for his cousin that he had been deceived?

'If that is so, you must proceed with your plans before Cecil reveals them,' she said, after a pause.

'That is beyond our power,' he said grimly. 'Parliament is prorogued until October. Nobody – not even Cecil – could persuade the king to abandon his plans for the summer so that it might meet earlier. He will be visiting some of the best hunting grounds in the kingdom. The queen says that he has talked of little else for months.'

Frances looked at him bleakly. 'Then you have no choice but to set aside your schemes – for now at least. There can be no proof of what you intended.'

Tom shook his head again, more slowly this time.

'There are many who would testify – under torture. Robin has been gathering more supporters to our cause, my own brother included.'

He fell silent and stared down at the ground. Frances felt her heart lurch with pity. He looked stricken. There were dark shadows under his eyes, and his linen shirt, which hung from his wasted torso, was smeared with dirt.

'Already, we were in a state of confusion,' he continued, after a long silence. 'This birth has led some to question whether we should abandon Princess Elizabeth in favour of her new sister, born on English soil. And now this. It seems that God has utterly forsaken us.'

Frances reached for his hand.

'You must leave England – you and your companions,' she said quietly. 'You have friends abroad. They will shelter you until all of this is forgotten – which will be soon enough,' she added quickly, seeing his doubtful expression. 'The king's obsessions burn brightly, but are soon extinguished. Even now he is preparing to leave court for the hunt.'

'And what of you?' he asked, his eyes scanning hers. 'Will you come with me?'

She looked steadily back at him.

'I cannot leave the princess,' she replied at last. 'The love that I bear for her is the only truth I know at this court. I will not relinquish it.' Though she kept her voice steady, she felt as if her heart was breaking. Every instinct told her to go with Tom, to leave this court – leave England – far behind. But she knew that she would never find peace if she abandoned her young mistress now, her own father too, amidst so much danger and uncertainty. She also knew that Tom's chances of escape would be much greater if he were not accompanied by a woman whose recent notoriety made her so recognisable. There was no choice but to sacrifice her desires and remain at court.

Tom was staring at her intently, conflicting emotions flitting across his face. At length, he raised her hand to his lips and held it there for a few moments, his eyes closing as he breathed in her scent.

'Then I too shall remain,' he said solemnly.

Frances opened her mouth to protest, but he continued. 'Robin must know of Sir Everard's betrayal. We will let him believe that he is still part of our plans, but we will share the truth with those closest to us. If God wills it, we might yet prevail.'

Though he spoke with conviction, his eyes were filled with uncertainty as he gazed at her. She wanted to believe that God was on their side, that He would see justice carried out, but at that moment He had never felt more distant.

'I will pray for you – for us,' she whispered at last.

Tom dipped his head to kiss her again, then, with an obvious effort, stepped away from her.

'I wish with all my heart that I had not brought you to this,' he said, his face ashen. 'Goodbye Frances.'

With that, he turned, and began to walk away from her, towards Westminster. Frances reached out to pull him back, but then let her arm fall limply by her side. She watched his retreating form until long after he was out of sight. Eventually, she looked back towards the place where he had waited for her, as if expecting to see some trace of their presence. It was deserted. Their encounter suddenly seemed as insubstantial as a dream.

CHAPTER 37

2 October

Frances grasped the letter that the groom held out to her and dismissed him with a brief nod of thanks. Closing the door behind her, she crossed over to the bed, her breath catching in her throat. She had not seen Tom since their meeting in Greenwich five months before, and it had been many weeks since he had written. For all she knew, he and his companions had fled to the Continent, though Tom's last letter had made it clear that they were still intent upon their course. The terrible anxiety that had plagued her after their last meeting had gradually receded into a constant hum of apprehension that made her fretful and short-tempered. She had forgotten what it felt like to live free from fear.

Cecil had made no move to uncover their plot, though he must have known of it for at least nine months, if not longer. Even a cat would have tired of playing with its prey by now, and devoured it long ago. The more time passed, the more Frances wondered if she had imagined the whispered conversation in Sir Everard's chambers, or confused the scent of ambergris for something else. Musk, perhaps. Or beeswax. But her instinct told her that it had been Cecil.

At last daring to look down at the handwriting, her heart sank. With a sigh, she sat down on the bed and broke the seal. Her uncle's script was as indecipherable as ever, and she had to read it over several times before she could get the sense of it.

The letter began without preamble:

The king has been in a foul temper since his return from the progress. Cecil has angered him again, and Northumberland holds sway in council now.

Frances's heart lurched as she read on.

The sickness has finally abated, so it is expected that Parliament will any day now meet. It is like to prove Cecil's undoing.

'And that of many others besides,' Frances whispered, crossing herself.

She stood abruptly, and the letter wafted silently to the floor as she walked over to the window. She would light a fire and burn it later, as she did all her letters, save those from her mother. It had barely grown light all day, and the clouds hung so low that they seemed to touch the hedgerows that bordered Lord Harington's estate. That morning, she had witnessed a strange phenomenon: the sun, which had been bright in the sky, had suddenly been thrown into half shadow, as if a dark cloak had been cast over it. Though the Reverend Samuels had railed against the superstitious nature of his flock, knowing that it made them distrustful of his remedies, she could not help feeling a creeping sense of dread. Her late mistress had taught her to respect the world that lay beyond sight and reason, to listen for the warnings that it whispered. She knew that she would not be alone in this. The atmosphere at court must be even more oppressive than usual, as rumours of the latest treason echoed along its corridors.

Was Tom even now hiding in those lodgings close to St Stephen's, ready with his companions to strike as soon as the king entered Parliament? A shiver ran through her. It all seemed so far away, here in Warwickshire, where the only thing likely to disturb the peace was a sudden clap of thunder. But if their plan succeeded, this slumbering countryside would soon be overrun with Catesby's supporters. Frances imagined them now, bearing down on the abbey with flaming torches and swords at their belts. She felt a pulse of excitement.

Perhaps Cecil is too preoccupied with securing his place on the council to pay close attention to Catesby and his plot, she reasoned. Although her uncle was given to exaggeration where his rival was concerned, she had heard enough to convince her that the Lord Privy Seal was clinging to power by his fingertips. And who knows how many other plots he and his spies had been distracted by? Thinking of Cecil in this light, embattled and over-burdened, gave her fresh hope. For so long he had seemed a constant, menacing presence. But had she given him more power than he actually possessed?

Turning away from the window, she began pacing the room, her steps keeping time with her thoughts. The pale glimmer of silver from the carriage clock on the shelf caught her eye, and she stopped to peer at it in the gathering gloom. It was almost six. Lord Harington was always prompt with his hours of dining. Hastily, she crossed to the ewer and splashed some water onto her face, then quickly changed her gown and swept out of the room.

'How pale you are, Frances,' Elizabeth exclaimed as soon as she entered the parlour. Frances forced herself to give a smile of reassurance and bobbed a curtsey to her mistress and host, both of whom were already seated.

'I had a slight headache and am still a little fatigued ma'am,' she replied. 'But I am sure that Lord Harington's excellent table will soon restore me.'

A few moments later, two grooms entered, each carrying a large silver tray bearing a selection of dishes. Though she had little appetite, Frances helped herself to some venison pottage and roasted capon, then took a sip of the Burgundy wine that their host always kept in plentiful supply.

Lord Harington broke the silence. 'I am particularly glad to hear such praise, since we are soon to receive some distinguished guests.'

The princess sat up in her chair and looked at their host with barely concealed anticipation. Though Frances had done her best to entertain her since their return from Greenwich several months before, she knew that Elizabeth found life here very dull and longed for the company and diversions that were always on offer at court. There were only so many rides into the country and games of cards to be played, and Lord Harington's library had already been exhausted of anything but the most turgid volumes.

'I received word from Sir Everard Digby today that he will soon be taking possession of Coughton Court, which is less than a day's ride from here. I invited him to visit us, of course,' he said airily.

Elizabeth clapped her hands with delight.

'How wonderful! I have longed for some new company.' She flushed. 'That is – somebody from whom we might learn news of court.'

'Quite,' Lord Harington said with a grin.

'You implied that Sir Everard would not be travelling alone?' Frances asked quietly.

'Indeed. He will be accompanied by Lady Anne Vaux and her sister Eleanor.' He paused and took a sip from his glass, but did not take his eyes off her. 'And a priest, I understand.'

'A priest?' the princess asked in dismay. 'Why would he wish to bring him? It will not help make our party very merry to have a stern old Puritan in attendance.'

Lord Harington smiled.

'Ah, then you need not concern yourself, Your Grace, for Father Garnet is a Catholic priest. I am sure he will be content to make as merry as you please.'

Frances shot him a look.

'You surely do not propose to receive a Catholic priest in your household, especially when the princess is in residence?'

'Please do not trouble yourself, Lady Frances,' he said sooth-ingly. 'Sir Everard sought permission from the Earl of Salisbury, who was most obliging. We must promise not to hear mass, though, of course,' he added, with a sly smile.

The princess giggled. Frances set down her fork and slowly dabbed at her mouth.

'Forgive me, Your Grace, Lord Harington, but the headache has returned. I think I must take my rest.'

Lord Harington looked at her closely.

'I do hope it was not all this talk of parties and papists, Lady Frances.'

He stood and offered her his arm as she made to leave. She nodded her thanks and gave a brief curtsey to the princess, who was busy devouring an almond tart and hardly seemed to notice her departure. As she closed the door behind her, she leaned against it for a moment and looked around the empty hallway.

Why would Cecil so readily give his permission for the princess to receive a known Catholic into her household? If, as her uncle claimed, he was already out of the king's favour, then this would surely make things worse? A new thought occurred to her: perhaps Sir Everard was no longer so well acquainted with the plot as she had supposed? Tom would have told Catesby of his betrayal at the earliest opportunity, so they may have spun a web of lies to divert him and Cecil from their course? Father Garnet's arrival at Coombe just days before the convening of Parliament would certainly draw attention away from events in Westminster. The more she reflected on this, the more credible it seemed. Again, she felt hope surge through her. Clasping her hands together, she uttered a silent prayer – for the princess, for herself, and for Tom.

CHAPTER 38

20 October

The princess watched, transfixed, as Lady Vaux's delicate white fingers plucked expertly at the strings of the lute. The haunting tune filled the gallery, disguising the sound of the rain as it dripped from the windows. It was a cold autumnal day, and the wind was already whipping some of the leaves from the trees. Their plans for a picnic had soon been abandoned, but at the princess's request Lord Harington had arranged for their luncheon to be served up here in the gallery. A fine linen tablecloth had been laid out, and large velvet cushions scattered around it for the guests to sit upon. Frances ran her fingers along the beading of her cushion as she listened to the music.

When the last note faded into silence, everyone applauded – the princess most enthusiastically of all. Lady Vaux inclined her head. She was seated on a high-backed chair, and the ivy green satin of her skirt was spread elegantly around her.

'You play beautifully, Lady Vaux,' Lord Harington remarked. 'It is a pity you are not more often at court. I am sure the queen would delight in your skill.'

'Thank you, my lord, but we have enough company in Enfield Chase to keep us amused. Besides, I am sure there are plenty of musicians to delight Their Majesties.'

'Does your sister play as well as you?' the princess asked eagerly.

Eleanor blushed and shook her head.

'By no means, Your Grace. I am equipped only to listen.'

Frances looked across at her. She was younger than her sister, and plainer in appearance and dress, but had a pleasant expression that made her more appealing.

'Not at all, my dear. I have heard you play many times, and always to perfection,' Father Garnet said softly. His kind eyes wrinkled at the corners when he smiled, reminding Frances of her father. His grey hair was thinning at the temples, and he had a small, neatly clipped beard at his chin. The simple black robes that he wore contrasted with the rich and vivid colours that surrounded him.

'Have you visited many places on your journey, Father?' Frances enquired.

'We have been fortunate to receive some excellent hospitality – not least at Richmond,' he said with a smile.

Frances felt her stomach tighten.

'I trust my parents were in good health?' she asked lightly.

'Excellent health – your sisters too. They had but lately returned, so I feared our visit would be an inconvenience, but we were made most welcome.'

'More welcome than at Rushton, certainly,' Lady Vaux cut in.

Father Garnet looked uncomfortable.

'Ah yes, our timing was unfortunate. You will have heard the news of Sir Thomas Tresham's death? Most regrettable – he was a fine man. His son was in London, for the parliament which has been postponed again so was not able to receive us, but we managed well enough.'

'I fancy this rain will soon clear,' Sir Everard announced, taking another bite of an apple. He was standing at the large window that overlooked the park. 'We could go hunting after all.'

'Don't be ridiculous, it will be far too wet underfoot,' Lady Vaux chided. 'And we must not tire the horses before we make the journey to Harrowden.'

Sir Everard threw the apple core into the grate with such force that it sent a shower of sparks across the rug.

'Very well, Lady Vaux. But I have promised the princess that we shall hunt – and I never forget a promise,' he said, with a rakish grin. 'Your Highness, I shall send word when I have taken up residence at Coughton Court. The parkland there is without equal in these parts. We will make a merry hunting party.'

Frances felt a jolt of unease, but Elizabeth was beaming with delight.

'I should be pleased to join you, Sir Everard.'

'Then it is settled,' he said firmly. 'Well now, should we take a walk? You mentioned that the abbey ruins lie in a beautiful spot. I should very much like you to show me them, Your Grace.'

The princess sprang to her feet at once and threaded her arm through his. The rest of the company followed as they walked briskly out of the room.

Frances looked out at the sky, which was still dark grey, and went to fetch Elizabeth's cloak and boots. But by the time she came down the stairs into the entrance hall, only Father Garnet was there.

'I fear I am not so quick on my feet as the rest of the company,' he said, with a rueful smile. 'But if you are content to walk with me, I should be delighted.'

Frances returned his smile and drew on her cloak. As they emerged into the courtyard, a few spots of rain still fell, and the air was chilly. She peered anxiously into the distance, but the princess was too far ahead to hear, so she folded the girl's cloak over her arm and hoped that she would not catch a chill before she was able to give it to her. Father Garnet looked out appreciatively at the gardens, and occasionally paused to remark upon a flower or shrub. When they reached the bridge, Frances peered into the distance, hoping to see the princess, but she was out of sight.

'Lady Vaux and her sister will keep her safe, Lady Frances,' Father Garnet said quietly, as if reading her thoughts. 'They know that there are matters I would speak to you about.'

She said nothing, but waited.

'Your father is a man of great integrity, Lady Frances,' he continued quietly. 'He has been a friend to many of the true faith, myself included. Richmond has become a haven for our cause.'

'My father has always been a loyal subject,' she replied carefully.

'He is most loyal to those he loves,' Father Garnet agreed.

He stopped walking and took her hands in his. They felt warm, comforting.

'His thoughts are always with you, Lady Frances. He asked that I would tell you to be of good courage for what lies ahead.'

Frances drew in a quiet breath, but continued to stare straight ahead.

'Already, you have proved a great support to this undertaking. If you had not discovered Sir Everard's treachery, their plans would already have ended in disaster, and Cecil would have secured ample proof to have them put to death.' He paused. 'When I first heard of this plot, I could not but think it a most horrible thing – the like of which was never heard. Surely no regime can flourish that is built upon the murder of an anointed sovereign, and hundreds more besides. And if it fails, Catholics will face even greater persecution than they do today.'

Frances felt a pang at his words. In these endless weeks of waiting, the same thoughts had begun to creep in, robbing her of sleep in the hours before dawn. Only the love that she bore Tom and her father had kept her to her course.

'But the evil that has flourished in the realm since this king came to the throne is now so great that it can only be destroyed by a blaze more intense than the fires of hell. He proclaims himself to be the instrument of God, yet he spreads fear and hatred across the kingdom, deepening the divisions between those of the old faith and those who promote the cause of reform.'

Frances stole a glance at her companion, whose placid features were now flushed with fervour. Suddenly, he turned and gripped her shoulders.

'Lady Frances, you must hold firm,' he urged, his eyes blazing. 'The time is fast approaching when you will play your part. As soon as he heard of Sir Everard's betrayal, Catesby set me to watch him. I have been his constant companion ever since – though he has made no secret that he tires of my company,' he added with a smile. 'He does not know what role I play, or that he has been discovered.'

'So he still keeps Cecil informed of everything that passes?' Frances asked, casting a glance in the direction that Sir Everard had walked with his companions.

'Yes – or at least, of those things that Catesby wishes him to know. But Sir Everard lacks the patience of his master, and grows careless with these long days of waiting. I have intercepted some of the messages that have passed between them. Cecil instructed Sir Everard to come to Coughton Court at this time so that he is poised to seize the princess as soon as he gives the signal. He knows that the success of the plot rests upon crowning your young charge as queen. She is popular throughout the kingdom, and can win support for their cause, even amongst the reformers. Without her, they are nothing. Cecil means to snatch their prize from under their noses.'

Frances fell silent for a few moments, considering.

'But if the princess is taken too soon, before the plot has been put into action, then Cecil will lack the evidence with which to convict Catesby and the rest,' she said at length.

'Precisely so,' the old priest agreed. 'Which is why Cecil intends to wait until the plotters are assembled beneath the chambers of Westminster Hall, with all of the gunpowder in place, before sending word to Sir Everard. It will not be long now. Parliament has been delayed again, but will meet on the fifth of next month.'

He tightened his grip on her shoulders so that she winced with pain. The old man immediately looked repentant.

'Forgive me, Lady Frances,' he said in a softer voice, his fingers relaxing slightly. 'But the part you are to play is vital now. Whereas before you were to deliver the princess into Sir Everard's care as soon as Catesby gave the signal, now you are to keep her from him at all costs – even if it puts your own life at peril. I will send word as soon as I hear that the enterprise has been set in motion. You must then keep the princess at Coombe, ready for Catesby and his men to ride north and claim her when they have destroyed the king and his Parliament.'

'But if Cecil knows of the plot, how can they be sure of success?' Frances demanded.

'Catesby has given Sir Everard false details about the chambers in Westminster. God willing, by the time that Cecil's men discover their location, it will be too late.'

Frances stared at Father Garnet. Though his mouth was set in a determined line, his eyes betrayed the same fear that was coursing through her own body.

'I will give my life to protect the princess, to help restore freedom to the people of this kingdom,' she vowed. 'But am I to face Sir Everard alone? I do not believe that Lord Harington can be trusted to support us.'

'Lord Harington will turn with the wind,' the priest replied with a grimace. 'If he is assured of Catesby's success, then he will do everything in his power to keep the princess at Coombe and claim some of the glory when she is crowned.'

'And if he is not?' The words came out as barely a whisper.

'Then you must take courage, as your father says.'

He reached inside the folds of his gown and pulled out a narrow object sheathed in cloth.

'You will not be entirely defenceless,' he said, handing it to her.

Slowly, Frances pulled back the material and gave a small gasp as the sun reflected off the blade in her hands. Though small enough to conceal in her pocket, the dagger looked deadly sharp, and the cloth was frayed where it had been wrapped around the point. In the hilt, a red jewel glittered.

'It was my father's,' the priest said softly. 'He had the stone set into it as a symbol of our name. I have been fortunate never to have used it, though its presence has given me comfort these past months. I hope it will do the same for you.'

Frances kept her eyes fixed upon the jewel.

'Thank you, Father Garnet,' she whispered at last. Slowly, she wrapped the cloth around the blade again, and carefully slid it into the pocket of her dress. Turning, she began to follow in Sir Everard's wake. With every step she took, the dagger nudged against her thigh. Even through the layers of material, she felt it cold and hard as a tomb.

CHAPTER 39

29 October

Frances slowed her horse to a trot as she glimpsed the red sand-stone turrets of Kenilworth Castle ahead. The imposing fortress reminded her of a vast eagle, sitting, wings outstretched, atop its eyrie, looking down on its prey. As the wind whipped about her, stinging her face and blowing a loose strand of hair across her eyes, she felt a shiver of foreboding.

The princess had ridden ahead, but drew up her horse now.

'Isn't it magnificent, Frances?' she called over her shoulder. 'I wonder that she could have refused him!'

Her cheeks were flushed, and Frances could see her little chest rise and fall as she caught her breath. Thanks to their frequent after-noon excursions, she had become an accomplished horsewoman.

As Frances drew level with her, she looked back at the castle. The weathervane on top of Leicester's magnificent gatehouse glittered briefly as the sun emerged from the clouds. The earl had lavished great expense on the place in one final effort to persuade Queen Elizabeth to marry him. Frances's mother had been there, and had often described the splendid banquets, masques, and fireworks. But it had all come to nothing. The queen had given only smiles and promises, and her favourite had been left disap-pointed, as well as near-bankrupt.

This morning's excursion had been the princess's idea. Sir Everard and his company had left for Coughton the day after their arrival at Coombe, much to the girl's disappointment. She had done little to conceal her boredom ever since, and even Lord Harington had grown impatient with her heavy sighs and petulant outbursts. Though Frances had had some misgivings about straying so far from Coombe, she felt a certain relief at being no longer confined to its gloomy chambers. The constant waiting and watching made the hours pass by so slowly, and at times she fancied that the walls were gradually closing in on them.

Lord Harington had enquired closely into every aspect of their ride. He had even suggested joining them, but to Frances's relief the princess had insisted that he stay behind. 'He would slow us down terribly,' she had whispered to Frances as soon as he had left the room. 'He blames the pain in his leg for riding so badly, but I fancy he has never been a good horseman.'

Though Catesby had assured her that Harington was a true Catholic and could be relied upon to support the plot when the time came, Frances had her doubts. For all she knew, in this world of endlessly shifting allegiances, he could just as easily be in Cecil's pay too. They had never spoken of the plot, though she had been in his household for seven months now. The more time passed, the less inclined she felt to test Catesby's assurance.

A sudden thundering of hooves behind them made Frances start. Instinctively, her hand flew to the dagger concealed in the folds of her gown, while with the other she reached across to grab the reins of the princess's horse. Turning around, they saw Carter approaching over the hill. The wind must have whipped the sound of his approach away until now, because within a few moments he had drawn level with them. There was a sheen of sweat on his brow, and his hair was matted at his temples.

Briskly, he raised his cap, then addressed the princess.

'Your Grace, Lord Harington commanded me to bring you back to the abbey without delay. He has received grave news from the court.'

Elizabeth grew pale.

'Is it my mother?' she asked in a small voice. 'My little sister?'

Carter paused before replying, clearly enjoying his moment of power, however fleeting. Frances felt a stab of loathing.

'No, Your Grace. But I am not at liberty to reveal anything further. Lord Harington wishes to tell you himself.'

'Well, whatever it is, I am sure that it can wait until we have returned from our ride, Mr Carter,' Frances interrupted curtly. 'The princess was greatly looking forward to it, and I am sure you have no wish to displease her.'

'Of course not, my lady,' Carter cut in quickly. 'But my orders were to convey you to the abbey at once.' He drew himself up before adding: 'Lord Harington is acting upon orders from the Earl of Salisbury, who represents the king in this matter.'

Cecil. The mention of his name sent a jolt of fear through Frances. Was this a trick? Were they being lured back to Coombe so that Sir Everard could seize his prey?

'You are quite sure my family are all well?' Elizabeth persisted.

'I have heard nothing to the contrary, Your Grace,' he replied.

The girl's shoulders dropped, and she sighed deeply. She glanced up at Frances with a look of resignation.

'Very well. Then we will come with you. But it had better be worth the trouble,' she added with a glare, then pushed her horse forward at a good pace. Frances had no time to protest, but spurred her own horse on, and followed close behind.

Lord Harington was standing at the door as they rode up the drive. His face was grave. After a cursory greeting, he asked the princess and Frances to accompany him to the library. Carter made to follow, but was swiftly dismissed. Frances could not help feeling a prick of satisfaction as she watched him strut resentfully away.

A fire was roaring in the grate, but the room was dimly lit. A solitary candle burned on Lord Harington's desk, illuminating a folded letter. Frances noticed that it bore a large seal, which had been broken. The old man gestured for them both to sit. Frances flashed a quick smile of reassurance to the princess, who had not regained her colour, even after the rapid ride back to the abbey.

'Your Highness, the Earl of Salisbury has discovered a most horrible conspiracy against your father the king.' Lord Harington remained standing as he spoke, his voice low. 'He has ordered me to keep you under close guard here at Coombe.'

Frances felt her throat constricting.

'Do they mean to murder me too?' Elizabeth whispered, her eyes wide.

The old man regarded her kindly. 'No, ma'am, but the earl wishes to take no chances.'

'There is always talk of conspiracies, my lord,' Frances observed quietly. 'What proof can Salisbury have that this one is cause for alarm?'

She saw Lord Harington's eyes flick across to his writing desk.

'Lord Monteagle received a letter from one of the conspirators,' he replied.

Frances knew the name at once, though she had never met him. He was the brother-in-law of Francis Tresham, and, despite his Catholic sympathies, a member of the House of Lords. Tom had spoken of him warmly.

'It seems that their plans centred around Parliament, which will meet on the fifth.' Lord Harington continued. 'Whoever wrote the letter warned Monteagle not to attend. Fortunately he did not hesitate to take it straight to Cecil.'

Elizabeth started. 'Henry is to attend that too,' she whispered, almost to herself. Frances reached forward and stroked her hand, which was icy cold.

'Do not concern yourself, Your Highness. He can come to no harm, now that the plot has been uncovered.' She turned to Lord Harington, her mouth suddenly dry. 'Does Salisbury know who the conspirators are?'

'He did not say so, Lady Frances.' He held up his hand when he saw that she was about to speak again. 'I know of no further details. The purpose of his letter was to instruct me to safeguard the princess.' He returned her gaze unflinchingly, but she did not know if he spoke the truth.

'So I am to be kept prisoner here?' Elizabeth's voice cut through the silence. It was laced with indignation.

'Only until the danger has passed, Your Grace,' Lord Harington replied soothingly.

The princess looked appealingly at Frances, but her attendant was lost in thought. With a heavy sigh, the girl stood up abruptly and gave a curt nod of farewell to their host, then swept from the room.

'Lady Frances?' Lord Harington's voice made her start.

'Forgive me,' she said hastily, getting to her feet. 'I must attend the princess.'

She made to follow Elizabeth, but the old man caught her arm. His grip was surprisingly strong.

'Now that it is discovered, this plot cannot succeed, my lady. All those who thought to support it would be well advised to show their loyalty to the king.'

His eyes bored into hers, and he made no move to release his grip. Frances felt her heart quicken. Not trusting herself to speak, she gave a curt nod, and, pulling her arm free, walked briskly from the room.

CHAPTER 40

1 November

The sound of horses' hooves made Frances jolt as she and the princess sat quietly at the breakfast table. Elizabeth shot her an anxious look, then crossed over to the window.

'He is not wearing palace livery, at any rate,' she said as she peered out, and then, with a nonchalant air, resumed her seat.

Frances noticed that the girl's hands trembled slightly as she cut herself another piece of cheese. They lapsed back into silence, both straining to listen as the visitor was admitted. There was a brief exchange, then the sound of the door closing and the man riding back down the drive. A moment later, Lord Harington walked slowly into the room. He was leaning heavily on his staff, and he seemed to have aged overnight. His face was pallid, and there were dark rings under his eyes. None of them could have had much sleep the previous night. She pulled out a chair for him, and he gave her a grateful smile. After he had caught his breath, he handed the princess a small folded note. She hesitated before opening it, studying the seal carefully.

'Do not be alarmed, Your Highness,' he said kindly. 'I believe it is an invitation from Coughton Court.'

Elizabeth brightened at once and ripped open the seal.

'Sir Everard is holding a great feast this evening, and wishes me to attend!' she exclaimed excitedly. 'All of his companions will be there – Catesby, the Wrights, Tom – as well as our new acquaintances, Father Garnet, and the Vaux sisters.' She turned to Frances. 'I think the blue silk gown, do you, Frances? It will look so pretty with the silver necklace that Sir Everard gave me at Hampton Court. Or perhaps the purple . . .'

She chattered on, oblivious to the expression on Lord Harington's face.

'I am sorry, Your Highness,' he broke in at last. 'But I am afraid it is quite impossible for you to attend.'

Elizabeth looked across at him in dismay.

'Whatever do you mean, Lord Harington?' she demanded. 'It is not as if I have any other engagements. God knows there is little enough company in these parts.'

Frances knew she had not forgotten that she was obliged to remain at Coombe until Lord Harington received further instructions from court; she was simply ignoring the fact. It was a tactic she had often employed when attempting to avoid one of Lady Mar's many unwelcome strictures.

The old man shifted uncomfortably in his seat.

'Your Highness, I regret that my orders are to keep you here at Coombe. You know that it is for your safety,' he added quickly.

'But I am only visiting a neighbour for the evening. Where is the danger in that?' the princess demanded.

'Coughton Court is some thirty miles away, ma'am. It is half a day's ride at least, so you would be absent from Coombe for a good deal longer than an evening.'

Elizabeth waved away his objections. 'Sir Everard would be offended if we turn down his invitation. He knows we live very dull lives here at the abbey.'

Lord Harington opened his mouth to reply, but Frances seized her opportunity.

'You are quite right, Your Highness. So in order to avoid causing offence, I will go in your stead.' She shot an appealing look at
their host.

'That is an excellent suggestion, Lady Frances,' he said with
relief. 'I will arrange a carriage for you.'

'There is no need, Lord Harington. I will enjoy the ride.' She
glanced across at the princess, who was scowling. 'Well then, it
is settled,' she said briskly. 'If you will excuse me, I will make
ready.'

The sun was low in the sky by the time Frances reached the parkland surrounding Coughton Court. There had been a hard frost
that morning, and it had barely thawed all day, which had made
the ride much faster than it might otherwise have been. Frances
was glad of it. She had hardly noticed the gently undulating fields
and valleys as she sped past, so lost had she been in her thoughts.
If the news had not already reached Tom that the plot was discovered, then she must be the one to deliver it.

She felt her stomach knot with anxiety at the thought of what
awaited her, but she also experienced the old rush of excitement
at seeing Tom again. She had no idea where he had been living
these past few months, but she could not imagine that it was in
any great luxury. She pictured him, pale and emaciated, his cheekbones sharp through his long beard, then shook the thought away.
Already, her fingers tingled to touch the smooth skin of his hands,
or stroke the hair that curled at his neck.

Frances spurred her horse on, dipping her head close to its neck
as they gathered speed. Only when she reached the top of the
drive did she slow it to a canter. As she rode along it, she rehearsed
her plan again. She would seek out Tom before dinner, and this
time she would insist that Catesby came too. He must hear the
truth from her own lips. If the gathering was as great as Sir
Everard implied in his invitation, then there would surely be
ample opportunity to slip away unnoticed to a quiet corner, where
they would not be overheard. She must take particular care not to

arouse Sir Everard's suspicions. He would no doubt be reporting everything back to Cecil.

The house came into view as she rounded the next corner, the last rays of sunlight illuminating the golden stone façade. It reminded her a little of Hampton Court, with its turreted gate-house and low, elegant ranges at either side. The Throckmortons had profited from their years at court, despite the taint of treason that had hung about their name since one of their number had led a conspiracy against the old queen. A torch blazed on either side of the great archway that led through into a courtyard.

Frances glanced around. She had expected it to be filled with carriages, but it was empty save for a mounting block, next to which a pageboy was waiting patiently to help her climb down from the horse. Neither was there any sound of revelry within the house. Had it not been for the lights that shone from the tall windows of the main range, she might have begun to think that the place was completely deserted.

After she had dismounted, the boy gestured towards a small doorway in the corner of the courtyard, where a footman was waiting to escort her. Frances nodded her thanks and followed him up a wide stone staircase, the walls either side of which were hung with faded tapestries. As they reached the landing that led into the hall, she heard subdued voices within. Her heart was racing by the time that she stepped over the threshold.

'Lady Frances Gorges,' the footman announced.

She stood for a few moments, her eyes scanning the room. Instead of the bustling reception that she had expected, there was just a handful of guests, all seated by the fire. Sir Everard stepped forward.

'You are most welcome, Lady Frances,' he said with a small bow. 'As you can see, we are rather few in number this evening.'

She followed the arc of his hand and saw Anne Vaux and her sister. Lady Vaux's expression did not alter as she looked back at Frances, but Eleanor forced a weak smile. Next to them was a pretty young lady with blonde ringlets and a small, heart-shaped face. She got up from her chair and bobbed a curtsey.

'I do not believe you have met my wife?'

Frances inclined her head. 'Lady Digby.'

She caught a movement out of the corner of her eye, and a figure emerged from the window embrasure, which was in shadow. Frances's heart leaped, but then she saw that it was Father Garnet. His face was ashen.

'The rest of our friends were unable to join our celebration after all,' he said quietly. 'Important business has detained them in London.' His eyes bored into hers.

'So our party is complete?' Frances asked as she glanced back towards Sir Everard and the ladies.

'I fear so, Lady Frances,' their host said, with a rueful smile. 'By the time we heard from Catesby, it was too late to send word to you. But we will do our best to make a merry party, eh ladies?'

His wife beamed adoringly at him, and Eleanor Brooksby nodded obligingly. Lady Vaux regarded him coldly and remained silent.

'Lady Frances, will you take some spiced wine before we go in to dinner?' Lady Digby addressed her shyly.

Frances thought quickly. It was enough that she had been robbed of the chance to warn Tom in person; she could not bear the prospect of waiting until after dinner for an opportunity to speak to Father Garnet.

'Thank you, Lady Digby, but I have a message from the princess to convey to Father Garnet and would rather do it now, before I get diverted by the delights of your table.' She smiled pleasantly. 'It is of a personal nature, so I would be grateful if you would excuse us for a few moments. It will not take long,' she added, when she saw Lady Digby glance anxiously at the clock.

'Of course, my dear,' Father Garnet cut in. 'We must always put spiritual affairs ahead of those of the flesh, eh, Sir Everard?'

Their host was scowling, but he forced a tight smile and bade them follow him to a small antechamber along the corridor. He lingered in the doorway after they were seated, and for a moment Frances feared that he was going to insist upon joining them. Eventually, though, he sighed and gave a small bow as he closed the door behind him. Frances waited until she had heard his foot-steps fade.

'So Cecil has revealed the plot already,' the priest said in a low voice before she could speak.

Frances nodded, her expression bleak.

'Monteagle's letter gave him little other choice, I suppose,' Father Garnet continued. 'The king would soon have learned of its contents. But I had not expected betrayal to come from another corner. We were watching Sir Everard so closely that we neglected others, it seems. At least none of the plotters has yet been captured.'

Frances felt a flicker of hope.

'So they have made their escape?'

The old man turned desperate eyes to her. Slowly, he shook his head.

'Catesby will not give it up,' he whispered. 'He says it changes nothing, that Cecil already knew about the plot, but is still in the dark about when or where it will be executed – or by whom.'

Frances stared at him in horror.

'But he surely knows everything now. Lord Harington's instruc-tions suggest so – Cecil has told him to keep the princess under strict guard at Coombe.'

The priest gave a heavy sigh and ran his hand across his brow, as if trying to smooth away the deep lines of his anxiety.

'It is madness to forge ahead, I know, but Catesby is blind to it – or chooses to be. He believes that God is on their side and will hand them victory.'

'God has no part in this!' Frances retorted angrily. 'Catesby acts for himself alone. Well, his vanity will cost not just his own life, but that of all his confederates.'

She stood up and began pacing the room. Her fury was laced with frustration that after all these months of waiting, it had come to this. And she was utterly powerless to prevent the plot careering towards certain disaster. Surely Tom could see that it was doomed? How could he forfeit his life, and that of his brother, out of blind loyalty to their vain and foolish cousin?

Father Garnet grabbed hold of her wrist to halt her frantic pacing.

'I pray you, Lady Frances, be calm. We will not help them with anger. There is enough of that already.'

Frances rounded on him. 'Then how *shall* we help them, Father?' she demanded. 'When they seem so utterly bent upon their own destruction?'

The old man shook his head sadly. 'I fear they are beyond our help, Lady Frances. We can only help ourselves.'

She looked away, not wanting to hear what he might say next.

'I will leave this place as soon as I am able to do so without raising suspicion,' he continued after a pause. 'Sir Everard will shortly be moving to Dunchurch, a village that lies very close to Coombe Abbey. Cecil has no doubt instructed him to be ready to seize the princess, if Catesby and his men should think to come here. Coughton Court will be all but deserted, so I can make my escape. There are those who will gladly provide refuge in Flanders. I would urge you to follow me. When the plot fails, and Catesby and the rest take flight – assuming they are not apprehended immediately – every sheriff in the land will be sent to find them. Nobody will notice our absence until we are safely across the seas.'

Frances stared at Father Garnet in disbelief. As soon as the tide had turned against the plotters, he had left them to their fate. Could any man be trusted not to turn his coat?

She fell silent. Nothing would be gained from trying to persuade him to alter his course, or from revealing her own intentions.

'I will think on it, Father,' she said at last. 'Now, we must return to the company, before Sir Everard's dinner is ruined.'

The priest looked at her uncertainly for a few moments, then gave a small bow and walked out of the room. Frances watched his hunched form retreating into the shadows. An image of Tom flitted before her.

'I will not forsake you,' she whispered into the gloom.

CHAPTER 41

5 November

There was a light tap at the door, and one of the chamber women entered the parlour with a burning taper. She padded quietly over to each of the sconces and lit them, taking care not to drip any wax on the fine Turkey carpet. Frances glanced out of the window. The light was fading fast, though the clock on the fireplace had not yet struck four. A square of embroidery lay limp on her lap. Now that she had light to work by, she picked up her needle again, but her fingers trembled so much that she was unable to thread it. She set it back down with an impatient sigh, and picked distractedly at the tiny stitches that she had sewn a few hours before.

'You are such a dolt today, Frances!' the princess exclaimed scornfully as she laid down her cards and cupped her hands around the coins in the centre of the table, dragging them over to add to the large pile in front of her. 'I would have done better to challenge Patch to a game.'

The Irish wolfhound raised his head expectantly at the sound of his name, then lowered it back down onto his paws and gave a small whine. Frances reached down and patted his soft grey back. His tail beat the floor a couple of times, then he gave a wide yawn and lapsed back into sleep.

'Forgive me, Your Grace,' she replied quietly. 'I couldn't sleep for most of the night, so I am a little tired.'

That at least was the truth. As soon as she had retired to bed, thoughts of what might be transpiring in London had come closing in, and she had known that any attempts at sleep would be hopeless. She had risen early, before it was light, and, though she had busied herself with various dull but time-consuming tasks throughout the day, her mind had been drawn inexorably back to it. Were Tom and his fellow conspirators even now in that dark cellar beneath Westminster Hall, carefully lifting another barrel of gunpowder into place, while the king presided over his Parliament in the chamber above? Were James and his ministers already dead, their corpses burning to cinders in the scorched ruins of St Stephen's Chapel? Or had Catesby finally realised the madness of his schemes, and fled for the Continent with his followers in tow? Again and again, Frances willed her mind to picture Tom on board a boat as it sailed across the Channel to safety. But the image would fade as soon as it appeared, like a fleeting glimpse of the sun in a stormy winter sky. In its place came a vision of Tom, a rope tightening around his neck, his face slowly turning blue as he fought for breath.

Frances shook the thought away again now, and, with trembling fingers, reached for her goblet. As she did so, she brushed against the house of cards that the princess, bored of playing such a distracted opponent, had been carefully building. They collapsed in a heap. Elizabeth gave an exasperated sigh.

'Really, Frances. It is too much to bear. I am kept here like a caged bird, while you are free to go riding, visit acquaintances, and anything else that takes your fancy. And when you do at last stay to keep me company, you are as dull as one of Lord Harington's statues.'

Frances felt a surge of impatience as she stared back at her young mistress, who had turned away from her and was idly toying with a ribbon that she had pulled loose from her hair. She bit back a retort, and fell into a resentful silence.

The opening of the door made them both start.

'Ah, Lord Harington, perhaps *you* would care to play cards with me?' the princess asked, before he had the chance to speak.

He smiled tightly and glanced across at Frances.

'Gladly, Your Grace, though I would not wish to deprive Lady Frances of her place,' he replied.

'You need not worry on that score,' Elizabeth retorted indignantly. 'She has no interest in keeping me company today.'

Feeling suddenly cold, Frances stood abruptly and moved to the seat next to the fire. She was only vaguely aware of the princess's endless chatter as she and Lord Harington began their game. Drawing her chair closer to the fire, she held out her palms and felt them tingle against the heat. As she stared into the grate, she suddenly saw an image of Tom writhing in torment, his skin blistering as the flames licked higher, the acrid smoke filling his lungs so that he choked for breath. Without warning, a log suddenly fell from the fire, landing on the stone hearth, sending sparks flying across the carpet. Patch leaped to his feet and began barking furiously. Quickly, Frances whipped the shawl from around her shoulders and threw it across the smouldering embers, stamping on it until each one was extinguished.

Lord Harington grabbed his dog by the collar and gave the howling animal a sharp tap across his flank. Patch yelped, then began to whimper quietly, hanging his head low as he skulked away into a corner. A plume of smoke rose from the charred rug and the fallen log, and the princess was seized by a dramatic fit of coughing. Frances busied herself with brushing the sparks from the carpet, then reached for the fire tongs and carefully placed the log back in the grate.

'Well, that has given us all a stir,' Lord Harington remarked as soon as order had been restored. 'You are recovered now, Your Grace?'

Elizabeth nodded, and gave another little cough. 'I am quite well, thank you. Besides, I was glad of the diversion. Lord knows there are little enough of them here,' she added sulkily.

Lord Harington looked chastened. 'I am sorry, ma'am. I know that I can offer few of the entertainments that you are accustomed to at court. But you are safest here for now.'

'Is there any news from London, my lord?' Frances cut in, her heart pounding.

The old man shook his head. 'Nothing yet, Lady Frances. Parliament was due to meet today, as you know, but I have had no word of whether or not it did. Pray God it has passed without incident.'

Frances traced a cross on the palm of her hand and mouthed a silent 'Amen.'

'When will I be permitted to leave this place?' the princess demanded brusquely. Frances shot her a look of reproof, but the girl refused to meet her eye.

'As soon as I receive word from the king your father,' Lord Harington replied quietly. 'In the meantime, I will try to ensure that you have everything that you require for your comfort and entertainment.'

Elizabeth gave a curt nod, then got to her feet and smoothed down her skirts.

'Please excuse me,' she said in a lofty tone. 'I am going to write a letter to my mother. She will be anxious for news of how I fare.'

Before either of them could answer, she swept from the room and slammed the door behind her.

Frances jolted awake, her heart pounding. She listened. Another volley of thuds sounded in the distance, followed this time by hurried footsteps. She hastened out of bed and lit a candle from the dying embers in the grate. Glancing at the clock, she saw that it was just past two in the morning. She wrapped her cloak around her and padded quickly along the corridor.

At the top of the stairs that led down into the entrance hall, she could hear muffled voices. She strained to listen as she peered over the bannister, but a moment later the door was closed and she saw

Carter running up the stairs towards Lord Harington's apartments in the opposite wing of the house. Instinctively, Frances
drew back into the shadows. She waited, her heart still racing. A
few moments later, Lord Harington came hurrying towards the
princess's rooms. The light from the candle that he carried
illuminated his stricken features, and as he came closer she could
hear that his breath was short and laboured. When he drew level
with her, she reached out and touched his arm. He jumped back
as if scorched.

'Forgive me, my lord, but I was woken by the knocking at the
door,' she said quickly. 'What has happened? Is it the king? Is
he—'

He drew her into a window embrasure and glanced over his
shoulder before replying.

'It was my neighbour's steward. A group of papists has
ransacked Lord Jeffrey's estate and stolen his horses. The men
were armed,' he added, his eyes wild with fear. 'He sent to warn
me that they might be heading this way. The plot must have
succeeded.'

Frances's hand flew up to her mouth. The king was dead.
Already Catesby, Tom, and the others must be riding north and
had sent word to their supporters here to raise arms in readiness.
She felt a mixture of elation and fear, though it hardly seemed
real.

'We must convey the princess to safety,' Lord Harington continued. 'There is no time to lose.'

Frances's mind was racing. If Catesby's men arrived at Coombe
to find that their prize had been snatched from them, the plot
might still fail, even though they had succeeded in destroying the
king and his Parliament.

'No.'

Her voice was quiet but commanding. 'If you leave now, you
will be exposing the princess to even greater danger. The safest
place for her is here at the abbey. Your retainers are already
prepared for a siege, after all.'

As she held the old man's gaze, her mind raced on. If the plot had succeeded – as it surely must – then by the time that Catesby and his followers reached the Midlands, they might have amassed a huge body of supporters. Lord Harington's men would be able to offer little resistance.

He eyed her doubtfully. 'But there is little time. The plotters might already be surrounding my estate.'

She shook her head. 'If they had planned to ride straight here from your neighbour's estate, then they would have arrived by now.'

She opened the window so that they might both listen. The chill breeze made Lord Harington's candle gutter. He shivered, but leaned towards the window. They strained their ears for the sound of horses' hooves approaching, but the dark countryside beyond was as still and quiet as the grave.

'Besides, you have had strict orders to keep the princess at Coombe until instructed otherwise,' Frances urged when she saw that Lord Harington still hesitated.

The old man sighed. 'Very well,' he said, after a pause. 'We shall remain here for now. But we must be ready to leave at a moment's notice – as soon as we find out which way the wind blows,' he added, regarding her closely. He glanced across to the princess's chamber.

'She will still be sleeping,' Frances said, anticipating his question. She forced a smile. 'We would have been left in no doubt if she had been awoken.'

Lord Harington nodded, but did not return her smile. 'I shall send word to my retainers straight away.' He stood up and walked stiffly away. Frances stood listening until his footsteps had faded away downstairs, then hastened back to her room.

Closing the door softly behind her, she walked over to the window and peered out into the darkness. As her eyes became accustomed to the gloom, she gradually picked out the silhouettes of the sycamore trees that bordered the estate, and the dark hills beyond. Once or twice, she thought she saw a glimmer on the hillside, to the south, and strained her eyes, expecting to see it grow brighter and multiply into a hundred blazing torches being carried aloft by Catesby's supporters. But when she blinked, it had gone.

Eventually, she turned away and walked silently over to the bed. Drawing her knees up to her chin, she closed her eyes and whispered a prayer.

The moment had come. Tom and his companions had prevailed in Westminster. Now she must ensure that their prize remained safe for them to claim as soon as they arrived at Coombe. It could surely not be long now. Parliament had been due to meet the previous morning. As soon as the gunpowder had been ignited, Catesby would have used the cover of the ensuing confusion to flee north with his men. If they rode hard and changed horses halfway, they would be here soon after dawn.

Her thoughts ran on. Had Sir Everard also received news that the plot had succeeded? If he had, then he might already be preparing to join his victorious companions at Coombe, unaware that they knew of his treachery. Or was he still waiting for the signal from Cecil to seize the princess and convey her to whichever hiding place they had arranged?

Cecil.

With a jolt, Frances realised that he was probably dead too. When Lord Harington had told her the news, she had thought only of the king. Yet his chief minister had plagued her ever since her arrival at court, his sinister, threatening presence a constant reminder of her vulnerability. She felt a searing rush of relief at the thought that she might never see him again.

But she must remain on her guard. Sliding her hand under her pillow, she felt the cold shaft of Father Garnet's dagger. The priest must be many miles from Coughton Court by now. She was angered by his faithlessness. Well, by acting precipitately, he had deprived himself of a share in the glory. A zealot like Catesby would not take kindly to those who proved to have weaker convictions, she knew.

The soft chiming of the hall clock echoed along the silent corridor, making Frances's heart lurch. As the third stroke faded into silence, she rose from the bed and began to get dressed. When Tom and the rest arrived, she must be ready.

CHAPTER 42

7 November

Frances glanced around. The woods were eerily silent and still. Overhead, the steely grey sky seemed to be closing in, shrouding the forest in gloom. It could be little more than two o'clock: she had set out directly after lunch on the premise of gathering some herbs that the cook had requested. In truth, she had been unable to bear Lord Harington's obvious unease, or the princess's resentful silence, broken only by the occasional scornful remark or complaint, bitter as bile. Her own restlessness had grown unbearable. There had been no news since the steward had raised the alarm the night before last. No plotters had descended upon the abbey as Lord Harington feared – and she had hoped. They would surely have been here long before now if they had ridden straight from London. But the abbey and its surrounds had been as still as the grave. Frances began to feel that any tidings – good or bad – would be preferable to this agony of waiting.

She had chosen these woods deliberately. They lay to the south of the abbey, close to the track that led to the Coventry road. Any travellers from either London or Coughton Court would pass by this way. Stooping down to pluck a sprig of ivy, its dark shiny leaves edged with brown, she paused and listened. For a moment, everything was silent. She held her breath. There it was again.

The distant rumble of horses' hooves was unmistakable now. Running to the edge of the woods, she looked out across the open fields to the south and caught movement in the distance to the west of the spires of Coventry. Even from here, she could see that the rider was travelling at breakneck speed.

Casting the herbs aside, Frances gathered up her skirts and ran back into the woods, towards the abbey. The crack of twigs underfoot seemed to echo around the forest, sending birds flapping from their shelter in alarm. Once or twice, she stumbled on the gnarled roots that weaved across the forest floor, her ankles twisting painfully, and the palms of her hands prickling with blood from the brambles that she grasped to stop herself from falling. But she ran on, her heartbeat pounding in her ears, and her back damp with sweat.

When the abbey at last came into view, she could no longer hear the horses' hooves. Whoever had come must be inside the house now. In her mind's eye, she pictured Sir Everard dragging the princess towards his waiting horse. She chided herself for her impatience. She should have stayed at the abbey. Though her legs now felt like water, and her lungs seemed fit to burst, she surged forward along the drive.

She reached the door, panting heavily, and held onto its heavy iron handle for a moment, fearing that her legs would buckle under her. There was no outward sign of any disturbance, and she could hear nothing from within. Taking one last, uncertain breath, she twisted the handle and pushed open the door.

The hallway was empty, but she could hear voices in the parlour. One of them was Lord Harington's, but the other she did not recognise. Not pausing to consider, she walked briskly towards the room, and, knocking sharply at the door, entered before anyone could reply.

Lord Harington was pacing up and down before the fire, but stopped abruptly when he saw Frances, his face ashen. A young man she didn't recognise was standing close by, his face and clothes spattered with mud. His back heaved, and there was a sheen of sweat on his neck. Turning to look at Frances, he bowed abruptly, then strode from the room.

The old man ran his fingers distractedly across his brow. His gaze darted from Frances to the door, which the messenger had left slightly ajar.

'Carter!' he shouted so suddenly that Frances started. She opened her mouth to speak, but he held up his hand. A moment later, the attendant appeared.

'Tell the servants to make ready. We must leave this place before nightfall.'

Frances noticed the steward's eyes widen, but he merely bowed and left the room. The sound of barked commands and rapid footsteps could soon be heard in the chambers beyond.

'What is the meaning of this, my lord?' she demanded.

'One of the conspirators has been captured. He was discovered in a cellar beneath Westminster Palace, moments from executing his evil work. A huge quantity of gunpowder was hidden there. They meant to destroy the king and his entire Parliament.'

Frances felt the blood drain from her face. She gripped the edge of the chair in front of her. *Then they have failed.* The hope that she had cherished for the past two days was crushed so suddenly that it took her breath away.

'Do you know his name?' she asked at length, her voice barely more than a whisper.

Lord Harington nodded. He was watching her closely. She held her breath.

'John Johnson.'

The answer was so unexpected that for a moment she was unable to comprehend it. She had never heard that name before, and she was sure that she knew all of Catesby's close associates. It was possible that he had joined the plot after she and the princess had left London, but it seemed unlikely that they would trust its execution to a newcomer.

'A false name, of course,' Harington continued, noting her confusion. 'But it will not be long before he spits out the real one.

The king has had him taken to the Tower. If he refuses to speak his name, and that of his fellow conspirators, His Majesty will not hesitate to have him racked.'

Frances shuddered. Had this man already led them to Tom? Was he even now shivering in a dark cell beneath the White Tower as he awaited his interrogators? No. She felt sure that he was not, though she had little reason upon which to base her conviction. It was only instinct that told her he still drew breath – the same instinct that had drawn her to him since their first meeting. But what of her father? Were Cecil's men now galloping west towards Richmond? She swallowed hard.

'Then why must we leave? If the plot has been foiled and one of its leaders arrested, we must surely be safe, especially so far from London?'

Lord Harington shook his head.

'There has been a raid on Warwick Castle by a group of papists. A great cache of arms and horses has been taken. I cannot risk the princess's safety by keeping her here,' he broke off, his gaze intensifying, 'where everyone knows she resides.'

Frances's mind was racing. Catesby must be forging ahead with what was left of his plot, regardless of the catastrophic failure in Westminster. Surely he could not hope to raise enough supporters in the Midlands to take London by force? He and his associates should be halfway across the Channel by now. It was their only hope of survival. But she knew with a sickening certainty that Catesby would stay and fight to the death rather than turn tail and flee to safety.

If they would not escape, then there was still time for her to do so. It would surely not be long before Cecil's men came to find her. But for now, everything was in confusion, as Father Garnet had predicted. By the time that her absence was noted, she could be riding south, to the coast. There was another way to save herself, she realised, her thoughts racing on. If she meekly complied with Harington's command and went into hiding with the princess, then by the time she emerged, Catesby and his friends might have been rounded up and put to death – Tom included. Unless one of them betrayed her, she could live out her days in comfort in the service of the king's daughter.

The king. She pictured him now, cowering in his privy chamber at Whitehall, his clammy white hands grasping for a sword whenever a floorboard creaked or a clumsy page sent a glass clattering. Now his face was close to hers, his spittle wet on her cheek as he whispered his foul threats. She felt her throat begin to tighten, as it had that night at the Tower, while the fire crackled in the grate, and James's witch pricker had sharpened his dagger.

No. She could not do it. For all the love she bore the princess, a life lived in the glittering cesspit of court, watched over constantly by Cecil and his men, would be more of a torture than anything she could suffer as a result of helping Tom and the reckless schemes in which he was embroiled. If there was even a glimmer of hope that their plot might yet succeed, she must do her utmost to assist it.

'Have you received instructions from the king to remove his daughter?' she demanded with a new resolve.

Lord Harington looked momentarily shamefaced, but soon recovered himself.

'No, my lady. But I cannot take the risk of staying here, surrounded by papists on all sides.'

'Where will you go?'

'To Coventry. There is a house belonging to a merchant in the heart of the city, close to the cathedral. We are assured of safety there, and it is large enough to accommodate the rest of my household.'

Frances thought quickly. If she left now, there would be no means of getting word to Tom of their whereabouts. Though she would be placing herself in danger by staying at the abbey, she would not doom the plot to failure by deserting it.

'I will remain here – for a night at least,' she said firmly.

'My lady—' Lord Harington began to protest, but she held her hand up to stay his words.

'You are leaving without the king's permission or knowledge,' she continued. 'If he should send word to you or the princess, there will be nobody here to receive it. Once you are settled safely in Coventry, you can dispatch a messenger to court with news of your whereabouts. It carries too great a risk now, with so many papists abroad who might intercept it.'

The old man fell silent, considering. He resumed his restless pacing, though Frances could see it gave him pain.

'You must leave me directions to the merchant's house, so that I might join you there as soon as I am able,' she continued. 'It will not be long, God willing.'

Lord Harington gave a heavy sigh.

'Very well, Lady Frances,' he said at last. 'But you must know that you will reside in this house alone – and in great peril. I will order one of the stableboys to stay – he at least will be able to keep watch from his room above the stables. But I will not put any more of my household at risk. I intend to send all but a few back to their homes for now.'

Frances nodded, her eyes ablaze. With one last, doubtful glance at her, the old man hastened from the room.

Frances watched as the last of the carriages rounded the corner towards the end of the drive, the torches that had been lit on its canopy slowly fading into the darkness. She exhaled deeply, her breath misty in the chill night air. After a pause, she turned and went back into the house, pushing the door quietly closed behind her.

The stillness within unnerved her, and she was seized with a sudden impulse to run after the carriages as they rolled quietly through the sleeping countryside. The thought of the boy in his lodging above the stables offered little comfort. For all she knew, he was already slumbering amongst the hay.

She stood for a few moments, her eyes scanning the dark corners of the entrance hall. The fires in most of the grates had been extinguished, and only a few candles still flickered in their sconces. They would burn out soon enough, she knew. She crossed to the small table next to the clock and took one of the candlesticks, lighting it carefully from one of the sconces nearby, before padding quietly upstairs.

As she drew level with the princess's chamber, she saw that the door was ajar. Pushing it open, she held her light forward so that she might see inside. It was in some disarray, dresses and cloaks strewn over the bed and chairs, and a pile of books lying scattered on the floor. Elizabeth had been the only member of the household to feel any excitement at the prospect of leaving for Coventry. As soon as Lord Harington had told her the news, the sombre and irritable mood that she had laboured under for days had lifted, and she had set Frances to work in packing her coffers. With wide-eyed wonder, she had speculated about the whereabouts of the plotters, relishing her newly cast role as a heroine, escaping from their evil clutches in the dead of night. Her only misgivings had been for her mother and baby sister, and she had plagued Lord Harington for assurances of their safety. The thought of leaving without Frances had also pained her, and she had made her attendant promise to follow the very next day.

Frances pulled the door quietly closed, promising herself that she would tidy the princess's room as soon as it was light. Once inside her own chamber, she felt a little calmer. Setting the candle down on the table by the fire, she stoked the embers and reached for another log from the basket. It sparked and hissed when she put it in the grate, but eventually the flames took hold, and it began to burn brightly, filling the room with warmth. She reached behind her back and began unlacing her bodice, then untied her skirts, and let the heavy fabric fall to the ground. She laid the clothes carefully over the chest by her bed, then pulled out her nightgown and shawl. Crossing to her dressing table, she sat down in front of the mirror and unpinned her hair so that it fell about her shoulders. Slowly, she ran the comb through the tangled tresses until they shone, smooth as silk, in the candlelight. The familiar movements calmed her, and at last her thoughts grew still.

When she had woven her hair into a loose plait, she stood and looked over to the bed. Though the panic had subsided, sleep still seemed a distant prospect, so she decided to sit by the fire and read for a while. As she looked at the volumes on the shelf, her gaze alighted on *Arcadia*. Her heart gave a lurch. She had not picked it up for months, unable to bear the memories that it stirred within her of a happier time, filled with hope for the future. But she reached for it now, desperate for the comfort and escape that it had once offered. Drawing her shawl around her, she pulled her chair close to the fire, which was now roaring in the grate, and began to leaf through its familiar pages.

Though she enjoyed feeling the weight of the book on her lap, she was so agitated that the words seemed to leap about on the page. After a few minutes, she closed it with a sigh. They would have reached Coventry by now. It was only six miles from Coombe, and the roads were good. She whispered a prayer for the princess's safe keeping. God knew when she would see her again. She picked up the book again and began to read, but her eyelids soon grew heavy, so she set it down on the table and curled her legs under her. Before long, her thoughts became disordered, strange visions remaining just out of her grasp so that when she tried to decipher their meaning, she found that they had already disappeared. Breathing deeply, she surrendered herself to sleep.

'Frances.'

She smiled at the familiar voice, but her eyes remained closed. He reached forward and closed his hands over hers. The coldness of his skin made her start. Her eyes sprang open. She blinked several times, unbelieving.

'Tom.'

She stared at him, unable to speak another word. He was kneeling at her feet, his eyes filled with uncertainty and longing. His skin was deathly pale, and the beard that had grown full since she had last seen him did not quite disguise how gaunt his face had become. His hair was matted, and Frances noticed that his clothes were flecked with mud.

He bent his head and kissed her fingers. His lips were as cold as ice.

'We are undone,' he said quietly, his head still bowed.

Frances struggled to control her breathing. She still did not know if this was real or a dreamlike fancy, conjured up by sleep. Tentatively, she reached out to touch his cheek. He grasped her hand and held it there, breathing in her scent. After a few moments, he laid it gently down on her lap, his own hand closed over it.

'Guido was discovered beneath the house in Westminster. Everything was in readiness. We needed only a few more hours for our plan to succeed. But Cecil knew more than we hoped, even though we have kept Sir Everard in ignorance since you told me of his betrayal.'

'Guido gave a false name?' Frances whispered, her voice cracked.

Tom nodded. 'But they got his real one out of him soon enough, thanks to the gentle tortures that the king bade them use.' His mouth twisted. 'It will not be long before those same tortures draw out the names of his associates.'

'What shall you do?'

He gave a heavy sigh and sat back on his heels.

'There is only one thing we can do: stay and fight. There are many in these parts who stand ready to take up arms. Already they have been gathering weapons and horses. We may yet be victorious,' he added without conviction.

Frances watched him closely. She knew it was pointless to try to persuade him again to flee. They were sworn to fight their cause to the death, no matter how slight the chances of victory.

A sudden thought occurred to her.

'Did you ride by the stables?'

Tom shook his head. 'No, the noise would have awoken the servants. I rode only as far as the woods to the south of the abbey. My horse is tethered there.'

'Only one servant remains here – above the stables. I am in the house alone.' She paused. 'The princess has been taken to Coventry. Lord Harington feared for her safety here, so he has taken her to a house of a trusted associate. I can direct you there, should you need it.'

He pressed his lips to her hands again. They were warmer now.

'I am indebted to you. You have shown greater loyalty to our cause – to me – than I deserve,' he replied earnestly. 'But our hopes for the princess are unlikely to bear fruit. Even now, Catesby and the rest are preparing to withstand a siege at Holbeach. It is rumoured that the sheriff has mustered hundreds of men.' He paused and looked at her steadily, his eyes grave. 'I must join them there before daybreak.'

Frances felt her heart contract in her chest.

'But you will be riding to your death.'

'You forget that we are trained soldiers, with many years' service. Besides,' he added with a slow smile, 'there have been even more ill-matched encounters than this, many of which have favoured the smaller force. King Harry's archers at Agincourt are testament to that.'

Frances did not return his smile.

'I cannot let you go.'

Tom reached up and gently brushed her cheek.

'I have no choice, Frances. Would that it were otherwise. God knows I have prayed that it might be.'

'So you have come to say goodbye?' Her voice caught painfully in her throat, but she stared back at him, her gaze unwavering.

He did not reply, but his eyes told her the truth of her words. They lapsed into silence and listened to the soft crackle of the small flames that still flickered gently across the embers. Soon they would die out, and the room would grow cold and dark. Frances gave a slight shiver.

Tom got slowly to his feet. She felt her composure begin to crumble. A tear weaved its way slowly down her cheek, and she brushed it away. She reached out and touched his hand.

'Do not go – not yet.'

Slowly, she uncurled her legs and stood up. His hands were trembling slightly and his breathing was rapid, but his eyes never left hers. She took a step forward so that their bodies were almost touching, then tilted her head upwards and softly kissed him. His lips were unyielding at first, but as her mouth became more insistent, his resolve seemed suddenly to weaken, and he clasped her to him, his kiss becoming deeper, his desire more urgent.

With impatient fingers, she fumbled with the ties of his cloak and doublet until they eventually fell slack and she was able to ease them off his shoulders. She slid her hands under his shirt, feeling the soft warm flesh of his back as he leaned forward to kiss her neck. His hands were warm through her linen shift as he caressed her back, her hips and thighs, and she was filled with an almost unbearable longing.

All at once, he pulled away from her, his breath rasping in his throat.

'Forgive me,' he said in a low voice, his chest heaving silently. He dropped his gaze to the floor.

Frances watched him steadily for a few moments, then slowly untied the collar of her shift and eased it down over her shoulders, letting it fall noiselessly to the floor. She saw Tom's eyes flick towards it, then move slowly up her body, savouring every gentle curve of her flesh as if wishing to commit it to his memory for ever. When at last his eyes met hers, they were blazing with desire.

Without speaking, she moved towards the bed, her gaze never leaving his. She lay back onto the thick coverlet and watched as he pulled off his shirt and hose. When at last he lowered himself gently down onto her, she raised her mouth to his and wrapped her legs around him, drawing him into her. The shock of the pain soon subsided into a delicious, rising pleasure that drove her to meet his rhythm, pushing her hips against him with an increasing urgency. As she cried out, he gave a shudder and collapsed onto her, his head buried into her shoulder.

They lay like that for a long time, their fingers idly caressing each other until they became impatient for more. At last they fell into a sweet, exhausted sleep, Frances cocooned against Tom's chest, his arms enfolding her and his mouth nuzzling the back of her neck.

She awoke with a start and shivered, suddenly cold. Tom was no longer there, and she sat up in panic, her eyes casting about the room. As they became accustomed to the dim light that was beginning to steal through the shutters, she saw his silhouette at the end of the bed. Relief flooded through her, but was instantly replaced by dread.

'I must leave you now, my love,' he said softly.

For a few moments, she was unable either to speak or to move. Then she slowly drew the coverlet around her shoulders and looked up at him. Though she could not make out his features, she knew that he was watching her intently.

'Please stay,' she whispered. 'Or if you must leave this place, then make your escape. Do not join the others at Holbeach. You know that you will not leave it alive.'

His shoulders sagged slightly, and he sat down next to her, his hands warm as he drew her to him.

'And you know that I cannot desert them,' he murmured into her hair. 'I have pledged to take such part as they do, even if it means forfeiting my life.'

Gently, he brushed her cheek with his thumb, and kissed her mouth. As he drew away, she could still feel the warmth of his lips. She pressed her own together as she struggled to swallow back her tears. She watched as he walked over to the door, then stopped and turned.

'I love you, Frances,' he said quietly. 'I always have. God go with you.'

'And with you,' she whispered.

He paused for a few more moments, then, with a sudden resolve, walked briskly from the room, closing the door behind him. Frances sat quite still and held her breath as she listened to his retreating footsteps.

'Come back to me,' she whispered as they faded into silence. 'Come back.'

CHAPTER 43

9 November

The rain was falling heavily by the time Frances reached the door of Holy Trinity church. It had not relented for two days now, and there were reports that the Avon had burst its banks at Warwick, washing away some of the poorer houses on the edge of the town. It was a blessing that Lord Harington had chosen Coventry as their refuge instead, though even here the streets were water-logged. The hem of Frances's gown was sodden, and her leather shoes had provided little protection from the large puddles that lay in a patchwork across the cobbled streets of the city.

Few other people had ventured abroad this morning – as much, perhaps, from fear as from a desire to stay warm and dry in their homes. It had meant that she could steal out of the merchant's house unnoticed. For once, Elizabeth had shown no inclination to accompany her. Besides, Lord Harington would never have let her out. He had succeeded in installing her in the house without attracting attention, and he was determined to keep her there until the danger had passed – if it ever did.

Frances twisted the old wrought-iron handle and heard the heavy latch lift on the other side of the door. Pushing her shoulder against it, she opened it just wide enough to walk through, then closed it silently behind her. Drawing off her cloak and hood, she paused for a moment, entranced by the serene beauty of the place. The aisle was flanked by a series of columns and archways, all perfectly symmetrical, with a gallery high up above. The ceiling was painted an azure blue, interspersed with beams and trefoils picked out in gold. At the top of the nave was a huge stained-glass window that filled the church with light, even on this gloomy day.

Frances glanced from side to side as she walked slowly up the aisle. Every pew was empty, and there was no sound except for the dripping of the rain from the gables outside. She took a seat opposite a small side chapel and bowed her head in prayer. But the moment she closed her eyes, images of the last night she had spent at Coombe came crowding in. She had pushed them away until now, busying herself with unpacking Elizabeth's and her own belongings, ordering the rooms that the merchant had given them, and doing her best to keep her young mistress from fretting. By the time she had retired the previous night, she had been so exhausted that she had slipped into a dreamless sleep, but she had woken early, her ears straining for the sound of a messenger arriving with news of the plotters. Even now she flinched at every echo of a horse's hoof on the cobbles outside. She rubbed her neck, as if to ease away the anxiety. She was thankful that Lord Harington had granted her permission to take a walk in order to clear the pains in her head.

She closed her eyes and saw Tom's face so close to hers that she could feel his breath on her lips. If she reached out, she felt sure that she would touch his chest, warm through his linen shirt. Her breathing started to quicken as she felt his fingertips brush her cheek. But then, suddenly, they turned to ice, and he stood motionless before her, his face as pallid and sombre as a death mask.

Frances snapped her eyes open to dispel the image, but it remained there, torturing her with its clarity. The pulse at her temples was throbbing painfully, and she struggled to subdue the sense of panic that threatened to engulf her. Casting about the church, her eyes alighted on a wall painting above the archway that spanned the aisle. She forced herself to focus on the vermilion of the disciple's coat, the look of supplication on Mary's face as she knelt before her son, Christ's outstretched arms as he sat in judgement, apparently oblivious to the pleas of those who crowded around him.

Her eyes then moved down to the wretched souls below. The tangle of bodies trying to climb towards the salvation of the Lord, their nakedness a sign of their sinful lives. The demons lurking at the mouth of hell seemed to watch their futile attempts in amusement, biding their time before dragging them back to the torments of eternal damnation.

Frances stood abruptly, sending the prayer book in front of her clattering onto the stone floor below. She glanced up again at the painting then, crossing herself, walked briskly out into the rain. As she made her way back through the deserted streets of the city towards the towering red-stone edifice of the cathedral, the bell began tolling the hour. As the ninth strike faded into silence, it was replaced by a faint tapping that grew more distinct as Frances hastened along the street, her head cowed against the falling rain. She rounded the corner onto Bayley Lane and saw a figure up ahead, shrouded in a long cloak. He was nailing something onto the walls of the Guildhall. She slowed her pace as she drew closer, peering at the notice. At the sound of her footsteps, he turned around, his hammer suspended above the final nail.

'Wicked business, miss,' he remarked with a shake of his head. A droplet of rain ran along his cap and onto his nose. He brushed it away, then turned back to his task. Over his shoulder, Frances could see that 'Proclamation' was printed in large letters at the top of the notice. She stepped forward so that she could read the words below.

IT HAS LATELY BEEN DISCOVERED THAT A HORRIBLE TREASON WAS CONTRIVED AGAINST HIS MAJESTY, WHEREBY THE UPPER HOUSE OF THE PARLIAMENT, ATTENDED BY THE KING, THE PRINCE, ALL HIS NOBILITY AND THE COMMONS, WAS TO HAVE BEEN BLOWN UP WITH A GREAT QUANTITY OF GUNPOWDER. THE PERPETRATORS OF THIS

DAMNABLE CONSPIRACY WERE SEVERAL CATHOLIC GENTLEMEN BY THE NAMES OF ROBERT CATESBY, AMBROSE ROOKWOOD, THOMAS WINTOUR, JOHN AND CHRISTOPHER WRIGHT, JOHN GRANT AND THOMAS PERCY, A GENTLEMAN PENSIONER TO HIS MAJESTY. THE SAID CONSPIRATORS HAVE SINCE FLED, AND THE KING COMMANDS ALL HIS OFFICERS AND LOVING SUBJECTS WHATSOEVER, TO DO THAT WHICH HE DOUBTS NOT BUT THEY SHALL WILLINGLY PERFORM, NAMELY TO MAKE ALL DILIGENT SEARCH FOR THE SAID TRAITORS.

Frances was only vaguely aware that the man had spoken again. Her eyes were drawn back to the proclamation.

Thomas Wintour

So Cecil had secured Fawkes's confession. She shuddered as she imagined the ropes of the rack tightening, the crack as the prisoner's joints were wrested from their sockets. But Tom was not yet captured. The notice only said that he and the rest had fled. Perhaps they had somehow overcome the sheriff's men and escaped to safety. Then her eyes alighted on the date at the foot of the page.

7 NOVEMBER 1605

'News travels slowly in these parts,' the man said, following her gaze. 'News they want us to hear, at any rate. But we know what passes well enough. We have eyes and ears as sharp as those in London.'

'They are apprehended, then?' Frances asked quietly.

'More than that,' the man replied, a note of pride in his voice. 'The sheriff's men had them surrounded at Holbeach. There was a fierce battle yesterday – they say the gunshots could be heard as far as Bridgnorth. The papists were few enough, but they fought like wild dogs. They must have known it was their last stand. Better to die there than at the gallows.'

Frances gripped the fencing that stood between her and the noticeboard. Her skin prickled with a sudden heat, though she was soaked through to the skin, and a chill wind had whipped up from the east. She ran her tongue around her lips and swallowed hard.

'So they are dead? All?' The vision that she had seen now blurred with the painting in the church, so that Tom's lifeless body was being dragged down to hell by a smiling demon.

'Yes, miss.'

Her grip tightened as she felt her legs begin to buckle.

'At least, the leader of them is, and several of his men,' he continued. 'The rest are captured and already on their way to the Tower.' He gave a chuckle. 'They'll soon wish their hearts had been stopped by one of the sheriff's bullets too.'

Frances tried to control the pounding in her chest as the man busied himself with packing away his tools. She did not know which was the greater torment to imagine: Tom being shot dead, or being bundled into a cart and taken, bound and gagged, to face an even worse fate in London. Either way, he was surely lost to her for ever.

The man straightened up and gave a groan as he rubbed the base of his spine.

'I fancy this rain has seeped into my very bones,' he complained. Frances did not reply, but continued staring straight ahead. He gave a shrug, then trudged off down the street.

The rain began falling more heavily. Frances's hair had come loose from its coif and lay in drenched tendrils around her shoulders. Large droplets of water ran down her face and stung her eyes as the wind whipped across the courtyard, but she remained as still and lifeless as the carvings above the entrance to the ancient hall.

The cathedral bell chiming the quarter seemed to rouse her, as if from a trance. She looked again at Tom's name on the proclamation, then with a sudden resolve ran back along the street.

She heard Lord Harington conversing with the princess behind the closed door of the parlour, and made towards the stairs, intent upon gaining some time alone in her room. But something about the girl's voice made her pause. It sounded clipped, almost shrill, and Lord Harington's soothing replies were rapidly interrupted each time.

Crossing to the parlour door, Frances knocked lightly and entered the room. The princess was seated on a chair in the far corner of the room. Her face was pale and agitated, and she barely glanced at Frances as she made her curtsey. Lord Harington looked askance at Frances's dishevelled appearance, but said nothing.

'Is something amiss?' Frances addressed the question to him, seeing that her mistress was too distracted to give a reasoned answer.

'I have just relayed news of the conspirators to the princess. They have been named in a proclamation. Her Highness is greatly troubled,' he replied shortly, glancing across at the girl, who was now staring down at her trembling hands.

'Robin,' Elizabeth muttered, as if to herself. 'And Tom, Kit, and Jack. Traitors all.' She stood up abruptly and crossed to where Frances was standing.

'It must have been a great shock to hear the names of those involved, Your Highness,' Frances replied quietly.

'They proclaimed their friendship, their loyalty, but it was all lies,' the girl spat back, her eyes flashing. 'I wish that I had never met such false wretches.'

'Their loyalty to you was true enough,' Frances replied firmly. Lord Harington shot her a fierce look, but she continued. 'They wanted to set you on the throne.'

'Not before they had murdered my father and brother.' She gripped her attendant's hands in her own, which were ice cold. 'I would rather have perished in the Parliament house than wear the crown on such condition.'

Frances gently pulled her hands away and looked steadily at the princess.

'Well, now they have died for it,' she said in a low voice.

'Not all,' Lord Harington interrupted. 'Four were killed by the sheriff's men, others were arrested, but a small number escaped.'

Frances felt her heart quicken.

'Do you know who?'

'Digby, Percy, and Bates.' He watched her closely. 'And Wintour.'

All of the colour drained from Frances's face, and she sank down into a chair. She had to remind herself to breathe as her vision began to grow blurred.

'*Robert* Wintour,' Lord Harington added, after a long pause, during which his eyes never left her. 'His brother Thomas was shot in the siege, and run through with a sword.'

Frances gripped her stomach. The room grew suddenly dark, and she swayed in her chair. The princess quickly poured her a glass of water and gently brought it to her mouth.

'See how you have startled her, as you did me!' she cried, rounding on Lord Harington. 'I'll wager that you wish to frighten us both to death.'

The old man spread his hands in a gesture of apology, but did not look entirely abashed.

'Have the dead been laid to rest?' Frances's voice was barely a whisper, and her eyes remained lowered.

'For now,' Lord Harington replied. 'Though there is talk of having them exhumed and displayed as a warning to all Catholics.'

Frances pressed her fingers to her mouth.

'What of those who have fled?' Elizabeth asked, her voice edged with fear. 'Are they likely to try to find me?'

Lord Harington shook his head. 'Do not trouble yourself unduly, ma'am. My Lord Salisbury has dispatched hundreds of officers to search every inch of land surrounding Holbeach. And he will be interrogating Wintour in person, so he can apply pressure to find out where his brother is hiding.'

Frances's head shot up.

'Wintour? Thomas Wintour? But you said that he was dead.'

'Not dead, Lady Frances: injured. Gravely, at that. But he is young and fit enough to survive for a time at least, assuming the wounds are well tended in the Tower,' he added with a smirk.

Frances's hand shook as she reached for the glass that the princess had brought her. She forced herself to take a few sips, and tried to order her thoughts as she did so. That Tom was alive seemed even more miraculous after she had believed him to be dead just a few moments before. Although she knew that his life was in the gravest possible danger, she could not help feeling giddy with relief and joy that he still drew breath. If he recovered from his wounds and proved sufficiently penitent, then perhaps the king would be merciful yet. She must cling on to that hope, for therein lay the breath of life.

'Ah, I almost forgot,' Lord Harington said after a long pause. He crossed to the table and picked up a sealed note. 'The messenger brought this for you, when he arrived with the news from Holbeach,' he said, handing it to Frances. She looked up at him in confusion, but his expression remained impassive. Her first thought was that it was from Tom. But she knew that was impossible. Even if he had been able to write at such a time, he would never risk implicating her. Turning the letter over, she drew a quiet breath as she recognised the royal seal. For a moment, she considered taking it to her room so that she might read it in private, but she knew that this would only court further suspicion from Lord Harington, so she broke it open and began to read.

Lady Frances,

The late events have occasioned great unease for His Majesty and myself. We had judged that the princess Elizabeth would be safest at a distance from court, but now that the conspirators are so close at hand, we think it best that she should return to London, where we may be more assured of her protection. To that end, we require you to make haste to Greenwich Palace so that I can instruct you about the princess's new lodgings. You

*may then prepare for her arrival, which will be arranged a short
while later. I have written to advise Lord Harington of the same.*

*Given under our signet at the Palace of Greenwich, this eighth
day of November.*

Anne R

Frances carefully folded the letter and tucked it into her pocket.
'Well, my lord,' she said at last. 'You already know its contents.
Have you informed the princess?'

'He has,' Elizabeth cut in. 'And I am sorry for it. I would sooner
keep you with me here, so that I might be assured of your safety
– and mine. I cannot think why Mama would wish you to leave
me here alone.' Her tone was indignant, but Frances caught the
apprehension in it.

'It is only for a short while, ma'am, then you will follow,' she
assured her. Turning to Lord Harington, she told him that she
would be ready to leave within the hour, and asked him to arrange
a carriage. The old man nodded his assent. Frances gave a brief
curtsey to her mistress, then hastened to her room.

As soon as the door was closed behind her, she sank back
against it and closed her eyes. In the few short hours since she had
left this room, it seemed that her entire world had shifted. She had
known few enough certainties before, but now even these had
vanished. Though she feared what lay before her in London, she
strained to return there with every fibre of her being. It was foolish to think that she would be permitted to visit Tom, but she
longed to be close to him, for however long – or short – the time
left to them both might be. She felt deeply grateful to the queen
for summoning her back, though she little believed the reason.
But she had no time to think on that now, as she opened her eyes
and tried to focus on the task in hand.

Less than an hour later, she was sitting in the carriage that Lord
Harington had arranged. Her sodden clothes she had left draped
over a chair close to the dying embers of the fire. She was glad of
the fresh, dry linen that now lay against her skin, and the warmth

of the gown that covered it. Glancing back down the alley, she saw neither flicker of life nor light within the house. Lord Harington would be hard-pressed to keep the princess calm during her absence, even if he was minded to do so, which she somehow doubted. It was as if he wished to punish the girl for her acquaintance with the plotters, overlooking the fact that his own had been far more damning.

With a jolt, the carriage started forward. Progress through the streets was rapid, for barely a soul stirred out of doors, even though it was almost eleven o'clock. By the time that Frances caught the striking of the hour, the tall spire of Holy Trinity had faded into the distance. She turned back to face the road ahead, and muttered a quiet prayer for what might await her there.

CHAPTER 44

12 November

Frances stood for a moment on the threshold of the queen's presence chamber so that her eyes could become accustomed to the gloom. The curtains had been drawn across every window, keeping out the meagre light from the leaden sky beyond.

'Lady Frances, you are welcome indeed.'

The voice came from beneath the canopy at the far end of the room. Frances swept a deep curtsey, then walked slowly forward. As she neared the raised dais, she could see Anne's form gradually begin to emerge from the shadows. She was dressed in her favourite slate grey, with a fine black lace shawl around her shoulders. On either side of her was a lady-in-waiting, dressed even more sombrely. Frances wondered fleetingly if the court was in mourning.

'Your Grace,' she said as she reached the steps of the dais, and dropped another curtsey.

'How fares my daughter?' the queen asked in her familiar, clipped tones.

'The discovery of the Powder Treason, as they are calling it, has greatly unsettled her, ma'am, though she is in safe keeping.'

'It has unsettled us all – the king most of all,' Anne replied. Frances thought she detected a note of disdain in her voice. 'He has been in a perfect terror ever since, and keeps mostly to his rooms, with only his Scottish servants in attendance. He swears that every Englishman countenances his death.'

One of the ladies made a small cough.

'Well, well, I must not speak of such matters,' the queen said quickly. 'We are all unharmed, God be praised, and I am indebted to you for keeping our daughter safe too.'

Frances inclined her head, but remained silent. She flicked her gaze towards the two attendants, who stared impassively ahead. After a few moments, Anne gestured for them to leave. They bobbed a swift curtsey, then stepped down from the dais, their skirts rustling as they passed. As soon as they had closed the door behind them, the queen gave a deep sigh.

'They came so close to success, Frances,' she said quietly. 'They lacked but a few hours.'

Frances paused so that she might choose her words carefully.

'It was a hazardous enterprise, ma'am.'

'But a noble one!' the queen exclaimed suddenly. 'If they had not been betrayed, then they would surely have accomplished everything they had planned. But now – now all is in ruins.' She shook her head impatiently. 'Cecil is like a cat who has cornered a mouse. He relishes the game of tormenting it before he pounces. Fawkes has already confessed; Wintour will soon follow. Though they say that he will not need to be racked: he is wounded and helpless enough as it is.'

A tear wound its way slowly down Frances's cheek. She had not shed a single one since hearing the news of his capture, for fear that if she gave way to her grief, it would have no end. But now that the queen had spoken of his pain, his helplessness, she could no longer contain it.

'I am sorry for it, my dear,' Anne said, her voice softer now. 'I know how deeply you loved him – and he you. He was a fine man, and brave.'

'He is still,' Frances replied defiantly, then cast her gaze to the ground. 'Might he yet be spared?' she asked in a small voice. 'If he gives Cecil the information that he seeks? Surely the king will wish to be hailed as merciful? His enemies have shed enough blood already.'

'If Wintour gives Cecil what he seeks, then we are all destroyed. All.' Frances caught the fear in her voice, as well as the anger. 'Cecil knows that they have a powerful patron at court, and has long suspected that it is me. But I have been careful to give him no proof, and even he flinches at the idea that a woman would collude in the murder of her own husband and son.' She stared at Frances, her eyes filled with bitterness. 'But suffering and violence and humiliation will drive us to take extreme measures. I acted as my conscience dictated.'

Frances paused for a moment, considering. Her mind went back to that morning at Hampton Court when she had visited Sir Everard's chambers.

'Did all the plotters know of your involvement, Your Grace?'

The queen shook her head. 'Just Catesby and Wintour. The knowledge was too dangerous to be shared more broadly. Catesby has taken it to his grave, or rather—' She broke off and shuddered, then took a breath before continuing. 'So my fate rests with Tom. His confession is expected every day.'

'He is a man of honour, ma'am,' Frances assured her quietly. 'He will not betray you – or anyone.'

'Who knows what a man will do when faced with the terrors of torture?' Anne countered impatiently. 'The king showed me Fawkes's confession, signed after torture. His signature is barely decipherable. He will have to be carried to the scaffold and held aloft while they tighten the noose around his neck.'

Frances looked down at her hands, which were clasped tightly together. They felt clammy and cold, despite the heat from the fire. She cared little for herself, but if Tom did name the queen, or worse still her father . . . She swallowed hard.

'Forgive me,' the queen said with a sigh. 'I should not speak so frankly. It is a failing in me – at least, with those I trust. With the king and his minions, I am a perfect queen of ice.' She paused. 'I just need to prepare myself – and you – for what might happen.'

'Is there nothing we can do to help him?' Frances asked, her eyes pleading. 'The king knows that he lacks the love of his people. If you could persuade him to show clemency—'

Anne reached forward and squeezed her hands.

'If I thought I had that power, I would not hesitate to use it,' she replied with a sad smile. 'But I am the last person of whom my husband will take heed. He wishes I would be carried away by a fever, or else in childbed, so that he could be left to enjoy his favourites in peace. My word is nothing to him.'

'Then we must only wait and hope?' Frances asked. Her eyes pricked with tears of frustration, and she brushed them angrily away.

'And pray,' the queen added softly. 'Pray that Tom will be taken by the Lord before he meets the crueller death.'

Frances bowed her head and closed her eyes, though not in prayer. She could no longer bear to look at the queen, nor hear the cold comfort that she offered. They sat in silence for a long time, then at last Frances roused herself and dropped a brief curtsey.

'Forgive me, Your Grace, but I am tired from my journey, and will seek whatever chamber has been reserved for me.'

The queen nodded, but did not reply. Frances had almost reached the door when Anne spoke her name. She stopped, her hand suspended above the door handle.

'I will do everything I can to save him,' she said quietly.

Frances did not turn, but stood still for a few moments, struggling to maintain her composure. At length, she gave a small nod, then slipped silently from the room.

As she passed through the succession of public rooms beyond, she was struck by the quietness. The court was usually crowded with ambitious place-seekers, visiting dignitaries, and household servants, but Greenwich was almost deserted. The few courtiers who lingered in the Great Hall had an air of despondency, but as Frances caught their eye she saw watchfulness too. She nodded her acknowledgement to those she recognised, but continued on to her chamber without stopping for conversation. She had no appetite for pleasantries, and even less for being drawn into discussing the late treason.

By the time she reached her apartment, the sun was dipping low on the horizon, and the room was suffused with a deep red glow. She crossed to the window and looked out towards the river. The tide was high now, and the waters threatened to spill over onto the edge of the formal gardens that swept down towards the riverbank. Frances craned her neck towards the city. Shielding her eyes against the dazzling rays, she tried to catch a glimpse of the Tower, but the snaking river afforded only views of the meadows that stretched out beyond the palace and across the north bank.

Sighing, she pulled the pane closed and sank down onto the bed. The princess would be here in a few days' time, and, although the queen had instructed Frances to arrive early in order to prepare the girl's apartments, she knew this was the work of only a few hours. She would have ample time to go to Whitehall, where the king and his court were residing, and could petition him herself for clemency.

Her mind ran on, imagining the words she might employ to persuade him. They sounded weak even to her ears, and as she lay back onto the pillows, she was overcome with a sense of hopelessness. The tears flowed freely now as she thought of Tom, shivering in whatever dark corner of the Tower he had been thrown into. Did he still draw breath, or had he bled out from his wounds, surrendering himself to the kinder death? She could not bear to think of him there, utterly deprived of hope and comfort.

Hear me, Lord, and answer me.

She mouthed the familiar words of the psalm as she pressed her hands together.

In this time of trouble I call.

She paused. Countless times she had recited the prayer. It had been a favourite of her father, and he had made sure all of his children knew it by heart so that they could draw comfort during any future suffering that might afflict them. But as she searched for the next line, she found only silence. She lay there for a long time, hoping that the words would suddenly return, but eventually, exhausted and resigned, she fell into a restless sleep.

She was down at the riverside before daylight. It had been easy enough to steal out of the palace unnoticed. There were few guards in attendance: most would be stationed at Whitehall, Frances supposed, in order to protect the king from any papists who still lurked in the city. The queen was of comparatively little importance, her favourite retreat a backwater. Frances had been hard-pressed to find a boatman to take her upriver.

The eastern stretch of the Thames was quiet, and soon Frances could see the turrets of the Tower silhouetted against the pale grey sky. She shivered, but her gaze did not waver as she surveyed the imposing white stone keep that towered above the thick walls encircling it. The oarsman eyed her uncertainly as she sat there, transfixed, twisting her body around as they passed the fortress so that she could watch as it gradually faded from view. Only as they were drawing level with the gates of Whitehall did she turn her head, suddenly aware of her surroundings. She looked at the steps that led up to the labyrinthine passages and courtyards, and the memory of following Tom there came back to her so vividly that she had to catch her breath. It had only been a few months before, but it felt like a lifetime.

Then she looked along the walls of the palace towards the Parliament buildings, and something caught her eye. Surmounted on two of the turrets there seemed to be a pair of moving orbs or weathervanes. Curious, Frances disembarked and walked towards the turrets. At first, she could not make out the ragged shapes on top, but then a stiff breeze whipped up from the Thames, twisting the poles around. She felt the bile rise up in her throat as she recognised the decaying heads of Robert Catesby and Thomas Percy. Their hair was matted and clumped, and the dark grey skin of their faces had a slack, waxen appearance, like a mask that had been melted by fire. The sockets of their eyes were hollow, and their mouths were downturned as if in perpetual lament. The skin around their necks was jagged and uneven from where it had been hacked away from their lifeless bodies.

Frances stared in horror for a few moments, unable to wrest her gaze away from the hideous sight. Then the splash of an oar on the river behind her broke the spell and she turned away, retching into the water. Crouching down, she clutched her stomach and tried to still her breathing to stop herself from fainting. Though she cast about for something to distract her thoughts, the faces of the two men seemed to be imprinted onto her mind's eye, and she clasped her hand over her mouth as a fresh wave of nausea swept over her.

After a few minutes, she raised herself up to standing and took a couple of tentative steps towards the palace. Desperation to escape the hideous spectacle gave her the strength to move forward, and she quickened her pace so that by the time she reached the riverside gate she was breathless from the exertion.

The yeomen guarding the entrance were busy interrogating a man who was trying to get in. As Frances approached, one of them turned and gave her a long, appraising stare. She had seen him several times before, and was grateful for having taken care to be courteous in the past, for he nodded at her now and lifted his halberd so that she could pass through.

The courtyard within was the usual bustle of officials and attendants. Frances kept her eyes fixed straight ahead as she walked across to the doorway that led into the palace, hoping that none of them would stop to question her as to the nature of her business there. Her sex was an advantage for once, she acknowledged bitterly, as she emerged into the first of the public rooms. Few would concern themselves with a mere woman.

As she neared the Great Hall, the aroma of freshly baked bread filled the air. Though the idea of eating made Frances's stomach heave, she craved a cup of water to cleanse her mouth. She therefore joined the ranks of courtiers who were crowding onto the long wooden benches that had been set out next to each table.

She was about to take a seat on the end of a row when she felt a hand press down on her shoulder. She turned sharply and saw her uncle standing before her, his face a mask of disapproval.

'What business have you here, niece?' he demanded as he clasped her elbow and steered her towards a quieter bench close to the raised dais.

'I am seeking an audience with the king, my lord,' she replied evenly.

The earl gave a snort of derision.

'You would do better to seek an audience with the pope,' he sneered. 'His Majesty has not shown himself to the court since the discovery of the late plot. He keeps to his innermost rooms, and will have only Scotsmen about him. He says the English are like vipers in the nest; he trusts none of us – not even Cecil,' he added, his expression brightening for a moment. 'The lords of the council are as alarmed by the king's suspicions as by the plot itself. Everybody is jumping at shadows. You would have done well to stay in Warwickshire.'

'I had no choice, Uncle. The queen summoned me back to London. She wished me to prepare for the arrival of her daughter.'

'What the devil does she mean by having that milksop brought back to court?' he snapped. 'She has caused trouble enough where she is. I wouldn't wonder if she had been conspiring with the plotters from the beginning. No doubt they flattered her into thinking that she would make a fine little queen, once her father and brothers were blown to the heavens.'

Frances bit back a retort. She knew well that her uncle's rages would only be prolonged if they met with resistance.

'And what of you, niece?' he continued after a pause, his voice now dangerously low. 'That churl Wintour fawned about you ever since you came to court. Were you fool enough to believe he loved you, or have you been a willing accomplice to his wicked schemes?'

Frances felt a rising fury as she glared back at her uncle. She had never despised him more than at this moment, she realised, as she watched his face grow puce and the pulse at his temples begin to throb.

'Who is the fool, Uncle?' she asked quietly. 'Do you truly believe it is I, not the ranks of preening flatterers who flock to pay homage to the cowardly, depraved usurper who sits on the throne, hoping to feast from the scraps that he throws from his table? I would rather die than serve such a master.'

The earl seemed stupefied for a few moments and stared back at her, his mouth moving as if trying to form the words with which to reply.

'So Cecil was right, then,' he said at last. 'He has long suspected you of complicity in some plot against His Majesty. Sackville overheard him say that he had set that old fool Harington to spy on you at Coombe, and Dymock was only too happy to oblige when you were at Longford. No doubt they found matter enough to fill their letters back to court. And to think that I defended your honour. Again and again I have assured the king of your loyalty after Cecil had dropped poison in his ears. You will bring us all to ruin – your father and mother are halfway there already, eking out their miserable days at Richmond. How proud they will be of their treacherous daughter when they see her head set on a spike.'

Frances took a breath. Her uncle had said nothing that she had not known or suspected, but the mention of her parents had dealt her a stinging blow. She fell silent for a few moments, considering. When at last she spoke again, her voice held none of the bitterness with which it had been tainted before.

'I have never intended any harm to my family, Uncle. If I had been permitted to stay at Longford, then I would have served them well to the end of my days – I wish it had been so,' she added wistfully. 'But it was your will that I should come here to further our fortunes, and you must carry some blame for what has followed.'

She saw anger flare again in his eyes, but continued before he could speak.

'If God wills that I die a traitor, I will accept His judgement. But I will not forsake those to whom I am bound. The king must be persuaded to show clemency to the plotters. If he will not admit me to his presence so that I can petition him in person, then you must do so. As a member of the council, you cannot be denied access.'

'And why do you think I would wish to speak on behalf of proven traitors?' the earl demanded scornfully.

'Because it would lessen Cecil's power,' Frances urged, her eyes blazing. 'You lack allies: Northumberland can no longer be of any use to you. Even the king knows of his Catholic sympathies, and now that his cousin has been proved a traitor, he must be suspected of complicity.'

She saw her uncle shift uncomfortably. Sensing her advantage, she continued, her voice rising with conviction: 'If, as you say, Cecil is already falling from favour, then you can speed his decline. The king knows that he lacks the love of his people. Showing himself to be a merciful ruler will do more to strengthen his hand than any number of troops. I wager none of his council has had the courage to tell him so. You can set yourself apart as an adviser of greater wisdom and experience than they.'

Her cheeks were flushed and her breath came rapidly as she held her uncle's gaze. He looked back at her doubtfully, but at length he gave a heavy sigh, as if resigned.

'I will think on it, niece,' he said. 'But in the meantime, you must get yourself back to Greenwich and keep your head low, lest someone chooses to strike it off.'

Frances took a long sip from the cup in front of her and set it down with trembling fingers, then got to her feet and bobbed a curtsey.

'Good day to you, my lord. And God speed your endeavours.'

CHAPTER 45

20 November

The princess has fallen gravely ill from a fever occasioned by the late disturbances. The poor lady is very troubled besides, having not recovered from the shock. I fear that she will not be fit to travel for some considerable time.

Frances put the letter down and looked at the queen.

'Do you wish me to go to her, Your Grace?'

Anne shook her head. 'Lord Harington was always given to exaggeration. If my daughter is as ill as he says, then he would have written to ask that the court physicians attend her. It may all be a trick. Cecil has made little secret of wanting to keep the princess in Warwickshire, safe from my influence. He treats me like a pariah, and my husband is too far buried in his own chambers to notice – not that he would care greatly if he did. Rumours are spreading that I was involved in the Powder Treason, and it will take little to convince the king that his wife is intent upon his destruction.' She smiled bitterly and bent her head back to her embroidery, stabbing at the canvas with unnecessary force.

'Have you not seen His Majesty since we last spoke?' Frances asked, trying to keep her voice neutral.

'He refuses to receive me, and will not answer my letters,' the queen replied scornfully. Seeing Frances's expression, she continued in a softer tone: 'I am sorry that I have been unable to help Tom, or any of his fellow prisoners for that matter. I have written to beg the king to show mercy, but I do not know if my letters have even reached him. I would not be surprised if they have all ended up as kindling for Cecil's fire.'

Frances fell silent. There had been no word from her uncle either. She felt as if she might be driven to madness from the long hours of watching and waiting. At least there was one thing of which she was certain: Tom still lived. There had been a flurry of proclamations, all denouncing the evil of the plotters who were held in the Tower. Their names had been given out numerous times so that they were on the lips of every subject in the kingdom. Only Tom's brother Robert remained at large. He had not been seen since he had fled from Holbeach, having had a premonition of disaster, so it was said. Father Garnet had also gone to ground. Frances imagined him cowering in the priest hole of a wealthy Catholic estate. Perhaps she should have done the same. It would have spared her family the disgrace that was surely to come.

'Will you go to him?'

Anne's question was so unexpected that for a moment Frances was not certain that she had understood. The queen's gaze was unwavering as she waited for an answer.

'How can I?' she asked at length. 'The Tower must be even more of a fortress than usual, and I cannot think that Cecil would allow such notorious traitors to receive visitors.'

'But you are not without connections there, Frances,' Anne said quietly. 'There are those who might wish to make amends for former wrongs.'

Frances looked uncertain. Though he could hardly be held accountable, Sir Richard Berkeley had certainly shown a degree of remorse for her ordeal in the Tower. But she could not think that it would be enough for him to risk defying his orders by admitting a visitor to one of the most notorious prisoners in his custody.

'I could gain you admittance to the Tower,' she continued. 'My command still carries enough weight for that. And Sir Richard would hardly refuse to see a member of the princess's household.'

The prospect of seeing Tom again was overwhelming after the long days of trying to reconcile herself to the fact that he might be lost to her for ever. She turned doubtful eyes to the queen.

'But I would surely be placing you in danger, Your Grace, if word got out that a member of your daughter's household had visited one of the plotters? You said that rumours of your involvement are already beginning to circulate.'

Anne waved her hand dismissively. 'I care little enough for that,' she said airily, then gave a little smile. 'My life here is interminable. If the king saw fit to have me thrown into the Tower, it would at least provide some diversion. Besides,' she added gently, 'I too am in your debt. I have so far proved powerless to fulfil my promise to help Tom. The least I can do is provide some comfort to you both before—' She hesitated. 'Before God's will is done.'

Frances held her gaze for a moment longer, then slowly inclined her head.

Frances pulled up her hood and drew her cloak around her chin so that her face was almost completely obscured. The yeoman of the guard glanced at her again, then back to the letter that she had handed him, drawing his lantern closer so that he might study the seal.

'Wait there please, my lady,' he said, then turned and marched briskly across the drawbridge and out of sight, his footsteps echoing along the cobblestones.

Frances reached into her pocket. Her fingers closed over the tiny glass phial. She took a breath. *God give me the strength for what I must do.*

She looked about her, desperate for something to distract her from what lay ahead. The portcullis was just visible above the arch of the gateway, its spikes gleaming in the moonlight. The walls of this tower must be several feet thick, she calculated, and there were many more that followed in the ringwork of defences that surrounded the fortress. The king should have holed himself up here, rather than in the patchwork palace of Whitehall. He could live out his days safe from even the fiercest of attackers.

The guard returned a few minutes later and gave a curt signal for Frances to follow him. They stepped through the small opening in the iron-studded door, and Frances heard the sharp thud as it was closed behind them. She quickened her step to keep up with the guard, whose lantern provided the only light in the narrow passageway beyond. After a few more paces, they turned left under the archway of the Garden Tower, their way lit by torches fixed to the walls on either side of the stone stairs that led up to the green. With every step she took, Frances pushed back the recollections of the last time she had been within these walls. Her terror then could surely not have been greater than her apprehension now as they neared the door to the lieutenant's lodging.

Sir Richard opened it before the guard had the chance to knock. With a nod, he dismissed him and bade Frances enter. He showed her into a brightly lit parlour, where a fire roared in the grate. She lowered her hood, grateful for the warmth, and sat in the chair that Sir Richard indicated. An open book was turned face down on the table, a half empty glass of wine next to it. *He can hardly have welcomed such an unexpected guest at this hour.* Though he forced a pleasant smile as he sat down opposite her, she caught the panic in his eyes.

'Sir Richard, I have come to see one of the prisoners in your custody,' Frances began without preamble.

A fleeting look of relief crossed the old man's features.

'Sir Walter is a popular resident here. Prince Henry himself came to visit but three weeks ago. However, I fear the hour may be a little late—'

'It is not Sir Walter whom I wish to see,' Frances interrupted. 'It is one of the men suspected of involvement in the Powder Treason.'

Sir Richard blanched. He reached for his glass of wine and took a long sip, holding her steady gaze as he did so. Frances noticed that his hand trembled as he set the glass down.

'My Lord Salisbury has issued strict orders that they are to see and speak to no one except their interrogators. I cannot disobey him.' He spread his hands and gave a slight shrug.

Frances paused, but kept her eyes fixed on him. Her mouth felt dry, and she swallowed hard before continuing.

'You have ever been a faithful servant to Lord Salisbury, have you not?' she asked in a low voice. 'I am testament to that. He had an innocent woman tortured, and you delivered her to him, even though employing such methods is against English law. Tell me, Sir Richard, do you consider that just? Is that why you accepted the post of lieutenant, so that you could arrange the torture of innocent men and women?'

She saw him flinch at her words.

'The gunpowder plotters are hardly innocent, Lady Frances,' he replied quietly. 'Their guilt has been well proven, even before their trial.'

'And have they freely confessed, or was it wrenched out of them?' she demanded, her voice growing louder.

The old man shifted uncomfortably in his chair. He took another sip from his glass.

'They are obstinate papists, Lady Frances, and so committed to their cause that they would say nothing to hinder it.' He sighed and ran his fingers across his brow. 'Fawkes had to be racked. He would have rotted away in his cell without speaking a word otherwise. But Wintour maintains his silence.'

Frances took a breath and looked down at her hands.

'And has he been racked too?' she asked quietly.

Sir Richard shook his head. 'There is little point. He is tortured enough by his wounds.'

She felt tears prick her eyes, but blinked them quickly away.

'It is he whom I wish to see.'

'My lady, I have already explained the impossibility—'

'As lieutenant of the Tower, it is in your gift, Sir Richard. The hour is late, as you say, and there can be no one here who would recognise me. You can tell the guard that I am his sister, come to pray with her brother before his trial. This should keep his silence.' She drew a bag of coins out of her pocket and placed it on the table in front of him.

Sir Richard fell silent again, his gaze fixed upon the purse.

'Very well,' he said at last. 'But for a few moments only.'

The smell of damp grew stronger as Sir Richard led her down the winding stairs, their only light the small lantern that he carried. At the foot of the staircase, there was a long narrow passageway with a number of doors on each side. As they walked along it, there was a sudden clattering of keys as a guard at the far end scrambled to his feet. When they reached him, the lieutenant leaned forward and spoke quietly in his ear, then pressed the bag of coins into his hand. The man nodded and unlocked the door next to him.

Sir Richard turned to Frances. 'I have told him you are to stay for a brief time only. I will leave you now.'

He turned on his heel and walked briskly back along the corridor before she could thank him. The guard lifted the latch and pushed the heavy iron door open. Frances stepped forward uncertainly. She stood on the threshold, blinking into the gloom.

'Take this,' the guard said, as he thrust a lamp towards her. A moment later she heard the door slam shut. She jolted forward and almost dropped the lamp. The candle flickered as she reached out to steady herself, and her hand brushed against a rough wooden post. Slowly, she lifted the light, and her breath caught in her throat.

Lying on the bare pallet that she had touched was a man, his legs drawn up to his chest. He wore a long linen shirt and breeches, and there were dark stains around his shoulder and stomach. His face was obscured by his arms, which were drawn over his head as if to shield him from a blow.

Frances drew in a deep breath. The air was dank and smelt of decay. She took a few steps so that she was level with the man's face, then knelt down on the cold stone floor. She lifted her lamp and gently reached forward to touch his arm. It felt as cold and still as marble. Her heart lurched, and she clasped her hand to her mouth. Hope and despair flared within her. But then he made a slight groan and shifted on the pallet.

'Tom,' she whispered as she leaned forward and stroked his hair, which was tangled and matted. She held her lamp closer to his face. His lips were dry and cracked, and there were smears of dark blood on his deathly white cheek. After a few moments, his eyelids began to flicker and he slowly opened them, blinking against the light. She set the lamp down on the floor and placed her hands gently over his. His eyes widened with recognition and he tried to speak, but the words rasped in his throat.

'Quiet, my love.' Frances pressed her fingers gently to his lips. She hesitated as she gazed into his sunken eyes, which were clouded with pain. Willing herself to find the strength that she needed, she reached into her pocket and drew out the phial. Her hand trembled as she eased the tiny stopper from the top.

'Here, drink this – slowly now.'

Tom lifted his head, wincing in pain as he did so. Frances could hardly breathe as she watched him take the phial from her hands and bring it to his lips. She longed to turn away, yet her eyes were fixed upon his mouth.

He tilted the phial, and slowly opened his mouth. Frances felt as if time had stopped. Her breathing came quick and shallow.

Tom paused, the liquid suspended at an angle in the glass. The acrid smell of foxgloves filled the air as he peered at the tincture, then at Frances.

'What is this?' he whispered, his voice cracked and hoarse.

Frances held his gaze.

'It is for your ease.'

Still, he watched her, but made no move to drink the potion. Frances felt as if the breath was being squeezed from her lungs.

'Please—' she whispered.

Tom gazed back at her with sadness and affection. She felt her resolve begin to crumble and her eyes welled with tears. Unable to look at him any longer, she lowered her head and began to sob. She was only vaguely aware of him taking the stopper from her and setting the phial down on the floor.

'Frances.' He reached out and stroked her hair. 'Did you mean to end my suffering – here, tonight?'

Her shoulders heaved with silent grief, and for several moments she was unable to answer. Then slowly she raised her bloodshot eyes to his.

'Forgive me,' she whispered. 'I have prayed – *prayed* – that God would take you before you leave this place. But it seems that he has deserted us.' Her eyes were wide with horror. 'I cannot let you suffer the torments of a traitor's death.'

Tom sank back onto the pallet, but grasped her hands in his, which felt deathly cold. He continued to regard her steadily.

'And I cannot let you forfeit your life for mine,' he said quietly. 'They know that my injuries are not enough to kill me – at least, not for some weeks yet. If they find me dead after you have left, they will have you arrested as a witch. Cecil let slip his prey once; he will not do so again.'

'But you know what awaits you. How will you bear it?' Frances whispered, her eyes filling with tears again.

Tom tightened his grip on her hands. His eyes shone in the pale light of the candle.

'For the love of you, I would suffer any torment. It cannot be greater than knowing that I had sent you to your death.'

Frances dipped her head to kiss his hands. When she looked up again, his eyes were glistening with tears.

'We have little time,' she whispered urgently, her face close to his. 'The queen has tried to petition her husband for clemency, but he refuses to see her. I have had no word from my uncle, and I fear he too has failed – if he even tried. You must do what you can to save yourself. If you give Cecil the confession he seeks, you may yet live.'

Tom gave a slight shake of his head.

'He will only be satisfied if I name those at court with whom we conspired.'

'Then name them!' Frances cried. There was the sound of feet scuffing on the flagstones on the other side of the door. She held her breath and waited, but the guard did not come in. After a pause, she continued in a low voice: 'The queen is weary of her life. She would gladly be free of it. Not that James would dare to have her executed for treason. It would make him even more ridiculous in the eyes of his subjects. He would send her away to a nunnery, where she could live out her days in peace.'

'And you?' He reached out and cupped her face in his hands. 'What would become of you?'

Frances looked at him steadily.

'Cecil knows that I am involved in this plot, and lacks only the evidence with which to persuade the king. If you give it to him, he will surely spare your life.'

'Or have us both put to death,' Tom said with a sad smile.

There was a sudden rattle of keys, and the door was flung open. In panic, Frances turned to face the guard.

'A few minutes more. Please,' she urged. 'We must have time to pray.'

The guard hesitated for a moment, then grunted and slammed the door shut behind him. Tom leaned forward and drew Frances towards him so that their faces were almost touching. His breath on her lips was barely warm.

'I must die knowing that you shall live, Frances. Only that will give me the courage I lack.'

A tear ran slowly down her cheek as she gazed back at him. He pressed his lips to it, then to her own. She clung to him as he drew her closer, wrapping his arms around her. The urgency of his kiss gradually subsided, and he lay back on the pallet, breathing heavily. She gently lowered herself down behind him and they lay like that for several minutes, her arms wrapped around his torso and her face pressed into his neck.

When she heard a movement behind the door, she kn[ew]
end. Battling every instinct in her body, she raised herself f[rom]
pallet and knelt down beside him once more. As the guard wa[lked]
in, she leaned towards Tom, whose eyes never left hers.

'I love you,' she whispered, then kissed him gently on the
mouth. 'I always have.'

Hearing his own words echoed back to him, Tom closed his
eyes. When he opened them again, she had gone.

CHAPTER 46

3 November

Frances pushed her way through the banqueting hall, which was crammed with courtiers chattering excitedly and craning their necks towards the empty throne on the raised dais. All of the windows were closed against the winter chill, and the air was stifling. A bead of sweat ran down her back as she surged forward, and when at last she found a relatively quiet corner next to one of the pillars, she was obliged to crouch down for a few moments to stop herself from fainting. Her breathing gradually became steadier, and she stood up slowly, holding onto the pillar. From her vantage point, she could see the lords of the council sitting grave-faced on two rows of chairs at the edge of the dais. Her uncle looked flushed and agitated, and every now and then he ran his finger along his collar in an attempt to loosen it.

She turned her gaze towards the large doorway behind them as a fanfare sounded across the hall. The lords immediately got to their feet and bowed low as the king swept past, a triumphant expression on his face. Behind him came the queen. Frances studied her closely, but she looked as impassive as ever. In her wake was Cecil. Though his head was bowed, she caught the smile that played about his lips. It made her blood run cold.

A hush descended as James walked to the front of the dais, flanked by six yeomen of the guard. Anne had sat down on her throne, staring straight ahead. To her left was Cecil, his hands placed neatly on his lap.

'Faithful subjects,' the king began, 'I have summoned you here so that I can relay news of the greatest import.' His accent was stronger than before, Frances noticed, no doubt thanks to having closeted himself away with his Scottish attendants. She strained to catch his next words, though she also feared what they might be.

'Ye will know that all but one of the plotters in the late devilish conspiracy have been captured and thrown into the Tower. They thought to elude punishment through their refusal to confess, but their obstinacy has crumbled before the skill of my interrogators. Guido Fawkes was the first to admit his guilt, and today the other leader has capitulated.'

Frances drew a sharp breath.

'Thomas Wintour has signed a full confession of the part that he – and others – played in the treasonous plot.' The king held a rolled parchment aloft with a dramatic flourish and smiled in satisfaction at the excited murmurs around the room. Frances's eyes darted across to the queen, but her expression had not altered. 'His words, written in his own hand, have provided my ministers with ample evidence to proceed to trial. This shall take place at Westminster Hall, where they intended to murder me and my Parliament, at a date to be assigned by us.'

He broke off again and looked around the hall to make sure that his words had taken full effect. The answering babble of animated voices assured him that they had. The guards who stood on either side of him were also scrutinising the faces of the crowd, but their expressions were anxious and watchful. Frances could no longer see any of them. Her vision had become clouded and her skin prickled with heat. She gripped the pillar tighter and willed this audience to end. Through the haze, she could hear the king's voice again.

'Lord Salisbury has seen to it that copies of Wintour's confession be distributed throughout the kingdom so that all my subjects might learn the heinousness of his crimes, and those of his fellow papists.' He nodded to Cecil, who handed several large scrolls to a group of attendants. They immediately began tacking them to each of the pillars, and, as soon as the king and his entourage had left the dais, everyone surged forward so that they might read the plotter's words.

Frances was jostled and pushed aside as a copy was fixed to the pillar next to her.

THE VOLUNTARY DECLARATION OF THOMAS WINTOUR OF HUDDINGTON IN THE COUNTY OF WORCESTER, THE 23RD OF NOVEMBER 1605 AT THE TOWER.

These were the only words she was able to read before the parchment faded from view. Desperate for air, she forced her way out of the crowds and ran for the doorway that the king had walked through a few moments earlier. As she rounded the corner at the end of the corridor, she came to an abrupt halt. Cecil was standing before her, his arms crossed in front of him, and an expression of mild amusement on his face.

'You are a fast reader, Lady Frances,' he remarked softly. 'Once Mr Wintour had broken his silence, the words came spilling out. My scribe was hard-pressed to keep up. He might as well have written his own death warrant, and that of his fellow papists. The trial will be over in a matter of minutes.'

'Did you loosen his tongue for him?' Frances asked, her voice dangerously low.

'Oh, there was no need,' Cecil retorted airily. 'The poor wretch is already bent double with his wounds. If we had pulled him straight on the rack, it would have stopped his breath before he could spit out the words.'

Frances felt the colour drain from her cheeks as she glared at him. Cecil took a step closer and leaned towards her.

'He did not name you – or your treacherous queen,' he whispered in her ear. Then suddenly he gripped her arm, squeezing it so that Frances winced with pain. 'But I know you were up to your necks in it,' he hissed, the spittle falling on her cheek.

He held her there, his breathing hot and rapid against her neck as she struggled to free herself. 'Sir Everard kept me well informed – for a time at least – and I made a show of having lost interest in the plot so that they would keep to their course. It would have been so disappointing if they had lost their nerve and lived out their lives in peace, don't you think?'

Frances wrenched her arm free and sprang away from him, her eyes filled with loathing. Her chest heaved as she gasped for breath. Cecil's smile broadened.

'I could not bring the king's witch to the gallows, but I will see her lover suffer the torments of a traitor's death,' he sneered.

Without pausing to think, Frances lunged forward and slapped him sharply across the face. The sound reverberated along the marble corridor as Cecil put his fingers up to his cheek, his eyes blazing with shock. When he lowered his hand, she saw a deepening red welt, and felt a stab of triumph.

'I wish that I were a witch,' she said quietly. 'I would curse you and your wretched schemes to hell.'

She stepped slowly forward so that she was standing directly before him, her eyes alight with fury. Her mouth lifted into a slow smile, then, without warning, she spat in his face. Barely registering the look of rage that suffused his features, she pushed past him, striding briskly down the corridor and out into the bright winter sunshine.

1606

CHAPTER 47

27 January

The angel's eyes were closed, and he wore an expression of quiet bliss. A crown of perfectly symmetrical curls framed his peaceful face, and clasped in his hands was a large shield bearing the arms of England. On his back was a pair of wings, stretched out wide as if ready to take flight.

'Do you think it will begin soon?'

Frances wrested her gaze from the heavenly vision in the magnificent ceiling above and looked down at the princess. The girl's delicate brow was creased with worry, and her fingers moved fretfully along the lace edging of her handkerchief.

'It cannot be long now,' Frances replied quietly.

The murmurs from the crowded hall below were growing steadily louder. Frances looked along the row of seats, and saw the king fidgeting impatiently as he peered down over the balcony. On his right sat Prince Henry, a scowl on his face. To the other side was Charles, who was leaning against his mother. His features were sharper than when she had last seen him, and his legs had grown long and spindly. He wore a solemn, watchful expression, and every now and then he glanced nervously up at his father.

Frances wished herself far away from this place. She had not for a moment thought that she would have to suffer the ordeal of watching the trial: such matters were usually restricted to the male members of court. But Cecil had persuaded the king that his wife and eldest daughter should be present so that they too might witness the execution of justice in his realm. James had agreed, on condition that they all be hidden from view, for fear that there might be papist assassins amidst the crowded courtroom.

Four loud knocks suddenly echoed around the ancient hall. Immediately, the chatter ceased, and all eyes turned to the doorway that led from the outer courtyard. An official in heavy black robes walked solemnly forward, a large staff raised before him. In his wake came a grim-faced man with dark hair and a reddish beard. He wore a long violet silk robe edged with ermine, a hood and cowl covering his shoulders. Frances's heart sank as she recognised Sir Edward Coke, one of the most feared judges in the kingdom. He had sent many men and women to their deaths during the old queen's reign, and his severity had shown no signs of abating now that James was on the throne. He took his seat in the centre of the raised dais, and the Lords Commissioners fanned out on the benches at either side. Frances noticed that the Earl of Northumberland was absent. She had heard that he was in the Tower. Cecil must have delighted in the opportunity to have one of his chief rivals removed so easily. The Lord Privy Seal entered the hall now, wearing the full robes of his office, and took a seat at the far left of the dais.

The summoning official rapped his staff on the floor again. Frances held her breath. The sound of shuffling footsteps could be heard approaching the hall, and a few moments later the first of the accused men appeared. Leaning forward in her seat, she recognised the swaggering gait of Sir Everard Digby. As he strolled nonchalantly past the assembled lords, trailing tobacco smoke from a pipe that protruded from one corner of his mouth, she caught the fleeting look that he exchanged with Cecil. The king immediately started to mutter, furious that his proclamation against tobacco smoking should be so publicly flouted.

Frances's eyes flitted across the men who followed, then stopped as they alighted upon Tom. He was staring straight ahead, his bearing erect, as he walked slowly towards the bench that faced the judge and his commissioners. His right arm was supported by a rudimentary sling fashioned from a dirty piece of linen, and his chest and stomach were obscured by a cloak flung over his shoulder, hiding his other wound from view. Even from this distance, she could see that his face had grown pinched and his eyes hollow.

Walking alongside him was his brother Robert. His hair and beard were much longer than when she had last seen him, and he too had grown thinner. News of his capture had reached the court a little over two weeks before. He had been hiding out in a succession of houses and barns since fleeing the siege at Holbeach, and the effects of spending a harsh winter mostly out of doors showed in his haggard appearance.

The last member of the sombre procession was Guido Fawkes, who was supported on either side by a court official and dragged, rather than walking, to join his fellow conspirators. His arms and legs hung as limp as a ragdoll's, and his neck lolled forward with every step that they took. Frances shuddered and sank back in her chair, but she could not hide from the view thanks to a large scaffold that had been erected for the eight men to stand on. They shuffled up the steps now, and stood in a line facing the crowded hall. Fawkes was carried by the officials, his feet banging against each step as they hauled him to the platform.

There was utter silence in the hall as the men stood on the scaffold, some with their heads hanging low, others surveyed the room with a fierce, almost triumphant expression on their faces. Frances's eyes were drawn to Tom. He looked neither fearful nor resigned, and there was a stillness about him that suggested a calm acceptance of what lay ahead. She glanced down and saw that in his right hand was clasped a string of beads, which he was slowly pressing between his fingers.

'The tongue of man never delivered, the ear of man never heard, the heart of man never conceived, or the malice of hellish or earthly devil ever practised such a treason as these men who stand before us.'

The commanding voice of Sir Edward Philips, Speaker of the House of Commons, rang out across the hall, causing several members of the audience to jolt in their seats.

'For if it is abominable to murder the least of God's creatures, then how much more so to murder a king, a prince, a state, and a government?' He paused to enable the crowd, who had recovered themselves, to begin murmuring and calling out against the eight men on the platform. 'These same traitors who stand before us are named in the indictment as follows: Thomas Wintour, Guido Fawkes, Robert Keyes, Thomas Bates, Robert Wintour, John Grant, and Ambrose Rookwood.'

Frances looked across at Sir Everard, who was now grinning widely. Had Cecil already ensured that he would escape punishment? If so, then this trial was an even greater charade than she had imagined.

'Sir Everard Digby will be tried by separate indictment,' the Speaker continued, 'for he alone has pleaded guilty to the charges set before him.'

Sir Everard's smile had not wavered. Perhaps he and Cecil hoped by this to secure a pardon, Frances wondered.

'The Lords here present should also be notified of three other traitors who are not yet taken,' Sir Philip continued. 'Father John Gerard, Father Oswald Tesimond, and Father Henry Garnet. Be ye advertised that as soon as these Jesuit priests are apprehended, they shall face trial by like means.'

Frances had heard nothing of Father Garnet since their last meeting at Coughton Court. Whoever was sheltering him must have a very ingenious hiding place. Or perhaps, with luck, he had escaped to the Continent with the others mentioned, and would live out his days in peace, far from the contagion of fear and suspicion that was threatening to engulf his native land. But if he were arrested, what might he tell Cecil and his interrogators? He was the only man living, apart from Tom, who knew of her involvement. Catesby had taken the secret to his bloody grave. As she looked across again to Tom, she found herself almost willing the truth to be known. She no longer cared what might befall her.

With an effort, she turned her attention back to the Speaker, who was now setting out the details of the case in lurid and scandalised language, interspersed with dramatic pauses that elicited cries and jeers from the crowd. Frances dug her finger-nails into her palms each time, willing him to finish. When at last he had taken his seat, Sir Edward Coke stood to begin his preamble.

'My Lords, you are here to witness the trial of these Catholic gentlemen who are accused of conspiring the death not only of His Serene Majesty King James, but of his sons, Henry Prince of Wales and Charles Duke of York, together with the entire Parliament of the realm.'

He paused, and there was an answering cacophony from the crowd, with shouts of 'Burn the traitors!' and 'Kill all papists!' Sir Edward surveyed the room, a satisfied smile on his face, then raised his hand to bring the court to order.

'Let there be no doubt that this devilish plot was part of a much wider contagion inspired by that antichrist, the Pope of Rome, and all of those who swear fealty to him instead of to our rightful King and Lord. If these same gentlemen who stand before you today are not punished with the utmost severity that the laws of this land will allow, then be sure of this: the contagion will spread until the entire kingdom is in the grip of the Devil and his minions.'

The shouts and jeers grew deafening again. Frances closed her eyes. She hardly heard the rest of the speech as it droned on, whipping the crowd into a frenzy of anger, fear, and bloodlust. The outcome was already assured.

'And so that there be no doubt as to the means of punishing these wicked traitors if this court should find them guilty, then let me here declare them. On the day appointed for their execution, each of the prisoners shall be drawn along the streets backwards at a horse's tail as a sign that he hath been retrograde to nature.'

Frances swallowed hard and looked across at the angel, willing herself to block out the judge's words as she studied the serenity of the carving.

'He will then be hanged by the neck until he is halfway between heaven and earth, as being unworthy of both. He will be taken down and his privy parts will be cut off and burned before his face since he himself hath been unworthily begotten and is unfit to leave any generation after him. While he still draws breath, his bowels and heart which had conceived of the wicked treason will be sliced out and the head which had imagined such evil doings will be cut off. Thereafter the parts of his body will be set on posts around the city so that they might become prey for the fowls of the air.'

The princess let out a small gasp, but quickly fell silent when her mother shot her a reproving look. Frances reached for her hand, which was cold and clammy, like her own. She tried to breathe deeply, but felt as if her throat was constricting. Taking care to keep her gaze from the platform, she cast about the hall.

It was then that she saw him. Sitting towards the back of the room, close to the doors that led out onto the public courtyard, was her father. Unconsciously, she tightened her grip on the hand of the princess, who looked up at her in surprise. But Frances was staring intently at her father, straining her eyes so that she could capture every detail of his appearance. His gaze was steady, and his expression unreadable as he looked towards the scaffold. While the people around him whispered among themselves or cried out in response to the judge's words, he remained perfectly still. Frances drew comfort from his presence, but it gave her pain too. It reminded her that she should not hold her life so lightly; that there were those who would grieve deeply if her part in the plot was revealed and she met the same fate as these men were certain to.

It was several moments before she realised that the hall was now silent. Looking across to the platform, she saw that Sir Edward had at last resumed his seat, and one of the officials was standing next to the scaffold, a sheaf of papers in his hand. He began to read out the 'Examinations, Confessions and Voluntary Declarations' of each of the accused men in a slow and ponderous manner, his tone never lifting, so that even the most ardent of the spectators started to fidget in their seats.

Frances listened carefully to Tom's, which was by far the longest, trying to catch at any familiar words or phrases. There were none. She knew that it was rumoured to be a forgery, drafted in desperation on the orders of Cecil, who had tired of waiting for him to capitulate. But if this were true, then Tom had held firm about those named within, for it listed only the men who had already been arrested. Frances wondered if Cecil had tried to make him sign another version, with herself and the queen named as conspirators, dangling the prospect of a pardon if he did so. She felt a rush of love for Tom that he had refused to betray them, though she would gladly have forfeited her life for his.

When the last of the statements had been read aloud, Sir Edward turned to the accused and told them that they might speak if they wished. Frances leaned forward in her chair again. As she looked down on Tom, his face still impassive, she felt Elizabeth's hand squeeze hers, and turned to see her young mistress's eyes shining with tears. She clasped her hand over the girl's delicate fingers.

Ambrose Rookwood was first to speak, but uttered only a brief declaration of his love for Catesby, his eyes fixed on the floor the whole time. There was a pause, and several of the men shifted about on their feet.

'My Lords, I do not wish to alter my confession nor plead for clemency.'

Tom's voice, though low, could be heard across the hall. Frances drew in a quiet breath.

'I ask only that I might be hanged for my brother, as well as for myself.' He looked across at Robert, who was visibly shaking. 'He wanted no part of this conspiracy, and if His Majesty should see fit to spare him, he will prove as loyal a subject as any here today.'

'God's wounds I will not!' the king muttered to himself. Frances glanced across, and saw that his face was flushed with rage. When she turned back to Tom, he had fallen silent once more, his gaze fixed on the doorway at the end of the hall, close to where her father was sitting. His fellow prisoners took their turns to speak, some pleading for mercy, others terse and unrepentant.

When the last had spoken, the judge conferred with an official, and then stood to address the hall, his face grave. Frances uttered a silent prayer as she waited for him to pronounce the verdict.

'My Lords, we shall now pass to the trial of Sir Everard so that his verdict shall be heard immediately after the rest.'

Frances saw Sir Everard's smile falter as he darted a look at Cecil, who shifted uncomfortably in his seat. Without pausing, Sir Edward proceeded to read out the indictment, which was no less damning than the one before. By the time that he had finished, Sir Everard was ashen-faced. When asked if he wished to speak, he looked in confusion at Cecil, his mouth working as if trying to form the words with which to defend himself.

'Good people,' he said at last, his voice uncharacteristically high. 'I pray mercy for my offences, but profess that I acted out of the love I bore to he who incited me to join this conspiracy' – he darted a look at Cecil, who stared grimly ahead – 'and that had the promises made to me not been broken, I should sit amongst you now, rather than standing here on this scaffold.'

This sparked a chorus of jeers from the crowd, with shouts of 'heretic' and 'traitor'. Sir Everard raised his voice so that he might continue his plea, but his words were drowned out by the growing cacophony, and the judge was obliged to lift his hand in order to bring the hall to order.

'I pray that you will be merciful to my wife and children, for they do not share in my offence,' Sir Everard said in a faltering voice as the noise died down.

''Tis a pity you thought nothing of His Majesty's children,' bellowed Sir Edward scornfully, 'but instead countenanced the deaths of those tender princes.' There was an answering cheer, and, warming to his theme, the judge quoted from the Psalms: 'Let his wife be a widow, and his children vagabonds, let his posterity be destroyed, and in the next generation let his name be quite put out.'

As Frances looked down on the hapless prisoner, she tried to summon up the loathing she had felt for him ever since she had discovered his betrayal. But she knew now that he had been as much at Cecil's mercy as she, and could feel only pity. Neither could he save himself by proving that he had been acting on Cecil's orders. What proof could there be? His patron was too careful for that, and the only person who would corroborate his story was a woman known throughout the court as a witch.

When at last the crowd had descended into silence once more, Sir Edward commanded the jury to consider its verdict. The dignitaries duly rose from their seats and retired from the hall. Frances let out a slow breath.

'Must we remain here, Father?' Prince Henry asked in his high, nasal voice. 'They may be gone for hours.'

James, his face still flushed, dealt his son a stinging blow across his thigh. 'Of course we must, damn ye!' he cried scornfully. 'Do you care so little for the fate of those wretches who would have blown us both to the heavens?'

Frances saw Henry's own cheeks redden, but he fell into a resentful silence.

'Will their suffering really be so great, Frances?' the princess whispered, her eyes wide with terror.

Frances paused. 'Let us pray they are granted the swifter death,' she replied at last.

Elizabeth opened her mouth to speak again, but at that moment the lifting of a latch echoed around the hall, and all eyes turned expectantly to see the solemn-faced commissioners walk slowly back into the room. Frances looked to where her father had been sitting, but he was no longer there. With rising panic, she scanned the room, desperate to see his reassuring presence. As Sir Edward began to speak, she drew her gaze back to the scaffold.

'Sir John, do you bring a verdict?' he demanded, addressing the Lord Chief Justice.

Her eyes rested on Tom, who was now gazing down at the floor. She saw his shoulders lift slightly and his lips part as he drew in a breath.

'I do, Your Worship.' Sir John paused and surveyed the room, clearly enjoying the moment. At length, he turned back to Sir Edward. 'We find all eight men guilty of high treason.'

'No!'

The cry came from the platform, where Sir Everard had sunk to his knees and was holding his hands aloft in desperate supplication.

'Have mercy!' he shouted, his eyes wild with fear. 'Forgive me, Lord! God save me!'

Sir John nodded towards an official, who mounted the scaffold and dragged the prisoner roughly away. His screams could still be heard when they had disappeared from view. The rest of the prisoners were then led away, their heads bowed and the shouts of the crowd ringing in their ears. Frances's eyes followed Tom as he shuffled silently along, the rosary still gripped tightly in his hands. As he slowly descended the steps from the platform, she saw him press the beads to his lips.

'They will suffer the torments of hell,' the king muttered, his eyes glinting, then he rose abruptly and stalked out of the chamber. His children followed dutifully behind him, the princess dabbing at her eyes with a silk handkerchief. Her mother walked slowly in her wake. As she reached the doorway, Anne turned, and looked back at Frances.

'May God go with them,' she whispered.

Frances kept her gaze fixed on the empty platform. She remained there long after the last of the crowds had filed out into the winter sunshine, the echoes of their footsteps reverberating around the silent hall.

CHAPTER 48

31 January

The bells of St Paul's began to toll. Frances counted. The streets were still in darkness, and there was not a breath of wind, so the sound carried easily.

One, two, three

She drew her knees to her chest and looked up through the open window. The moon was beginning to wane, and the stars had faded from view. Frances had watched them, straining her eyes to catch the last light that they left behind.

Four, five, six

Silence.

Could it be so close to the hour already? Though she had not slept, the time had passed too quickly. She had lain for a while on the small pallet bed that Elizabeth Rookwood had provided for her here in the garret of her husband's lodgings on the Strand. She could have enjoyed greater comfort in one of the chambers below, but she preferred the solitude of this dark attic. The oak beams of the gable roof were high enough at their apex for her to stand upright beneath them, but she was obliged to crouch down if she moved to another part of the room. A few dusty chests were piled on top of each other in one corner, but otherwise the room was bare of furnishings. Frances welcomed the simplicity. The ostentation of court had seemed even more distasteful to her since her visit to the Tower. Even this tiny garret was comfortable by comparison, its timbers warmed from the fireplace below, and its lofty position keeping the walls free from damp.

Frances had brought nothing but the clothes she had been wearing, and a tiny book of hours, tucked into the pocket of her dark grey dress. The queen had arranged the lodging for her as a gesture of kindness – or repentance, perhaps. She too had worn sombre clothes since the trial, obliging the ladies of her household to follow suit. The king would hardly have approved if he had seen his wife and her ladies dressed as if for a wake, but the court at Greenwich was now so depleted that it passed without notice. News of Father Garnet's arrest had prompted the few courtiers who had remained there to hasten to Westminster so that they might see the 'Jesuit traitor,' as Cecil called him, brought before the Privy Council.

The priest had finally been discovered on the day of the trial. He had only made it as far as Hindlip Hall, which lay some fifteen miles west of Coughton Court. The king's messenger had been waiting outside the chamber at Westminster to relay the tidings of his arrest. Frances guessed that her father had been told before the proceedings came to an end, hence his hasty departure.

The queen had dispatched a groom of her household to find out the details. The boy had arrived in time to see Father Garnet being escorted from his carriage. The old man had apparently been so frail from his long weeks of hiding that he could barely stand. Frances had heard that the priest hole had been so small that he had been unable to lie down, and the sheriff's men had been obliged to pull him out by his shoulders. She wished that she could have made a poultice to reduce the swelling in his legs. Root of mandrake, ground with a little basil, would have soon worked its effect. Perhaps a little felwort to thin the blood and speed its progress to the heart. But her salves seemed of little use now. They were part of another, more innocent life, and when she tried to recall the comfort that they had once brought her, it was like grasping at a long-faded dream.

The rumble of a cart on the street below disturbed her thoughts. Wincing from the stiffness in her joints, she slowly straightened and crossed to the window. Already, ropes had been positioned along the Strand in order to hem in the thousands of spectators who would soon be jostling for a view of the four remaining traitors as they were dragged from the Tower to Westminster. The place of execution had been hastily changed after the other four men had been put to death the day before. It was rumoured that the king had been disappointed by the lack of spectacle at St Paul's Churchyard, so it was decreed that the remaining traitors should meet their end outside the place of their intended crime.

Frances wished that she could have closed her ears to the reports that had reached the queen's presence chamber on an almost hourly basis the previous day. The first to die had been Sir Everard Digby – a meagre compensation for Cecil's betrayal, perhaps, that he should thus be spared the sight of his fellow traitors being ripped apart before he met his maker. Lady Mar whispered that when the executioner had cut out his still-beating heart and declared to the baying crowds that it belonged to a traitor, Sir Everard had cried 'Thou liest.'

Tom's brother had been next to mount the scaffold, but little had been said about the manner of his death, except that he had gone to it quietly, muttering prayers to himself as the executioner's blade did its work. John Grant had followed in his bloody footsteps. He had had to be led up the ladder to the halter, having been blinded by an explosion of gunpowder before the siege at Holbeach. But his spirit had been unbroken, and he had died insisting that he had not sinned against God. Thomas Bates had been less stoical, but he, like the rest, had upheld his Catholic faith to the end.

A pale light was beginning to steal over the rooftops of the city now as Frances peered out of the small casement window. A steady trickle of spectators and stallholders was starting to fill the pavements below, and, as she glanced westwards, Frances could see a procession of guards approaching. She guessed that they would be stationed at intervals along the route to prevent any of the condemned men's friends or family members from saying goodbye – or, worse, staging a reckless attempt at rescue – as their loved ones passed by.

The bells of St Paul's tolled again, but the sound was obscured now by the gathering cacophony below. Frances turned her back on the window and crossed to the middle of the room so that she might straighten out her aching limbs. Reaching into her pocket, she drew out her prayer book. There was just enough light to make out the tiny script.

> He discovereth deep things out of darkness,
> and bringeth out to light the shadow of death.

She traced the exquisite illumination that ran alongside the familiar passage, her fingers weaving along the intricate briar with its tiny red and white roses. She mouthed the words silently as she read, then closed her eyes and repeated them over and over again, trying to shut out the growing noise from the street. Tears streamed down her cheeks, and her hands trembled as she pressed them tightly together.

By the time she opened her eyes, the room was filled with a pale grey light. As she wiped the tears with the linen of her sleeve, something caught her eye on the beams overhead. She looked closer, and saw that a series of upturned 'V's had been carved into the wood. At first, she wondered if they were the initials of the carpenter who had built the dwelling, but their order was too random. As realisation dawned, her mouth slowly lifted into a smile.

Witches' marks.

Whoever had had this house built had taken care to protect its occupants from the workings of Satan's whores. Similar markings would no doubt be found in the eaves of houses across the kingdom, Frances knew. She remembered her father showing her some in the attics of Longford when she was a girl. He had held his candle perilously close to the heavy oak beams so that she could glimpse the strange shapes carved into their smooth surface. Quite what protection they could offer had been as great a mystery to her then as it was now. Clearly, they had failed in their purpose, she thought, for a witch had dwelt beneath them for a full night without any harm befalling her.

There was a sudden shout from the street below, followed by another. Soon the whole of the Strand seemed to be in uproar. The smile faded from Frances's lips. They must be in sight.

She crossed to the window and took a deep breath before looking down. The pavements were now thronged with people, and the king's guards were hard-pressed to contain them as they pushed and jostled their way closer to the front. Frances craned her neck so that she could look eastwards, beyond the edge of the windowpane. In the distance, she could see the first horse making its slow, plodding progress along the Strand. There was a harness around its neck that was attached to a rope on either side, and, although the bulk of its flank obscured whatever it was that it pulled behind, Frances knew with a sickening certainty that it was the first of the prisoners. The other four men had been dragged to their deaths in this manner, each strapped to a wicker hurdle rather than being pulled along the ground as Sir Edward had stipulated, for fear that they would already be dead by the time they reached the scaffold.

The first of the horses was almost level with the house now, and Frances caught a glimpse of the ragged boots worn by the prisoner as they bumped along the rough cobbles. Quickly, she drew back from the window, appalled by the sight that was unfolding beneath her. But she forced herself to look down again, and recognised Guido Fawkes, his face twisting into a grimace as his limp body was jolted agonisingly along the street. He hardly seemed aware of the hordes as they jeered and spat when he passed by, so lost was he in bodily torment.

The second horse followed so close behind that its hooves occasionally brushed against the soles of Fawkes's boots. Robert Keyes strained at the ropes that tethered him to the hurdle, his head jerking from side to side and his eyes wild with fear. Frances made the sign of the cross over her breast as he passed by. As the next horse drew level, she heard an anguished cry from the window below. Ambrose Rookwood raised desperate eyes.

'Pray for me, pray for me!' he shouted.

The crowd fell silent as his wife called back: 'I will, and be of good courage!'

One of the guards jerked his head up to the window, furious at the flouting of the king's orders that none of the prisoner's wives should see them before they died. But Frances's eyes were already upon the next hurdle, which was slowly coming into view. Tom's wasted limbs were strapped tightly to it, his right arm still covered by a sling. His face was deathly pale, and his eyes were closed, but she saw that his lips moved in silent prayer.

'Offer thyself wholly to God!'

The shout came from the window below, as Elizabeth Rookwood tried desperately to comfort her husband before he moved out of earshot. Tom's eyes flickered open.

'I, for my part, do as freely restore thee to God as He gave thee unto me,' she continued.

Tom looked up to the source of the voice. Instinctively, Frances reached out her hands, as if to touch him. Catching the movement, his eyes flicked to the window above. When he saw her, his mouth slowly lifted into a smile. As she held his gaze, Frances could no longer hear the noise of the crowd below. It was as if the whole hideous spectacle had faded away, and she and Tom were standing before each other on the stage of the Banqueting House, his brown eyes dancing with amusement as the rest of the masque was played out around them.

She gave an answering smile, and pressed her fingers to her lips. He nodded slightly, his eyes still bright, then slowly turned them up to the sky as the horse pulled him out of sight.

One by one, the guards stepped from their stations and fell in line behind the procession. The crowds followed in their wake, eager to gain a good vantage point when they reached the court-yard in front of Westminster Hall. Frances knew that it would already be thronged with people. They would come along in their thousands to watch the execution of common felons. How much greater the prospect of witnessing the grisly fate of the traitors who had plotted to blow up the king and his entire Parliament. The whole of London would have turned out to see it.

Before long, the Strand was deserted, and an eerie silence had fallen, interrupted only by the occasional sob from the chamber below. Slowly, Frances turned from the window and walked across to the pallet bed. Kneeling beside it, she closed her eyes and started to pray.

The bells began to toll again. She held her breath. As the eighth toll faded into silence, a sudden roar rose up from the distant crowds.

30 March

An uncertain grey light had begun to creep along the quiet streets as Frances passed under the Holbein Gate. The cobbles glistened in the glow of the sconces on either side of the towering gateway. The onset of spring had brought no respite from the rains that had arrived two months before, dousing the city with an endless deluge so that its very walls seemed to weep, and its swollen river threatened to burst its banks. They had abated for now at least, although, as Frances glanced up at the sky, she saw that it was already thickening with more dark clouds.

Quickening her pace a little, she drew up the hood of her cloak and kept her gaze fixed on the path in front of her. She felt a drop of rain on her face, soon followed by another. The vast expanse of St James's Park lay to her right. If the rain became heavier, she could shelter for a while among the tree-lined pathways. But for now, she continued straight ahead, eager to reach her destination before the streets began to fill with people.

Though she had only walked a short distance, her legs felt heavy and her shoulders ached. She had slept a great deal since Tom's death, retiring early from the evening entertainments so that she could take her rest, and sometimes arriving late to attend the princess in the morning. Even when she had a few moments of leisure to pick up Master Gerard's book, which she no longer troubled to conceal, her eyelids would soon grow heavy, and she would be able to read only a few pages before the words started dancing in front of her eyes. *Arcadia* had lain untouched on her shelves for many weeks, but not for the same reason. More than once, Elizabeth had become vexed with her favourite attendant, upbraiding her for being dull or neglectful. But the queen had been patient and solicitous, sending comfits or other delicacies in an effort to lift her melancholy.

The tower of St Stephen's was clearly in view now. Frances slowed her pace as she approached it. She had not set foot in Westminster for months, though it had been often in her thoughts these past weeks. Glancing over to her right, she saw the towering abbey silhouetted against the gloomy sky. She might go there to pray afterwards, though God seemed to have forsaken this miserable city. Certainly the king had deserted it, bored of the interminable debates in Parliament about the depleted treasury; bored even of the constant rumours of a fresh Jesuit conspiracy. Better to turn his back on it all and take his pleasure in the hunt, or in the yielding flesh of the latest young man to catch his eye.

Frances crossed into the courtyard next to Westminster Hall and stood on its periphery. The ropes were still strung across the entrance to the hall, where the trial of Father Garnet had taken place two days earlier. The queen had attended in her husband's absence, and had returned, ashen-faced, with tales of the priest's eloquent and spirited defence, of his frail old body broken from the torments of the rack. He had been found guilty, of course, though Anne said the crowds had fallen silent when the verdict had been declared.

The rain was falling heavily now, but Frances hardly noticed as she walked slowly over to the centre of the courtyard. The scaffold had been here. She had seen the pamphlet that had appeared at court within days of the executions, its pages filled with detailed drawings of the gruesome spectacle. Tom's blood had long since been washed away, she thought, as she gazed down at the cobbles. She lowered herself to the ground and reached out to touch the smooth stones. The torrent of rainwater had pooled around them, and was now rising so fast that it threatened to engulf them altogether.

She was to return to Longford tomorrow. Though the princess had objected furiously to her request that she might take her leave from court, the queen, guessing the reason, had swiftly agreed to it. Cecil had raised no opposition; he no longer had any use for her, after all. For all the terrors that he had suffered in the Tower, Father Garnet had refused to name her, and he was hardly likely to do so now. Neither had her father been implicated, but had returned to Richmond soon after Tom's trial. He and her mother were there still, tending to the gardens and palace as if the plot had never existed. Even the king had lost interest in the idea that there were still conspirators at large, and had told Cecil to let the matter rest. Besides, Frances reflected, the chief minister had enough to do in trying to claw back ground from Sackville, who was rapidly beginning to eclipse him in power and favour.

The sound of horses' hooves echoed around the courtyard as a carriage passed by. The streets surrounding the ancient hall were starting to come to life now as people emerged from their houses, scowling up at the heavens. Frances looked down at the stones by her feet once more, then gathered up the sodden hem of her dress and slowly stood upright.

As she turned back towards the palace for the last time, she paused and placed her hands lightly over her stomach, closing her eyes as she did so. The child had grown quickly this past month, though it was still concealed by the folds of her gown. God willing, it would open its eyes to a bright midsummer sky as the sun gently warmed the old stone walls of home.

ACKNOWLEDGEMENTS

This, my first novel, has been a long time in the writing. It began as a conversation at the Harrogate History Festival a few years ago, and gradually evolved into a story with 'a beginning, a middle and an end', as my Dad would say. It is entirely thanks to the inspirational guidance provided by my agent, Julian Alexander, and my editor, Nick Sayers, that the novel was slowly transformed into its final incarnation. I am deeply indebted to them both for their creativity, insights and patience. I have also benefited hugely from the wisdom and experience of George Gibson, my editor at Grove Atlantic.

As ever, I have been supported by an excellent team at Hodder, notably Cicely Aspinall, Caitriona Horne and Rebecca Mundy. I am extremely grateful to Tom Duxbury for crafting such a beautiful cover. I would also like to thank my non-fiction editor, Maddy Price, for taking time out to read an earlier draft of the novel.

Longford Castle plays an important part in the novel, and is greatly beloved of its heroine, Frances. I am deeply indebted to William Pleydell-Bouverie, 9th Earl of Radnor, whose family has lived in the castle for three centuries, for allowing me to visit and for providing such an enlightening tour of his beautiful home. I am also very grateful to Alexandra Ormerod and Jane Pleydell-Bouverie for helping to arrange the visit.

I owe an enormous debt of gratitude to my friend Stephen Kuhrt, who read each chapter as soon as it was written, and sustained me throughout with his unstinting encouragement. It is thanks to Stephen's enthusiastic responses (usually received before I had even arrived home from the British Library) that my confidence in the story and characters increased as the novel took shape. My botanist friend Honor Gay supplied me with invaluable advice on the medicinal herbs and plants that would have been used in the early seventeenth century. I was also fortunate to draw upon the expertise of Mark Wallis and Kathy Hipperson of Past Pleasures Ltd with regard to ladies' riding styles and side saddles.

My final thanks go to the family and friends who have, yet again, lent their support. I am particularly grateful to my parents, my daughter Eleanor and my husband Tom for their practical help, encouragement and, at times, forbearance. Thank you.

AUTHOR'S NOTE

Although little is known of her life, Frances Gorges really existed. She was the third of eight children born to Elizabeth I's favoured attendant, Helena Snakenborg and her second husband, Thomas Gorges. The fact that precious few details about Frances survive in the contemporary sources makes her an ideal heroine for a novel. I have stayed true to those details, but have drawn upon my own imagination to fill the long gaps in between.

Frances's home, Longford Castle, still survives today and is one of the finest examples of the Elizabethan prodigy houses. Built in an unusual triangular formation, which was often a device to express an owner's Catholic faith, it was the inspiration for Philip Sidney's 'Castle of Amphialeus' in *The Countess of Pembroke's Arcadia*.

The historical context for Frances's story is also largely accurate, and I have drawn upon contemporary sources and quotes for the narrative. The early years of James I's reign were a dangerous time to be alive. The new Stuart king was cut from a very different cloth to his predecessor. Intolerant and dogmatic, he had no intention of upholding Elizabeth's policy of not 'making windows into men's souls'. It was soon obvious that he was going to stamp his extreme brand of Protestantism onto the English people, which spelt danger for any subject who still clung to the old Catholic faith.

The new king also brought with him the violent persecution of suspected witches that had seen thousands of innocent women put to the flames in Scotland. A woman had only to be unmarried, poor, or be practised at healing to be under suspicion, and an accusation alone was enough to bring her to trial. The horrors that thousands of women underwent in order to determine their guilt before they even reached the courts are not exaggerated in this book. They included the notorious practise of 'witch-pricking', whereby a blade would be thrust into every mark on the body of the accused. When one was found that did not bleed, it was declared to be the Devil's Mark. Other tortures included sleep deprivation and the notorious 'test by water', whereby a suspect's hands and arms would be bound together and they would be thrown into a body of deep water. If they rose to the top, they were guilty; if they sank, they were innocent and hauled out – although often not in time.

For all James's staunch Protestantism, with its emphasis upon virtue and restraint, the court over which he presided was shockingly decadent. In place of the cultural vibrancy and strict morality that had defined the Elizabethan court was drunkenness, depravity and excess in every form. Little wonder that James's new subjects soon harked back to the 'Golden Age' of Elizabeth and began nurturing a dangerous resentment against their new king.

James's consort, Anne of Denmark, is a fascinating character. She was just fourteen when she married James, then king of Scots, in 1589. She gave birth to Prince Henry, the vital son and heir, four years later, and went on to bear another six children, including the future Charles I. But despite their numerous offspring, Anne's marriage to James was in other respects a sham. Her husband made little secret of his homosexuality and flaunted a succession of handsome young favourites at court.

Anne bore the humiliation with admirable fortitude. But beneath her calm, somewhat aloof exterior, lay a woman who bitterly resented her husband's behaviour and beliefs. Although she had been raised a Protestant, it was rumoured that she had secretly converted to the Catholic faith. Pope Clement VIII sent her a rosary as a token of his esteem.

Whether Anne's Catholic sympathies drove her to support the Gunpowder Plot will probably never be known for certain. The plotters themselves hinted that some great person was behind their schemes. Historians have long since debated who this might have been. One theory is that it was Robert Cecil himself. The wily minister may have realised that the plot would be so abhorrent to most Englishmen that there would be a devastating backlash against the Catholics as a result. But Anne, too, had a strong motive for supporting the plot, viewing it as a means to rid herself of her husband and re-establish the Catholic faith in England.

I have stayed as close as possible to the known facts about the plot and those involved, with one exception. There is no record that the plotters ever met Princess Elizabeth, although they certainly intended to make her queen and their strong court connections make it at least possible that their paths might have crossed.

Thomas Wintour (or Winter) and his brother Robert were the sons of a Worcestershire gentlemen and cousins to the plot's leader, Robert Catesby. Thomas was a well educated and intelligent man, who could speak several languages and was trained as a lawyer. He served for a time in the English army, and fought in the Low Countries and France.

He converted to Catholicism in 1600 and became a fervent advocate for that faith, working tirelessly to secure Spanish support for an invasion on behalf of England's Catholics. When his pleas fell upon deaf ears, he threw in his lot with Catesby and they began plotting the murder of James and his entire government.

As I have related in the novel, Sir Everard Digby's role in the plot was to kidnap the princess. Catesby ordered him to rent Coughton Court, which was within easy access of where Elizabeth was staying at Coombe Abbey, so that he could be ready to seize her when he received the signal. There is no evidence that Digby was a double agent, but it is likely that one of the plotters turned informant.

Shortly before Parliament was due to meet, Lord Monteagle received an anonymous letter warning him not to attend. He showed it to Cecil, who alerted the king. It took little to ignite James's paranoia, and he immediately ordered a search of Westminster. His officials uncovered the plot just a few short hours from it being put into action.

When Guy Fawkes was arrested and a huge quantity of gunpowder was discovered in a cellar beneath the House of Lords, most of his fellow plotters fled from the capital. But Thomas Wintour held his nerve and went to Westminster to try to find out what had happened. Only when he learned that the King now knew all about the plot and those involved did he too flee north. He joined Catesby, Thomas Percy, John Grant, Ambrose Rookwood and John and Christopher Wright at Holbeach House in Staffordshire for a last, desperate stand against the sheriff's men. Thomas was first to be shot, in the shoulder, followed by the Wright brothers and Rookwood. Catesby and Percy were killed by the same bullet.

Along with the other surviving plotters, Thomas was taken to the Tower of London, where he signed his confession on 23 November 1605. Much of what is written about the Gunpowder Plot derives from this document, although there is reason to believe that it was forgery drafted by the King's officials.

The plotters were tried and condemned on 27 January in Westminster Hall, and they met their grisly deaths a few days later. Thomas was the first to mount the scaffold in the Old Palace Yard at Westminster on 31 January. Eyewitnesses observed that he was 'a very pale and dead colour'. When invited to say a few last words, he retorted that it was 'no time to discourse: he was come to die.' He did, though, ask his fellow Catholics to pray for him and declared his undying allegiance to the faith.